C000297882

BARBARA HANNAY

the Sister's Gift

MICHAEL JOSEPH
an imprint of
PENGUIN BOOKS

MICHAEL JOSEPH

UK | USA | Canada | Ireland | Australia
India | New Zealand | South Africa | China

Michael Joseph is part of the Penguin Random House group of companies
whose addresses can be found at global.penguinrandomhouse.com

Penguin
Random House
Australia

First published by Michael Joseph in 2020

Copyright © Barbara Hannay 2020

The moral right of the author has been asserted.

All rights reserved. No part of this publication may be reproduced, published, performed
in public or communicated to the public in any form or by any means without prior written
permission from Penguin Random House Australia Pty Ltd or its authorised licensees.

Cover design by James Rendall © Penguin Random House Australia Pty Ltd
Cover images: Woman by Jasmina007/Getty Images; girl and beach by
subman/Getty Images; palm fronds by Pratchaya.Lee/Shutterstock.com
Typeset in Sabon by Midland Typesetters, Australia

Printed and bound in Australia by Griffin Press, part of Ovato, an accredited
ISO AS/NZS 14001 Environmental Management Systems printer

 A catalogue record for this
book is available from the
National Library of Australia

ISBN 978 0 14379 421 9

penguin.com.au

For Liz and Marg,
my beautiful, talented and loving sisters

New beginnings are often disguised as painful endings.

—Lao Tzu

PROLOGUE

On the morning Freya went into labour, she told no one. She simply walked onto the Magnetic Island ferry, found a padded seat near an open window and focused on the seagulls lined up along the jetty. While the birds dived for fish among shell-encrusted pylons, Freya took deep, steadying breaths, just as she'd practised at the antenatal classes.

We can do this, Butterfly.

Fortunately, the ferry wasn't crowded, but it rocked as it left the island's sheltered bay and headed across open water to Townsville. The jerky movement brought a wave of nausea, accompanied by a fiercer and longer contraction. Biting back the urge to whimper, Freya closed her eyes and breathed even more deeply as she gently massaged her enormous belly.

Her solo journey had never been part of the Official Plan, but more a last-minute impulse. After nine long, often trying months, the baby girl was about to arrive, and Freya had been gripped by an unexpected need to experience the momentous event on her own.

Selfish? Perhaps, but there were limits to her generosity.

Just the same, she'd never expected the labour to progress so quickly. First babies were supposed to be drawn-out affairs, weren't they? As the island's boulder- and pine-studded headlands receded, another contraction came, closer and stronger than the last.

The twenty-minute ferry ride seemed to take forever and when the boat finally reached the dock in Ross Creek, the young fellow in charge of tying up to the pier was tediously slow. Tourists jostled on the wharf, impatient to hurry on board for a day on an idyllic tropical island. Freya swayed unsteadily as she stood, felt dampness down below and had a flash of panic.

Not now. Hang on, Butterfly. Please don't rush.

Praying that her waters would remain intact until she reached the hospital, Freya made her way down the ramp, moving slowly, cautiously, for the first time in her life hanging onto the railing like a little old lady. And as another contraction arrived, the decision to take a taxi to the hospital was a no-brainer. She couldn't possibly drive the little rattletrap Honda she kept in the ferry's car park for use on the mainland.

A mere three hours later, Freya made the necessary phone call.

'Pearl, she's here.'

'What? Who's there?'

'The baby. She's arrived.'

'Oh, my God. How —?'

'She's so cute. I think she looks a lot like Troy.'

'Freya!' Pearl's voice was frantic. 'Why didn't you tell me? You knew I wanted to be there. Troy's on night shift this week. He could have come, too. We both wanted to be there. You knew that.'

'Sorry.' Freya looked down at the bundle of miniature perfection in her arms, reliving the enormous sense of achievement and excitement that had overridden the pain when this little girl slipped sweetly into the world with only a minimum of assistance from the midwife. 'It was all a bit of a rush.'

'But we had everything planned. We told you so many times that we wanted to be there for the birth.'

Pearl's voice was sorrowful. Accusing. Almost certainly, she was crying, but Freya refused to feel guilty. 'She's here safely, Pearl. That's the main thing.'

'I suppose . . .' Her sister's voice squeaked and then, sounding more like her usual bossy self, 'Have you expressed colostrum?'

'Not yet, but I will.'

'It's very important, as you know.' Freya could imagine Pearl's stern frown now, the earnest expression in her pale blue eyes that could make her look years older than she was. 'Troy and I will be on the next ferry.'

'Lovely.'

'You won't actually breastfeed, will you?'

'No, Pearl. I'll stick to our agreement.'

'Right. Yes. Good.' Less certainly, 'Of course you will.'

'I promise, Pearl.' After a beat, 'She's yours.'

'Well, yes. Of course she is.'

Freya let out her breath slowly. She hadn't wanted to make trouble today. True, she hadn't obeyed the rules they'd set out, but she was sure she'd earned this treasured window of time alone with the small creature she'd carried for so many months.

She looked down at the baby's sweet pink perfection. Her skin was so soft, her tiny, tiny fingers and diminutive ears so exquisitely faultless. The baby screwed up her face and love swelled in Freya to the point of bursting.

'It's over to you now, Pearl,' she said bravely. 'To you and Troy.'

'Thank you.'

There was no mistaking the relief in her sister's voice.

CHAPTER ONE

Twenty-four years later, on the Sunshine Coast

If Freya had known she was leaving her home for the last time, she wouldn't have rushed. She certainly wouldn't have grabbed her car keys from the hook in the kitchen and dashed for the door, only stopping to briefly check her hair and lipstick in the hall mirror.

She would have taken time to admire the late-afternoon light as it bathed her front hallway in softness and warmth. She would have stopped for a final, loving look at the little English oak table she'd inherited from her grandmother. She might even have run her fingers over the collection of water-worn stones that she'd brought home from holidays abroad and set in a glass dish on.the table.

Or perhaps she would have smiled at the blue pottery vase filled with flowers she'd bought at the supermarket yesterday, simply because they'd looked bright and cheerful – and because she'd deserved a little cheer.

Actually, if she'd had any inkling of what was about to happen, Freya probably would have hugged the vase to her chest – and the bowl of stones and the little table – hauling them out the door to safety on the front lawn.

Or she would have raced back to the sunroom she'd turned into her studio and grabbed her artwork. Most certainly, she would have scooped up her little dog, Won Ton, and taken her safely into the car, instead of leaving her in the laundry with her basket and supper.

Sadly, the major events in life rarely come with a warning. Freya had learned this a year ago, when Brian had arrived home on a Friday night and made his shocking announcement. And now, this evening, she had no idea that another disaster lurked. Besides, she was running late, so of course she was rushing.

Which wasn't unusual. Freya had an aversion to arriving anywhere too early, so she often left her preparations till almost the last minute. Inevitably, this meant that getting ready for any event was a somewhat frantic business.

She knew it was a bad habit. It had driven Brian mental. During their marriage, each time they'd gone out, he'd hovered by the front door, scowling down the hallway, tapping a foot or jangling the car keys impatiently, with Freya still in the bedroom, desperately trying to finish her makeup, or her hair, or setting her scarf just right. Possibly, Brian's new wife found him just as impatient.

Was it terrible to hope this was the case?

But eventually, this evening, Freya was ready. As she backed her car out of the garage, leaving the door raised for an easy return – another thing that would have irritated Brian intensely – her thoughts were entirely on the evening ahead. A funny, feel-good movie was planned with her girlfriends, followed by a cosy meal and a good old chinwag at one of their favourite restaurants.

As she headed down the street, she did catch a glimpse of her house in the rear-view mirror, sitting sedately in the curve of a quiet cul-de-sac behind a lush, green clump of palms. Her home, with white weatherboards and large windows framed by pale-green French-style shutters, made her smile. It was still her happy place.

The one thing she had left.

The night was cold by Queensland standards, the café cosy and Mediterranean in mood, with rustic stone walls and floors warmed by glowing braziers. Tempting aromas of tomatoes, garlic and herbs wafted. A dresser bore oversized candelabras dripping stalactites of wax, and through the curving arches on the terrace, a clear winter sky glittered.

Freya, Daisy and Jo grinned as they clinked their wine glasses. Their movie had proved clever and droll, leaving them in a happily mellow mood.

'It's so good to be out with you girls again,' Freya told her friends once she'd taken her first delicious sip. 'Thanks, I really needed this.'

Daisy and Jo nodded with sympathetic smiles. They were trying to cheer her up, of course, a tactic not all that different from the one she and Jo had employed to help Daisy through her grief after her husband had died. A divorce wasn't quite the same as a death, of course, but for Freya it felt almost as bad.

Perhaps she was being self-indulgent, but in her case, there'd been a sense of shame about Brian leaving her, a feeling of failure and the underlying message that she'd been deemed unsatisfactory.

Hastily she axed these negative thoughts. 'I'm managing okay, truly.'

'Of course you are,' affirmed Jo. 'I've always thought you were wonderfully balanced and centred.'

Freya almost elaborated on how very unbalanced and off kilter she'd felt during the past months.

Luckily, Daisy launched a distraction. 'How are you finding the art classes?'

'I love them.'

'I didn't know you were artistic,' said Jo.

Freya laughed. 'Neither did I, really. I hadn't picked up a paintbrush since high school, but honestly, messing about with watercolours is so much fun. Really rewarding. I might even have a skerrick of talent.'

'I'm sure you have masses of talent.' Daisy was always wonderfully loyal.

'And I'm kind of getting into gardening,' Freya added. 'Not quite at your level, Daisy. I only really managed with pot plants while I was working full time, but I've started growing veggies. Well, just cherry tomatoes and lettuce, but at least I've started.' She might as well pile on the positives. It actually made her feel better to list these recent milestones.

'I don't suppose you've tried dating?' Daisy asked with a tentative, almost apologetic smile.

'I have, actually.' Freya grimaced as she admitted this. 'Just the once though.' She'd run into the fellow at the supermarket, a former customer, a widower, and he'd asked her out for a drink, which she supposed counted as a date. He'd caught her on a day when she was feeling bored and maybe a bit lonely, so she'd agreed.

'He wasn't my cup of tea,' she said. 'All he wanted to talk about was the stock market, his golf handicap and his amazing sons.'

Jo responded with a sympathetic eye-roll. 'Don't give up. I'm sure the right guy's out there, but in the meantime, I'm so glad you got to keep your house.'

Good old Jo, always practical.

But, yes, at least she had the house. Freya had tried to feel grateful that she'd kept her lovely home, while Brian and Amber were renting a two-bedroom apartment in Mooloolaba, several blocks back from the waterfront with no hint of a view whatsoever. Gratitude didn't bubble easily to the surface, though, after your husband had traded you in for a younger model.

Apart from the shock and the hurt, it was all such an embarrassing cliché, the sort of thing that happened to other people.

Not to Freya and Brian.

For heaven's sake, they hadn't been a run-of-the-mill married couple. They'd been lively and fun, throwing the very best parties, taking regular trips overseas, and they'd run a successful business together: Brian Bright's Electrics.

For twenty years, Freya had managed the office, fielding phone calls, handling all the paperwork, balancing the books, wrestling with tax, keeping the place spotless and inviting for customers, windows sparkling, floors gleaming, pot plants thriving.

And now. She hadn't just lost her husband, she'd lost her career. Replaced by Amber, a fluffy-haired, curvaceous blonde aged thirty-two.

Thirty-two? How ridiculous was that? And the biggest cliché of all – Brian had met Amber on the job, while fitting a new ceiling fan in her bedroom. Arrrgh. It was all so pathetic. And how on earth could Amber have fallen for a man past fifty, balding and grey, with a softening paunch?

It still hurt Freya to know she'd been so easily and eagerly replaced. She couldn't begin to imagine the kinds of conversation Brian might have with a woman like that. Perhaps there wasn't a lot of talk. It was all action of the bedroom variety, and she certainly didn't want to think about that, but her imagination could be a real pain in the proverbial.

Freya consoled herself with the belief that it couldn't possibly last.

Not that she would take Brian back. *Hell, no.*

'We should check out the menu,' she suggested now, having spent more than enough time dwelling on her issues. And once her friends had made their selections, she steered the conversation to their families. With no children of her own, she was always interested in what Daisy's and Jo's offspring were up to. Daisy even had a grandchild now, a dear, chubby little boy, just learning to walk.

Topping up their glasses, the women relaxed and let their chatter drift happily from the movie they'd just seen to Jo's kids' sporting achievements and Daisy's younger daughter's adventures in South America. Their meals arrived, wonderfully aromatic concoctions, artistically arranged on trendy stoneware, and Freya's taste buds tingled as she speared her fork into a succulent prawn.

Their conversation moved on, through food and fashion to their extended families. Jo's mother had moved into an aged-care facility. Daisy's sister was training for the one-hundred-metres freestyle in the Masters Games. Freya hadn't a lot to contribute, though, as she wasn't in regular contact with her family.

'I hear that Amber's pregnant.'

This bombshell came from Jo, and was dropped gently enough, but it still landed on Freya with almost nuclear force. She couldn't help flinching.

So. Word had leaked out.

'Yes,' she said dully. She'd been determined not to mention this news. It was just too painful to admit that Brian and Amber were to be parents. Brian – her Brian – was to be a father. Now. To another woman's child.

After all the heartache of the first decade of their marriage – the miscarriages and bitter disappointments – this information, delivered just last week, cautiously, almost fearfully, by her ex, had shattered Freya's heart.

'I'm pleased for them,' she said bravely now, but she couldn't quite manage to smile.

Daisy reached out and squeezed her hand, her warm, sensitive smile conveying gentle understanding.

Even so, Freya was sunk into blackest gloom. The news of Amber's pregnancy had been the absolute last straw, even harder to accept than the bald fact that her husband had grown tired of her. God knew, she'd been tired of him, too, but there was such a thing as loyalty, wasn't there?

Shaking her head to scatter these thoughts, she squared her shoulders and squeezed out a grin that she hoped didn't look too false. 'Have I mentioned that I've repainted my bedroom?'

'Now that's an excellent idea,' enthused Daisy. 'New furniture, too?'

Freya shook her head. 'I would have loved to chuck the bed, but I couldn't afford to be so rash. I bought a new quilt, though, and bed linen and cushions.'

'What's your new colour scheme?'

'Pink and orange.' Freya allowed herself a smirk of triumph. 'Not a shade of fashionable grey in sight. Brian would hate it.'

'Oh, wow. Now that's what I call sweet revenge. An orange and pink bedroom. I love it.' Jo, the only member of the trio who still had a husband, was grinning. 'Good for you, Freya.'

'I must say it does cheer me wonderfully to wake up and see those ridiculously bright colours.'

'Yes, it's a stroke of brilliance.' Daisy raised her glass. 'Here's to many more lovely bright mornings.'

As they clinked their glasses once again, Freya's phone rang. It had, of course, slipped from the little side pocket in her handbag and was lying at the very bottom, beneath her money purse, a tangle of old shopping lists, her sunglasses case and her hairbrush. The phone had almost rung out by the time she finally retrieved it.

'That's funny,' she said, as she glanced at the screen. 'It's from Louise Richards, my neighbour. Why would she be calling me at this time of night?'

CHAPTER TWO

Twelve hundred kilometres to the north, it was also a beautiful night on Magnetic Island. From the restaurant's deck, Billie could see the half moon sitting clear and bright in an inky sky and casting a silver path across the dark surface of the bay. This was North Queensland winter at its blissful best and she was almost glad she'd come home.

Of course, this island could never be quite the same as Santorini. Here, no vineyards sprawled beneath hills topped by blue-domed churches. No whitewashed buildings clung precariously to cliffs that rose steeply out of a sapphire sea, and never again would Petros be waiting to welcome her when she returned to their flat.

At least the brutal pain of Billie's heartbreak seemed to be fading, albeit far too slowly, and she might have actually enjoyed being back on Maggie, if she hadn't been run off her feet. So far she hadn't even had time for a swim in her favourite bay. By day she was sweeping and mopping and dusting the bistro, unstacking the dishwasher and polishing silver, and by night she was waiting tables.

Her friends thought she had it easy, being the only daughter of the successful owners of Island Thyme. They didn't know the half of it. This evening, Billie had Buckley's chance of stopping to enjoy the moon.

Gathering up a delicately balanced armful of empty plates and cutlery from table four, she hurried back to the kitchen where two servings of eight-hour lamb shoulder, a bowl of Persian lentils and a medium-rare steak were waiting under the warmers. These she delivered to table six, remembering to smile as she also topped up their wine glasses.

About to check on other diners nearby, Billie saw that a cluster of new arrivals had appeared at the top of the stone stairs that led from the beach. Stifling an urge to sigh, or to phone her parents and insist they find an extra waiter, Billie hurried over to the group.

'Belinda!' one of the newcomers cried before Billie could even ask if they had a reservation.

Eeek. Almost no one, not even her parents, called her Belinda these days. Just her luck, she now recognised her Year 7 teacher among these new prospective diners. Sonia Brassal's long straight hair was now completely grey, and she seemed to be hiding her middle-age spread beneath a capacious woollen cape. But her aura of warmth overlaid by unmistakable bossiness was exactly as Billie remembered.

That was the problem with growing up on a tiny island. It was as bad as living in a small country town. You ran into people from your past at every turn.

'Hello, Mrs Brassal.' Billie offered her brightest smile. After all, she'd had the lesson ingrained from her mum's repeated lectures. A successful eatery was all about good service. If you didn't smile and make people feel better for having come to your venue, they wouldn't remain customers for very long. 'How are you?'

'Wonderful, Belinda. Never better, thanks, and it's great to see you.' Sonia Brassal allowed her gaze to linger on Billie. 'You're looking very well, I must say. I hear you've been travelling overseas.'

'That's right.'

'Excellent. Travel is so good for broadening the mind and you always had so much potential.'

Potential? Really? Yeah, well . . .

'Although I'm sure your parents are very happy to have you home again,' she added.

'Yes.' Billie's smile this time was more polite than brilliant.

'And how nice that you can help them out. Island Thyme has become our favourite eating place, hasn't it, Thomas?'

A small, balding man with spectacles and a white moustache obediently nodded.

Billie also offered a little nod. 'I – er – assume you have a reservation?'

'Of course.' Sonia Brassal almost snorted as she pointed to the ledger on the nearby lectern. 'I'm sure we must be listed there. Under Brassal. Table for four.'

'Of course,' Billie smiled to cover her hesitation. Perhaps Gavin, their hardworking chef, had taken the booking. Without bothering to check the ledger, she picked up sufficient menus and gestured. 'If you'll come this way?'

Luckily, there was indeed a spare table at the edge of the deck. Ready and waiting with an immaculate white linen cloth and sparkling silverware, the table offered a perfect view of the little bay bathed in moonlight.

'Oh, how divine.' The other woman in the party was clearly in raptures as she took her seat, gazing at the view with an ecstatic grin and her hands clasped over her heart.

'My sister's from Melbourne.' Mrs Brassal leaned towards Billie to speak in a conspiratorial undertone. 'She's so envious of our beautiful winters. She's threatening to move here.'

'We've told her to try the summer first,' commented Mrs Brassal's husband.

'But it's so amazing here,' the sister from Melbourne protested as she gestured to the view. 'It's like being on a Greek island. Just so picturesque and romantic, but right here in Australia.'

Billie tried to ignore the painful clunk in her chest that came with the mere mention of Greece. *Forget him. Forget Santorini.*

Holding her smile carefully in place, she handed out menus and filled water glasses.

'I'll leave you for a few moments to look at the —'

Billie was stopped by a hand on her arm.

Sonia Brassal leaned closer and spoke again in an undertone. 'I just wanted to say that I think it's very good of you to help your parents out like this. They really need a break.'

It was on the tip of Billie's tongue to point out that her return to the island was only temporary – very temporary, in fact. She might even have joked that she was only working here because she needed the money, but she was silenced by the sombre message in Sonia's eyes. It was almost as if the woman was hinting that she was privy to knowledge that Billie didn't share. Knowledge about her own parents?

Billie had to admit, her parents had been a tad cagey since she'd come home. She'd assumed it was because she'd been away for so long and they'd fallen out of the habit of including her in their discussions. But was there more? Something she, their precious only child, should know?

This was hardly the appropriate moment to ask such a question, however. Billie simply nodded again and thanked her old teacher before hurrying away to see if table five had decided on desserts.

CHAPTER THREE

'Freya?'

The terrified note in her neighbour's voice sent a chill through Freya. 'Yes?'

'Oh, Freya, I'm so sorry, but it's bad news. You'd better come. Your house —'

'*My house?*'

'Yes. It's on fire.'

'Oh, God.' Shock exploded in Freya's chest. This couldn't be true. It wasn't possible.

'We've called the Fire Brigade,' said Louise. 'They're on their way.'

It was too much to take in. A moan broke from Freya. This couldn't be real, surely?

'Freya, what's happened?' Daisy's voice sounded now beside her. Scared. Uncertain. She touched Freya's elbow. 'What is it?'

Freya shook her head. She didn't want to answer. Perhaps if she didn't utter the terrible words, it would all go away.

On the phone, Louise Richards spoke again. 'I'm so sorry, Freya.'

'Is it – is it bad?' she managed to ask.

'Yes.' Louise sobbed. 'It's so scary.'

And then, overriding her neighbour's despairing voice, came the background scream of a siren, slicing through the airwaves, cutting straight through Freya's heart.

She disconnected, needing to be rid of it.

'Freya, what's happened?' Daisy and Jo were in unison now.

But she couldn't answer them. She was too frozen with panic, too desperately hopeful that this was some kind of nightmarish mistake.

'Hey.' Daisy spoke quietly, and gently patted Freya's elbow. 'We're here for you, honey.'

Swallowing to ease the burning in her throat, Freya forced her eyes open and was confronted once more by the pleasant restaurant and its happy diners. The scene was beautiful, bathed in soft candle-light, exactly as before.

Perhaps she'd imagined the phone call. Had a brain snap.

Then she saw her friends' anxious faces, watching her fearfully.

With a dazed shake of her head, she told them. 'My house is on fire.'

'Oh, God, no.' Daisy was on her feet in an instant, grabbing her handbag.

Jo was up, too, already heading for the entrance. 'I'll get the bill,' she called over her shoulder.

'Come on, we have to go.' Daisy gave Freya's arm an urgent tug.

Freya wasn't sure she could move. Her legs weren't steady enough to support her.

'We'll take my car,' Daisy said next, giving her a little shake and urging her to her feet.

'No, I'm okay.' Freya stood and her legs didn't give way. 'I can drive.'

'No you can't,' insisted Daisy. 'Not under these circumstances. Don't even think of it.'

Perhaps, given that her head was spinning, this wasn't the right moment to try to prove anything. Freya allowed herself to be shepherded outside where the cold night air hit her face. A moment later, she was in the front seat of Daisy's Volvo and classical music burst to life on the radio. Daisy quickly switched it off. Jo climbed into the back. Car doors slammed and the motor revved.

No one spoke as they roared out of the car park and down the curving hillside road to the Sunshine Motorway. It would take twenty minutes to reach Freya's house.

Twenty minutes! A house could burn up completely in that time. Twenty minutes of fire and flames, licking, burning and devouring.

'Oh, God, Won Ton!' Freya wailed, suddenly remembering her little silky terrier. 'I left her in the laundry.'

'There's a door flap, isn't there?' asked Jo.

Freya nodded. 'Yes.' But then she groaned. 'But what if she's too scared to use it? What if she's overcome by smoke?'

'I'm sure she would have got out.' Daisy sounded quite certain. 'She's a smart little dog. She'll be fine.'

'I'll have to ring Louise. Tell her she has to find her.'

Freya was still clutching her phone, but tears blinded her as she searched for her neighbour's number. She fumbled and swore, before she finally got through.

'Louise,' she asked fearfully, 'have you seen Won Ton?'

'Oh, dear.' This was so not the response Freya needed. 'Let me check for you. I'll see if I can speak to one of the fireys. I'll call you back, okay?'

'Okay. Thanks.' Sick with panicky dread, Freya let the phone fall into her lap and closed her eyes again as she sank back into the headrest. She'd always considered herself to be a coper – at work, with life in general, even with the divorce. Habitually, she'd taken difficulties on the chin and carried on. But now she felt utterly helpless. Useless. While her home, and possibly her little dog, burned.

She tried not to think about the ghastly bright flames leaping up into the black night sky, eating up her house. Her lovely home.

As Daisy sped down the motorway, no doubt exceeding the speed limit, Freya's agonised thoughts kept whirling. Hadn't the universe taken enough swipes at her already? First it had rendered her childless and then divorced. Surely this was one blow too many?

How could one person deserve so much bad luck?

Was it all her own fault? Bad karma? She'd made mistakes in her life, but she'd always had good intentions. Perhaps she should have noticed something amiss when she'd left the house just a few hours earlier.

Of course, she'd been dashing about. Bloody hell, she hadn't left the stove or the iron on, had she? Surely she couldn't have? It was unbearable to think that she might have avoided this disaster if she'd been paying more attention.

If only she could go back in time to check.

Freya's mind slipped and slid as she tried to remember those last careless minutes before she'd left the house. Why hadn't she taken the time to double-check the appliances and power points? And why hadn't she at least stopped for a moment, to take one last, loving look around her?

Perhaps she might have been alerted to danger, might have saved the photo albums or important documents?

A small wail escaped her now, as she thought of all the precious images from her past being gobbled up by flames. The baby photos, the school pics, the treasured photos of her mum and the shots of her first boyfriend, Seb, that she still liked to steal occasional peeks at.

Oh, help! Please let it only be a little fire.

The footpaths and bitumen were crowded when Daisy eventually turned into Freya's street. Cars crammed the gutters, stickybeak onlookers stood about in pyjamas and tracksuits, while two fire trucks were parked nose to tail in Freya's driveway. There was even a bloody TV cameraman. And there for all to see and gape at – the smouldering ruins of her home.

'Oh, dear God,' Daisy murmured as she pulled up on the bitumen behind a fire truck and turned off the motor.

It was hard to process, but one thing was clear. The fire was much, *much* worse than Freya had feared.

Shock dragged the air from her lungs as she saw the awful truth. Her house, her beautiful home – all of it – was —

Gone.

Only blackened walls stood, with gaping spaces where her windows had gleamed. Firefighters on ladders were spraying water through a hole where her roof had been.

Her lovely bedroom, her kitchen, described in women's magazines as the beating heart of a home.

Everything.

Gone.

Even with the evidence right in front of her, it was impossible to process.

Shaking, Freya forced the passenger door open and almost fell onto the footpath. After she'd managed to regain her balance, she turned to find Daisy and Jo beside her. She saw their sagging mouths, the sheen of tears in their eyes, and she just wanted to sink into the ground and disappear.

'Oh, darling.' Daisy held out her arms and Freya, crumpling, stumbled into her friend's hug.

And now Jo was hugging her, too, and despite being surrounded by her very worst nightmare, Freya found herself, with her friends' arms around her, quite unexpectedly, comforted. And when a familiar yip sounded close by, she turned to see a firefighter, huge and heroic in his helmet and protective gear, cradling a little furry bundle in his arms.

'Won Ton!' *A miracle, surely?*

The firey's face was blackened by ash, but his teeth flashed white as he grinned. 'Found her hiding in the shrubbery.'

'Oh, thank God.' Freya gave a shaky, teary laugh as he handed the shivering little dog to her. 'Thank *you*,' she added, as she hugged her canine baby and felt frantic heartbeats beneath her hand.

'You'll be okay, Frey. You will,' Daisy murmured beside her. 'You'll get through this.'

Freya didn't want to get through this – she just wanted it to go away. But life had already taught her several harsh lessons, and she knew already that she had no choice. She was grateful, though, that no one mentioned phoenixes rising from ashes.

CHAPTER FOUR

A curlew's mournful cry coiled through the night as Billie let herself into her parents' house.

Strange how she thought of this new place as her parents' house, rather than her home, as if she didn't really belong here. While she'd been away, her mum and dad had moved out of the house she'd grown up in. For years their home had been a modest chamfer-board and fibro cottage in the back streets of Picnic Bay. In her teens, Billie had helped her dad to paint it a reckless but cheerful aqua with bright yellow window frames. Now, her parents lived in a tasteful, architecturally designed rectangle of timber and glass perched on a rocky headland with magnificent sea views.

For Billie, while their new house with its picture windows, polished timber floors and stainless steel fittings was undeniably swish, and stunning proof of her mum's impressive years of frugality combined with good business sense, she didn't really feel that she belonged here. She'd driven past her old home yesterday to find it looking rather dilapidated, with the garden totally neglected, and yet she'd felt such a strong tug of nostalgia she'd almost stopped and knocked on the yellow front door.

She wasn't quite sure what she might have said if the new owner had actually answered. *I'd just like to take a peek at the back bedroom?*

The thing was, although Billie wasn't a kid any more, it still kind of hurt to know that her parents had cleaned everything out of her old bedroom, making high-handed decisions about what to toss and what to stow in boxes at the back of their new garage.

Billie hoped her mum hadn't been too nosy while she'd been packing. She hated to imagine her mum snooping between the covers of that embarrassing diary she'd kept in Year 10. And what about that dope she'd hidden in a shoebox at the back of her wardrobe and never bothered to remove?

So embarrassing.

Oh, well, her parents had never held back from speaking their minds when they'd been upset with her, so if they'd been bothered by any of these things, they would have said something by now.

This evening, however, as Billie let herself into the sleek new kitchen – double oven, induction cooktop, stone benches, natch – she had to wonder if her parents were bothered by *something* at the moment. The house seemed to be in darkness, so they must have already gone to bed. Which wasn't particularly unusual, given her dad's nursing shifts, but Billie fancied she'd sensed a subtle change in them since she'd returned after almost two years away.

She couldn't quite put her finger on what it was that she'd noticed. Her parents hadn't turned into snobs just because they'd moved house, or anything painful like that. Their favourite TV shows were still *MasterChef* and any adaptation of Agatha Christie they could find. Her dad, Troy, still worked at the Townsville General Hospital and caught the ferry to the mainland each day. But their new garage was no longer littered with his fishing rods and reels, cast nets and crab pots in the way their old garage had been.

As for Billie's mum, Pearl, she no longer put in the long hours on the day-to-day menial tasks in the bistro the way she had when she'd first started out, but she seemed to work almost as hard now as its manager. Billie had asked what this involved and had been somewhat stunned to hear her mum rattle on about monitoring cash flows and planning marketing strategies.

Even so, the change in her mum couldn't really be explained by a new skill set and a new vocabulary. There was palpable tension in the air and Billie had no idea whether this was caused by worry about finances – had they overspent on this house, or was the bistro no longer as profitable as it had been? – or whether her parents had some other concern that they weren't willing to share.

Of course, after her breakup with Petros, Billie knew it was possible that she was now viewing her parents through the filter of her own sadness and despair. She might have dismissed her worries if she hadn't seen the meaningful look in Sonia Brassal's eyes this evening.

Billie had caught that look again as the Brassals were leaving. Her former teacher had taken her aside and had spoken almost furtively, out of the corner of her mouth. 'As I said before, Belinda, it's very good of you to have come home to help your parents. I know they're very grateful, but just remember you shouldn't stay too long on this island.'

It was hard to know what to make of this. Billie hadn't viewed her return as especially big-hearted. She'd needed a job and a roof over her head until she worked out what she wanted to do next. And her parents hadn't shown any signs of over-the-top gratitude. If they were happy to have her come home to help, why should it concern Mrs B?

'What's wrong with the island?' she couldn't resist asking, hoping she didn't sound too naïve. 'You're still here, and you're happy, aren't you?'

'Of course,' she was told. 'But it's different for you, Belinda.'

'It is?'

Sonia Brassal narrowed her eyes and stared at Billie, as if she was trying to read her mind. Then she gave a slow nod. 'It is. Remember that. You've always had huge potential. Make sure you don't waste it.'

Then she'd sailed off into the night, her cape flowing about her, her husband, sister and brother-in-law trailing demurely behind her, leaving Billie to wonder what the hell she'd meant.

What was this about potential? Anyone would think she was some kind of brains trust, but she'd only been a slightly above-average all-rounder at school. In high school – on the mainland, as the island didn't run to secondary education – she'd become quite rebellious, changing from Belinda to Billie, and getting into all sorts of strife, so that her parents were somewhat relieved when she'd finally scraped through Year 12 with a very mediocre result and they hadn't pushed to send her to uni.

A lucky escape, she'd always told herself, although she had sometimes wondered.

CHAPTER FIVE

When Freya woke, she took a moment or two to work out where she was, but too soon, realisation dawned. Of course. This was a spare room at Daisy's house, which explained why the clothes Freya had worn out to dinner last night were now draped over a green cane chair in the corner. And why Won Ton wasn't in her basket in the laundry, but curled on a woven mat beside her bed. Why Freya was wearing a pink nightdress instead of her usual animal-print PJs.

In a sickening rush, everything else came flooding back in horrid images tumbling one after the other. The fire. The total devastation of her beautiful home. Plus the disquieting news from a firefighter that the blaze had probably started in solar panels on her roof, followed by the angry thought that bloody Brian had been so busy with his new and better life that he'd neglected the routine mainte-nance he'd specifically agreed to as part of their divorce.

Damn him to hell and back.

For a scant moment, it did occur to Freya that Brian would probably be upset about the fire. There'd been a time when he'd been both proud and fond of their home, and when he heard about the solar panels he was bound to feel guilty, but he'd soon get over the upset. He had pregnant Amber to comfort him now, while all Freya had left in the entire world were her dog and those clothes on that chair. And her car, presumably still at the restaurant's car park. Oh, and her phone, which Daisy had kindly set to recharge in the kitchen.

So little.

It was no good trying to tell herself that she'd only lost *things* and that no one had died. Somehow that wasn't any comfort when she was actually homeless.

With that thought, Freya's mood sank even lower. Was she now like the women she'd seen on TV, in the second half of their lives and reduced to couch-surfing or living in campervans and being interviewed by earnest journalists? Could she bear it?

She couldn't dredge up any excitement at the possibility of building a new house. She'd loved the one she had, thank you very much.

But never again would she wake to the warm, cheeky new colours in her bedroom. Never again could she wander through to her sunny, north-facing kitchen with gleaming stone benchtops and nifty pull-out shelves in the pantry. And what about the photographs? The paintings? Her clothes? The to-die-for grey silk pants she'd bought in Milan? The gorgeous floral summer dress she'd bought in harbourside Sydney?

Overwhelmed and flattened by fear and sadness, Freya lay very still. She felt numb, exhausted. Totally drained.

Life was simply too hard this morning and yet she felt weirdly bored, as if nothing mattered any more. Justice, equality, world peace, global warming? Nup, not interested, thank you. After all, the universe didn't give a damn.

She might have rolled over and tried to go back to sleep if there hadn't been a gentle knock on her door.

'Morning,' she called and Daisy appeared with a mug in her hand.

'Thought you might like a cuppa,' her friend said.

'Oh, thanks.' Freya tried for a grateful smile. 'Is it very late?'

'A bit after ten.'

Good grief. Freya propped herself up on one elbow as Daisy continued into the room and set a bright mug in tropical pinks and greens on the bedside table. 'After ten?' she said. 'Gosh, sorry.'

Daisy shook her head. 'No need to apologise. And no need to get up. I'm sure you must be exhausted. You probably took ages to get to sleep last night.'

'Yes, I did.' Freya had lain here for hours, boiling in a soup of anger and despair. 'But this bed's deliciously comfortable,' she added, not wanting to seem ungrateful.

'Good, then I'll leave you to enjoy your cuppa. I think I got it right. White with one?'

Freya took a sip. 'Yes, it's perfect, thanks. You're a darling.'

'And stay there as long as you like.'

She really wouldn't mind staying in bed all day. All week, for that matter. When life had beaten you into the ground, what was the point in getting up? No one would mind if she just wanted to curl up and retreat from the world.

But to her own surprise, Freya found herself saying, 'No, I should get up. I'll just sulk and feel sorry for myself if I stay here in bed.'

Daisy's response was a sympathetic smile. 'You're certainly entitled to sulk, but perhaps you're right. I've put towels in the bathroom, if you want to shower. Fresh clothes are a bit of a problem, though. I'm so much shorter and rounder than you. But Jo rang to say she's dropping a few things over and she's pretty much your size.'

'That's kind of her. What would I do without my friends? You've both been so thoughtful.'

'You know you'd do the same for us.'

Yes, Freya thought, and if they'd been younger, she and her girl-friends might have got stuck into the grog last night, but somehow, this level of misfortune had brought out the adult in everyone.

With another of her gentle smiles, Daisy turned to leave, but then she paused in the doorway. 'By the way, Brian rang. Your phone was in the kitchen and I could see it was him calling, so I answered. I hope you don't mind. He'd heard about the fire on the local morning news.'

'Oh.' Freya shuddered at the thought of her home's heart-rending destruction being broadcast on local radio news or TV screens in thousands of living rooms.

'He was pretty upset.'

'Yes, I suppose he would be.' Freya sighed. 'I'll ring him later.' She wasn't ready to deal with her ex's emotional fallout on top of her own.

By the time Freya emerged from the shower, wrapped in a towel-ling bathrobe and feeling slightly less fragile, Jo had indeed arrived, carrying a shopping bag and an armful of clothes.

'Just a few things to get you started,' she said. 'Jeans, T-shirts and a couple of sweaters. Oh, and undies in here,' she added, hold-ing up the bag.

Freya blinked. She'd never worn someone else's undies before.

'I grabbed them from Target on the way over,' Jo added, as if she'd read Freya's mind. 'I hope I got the sizes right.'

'Wonderful.' Freya made a quick check and the sizes were perfect. She'd assumed she would have to collect her car and go shopping straight away for staples. Instead, Jo had given her a little breathing space, while Daisy had made a pot of coffee and set out breakfast options – muesli, yoghurt, fruit, a pile of toast and a collection of spreads.

'Wow,' she said. 'How lovely.'

'You should start up a B&B, Daisy,' Jo added with a grin.

'My kids have suggested that more than once.' Daisy rolled her eyes. 'But no, thanks. All that housework every day. I'll stick to garden design.'

Coffee was poured and the trio sat on stools at the kitchen's island bench. Neither Daisy nor Jo was averse to a mid-morning helping of toast, so Freya felt quite comfortable about tucking in, having realised, with some surprise, that she was actually quite ravenous. She was normally careful about too many carbs, but this morning? *What the heck.*

It was while she was spreading delicious cumquat marmalade over a thick slice of buttery sourdough toast that Jo said, 'I've been doing a little research on the internet.'

Freya frowned. 'Research?'

'Yes. I hope I'm not being too pushy, but I thought I'd check out all the practical info. You know – about what to do after a fire.'

'Oh?' Despite an inner quaking, Freya gave a deliberately careful nod. 'Okay.' In theory, she liked the idea of being practical. It certainly beat moping. But in practice she wondered if it was necessary for her to be heroic so soon. The thought of all the work ahead of her was exhausting. Couldn't she take a day or two out to grieve?

'I guess you'd need to look into replacing documents like passports and birth certificates,' suggested Daisy.

Freya sighed again.

'The documents are important,' said Jo. 'But you also need to get yourself well prepared for the insurance people.'

'Oh, God, insurance.' Freya winced. That was another reason she would have to speak to Brian. Insurance was one of the issues covered by the divorce settlement. 'I hate to think what *they'll* need.'

'They want masses of info,' came Jo's unappetising reply. And with a small smile, she added, 'I'm assuming you don't have a photo of every item in your home?'

'You've got to be joking.' Freya's jaw sagged in horror. 'Don't tell me that's what they expect?'

'Apparently that's the ideal, but of course hardly anyone does it. But they say you should start listing everything you've lost.' Jo was consulting a sheet of paper, no doubt a printout from her computer. 'The advice here is that you should itemise everything, room by room, drawer by drawer, cabinet by cabinet.'

'I'm supposed to remember everything?' Freya echoed in disbelief. 'Drawer by drawer?'

Jo nodded. 'That's what it says here.'

'Bloody hell.'

'And you should include everything in the garage and the garden as well.'

Just in time, Freya stopped herself from snapping at Jo. 'And I suppose they also want to know how much everything's worth?'

'You can add in values later. Seems it's a good idea to just get everything listed first. Create a spreadsheet, perhaps.'

'I guess,' Freya said faintly. At least she'd spent years running an office and she'd mastered Excel.

'And I can lend you a laptop,' added Jo.

Brian rang again just as Jo was leaving. Freya's stomach tightened when she saw his name on her phone's screen. Waving to her friend, she took the phone back to the spare bedroom and plonked herself down on the end of the bed.

'Hello, Brian.'

'Freya, I'm so sorry about the fire.' Her ex sounded shocked. Shaken.

'Yeah.' What else could she say?

'I need to talk to you.'

Freya frowned. Brian was talking now, wasn't he? 'What do you want?'

'Ah —' He gave an awkward, throat clearing growl. 'Could you come to the office?'

Was that really necessary? More to the point, Freya needed to know if Amber would be there, but she couldn't bring herself to ask this. 'I – I don't have my car at the moment. I was out last night. Daisy drove me home.'

Now an impatient, or possibly desperate, sigh sounded in her ear.

Really? Whose problem was this? Freya's thoughts were spinning. What the hell did Brian need to talk about? Now, on quite probably the worst day of her life?

'Please, Freya, it's important. We need to meet. It's not something I want to discuss over the phone.'

Freya wanted to yell and snap that whatever his issue was, it couldn't possibly be more important than her problems. Not today, but she supposed this would nag at her unless she spoke to him.

'We were planning to collect my car shortly,' she said with excessive patience. 'So I suppose I could meet you in about an hour?'

'Okay. Thanks. See you then.'

Abruptly, Brian hung up before Freya could quiz him further. She sat for a moment, staring at her phone, wishing she didn't feel so rattled, so aware of an inner disquiet caused by her ex-husband's unexpected need to meet.

For the hundredth time she wished she could press a reset button on this whole horrible problem so it would just go away. And then, as her mind zigzagged crazily, she even wondered if the fire might not have happened if she and Brian had still been married.

Oh, for God's sake. Hadn't she moved on from that useless line of thought? She had moved on, of course she had.

*

At least, when Freya and Daisy arrived at the restaurant car park, her car was still there. Freya knew it was ridiculous to feel so inordinately relieved, but she almost cried when she saw her sturdy white Forester still parked exactly where she'd left it.

Given everything that had happened since she'd abandoned it yesterday evening, this felt like a huge achievement. Now, her ordinary, not very new vehicle, which wasn't nearly as prestigious as Daisy's Volvo, felt exceptionally special. After all, it was solid and undamaged and Freya owned it outright. Sure, an inanimate object shouldn't really warrant such a rush of fondness, but at times like this, just one intact worldly possession could be balm to a distraught woman's soul.

Her upbeat mood stayed with her as she farewelled Daisy and drove back along the Sunshine Motorway. It was a beautiful sunny day, in fact. The sky was an impeccable, spotless blue and the wattles on the median strip were bursting into fuzzy balls of golden glory.

Being a Saturday afternoon, there were no customers at Brian Bright's Electrics, which was a plus. Freya experienced a jolt, though, as she noted the changes in the office, no doubt adapted to suit Amber's tastes. Most of her carefully tended pot plants had disappeared and the few plants left were on their last legs, while a shiny Japanese Fortune Cat now sat on the counter with its paw raised, presumably to wave in loads of cash.

Brian was sitting in front of the computer in the chair that had once been Freya's. Three bottles of variously coloured, glittery nail varnish were lined on the desk in handy reach and a fluffy pink cardigan was draped over the chair's back.

Freya tried not to feel humiliated, but it still hurt to know she'd been so quickly and happily replaced.

At least Amber was nowhere in sight, so that was something.

And Brian leapt to his feet as Freya entered. It had only been a few months since she'd seen him last, but she was conscious of an extra roll around his middle and new grey flecks in his receding brown hair. There was also a decidedly harried expression in his pale hazel eyes.

Had he always looked so – ordinary? So lacking in earthy sex appeal?

She wondered how they should greet each other under these strained circumstances. Politely shake hands? Would Brian kiss her on the cheek?

He did neither, but simply remained where he stood and gave a nervous nod. 'I'm really sorry about the fire, Freya. It was such a shock.'

'It certainly was.' *And a way bigger one for me, pal.*

'It's so hard to believe.' His frowning gaze was intense, almost fearful. 'Do – do you know how it started?'

'The fireys seem to think it was the solar panels.'

Brian blanched at this news and Freya might have grabbed the opportunity to get stuck into him, to let out her anger and lay on the guilt, reminding him that he'd agreed to continue any electrical maintenance as part of their divorce settlement. His ashen complexion, however, suggested that he didn't need reminding.

'You'd better take a seat,' he said next, pointing to one of the padded chairs usually reserved for waiting customers. He, meanwhile, lowered himself back into the chair at the computer and began a nervous tapping on the desk.

'What's this about, Brian?' Freya couldn't help being alarmed by his manner as she sat where she was told. 'Why did you need to see me?'

Now he looked more worried than ever. He opened his mouth to speak, but then shut it again and swallowed, reminding her of a goldfish.

Thoroughly disconcerted, she sat straighter.

Brian cleared his throat. 'It's about the insurance.'

A zap spiked through her, an electric shock of pure terror.

'What about it?' she managed to ask. Before the divorce, the insurance for their house and these office premises had been automatic deductions from one of their business accounts. After the legal matters were settled, Freya had kept the house, but relinquished her share in the business. In return, Brian had grudgingly agreed to take care of her home's rates, insurance and general maintenance.

At the time Freya had thought it was a fair enough deal.

But now, her ex looked way too uncomfortable. Watching her, he gulped, making his Adam's apple jerk.

'Brian, for God's sake, don't tell me —' She couldn't voice her sudden fear.

'It's my fault,' he said. 'I should have reminded Amber. I should have checked.'

What the hell?

Freya leapt to her feet. 'Are you telling me my house isn't insured?'

'I'm so sorry,' Brian said again.

Shock robbed Freya of breath. As she stared at him, her heart banged as if she'd rushed up a dozen flights of stairs. 'You mean it, don't you? You haven't paid the bloody insurance?' She was gasping as she stood, fists clenched, shaking with rage. With disbelief. With utter despair.

Brian lifted his hands, feigning helplessness. 'Poor Amber's been distracted, with the pregnancy and everything.'

'Poor Amber?' Freya screamed. Was the man for real? Was he actually blaming ditzy Amber? 'Do you know what you've bloody done to me?' she roared next. 'You and your damn midlife crisis?'

'Freya, please —'

'Shut up, Brian. Bloody hell. Don't you dare try to make excuses, or tell me how to behave. For God's sake, it wasn't enough for you to dump me. You've taken away my job, my business – and – and now —' She was shaking so hard she could barely get the words out. 'Now, my home.'

Fuelled by more fury than she'd ever experienced in her life, Freya picked up a chair and hurled it across the office. As it crashed to the floor – missing Brian's feet by mere inches, worse luck – she burst into uncontrollable, noisy tears.

CHAPTER SIX

When her father found her, Billie was sitting on a huge smooth boulder, gazing out at the stunning blue vista of the Coral Sea. Monday was one of the two days in the week when Island Thyme was closed and she was free, so she'd followed her favourite walking track that wound around the rocky headlands and offered gorgeous glimpses of a succession of little bays below.

She was in a brooding mood. Brooding over Petros, of course.

Sitting on a sun-warmed rock, hugging her knees and staring glumly at the crescent of white sand that fringed a half-moon bay, she could almost imagine she was back in Santorini. When she drew a deep breath, she could just about catch the scents of oregano and basil, the aroma of Greek coffee and the salty-sweet clash of fish and ouzo.

With her eyes closed, it was all too easy to picture Petros, her own personal Greek god, striding towards her along a cobblestone pier. His long legs in sun-bleached jeans, dark hair lifting in a soft breeze, while his white teeth flashed in a brilliant smile.

The memories were so entrancing, Billie ignored the sound of approaching footsteps. After all, there were always plenty of hikers on this track. Day trippers, backpackers, divers with snorkels and flippers searching for the next bay to explore.

She just wanted to concentrate on Petros.

'We knew from the start that this couldn't really last,' he'd said at the end. 'It's probably best if we don't drag it out.'

But Billie hadn't known anything of the sort and Petros had never really explained why he'd wanted out. Surely she deserved to know?

'Billie.'

Her father's voice brought her whirling round, her thoughts spinning, her cheeks aflame. It was her dad's day off, too, but he'd been busy answering emails on his laptop when Billie had left the house. Now, with his jaw shadowed by a day-old grey-speckled beard, he was dressed in faded denim shorts, a loose, even more faded grey T-shirt and battered sandshoes, with an old red towelling hat that shaded his eyes. He smiled at her. 'Thought I'd find you here.'

'Yeah.' Billie edged sideways to make room for him on the rock. 'This is still my favourite spot. It's a gorgeous day.'

'Isn't it just?'

Her dad settled beside her and she was relieved that he seemed happy enough to sit quietly, soaking up the winter sunshine and admiring the glittering sea.

'Look,' she said, determinedly closing a door on her Grecian heartache as she pointed to a cute rock wallaby emerging shyly from between two boulders.

Troy grinned. 'Yeah, he'll be looking for a handout.'

'I didn't bring any food. Did you?'

'No, but he won't be hungry for long. The tourists are always feeding the wallabies. They can get quite cheeky and game.'

'Yeah, I remember.'

'Of course you do.' The lines around her dad's eyes deepened as he smiled again.

For several minutes, they remained sitting there in companionable silence, watching a yacht plough around the point, sails billowing, snowy white against the blue. Eventually Billie's curiosity forced her to speak. 'You know you can ask me, Dad.'

'Excuse me?'

'Well, you seem to have come looking for me, so I assume there's a question.'

He grinned broadly then. 'You always were too smart for your old man.'

Billie turned to him, remembering the thread of tension she'd sensed between her parents, and she felt nervous now. She kept her tone casual. 'So what's bugging you?'

'It's not a huge deal, Bills. I just wanted to sound you out.'

'Uh-huh?'

'You're doing such a great job at the bistro. The staff love you and, well, we – that is, your mother and I – thought maybe you could stay on for a bit.'

A bit? She had no idea what that might entail. 'Well, I wasn't planning to rush straight off.'

'We were actually wondering if you could stay, keeping an eye on everything, while we take a break.'

This was unexpected, not that her parents weren't entitled to a break. Billie couldn't remember the last time they'd gone away on a proper holiday. They'd often joked that living on Maggie Island was like being on a permanent holiday. Boredom of seeing the same old, same old had never seemed a problem for them.

'Your mum's got it into her head that she wants to take off. You know – do the lap of honour.'

'The *what*?'

'Heading around Australia in a caravan.'

'Really?' Billie blinked in surprise. She'd been thinking along the lines of a couple of weeks in Tasmania, or New Zealand, or even Bali perhaps. 'Like grey nomads?'

Her dad shrugged. 'Yeah, I guess so. We'd get one of those low-profile vans. They're not such a hazard on the road.' Picking up a small pebble, he rolled it between his fingers and thumb before flicking it to bounce from rock to rock. 'Your mum's been talking about it for quite a while now, actually. It's pretty important to her. Seems she's realised there's a whole country out there that she's never explored, while you've been travelling and your aunt Freya's had all sorts of overseas trips.'

'And Mum's been working her guts out on this island.'

'Yeah.'

'She's been hit by a major dose of FOMO,' said Billie.

'What's that?'

'Fear of missing out.'

'Well, yeah.' Momentarily, her dad's eyes lost their sparkle and took on a worried, distanced look instead. But then the moment was gone, making Billie think she must have imagined it, and he was grinning. 'FOMO. I'd say that's it in a nutshell, love.'

Wow. If this idea had been brewing for some time, Billie was surprised she'd heard nothing about it till now. 'Well, it would be fun for you both,' she said cautiously, as she juggled the warring concepts of family duty versus entrapment. 'You guys haven't done a lot of travel.' Then quickly, before she found herself too committed, 'How long would you be gone for?'

'Only six months.'

Six months. Yikes. At least it wasn't a whole year, but still. Twenty-six weeks. 'Can you *do* the whole of Australia in six months?'

'Your mum's been checking everything out and she reckons we can. I guess we'd have to pick and choose the places where we'd stay on for a bit and those that we'd more or less whiz through.'

'I guess. But what about your work, Dad? Can you take six months off?'

'Yeah, yeah. No worries. I'm well overdue for long service leave and I can add on my annual leave, plus all the other days I'm owed.'

'Right.' Billie had run out of questions for the moment, but she was still trying to take this in. It was so unexpected. Mind you, she'd known there was something in the wind. All those looks that had passed between her parents. The unmistakable tension. She was relieved it wasn't anything more serious. But had they really been nervous about broaching this with her?

It seemed her father had drawn the short straw when it came to raising this subject with her, but she supposed that made sense. Billie and her mum got on okay, give or take the usual mother–daughter flare-ups that had happened over the years, but her relationship with her dad had always been way more relaxed.

Perhaps he'd had it easy, though. During her childhood, her dad had taught her the fun stuff, how to swim and skin dive, how to throw a cast net or to build a camp fire on the beach. Her mum had been the one left to supervise her homework, her chores, her wardrobe and her social life, so there'd been inevitable friction.

These family dynamics had been laid down decades ago and Billie guessed they would remain the same when she was fifty.

'So what d'ya reckon?' her dad asked now, as the yacht they'd been watching disappeared around a northern headland.

Billie would have liked more time to think, but she was conscious that her father tactfully *hadn't* mentioned that it really was time for her to pull her weight, especially as she was their one and only and she had no other obvious plans. It wasn't as if they'd be dragging her away from an important career. And she didn't have any other work lined up at the moment.

The sad reality was that Billie had been drifting for years now, with no clear goals. Mind you, she'd started out with ambitions. At art college, she'd put in three and a half semesters before she realised she would never make a living out of painting and drawing.

After that, she'd worked in a shoe shop in the Townsville mall, travelling back and forth on the ferry each day, until she'd saved enough money to travel further.

Then she'd headed for Thailand and that had become the pattern. She would find a low-key, no-stress job and save until she had enough money to set off again.

'You'd have the house to yourself,' her dad said.

Billie slid him a sly, sideways smile. 'You can spare me the sales pitch.'

'But it's true, Bills. You'd be able to invite anyone you wanted to stay.'

Fair enough, but right now Billie could only think of one person she longed to invite and he'd made it heartbreakingly obvious that he wasn't available.

'And maybe your mum could stop worrying about you, if she knew you were going to be here, in one place, for a goodly stretch of time.'

'She worries about me?'

'You're joking, right?'

'Well, I guess I sort of knew.'

'Of course she worries when you take off for the other side of the world on a shoestring budget and then only communicate when the whim hits you.'

Her mum had certainly carried on when Billie first announced that she had her passport and was heading overseas, but when you grew up on a tiny island, you reached a point where you just had to get off.

'And this last jaunt,' her dad went on, 'I know you were on your way home and running low on cash, but – seriously, Billie – hitching a ride up the coast on a yacht with a stranger? When you do things like that, your mother can fret for Australia.'

'I wasn't just hitching. I was crewing,' Billie defended. 'It was a paid job.' Or at least it had been until the lecherous prick who owned the yacht had pressured her one too many times and she'd jumped ship in Shute Harbour. But her parents didn't need to hear every unsavoury detail. Her mum would have had a heart attack if she'd known the whole story.

'Anyway, about the bistro,' she said, steering away from that unpleasant topic. 'I can't imagine I'd be any good with the business side of things. I'm no bookkeeper.'

'Your mum's spoken to Aileen Jones about that.'

Aileen was an accountant who lived in Horseshoe Bay. Her daughter, Mandy, had been a great mate of Billie's, years ago in their school days. Sensible Mandy had become a school teacher and was now married with two kids and living in Brisbane. Most of Billie's old schoolmates were similarly settled. Billie was the failure among her classmates, it seemed. The black sheep. Or was that the lost sheep?

'But what about all the other managerial stuff?' she asked next. While she'd worked in offices, she'd only ever been a general dogsbody, typing, printing out documents, filing and fielding phone calls. 'I spoke to Mum and it sounded full on.'

Her dad's lips pursed and he gave a slow nod. 'There'd be a bit to learn, I must admit. But I reckon the most important thing is making sure Island Thyme continues to offer good service. Restaurants and cafés are mostly about serving others. Giving them a good experience.'

This was something Billie innately understood. 'So it's a bit like nursing?'

Her dad smiled. 'Yeah, a bit. And I reckon that's your talent, Bills.'

'Well, yeah, I can wait on tables, no sweat, and I can make tea and coffee – but —' She sighed. 'I really don't know about managing. Wouldn't you want someone with business experience?'

'That would be the ideal, of course, but your mum could show you the ropes. It's a small business, really. I don't think it's all that hard.'

Billie was about to protest. She had visions of her parents arriving home from this so-called lap of honour, sun-tanned and happy and looking more relaxed than they had in absolutely ages, only to discover their business was in all sorts of trouble, a financial disaster, simply because they'd had naïve faith in their precious child. And she hadn't measured up.

She might have blurted out this fear if Mrs B's words from a couple of nights ago hadn't echoed in her head.

You've always had huge potential. Make sure you don't waste it.

Yeah. Easy enough for an old Year 7 teacher to throw around a compliment, but did that potential include fast-track lessons in how to take over a business at short notice?

'Can I think about it?' she asked. 'I won't drag out my answer, I promise.'

'Of course,' came the speedy response.

In the distance she could now see the ferry chugging towards the island from the Townsville mainland. Before she lost her nerve, she asked, 'So what about you guys otherwise? You and Mum? Is everything okay?' She shot her father a quick searching glance.

'Sure,' he said, perhaps a shade too quickly. 'Why do you ask?'

Billie sighed again. 'I don't know. I thought you both seemed a bit strained.'

'You think so?'

Was it her imagination, or was his expression too carefully neutral? 'Yeah,' she said. 'I thought so.'

'Well, we thought the same about you.'

Clunk. Was her broken heart really that obvious?

Billie tightened her jaw, trying to look way tougher than she felt. 'I'm okay.'

'And so are we, love.'

If she'd been game to look her father in the eye, she might have seen the truth, but she was too busy hiding the precise state of her own emotions.

'I guess your mum's just been getting more and more impatient ever since she was struck by this mood to take off,' he said.

Billie nodded. 'I get that. Mum didn't even travel when she was young, did she?'

Her dad shook his head. 'For almost as long as I've known her, she's always been too busy with some project or other.'

Billie could remember this well. Instead of embracing the island's sarongs-and-sandals spirit, her mum had always shown an entrepreneurial bent. Even when Billie had been in kindergarten, her mum had worked hard at sewing and crocheting and bottling preserves, all of which she'd sold in street stalls, or at the weekend markets.

Later, when Billie reached mid-primary, her mum had opened a fish and chip shop on the Picnic Bay Esplanade and then finally, six years ago, she'd realised her dream of renovating a perfectly positioned cottage and turning it into a cute bistro with a lovely deck overlooking her favourite bay. And she'd made it a success, because she'd worked so damn hard.

'Mum's certainly earned her lap of honour,' she said quietly.

'She has, love. No doubt about that.'

'And so have you, Dad. You've worked just as hard. God knows how you put in so many years in the emergency ward.'

He merely grinned, then looped an arm around Billie's shoulders and dropped a warm kiss on her forehead. 'Well, anyway, give it some thought, won't you?'

CHAPTER SEVEN

The weekend was hellish – there was no other word for it – and several days passed before Freya found the strength to ring her sister. She'd been hoping that Pearl might ring her first, full of horror at what had happened, offering sympathy and help, the kind of assistance that any sister would readily provide.

Of course, it was more than likely that Pearl hadn't actually heard about the fire. Even if the story had made it to the newspapers or TV screens in North Queensland, not everyone was glued to the twenty-four hour news cycle, certainly not the busy owner of a thriving beach restaurant.

And anyway, the lag before sharing her news with Pearl was probably for the best. After her meeting with Brian, Freya had needed time to calm down. She'd been too shattered to think straight.

She'd staggered out of his office, distraught and sobbing and, no doubt, still screaming like a fishwife, and had driven to the nearest beachfront bar and ordered a succession of scotches without so much as a bag of potato chips to help line her stomach.

But honestly, what else could a woman do when she'd found herself left with nothing to her name? Not a frigging thing?

Not only had her lovely home, the one thing she had left after she'd lost her marriage and her career, been reduced to a block of land burdened by an ugly blackened ruin, but she'd also lost any chance to rebuild.

And now she'd lost her emotional framework as well. Her sense of security. Her trust in relationships, her sense of purpose, of being needed. She felt adrift in a cold and desolate sea with no sign of any bloody life raft.

Brian's offer to have the burnt-out rubble removed was such a ludicrous attempt at compensation that Freya's usual tipple of a glass of pinot gris, or even a gin and tonic, just couldn't have cut it that night. So, yeah, trying to obliterate herself with scotch wasn't her usual MO, but she'd been too blinded by despair to care.

It had been around midnight when Daisy had finally found her.

Poor Daisy. She'd been an absolute darling, yet again, gently but firmly steering Freya out into the chilly night air and into her car to bring her home. For the second time, Freya's car had been abandoned to be picked up the next day, while Daisy had dosed her with water and aspirin and helped her into bed.

Of course, when Freya had finally emerged from her hangover haze, she'd been aghast and so very contrite that she'd landed her friend with all that worry and trouble. But she'd been too overwhelmed by her own wretched feelings of utter hopelessness to bother about contacting her family. Besides, she was pretty damn sure that if she had tried to ring her sister, she wouldn't have been able to share her news without becoming an out-of-control sobbing mess.

Instead, Freya had tried to atone by cooking dinners for Daisy, vacuuming her floors and cleaning her windows till they sparkled. Daisy had protested, gently, until Freya assured her that the elbow grease was therapeutic.

Now, mid-week, feeling only marginally calmer, Freya dialled her sister Pearl's home phone number. She'd only seen photos of the new house with plate-glass windows and stunning sea views, but she could quite easily imagine it. No doubt Pearl would be gazing through one of those big picture windows now and admiring a spectacular view of sea and sky as she answered the phone.

'Hello, Billie speaking.'

Billie was home? This was unexpected. Freya hadn't even realised that her niece was back from Greece. Just showed what a closely bonded family they were.

'Billie, it's Freya,' she said, and she felt the kind of mellowing inside that she always felt when she was talking to Billie, a quiet kind of happiness, wreathed in memories of the special bond she'd once shared with her niece. Way back.

They'd seen each other infrequently over the years, but Freya knew Billie had grown into a warm-hearted and well-balanced young woman, despite her mother's tiresome hovering. The term helicopter parent might have been invented for Pearl.

'How are you?' Freya asked her.

'Not bad, thanks. Mum's got me working my legs off, but I guess I can't complain.' There was a smile in Billie's voice as she said this, so clearly she wasn't too bothered. 'How about you, Freya?' Billie had dropped the 'aunty' tag for Freya somewhere in her mid-teens, around the same time she'd rejected Belinda as her given name.

'Oh —' Freya hesitated. She'd expected to share her bad news with her sister first, which was why she'd chosen to ring before the bistro opened. 'I'm – ah – not great, to be honest. I was wondering if your mum's at home?'

'No, sorry. Mum and Dad are over in Townsville. They had an appointment.'

'Oh? Right.' If Pearl and Troy were in the middle of an appointment, Freya supposed she shouldn't ring Pearl's mobile either.

She felt even more flattened, if that were possible.

'Sorry you're not feeling so great,' Billie said gently. 'It's not the flu, is it?'

'No, no, my health's fine. I'm guessing none of you have heard.' Freya swallowed. 'My house burned down.'

'Oh, God!' The distress in Billie's voice was strangely gratifying. 'Oh, Freya. Oh, shit, I don't know what to say.'

'That's okay. There's not much to say, really.'

'But it's terrible. You poor thing. I'm so sorry.'

'Thanks.' An inadequate response.

'What can we do?' Billie asked next. 'Is there any way we can help? Do you have somewhere to stay?'

'I'm at a friend's place at the moment. She's been wonderful.'

Now was not the time to mention it, but Freya didn't plan to impose on Daisy for too much longer. On quizzing her friend closely, she'd learned that a rather special visitor from America would be arriving soon, a fellow Daisy had met while she'd been holidaying in Italy.

Daisy's coy smile when she'd spoken about him had been a dead giveaway, and the last role Freya wanted was to play gooseberry on the sidelines of an autumn-of-life romance. Consequently, she'd been considering her options. Jo's place was overflowing with her own family, and while Freya had other friends, she was reluctant to ask those who hadn't offered. A caravan park seemed the most likely prospect.

In her more upbeat moments, she told herself it would be fine – like going full circle – returning to her youth when she and Pearl had lived in van parks with Ruby, their single mum. It hadn't been all bad.

Not that she would burden Billie with this possibility right now. 'My friends have been fantastic,' she said.

'That's something, I guess. I don't suppose bloody Brian's been much help. Sorry, Freya, but I've been calling him "bloody Brian" ever since the divorce.'

'You and me both,' Freya retorted, forcing a laugh. In her head, her language regarding her ex had become considerably riper in the past few days.

'God, this is such a rotten thing to have happen,' Billie said next. 'As if you haven't had enough. It's just not fair. Mum's going to be so upset for you.' She hardly paused for breath. 'There must be something we can do. Are you going to build a new house?'

Freya closed her eyes. It still hurt to share this next bit. 'No,' she said quietly. She wasn't comfortable about burdening her niece with the true depth of her woes, but Billie would have to know sooner or later. 'The insurance has lapsed.'

Several seconds passed before Billie spoke. 'Fuck,' she whispered.

'Look, I'll try to catch your mum later,' Freya said. 'When do you think she'll be back?'

'Oh, probably on the four o'clock ferry.'

'Good. I'll ring after that. And don't worry about me, Billie. I'll get through this.'

'Yes, of course you will.' There was no missing the forced brightness that Billie injected. 'I'll let Mum know that you called and she can ring you, if you like.'

'Okay, thanks.'

'Love you, Freya.'

Freya's heart glowed with unexpected warmth. 'Love you, too, Billie.'

It was exhausting, trying to stay strong.

Freya had given herself plenty of lectures, reassuring herself, yet again, that she'd be fine. After all, her life to date hadn't been a bed of roses and she was used to disappointments. In the early years of her marriage, she'd had to deal with the death of her motherhood dreams. Then, last year, her marriage had completely disintegrated and she'd lost the job that she'd given everything to.

Despite these losses, or perhaps because of them, she'd learned that it was still possible to find a level of contentment and she reckoned she'd managed pretty damn well, all things considered.

Now, Freya tried to tell herself that happiness was still out there somewhere, waiting to be found and harnessed. She just wished the search didn't require so much effort. She was tired of strapping on armour to face each day.

When her phone rang, well before four o'clock, she was walking with Won Ton along Peregian Beach in the vain hope that fresh sea air, clear skies and the rolling thump of the surf might lift her jaded spirits.

She was expecting to hear Pearl's voice, but it was Billie again, and to Freya's surprise, her niece seemed to be bubbling with excitement.

'I had to ring back,' Billie said. 'Mum and Dad weren't home before I had to leave for work, but I know they'd agree with me.'

This was accompanied by a metallic clinking sound and Freya guessed Billie was multitasking, no doubt laying cutlery on tables with one hand, while she held her phone with the other.

'I have the perfect solution for you,' Billie said.

'Oh?' It was hard to sound equally enthusiastic.

'Sure. You should come and stay here with me and help me to run Island Thyme.'

Freya came to an abrupt halt, her bare feet sinking into soft damp sand as, for a golden moment, she found herself swept up in the fantasy Billie presented. A roof over her head, a job and someone who welcomed her company. All her wants catered for in one sweet solution.

Then reality dawned. 'Billie, honey, have you discussed this with your mother?'

'Well, no,' came the disappointing reply. 'As I said, I haven't had a chance to talk to Mum yet, but it doesn't really matter. I know she'll think it's a brilliant idea.'

Freya sighed. She was pretty certain Pearl would think it was the worst idea ever.

'She'd love it.' Billie jumped in before Freya could frame an appropriate response. 'Mum and Dad are taking off, you see, doing a grey nomad thing around Australia, and they're leaving me in charge of the business. Can you believe it?'

Freya was too surprised to respond straight away. No, she couldn't quite believe this. Pearl was such a micromanager – in her business and in her relationships – and now that she had her daughter safely home again, Freya would have expected her to keep Billie well within her sights, too.

Instead, she was taking off?

Really?

'I've got to tell you, I'm freaking out,' Billie said next. 'I can wait on tables, no sweat, but I know zilch about managing a business and, well – you're an expert, Freya. This is right up your alley.'

Again Freya couldn't produce a ready answer. She was too surprised, too swamped by a giddy tsunami of emotions. A flurry of hope and an equally strong dose of doubt. She looked down at Won Ton who was watching her with the same anxious expression that had haunted her little face ever since the fire.

'Just imagine,' Billie rushed on. 'We could have so much fun running this place together. And if that's not enough to tempt you, the bonus is, it's winter right now. You know how special Maggie Island is in winter.'

Yes, Freya did know this. She'd lived on Magnetic Island throughout her teens after their mum, Ruby, having taken their van as far north as Townsville, had discovered the island lying just off-shore and decided it was Paradise and they would go no further.

In next to no time, Ruby had landed a job as a barmaid at the Arcadia pub and she'd rented a tiny, ramshackle fisherman's hut right on the beach at Geoffrey Bay. And life had indeed been pretty damn glorious.

No one in their new community had cared or even seemed to notice that Freya and Pearl owned only one pair of shoes each and wore op shop clothes, including secondhand school uniforms. Remembering this now, Freya was aware of the irony that she would once again be reduced to op-shopping.

Back in their youth, she and Pearl certainly hadn't cared. They'd swum every day with the other island kids, they'd learned to snorkel and had discovered a magical coral wonderland right on their door-step. Even now, Freya could remember the utter joy of diving into that secret world of brilliantly hued fish. Bright-blue damsels and prettily striped angelfish, gorgeous yellow butterfly fish and orange and white clowns.

And for the first time ever, she and Pearl had gone to the same school for several years in succession, instead of moving on every few months. When they'd progressed to high school on the main-land, the daily ferry trips had been huge fun. Some days the ferry driver would actually stop the boat so they could watch the minke whales frolicking.

Even on the ordinary days, the island kids enjoyed a unique camaraderie, and each afternoon, they got to leave the city behind them and head back to their own private island haven. Word was, Townsville never looked better than from the back of an island ferry.

So, yeah, Billie was right. While Freya had loved living here on the Sunshine Coast with its magical surfing beaches and brilliant restaurants, she wasn't rapt about the unending miles of suburbia that stretched from Noosa to Brisbane and the Gold Coast. Maggie

Island, on the other hand, was special. If Freya closed her eyes, she could see the island now, with its green tree-studded hills and quiet villages nestled like jewels in a necklace along a scalloped fringe of luminous blue bays.

Of course, developers had swung their muscle, restructuring Nelly Bay Harbour and filling it with modern apartment blocks, but for the most part, the island remained unchanged. A sleepy haven of perfect beaches and white coral sand lined with coconut palms, with headlands covered in smooth round boulders, and simple timber and fibro cottages fronted by deep verandahs and gardens lush with banana and mango trees, clumps of bright bougainvillea and gaudy crotons.

And it was true. After decades of managing Brian's electrical business, she'd soon learn the ropes for the managerial side of running a bistro. Already her imagination was leaping ahead, doing cartwheels as she pictured the possibilities. A chance to regroup, a roof over her head, and a stunning roof at that. Plus a job she'd enjoy.

As for the chance to reconnect with Billie, to get to know her niece properly after all these long years of separation – the possibility made Freya's heart tremble with both joy and fear.

Pearl would be a stumbling block, though. She would never agree to leaving Freya alone with her precious daughter for six long months.

CHAPTER EIGHT

Billie was later than usual getting back from the bistro. A party of diners had wanted to linger on the deck, enjoying the balmy evening, watching the moonlight on the calm tropical water as they dawdled over wine with their dessert and then liqueurs with their coffee. Gavin, the chef, had become fed up with waiting and declared his shift over, so he'd taken off, leaving Billie to hang around until the party finally decided to call it a night.

Once they'd sauntered – or rather stumbled – off, on foot at least and not by car, Billie had finished tidying, stowing dirty linen into the laundry bags, wiping down tables and benches, stacking the final pieces into the dishwashers, closing windows and locking up.

By the time she arrived home, she was dead tired and looking forward to a mug of hot chocolate before she hit the hay. Her dad was on night shift, so she was surprised to find lights on and her mother waiting up for her, sitting stiffly on one of the new white sofas at the far end of the spacious open-plan living area. Billie wondered if her mother had heard about Freya's fire. That might explain her grim face.

'Hi, Mum,' she called from the kitchen as she set a saucepan on the stove and added milk. 'I'm just making a hot chocolate. You want one?'

'No, thanks.' Her mother rose from the sofa and crossed the expanse of polished timber flooring. 'I had a call from your aunt.'

So, she knew. At least that spared Billie from having to share the horrible news. Billie nodded. 'Isn't it terrible?'

'It is. I was shocked, of course. Poor Freya.' Her mother folded her arms across her chest and fixed Billie with a stern look that usually preceded some kind of telling off. 'But I got an extra shock when Freya told me you'd offered her a job.'

Billie gaped at her. She was in trouble for that? Seriously? 'Surely you don't mind?'

Her mother gave a defensive toss of her head and began to rearrange the fruit in the bowl on the counter with unnecessary precision. 'Don't you think you should speak to me before you start offering to employ people?'

Billie could feel her jaw dropping even further, as if a hinge had broken. 'But Freya's not *people*, Mum. She's not just anyone.' *For fuck's sake*, Billie wanted to snarl, but she resisted the temptation to swear out loud. 'She's your sister. And she's just lost her home. She's lost everything.'

'I'm well aware of that. I don't need a lecture, thank you.'

A lecture? Billie might have lost her temper if the milk hadn't chosen that moment to boil over on the stove behind her, giving a hiss as it hit the glass surface. Spinning round, she did swear this time, as she reached for a dishcloth and swiped at the hot spilt milk.

Through gritted teeth, she said, 'Freya's had masses of experience at running a business.'

'Not at running a bistro.'

'Mum!' Billie cried in despairing disbelief. 'Are you for real? I can't believe you're being so negative about your own sister.'

But even as she shouted this protest, a niggling inner voice reminded her . . .

Wasn't this how it had always been?

Billie had never understood the distanced relationship between her mother and her aunt. She'd always thought they were dead lucky to have each other. Billie would have loved a sister. She'd hated being an only child, the sole focus of her parents' worry and concern, and her mother's in particular.

From what she'd observed of her friends' lives, everything was way easier when the focus was diffused among brothers and sisters. Siblings gave you a built-in support system. Even when those siblings were pesky older brothers, they still gave you options at least. On your own, you had no one.

Gosh, when Billie was young, her imaginary friends had more often than not been imaginary sisters.

Word was, her mum hadn't been able to have any more children, but Billie hadn't quizzed her too hard about that. She'd learned when she was quite young that it wasn't a comfortable topic, and all she'd been able to glean was that her own birth had been trouble free.

'Oh, you arrived like a dream,' her mother would say on those rare occasions when Billie had enquired. 'It was when we got you home that the trouble started.' This was usually added with a wry, crooked little smile, almost as if it was a joke, or as close to a joke as her mother ever got.

But it was also because she had no siblings that Billie considered her aunt Freya so special. Along with the cards and presents that came from her grandparents at Christmas and birthdays, there'd always been chatty, warm phone calls from Freya, and the cards she'd sent had contained lovely notes – personal messages full of encouragement and love. Freya's gifts had been special, too.

Billie could still remember most of them – wonderful adventure books, an instant camera, glamorous bath melts, divine scented candles, a silver pendant with the cutest tiny sea turtle that she still wore all the time.

Her mother had often looked worried when Billie had excitedly unwrapped these presents, almost as if she'd feared her daughter might love Freya's gifts more than her own offerings. Secretly, this had been the case on one or two occasions, but Billie had been wise enough to never let on.

Now, however, the sisters' scales of fortune were so out of balance – with one totally homeless while the other lived in this gorgeous new stunner – her mother couldn't possibly feel threatened, surely?

'I had to tell Freya,' Billie protested as she poured what was left of the milk into a mug, added powdered chocolate, and began to stir. 'I was so excited. Inviting her to help is such a great idea and I was sure you'd think so, too. The perfect solution all round. For everyone. And anyway,' she hurried on before her mother could interrupt. 'If you're prepared to leave me more or less in charge of the bistro, I'm entitled to have some say in who helps me.'

'I suppose that's true,' her mother admitted, before her eyes acquired a puzzling, almost triumphant gleam. 'But Freya's actually turned us down.'

CHAPTER NINE

'You'd think I'd know better after all these years,' Freya moaned to Daisy. 'I'm used to Pearl. I know her ways. I can read her like a book. I was more or less expecting her to put up barriers, but instead of steering around them, I just lost the plot.'

'You didn't hang up on her?' Daisy asked.

'More or less.' Freya grimaced apologetically. 'I told her to forget the whole plan. I wasn't interested.'

Daisy's smile was rueful, but her eyes were soft with sympathy. 'It's perfectly understandable that you were tense. You've had so much stress.'

Freya sighed and stared into her glass, giving the ruby contents a swirl. Tonight, she should have been able to relax. After a delicious meal of seafood pasta, she was stretched on the sofa in Daisy's lounge room where a pot-bellied stove in a tiled recess emitted comforting warmth.

Won Ton was snoozing on a mat in front of the stove, and the women were polishing off a fine bottle of red. All the elements for a perfect night were in place, but then Freya's phone had rung.

And now she was still stewing over a call from her sister that she'd totally wrecked. Mind you, Freya wasn't sure if she was suffering from regret so much as self-righteous indignation.

Just as she'd feared, it was all very well for Billie to offer her a job that made her feel wanted and useful, while providing the bonus of a roof over her head for six whole months. But how could she possibly accept when Pearl had been so damn lukewarm about the idea?

Pearl hadn't opposed it outright, of course. How could she when her sister was in such dire straits? But she certainly hadn't been effusive and welcoming. There'd even been a warning note in her voice.

'It's kind of you to make yourself available, Freya, but I imagine you'd get many better offers from businesses on the Sunshine Coast.'

Freya, listening to this, had all too easily remembered her sister's stern frown and earnest expression.

'And you poor thing,' Pearl had added. 'You'd probably prefer to stay put, so you can be on hand to supervise the builders when they start on your new home.'

This had required the awkward explanation that there would be no new home in the foreseeable future, but Pearl had somehow managed to counter this with a dismissive comment, claiming that Billie really could manage on her own with the help of a bookkeeper, thus hinting that Freya really wasn't necessary.

'But of course, if you *need* to come —' she'd finished rather lamely.

At which point, Freya had declared she didn't *need* the work – which was a blatant lie – and of course she didn't want to drive all that long way north if it wasn't necessary.

Now, however, she was kicking herself for throwing away such a wonderful opportunity. Until she'd lost her home, she'd been managing on her savings, but now she was going to have to either pay rent for the rest of her life, or find a job and save for a new, very modest dwelling. The six months' breathing space that Billie had offered had been like a life raft.

Freya let out another sigh. 'It would have been different if I thought Pearl was happy to have me there.' She tried to sound off-hand, but she couldn't keep the tightness from her voice.

Daisy looked concerned. 'You only have the one sister, don't you?'

'Yep. My mum's over in Western Australia these days, so Pearl's all the family I have in Queensland. Pearl and Billie – and Troy, of course.'

'What about your father?'

Freya shrugged. 'Wouldn't have a clue about him. I can't remember him. I was a baby when he left and I've never seen him since. Mum would never talk about him.'

'Gosh, that's sad.'

'I suppose.' Freya shrugged. 'I honestly can't imagine a father in our lives. When we were kids, it just seemed right to be a family of three – Mum, Pearl and me.'

'And here am I, overrun by family,' said Daisy with a wry smile. 'Sisters, brothers-in-law coming out my ears. Nephews, nieces, countless cousins, all within a fifty-kilometre radius.' She took a thoughtful sip of her wine. 'I don't suppose you've seen much of Pearl either, when she lives so far away. I don't remember her visiting.'

'No.' The single syllable sounded perfunctory, but there it was, the unvarnished, not-so-pretty truth. Since Freya had left Magnetic Island she'd rarely been back and whenever she had made the trip north, Brian had accompanied her. Rather than crowding into Pearl and Troy's small cottage, they'd stayed at the Picnic Bay pub, and Pearl had always seemed relieved about that. And in all those years, her sister had made only two fleeting visits to see Freya at the Sunshine Coast, protesting that she was always too busy to get away for a proper holiday.

Yet now, after so recently moving into in her beautiful dream home, Pearl was planning to travel around Australia for six whole months. It didn't make sense.

And I didn't even ask her about that.

Taking a deep sip of wine, Freya stared at the fire as she considered this puzzle. Her sister's spontaneous urge to take off was so out of character. In the past, Freya had always been the reckless one, and during their childhood Pearl had dragged her out of trouble more than once.

With that thought, Freya's chest tightened and, once again, she was reliving that dreadful afternoon when she was just eight years old and they lived in a caravan park in Charleville in western Queensland. Without even closing her eyes, she could see every detail of the dark, weedy creek where she'd almost drowned.

She would never forget the breathless panic of the green water closing over her, the slimy weeds tangling around her ankles, dragging her down. Oh, God, she still had total recall of that all-consuming terror.

It was Pearl who'd rescued her. Despite their six-year age gap, Freya had been almost as tall as Pearl, and she'd thrashed her long arms and legs and almost pulled poor Pearl under the water with her. Somehow, against the odds, Pearl had managed to yank her to safety.

Landing on the muddy bank, gasping but alive, Freya had experienced a moment of huge gratitude. And fifteen years later, she had tried to repay her debt to Pearl.

But that hadn't gone quite the way she'd hoped.

Okay. Enough.

Freya shifted on the sofa, sitting up straighter and making a deliberate effort to clear her thoughts of the past. The present and the future were what mattered now.

After a bit, she said, 'I suppose I *could* try to apologise. Perhaps I should use the stress of the fire as my excuse for hanging up.'

'Of course,' Daisy said with a vigorous nod. 'No one could doubt you've been seriously stressed.'

'Hmmm . . .' Freya winced. 'I should probably ring back first thing in the morning and eat humble pie.'

'But only if you really want to go and help your niece,' Daisy added quickly. 'You're welcome to stay here. You know that, honey. While I do think that a spell on Magnetic Island could be just what you need, I'm certainly not trying to push you away.'

'I know you're not, Daize. You've been an absolute darling. But I won't stay here. Not when you have your dishy Charles on his way from New York.'

'I wouldn't mind.'

'But Charles might.' Freya shot her friend a knowing smile and had the pleasure of seeing her blush prettily. It was wonderful to know that Daisy, who was nudging sixty, was excitedly looking forward to a romantic liaison with a man she'd met while on holiday. For a giddy moment, Freya wondered about the possibility of someone like that for herself in the future. But heavens no, not with her track record with men.

'Honestly,' she told Daisy. 'I'm truly grateful for your generosity, but I really should ignore Pearl's mutterings and take up Billie's offer.' It wasn't just the appeal of a roof over her head and a job. This was also a chance, a dubiously slim chance admittedly, to reconnect with her sister in some small way. 'I'll just have to be super sweet and conciliatory to Pearl and she'll have to suck it up.'

'I can't imagine why she wouldn't want you there, but I know families can be tricky.'

'Ain't that the truth?' Freya suspected that her smile was a little too bitter, but her relationship with her family was a damn sad state of affairs. And in that moment, in Daisy's fire-warmed room, mellowed by wine and with her friend's willing, sympathetic ear, she was seriously tempted to spill about the whole sorry situation, to explain exactly why Pearl had always been nervous about letting her too close to Billie.

Unfortunately, Freya had promised she would never tell that story. And despite her many faults, she was a woman of her word.

CHAPTER TEN

Sitting on the edge of the bathtub, Billie stared at the two lines in disbelief. *No, no, no.* This couldn't be real. This mustn't be happening. It was a bad dream and at any moment now she would wake up and laugh with relief. She couldn't be pregnant.

In desperation, she closed her eyes and gave the testing stick a vigorous shake, but when she looked at it again, those two stubborn lines were still there.

Panic ripped through Billie. Not in any way was she remotely ready to have a baby. God, she'd already made a big enough mess of her life, but this would stuff it up completely.

I'll do another test, she told herself. She had no real understanding of how these tests worked, but perhaps there was a chance that her pee had been too concentrated, or something, and had given her a false reading. A girl could hope.

She stood and went to the bathroom sink, filled a tumbler with water and drank it down, then filled it and drank again. Okay.

After yet another tumbler of water, she waited ten minutes, pacing the bathroom floor anxiously, telling herself over and over that everything would be fine. She just had to stay zen.

The killer was, this was actually the second month now that Billie had missed her period. The first month she'd taken little notice. Her cycles had never been very reliable and she'd reasoned that the emotional fallout of breaking up with Petros could explain why she'd skipped a month, especially when the breakup had been followed by a regrettably stressful sailing experience as she'd travelled back up the Queensland coast.

But now, after another month, she was again overdue and those two blue lines were scaring the hell out of her.

Inhaling a deep and hopefully calming breath, she broke another testing stick out of the packet.

'Okay, here goes . . .'

This time her urine was as clear as rainwater and, with the stick well and truly dosed, Billie closed her eyes. The instructions on the packet said to wait three minutes, so she counted out one hundred and eighty impatient but careful seconds.

Don't let it be two lines. Don't let it be two.

She was almost too scared to look, but slowly, fearfully, she opened her eyelids just a crack.

And there they bloody well were. Two damn lines, and if anything, looking stronger and more self-importantly certain than ever. And now that she thought about it, her boobs had been a bit tender lately.

Crap.

How on earth had this happened? Surely not from those few days in Santorini when her prescription had run out and she'd missed taking the pill? Just a few days – three at the most – and anyway, women in her family were supposed to be hopeless at getting pregnant. Her mum could only have one kid and Freya hadn't been able to have any.

And yet.

Billie let out a heartfelt groan. And yet here she was, pregnant without even trying. How unfair was that?

Filled with gloom, she sank back onto the edge of the bath and her thoughts, inevitably, veered to Petros. Instantly, she could picture him, all Greek-god gorgeous with his coffee-dark eyes and glossy black hair, his smooth golden-brown skin and ridonkulously sculpted muscles. His slow, sexy smile.

But how would Petros react to the news of impending fatherhood? Would it soften the indifference he'd shown towards her at the end?

No question, he would look absolutely awesome with a baby in his arms, but would he want her and their child back in his life?

Sadly, Billie couldn't be confident about that. If she was totally honest, she had serious doubts.

She sighed heavily as she remembered the night she'd first met Petros at a beach party on Santorini. He'd been crazy about her and she'd never experienced such beautiful flirting. Admittedly, moonlight and ouzo had been involved, but dancing with Petros on the edge of the Aegean Sea, with gentle wavelets lapping at their ankles, had been the most incredibly romantic experience.

Within a week, Petros had begged Billie to move in with him, and every single thing about their life together had been beyond fabulous. Certainly, no girl could have asked for a more ardent or passionate lover.

It had been several blissful months before he'd begun to change, turning from god to grouch, complaining that Billie was untidy, even though he was perfectly happy to leave his jocks lying about on the floor, and suggesting that her cooking wasn't quite up to scratch, certainly not as good as his mother's.

Billie had known these were clues that he was getting tired of her, and perhaps she had mentioned Australia a little too often in those later conversations when homesickness crept in. No doubt she had banged on too much about Magnetic Island's beauty when she'd told him about her home. And perhaps it hadn't been wise to inform him about the huge numbers of Greeks who'd happily migrated to Australia.

Just the same, it had still been a huge shock when Petros had quite forcefully suggested it was time for her to leave.

'Billie, are you in there?' Her mother's voice, accompanied by a sharp knock on the bathroom door, roused Billie from her unhappy musings.

'Yep,' she called back. 'Coming.' Hastily, she shoved the pregnancy tests into the small rubbish bin beneath the sink. Luckily, the bin had a lid but, as soon as possible, she would have to get rid of the incriminating evidence properly. Her mother didn't generally use this bathroom, as she had an ensuite off the main bedroom, but Billie certainly didn't want her to find out about this latest disaster.

Not now, when her parents had already bought a caravan and were happily planning the fine details of their trip. Caravans weren't allowed on the island – the roads were just too narrow and winding – so there'd been many trips back and forth to Townsville to stock their van with linens and towels, cooking gear and pantry goods. Her mum had also spent all the hours she could spare on her laptop, haunting grey nomad websites and Facebook pages, making notes on the very best ways to approach their adventure.

'They say it's best to only drive about three hundred kilometres in a day,' she'd told Billie, her eyes gleaming with unnatural excitement. 'That allows time for stops for morning tea, lunch, et cetera. And if you get your distances right, you can settle into the new destination by around four in the afternoon.'

It was quite amazing the way her mum had rattled on lately, outlining all their plans. They would spend a couple of days in each main centre, soaking up the ambience of whatever town they were visiting, seeing its sights and touring its museums or galleries.

'And we won't stay in the caravan every night,' she'd added. 'I think we'll need to give ourselves a couple of nights each week in a hotel or motel, eating out, instead of cooking for ourselves, and enjoying hot showers without having to traipse through a van park.'

Her mother even had a pinboard in her office where she'd mapped the grey-nomad-friendly service stations with refuse and laundry facilities. And she'd written an actual bucket list. She wanted to try her hand at prospecting for gold and to see the Dog on the Tuckerbox near Gundagai. She wanted to go to the Kimberley and see Western Australia's wildflowers and the Morning Glory in the Gulf of Carpentaria. Seeing the tip of Cape York was also a goal, as well as the southernmost point in Tasmania, and she hoped to eat oysters in Port Lincoln in South Australia and to dine in a top gourmet restaurant in Melbourne.

It was going to be a busy six months for them. Billie wasn't sure they'd manage to fit all of the wish list in, but she was delighted to see her mum looking so happy and worked up, instead of worried and tense. The last thing Billie wanted was to cruel this excitement by sharing her pregnancy news. Glumly, she realised she wasn't ready to tell Petros about it either.

Fixing a smile on her face, she opened the door and went out to the living room. 'You wanted me, Mum?'

Her mother nodded. She looked a little pink in the cheeks, but her expression was guarded. 'I've just heard from Freya again.'

'Oh?' Billie tried not to sound too hopeful.

'Seems she's changed her mind.'

'You mean she's coming after all?'

'Yes.'

'Oh, wow.' Billie couldn't resist fist-punching the air. It was about time she had a little good news. 'That's great.'

'Yes,' her mum said again, but with markedly less enthusiasm, and she made a business of straightening the silk runner made from Indian saris that graced the dining table.

'That's awesome, Mum. I'll really appreciate Freya's help, and after the fire and everything, I'm sure she'll benefit from getting away and having a change of scene.'

'Yes, of course. I knew you'd be pleased.'

'You're pleased, too, aren't you?' Billie couldn't resist nudging.

'Yes, yes.' Her mother's expression changed and she seemed to be studying Billie, dropping her head to one side as she did so. She frowned. 'Are you all right, Billie?'

No. I'm freaking out. 'Yes. Fine.' Billie squeezed her cheek muscles to hold her smile in place and tried to blank her thoughts re the pregnancy dilemma. Yikes, if she went ahead with it, how enormous would she be when her parents returned in six months' time? And how would poor Freya react?

CHAPTER ELEVEN

The Forester was packed, a task that, sadly, had taken very little time, given the scarceness of Freya's possessions. Now her car waited at the kerb, rather like a patient packhorse, while Freya made a final pilgrimage to the remains of the home where she'd lived for close to twenty years.

She almost hadn't come. A tour of the wreckage would be an unnecessary downer when she was about to head north on a new adventure. There was something therapeutic about the beckoning call of an open road, and she was actually looking forward to the two long days of driving, passing through Rockhampton and then Mackay and Bowen, before she eventually reached Townsville. So she'd been tempted to skip this painful goodbye.

It had felt spineless, though, to leave without taking one last look, and Freya wanted, more than anything, to be strong. She'd read in an article in one of Daisy's self-help magazines that the worst day of your life could also be the best day. It was all about how you reacted and what you chose to focus on.

Freya wasn't sure she actually had a true focus at this point, but she would probably try to sell the block of land. And she was hoping that if she faced up, just one more time, to the harsh reality of her house's skeletal remains, she might find it easier to let go.

Poor Won Ton was a shivering wreck, though. As soon as Freya turned into the cul-de-sac, the little dog began to whimper and cower with her face between her paws. Freya hated to think of the trauma the poor animal had suffered on the night of the fire.

'I won't be long,' Freya promised, giving Won Ton a comforting rub behind her silky ears. Then, leaving her in the car with a window partly unwound, she resolutely marched up the drive to the tangle of twisted and blackened metal that had once been her garage doors.

Okay, let's do this.

The rest of the house was worse, nothing but rubble and soft grey ash that clung to Freya's boots. Miserably, she pictured the rooms as they'd once been. Her lovely kitchen had been right here in the centre, the heart of her home, but now, the beautiful stone benches that she'd kept spotless and perfect lay at her feet in cracked, black and broken pieces.

Tears stung Freya's eyes as she remembered the joyful day those gorgeous pale benchtops had first been installed. Remembered all the times she'd happily cooked and baked right here, chopping herbs, beating batters, rolling out pastry on the gleaming surfaces.

Oh, the sticky date puddings she'd made in this space, the fruit mince pies at Christmas, the seafood chowders and Thai curries. So many hundreds of hours she had spent here, preparing meals for herself and Brian, and her dinner parties had become quite famous within their circle of friends.

Just a few steps over was the spot where her favourite corner bench had caught the sunlight on winter mornings. God, how many mugs of coffee had she enjoyed there?

Now, all that was left were copper wires and pipes and unidentifiable rubble. Oh, and a burnt-out dishwasher. Almost angrily, Freya gave the door a wrench and scowled into its blackened interior.

Goodness. To her surprise she spied two of her favourite coffee mugs, one with orange and white stripes and the other decorated with autumn leaves. They almost looked okay and, when she pulled them out, she discovered they were only slightly blackened and hadn't even cracked. How amazing.

Clutching the unexpected treasures to her, she wandered on to the end of the house where her bedroom had stood, remembering her ridiculous excitement over its jaunty new look and how those pinks and oranges had put a smile on her face when she woke each day.

Ouch. How fragile those pleasures had been, based on a couple of pots of paint and a few bright swatches of fabric.

They were only things, she told herself as she had so many times in the past fortnight. *No one was hurt . . .*

Unfortunately, Freya still couldn't quite accept that earthly possessions weren't important. She wondered how many of the people who so easily preached this sermon had actually lost everything.

And in the next breath she found herself asking, *I wonder if the ring's still here?*

The question jumped out of nowhere, but almost immediately she knew deep down that this was why she had come. Next moment, she was crouching among the ashes, eyes alert, searching for the impossible. A small silver circle.

If a coffee mug could survive the fire, she reasoned, surely a diamond ring might stand a chance.

She looked around her again, taking careful stock of the twisted metal struts that had once supported her bed, as she tried to work out exactly where her bedside table had stood. It had been made of timber, with a drawer and a little cupboard underneath. The cupboard door had a small metal hoop instead of a knob. Oh, look, there was the fractured base of the lamp that had stood on the table to light her bedtime reading.

Setting the mugs aside and kneeling in the sooty ash now, not caring about the messy state of her jeans, Freya began to sift through the debris with the forensic care of an archaeologist. The ring she searched for was not the sapphire one that Brian had given her for their engagement. She'd sold that months ago and good riddance.

No, her interest in this other ring was quite hopelessly sentimental. Now, with no possessions to give witness to her life – no books or photographs or clothes. No photos of her mum and her grandparents. No high-school-formal dress that she'd kept for decades. No Ginger & Smart trouser suit that she'd spent a ridiculous sum on when she and Brian had gone to the Melbourne Cup. Now that she no longer possessed any of these things, this modest ring's importance seemed to have skyrocketed. For reasons Freya couldn't properly explain.

The little hoop door handle appeared first, buried in soft white ash, and she almost missed the other small metallic circle. As she carefully brushed more ash aside, however, there, by some kind of miracle, it was. A silver ring with a modest single diamond.

Trembling now, with a sense of awe, Freya picked it up. The band was blackened, but it would probably rub clean. The little diamond, however, was no longer bright and clear, but cloudy, no doubt affected by the intense heat of the blaze.

Goosebumps prickled her arms. Her throat tightened painfully and she suddenly wondered if searching for this had been a mistake. Even now, all these years later, she could still remember in excruciating detail the momentous afternoon on the beach at Picnic Bay, and she could still hear Seb's voice, rough and raw with emotion.

'But what you want to do isn't even legal in Queensland.'

Even now, she could hear the call of black cockatoos in the sea-almond trees and the soft splash of tropical waves, and she could see the glistening shimmer in Seb's grey eyes, the jerky motion of his throat as she'd tried to hand his engagement ring back to him.

'I need to do this, Seb. Pearl's desperate to have a baby.'

He'd refused to take the ring, even though he'd probably needed the money back in those days and should have at least hocked the diamond at a pawnbroker's.

'This is your decision,' he'd responded in a cold hard voice that Freya had barely recognised. 'I want no part of it.' And with an abrupt about-turn, he'd marched away, up the beach, past the line of palms, shoulders squared.

Never to look back.

Freya had, perhaps foolishly, kept this ring for decades, well hidden, of course, and an early, brief engagement with her high-school sweetheart was a chapter in her history that she'd never shared with Brian.

During their marriage, she'd tried not to think too much about Seb Hudson, but the internet was a jolly handy tool and she'd kept a weather eye on his soaring career. She knew that he'd left for America twenty years ago in a bid to further his art, and in California, he'd lived in some kind of artists' commune. And, well, actually, if she was brutally honest, she could probably win a *Mastermind* quiz if her specialist topic was the artwork of Sebastian Hudson.

Sure, she'd tried to consciously wipe him from her thoughts, and she'd achieved a measure of success in that regard. But only months ago, she'd stumbled on an article in the *Sunday Mail* along with photos of Seb's amazing paintings, and the report included the fact that he now lived in Spain.

With a heavy sigh, Freya almost slipped his damaged ring into the pocket of her jeans, but somehow that didn't seem quite safe enough.

It still fitted her finger, however – the finger of her right hand, that is – and when she gathered up the mugs and went back to the car, she didn't care about the diamond's blackened, cloudy state. Given the mess her life was in, a damaged ring from a long-lost lover seemed appropriately symbolic.

CHAPTER TWELVE

Billie turned from smoothing a muted grey and white striped cotton spread over the bed in the spare room to find her mother in the doorway with an armful of neatly folded sheets and pillowcases.

'Oh,' her mum said. 'So you've already made up Freya's room? Well, that's good, I guess.' But she didn't look particularly pleased.

Billie almost came back with a snappy retort, suggesting that she'd appreciate a little gratitude. She'd been feeling pretty damn tired lately, what with working long hours, as well as helping out at home, not to mention keeping her scary pregnancy news under wraps. Now she held her tongue, however.

She knew her mum was tense about Freya's arrival. Earlier at breakfast, she'd seen a flash of something close to panic on her mum's face when Freya had texted that she would arrive on the ten o'clock vehicular ferry. But whatever was behind the tension between her mother and her aunt, it had begun long ago and the situation was unlikely to change in the next couple of days between Freya's arrival on the island and her parents' departure.

'Would you like some flowers for this room?' Billie asked, thinking that while her mother's preference for linens in faded dust-bowl colours was currently very fashionable, it didn't really match her memories of her vibrant, colour-loving aunt.

Her mum gave a brief eye-roll, accompanied by a one-shouldered shrug. 'I'm sure Freya would like them.'

Billie suppressed an impatient sigh. 'I'll pop down to the super-market. They had lovely buckets of sunflowers yesterday. With luck, they won't be all gone. I might grab a pawpaw as well and we could do with more butter.'

'Thanks, love.'

This was said more gently and her mum gave a tired smile, which worried Billie, but she couldn't ask again if her mother was all right. She'd had that question rebuffed too many times already. Even her dad had shrugged her concerns aside.

'Your mum's fine,' he would say, if Billie enquired. 'She just needs a good holiday.'

Billie didn't feel she could argue. He was a nurse, after all.

She was waiting on the wharf at Nelly Bay when the barge from Townsville pulled in loaded with vehicles in neat rows. Freya had texted that she was driving a white Forester and Billie could see at least five white SUVs in the line-up, but it was impossible to make out their drivers from this distance.

She was surprised by how excited she felt. Excited, relieved and just a little nervous. Being responsible for her parents' business was still a daunting prospect, and Billie knew that Freya would be a gen-uine support in that regard, but she'd also be great company, too.

If only I didn't have the pregnancy to worry about.

Billie's breathing snagged at the very thought of having a baby. Big decisions awaited and she suspected – maybe hoped – that she'd find herself discussing her options with Freya. But she certainly wouldn't burden the poor woman with her problems the minute she arrived.

At least it was a beautiful day, spectacularly beautiful, in fact. The sky stretched overhead like a spotless, vivid blue sail and the aquamarine sea was at its sparkling best. On the headlands the hoop pines stood tall and proud among massive granite boulders. And now, the first cars were moving cautiously off the ferry and up the ramp.

Billie edged closer to the railing, her eyes darting from white car to white car, searching for Freya. Then she saw a long arm waving madly and she found herself grinning as she waved back. It was a matter of being patient then until Freya had at last driven up the ramp and found a place to park.

'Billie, how lovely to see you, darling.' Slim arms extended, Freya swept Billie into a warm embrace. 'It's been too long.'

'I know. Ages.'

'How are you?'

'I'm fine. How are you? How was the trip? It's such a long way to have to drive.'

'Oh, it wasn't too bad. I listened to all sorts of programs on Radio National.' Freya laughed. 'Ask me anything about climate change, gut health, North Korea. I'm all clued up.'

Trust Freya to be so positive in spite of everything that had happened to her. She looked wonderful, too, as slender as ever in skinny jeans and a loose-fitting lime-green linen shirt, with a bright scarf tied around her auburn hair and knotted on top. She'd always dressed with flair, Billie remembered.

'You look great,' Billie told her.

This brought another laugh. 'You can actually find amazing bargains in the op shops on the Sunshine Coast.' Then, more seriously, she asked, 'So how are your mum and dad?'

Billie hesitated now, wishing she still didn't have the gnawing sense that things weren't quite as perfect as her parents were making out. 'They're fine.' What else could she say? 'You'll see for yourself very soon.'

Freya's gaze narrowed as she processed this response. She looked, for a second, as if she would have liked to ask another question, but she must have changed her mind. 'Righty-oh,' she said brightly instead. 'Let's go then. Do you want to hop in my car, or did you drive here?'

'I drove.' Billie pointed to the little blue Honda parked a bit further along. 'Probably best if you follow me.'

'Lovely.' Freya looked around her, letting her gaze sweep over the little harbour with the ferry and yachts at their moorings and the tourist buses parked outside the terminal. She looked out to the shimmering sea beyond the harbour wall and then back to the island's green tree-covered hills, and she took a deep, long breath, as if she needed to fill her lungs with fresh and salty sea air. She let the breath out slowly.

'It's so good to be back,' she said and, for a moment, her eyes glinted with a hint of tears. 'I still think of this place as home.'

Her smile was a tad shaky as she climbed back into her car, but then she winked and sent Billie a wave. 'Lead on.'

CHAPTER THIRTEEN

'And, of course, I'd really appreciate it if you could manage to keep these pot plants alive.'

Freya stiffened. *Bloody hell.* This latest request from Pearl was one dig too many, thank you.

The tension between the sisters had begun, of course, with Freya's arrival.

'Oh, no,' Pearl had said the very moment Freya emerged from her car. 'You haven't brought a dog?'

'Lovely to see you, too, Pearl,' Freya had replied, nursing poor little Won Ton to her chest like a baby. 'She won't be any trouble. She's house trained.'

'She's an inside dog?' Pearl managed to convey an air of greatest tragedy.

Freya, parked on the steep driveway, looked to Pearl's house, cleverly wedged between granite boulders and poised above a dramatic drop to the sea below. No yard. No sign of a fence.

Perhaps she should have warned Pearl about Won Ton, but what would she have done if her sister had said no?

'She's a very good little dog,' she said. 'I'll take her outside to do her business. She's been staying at a friend's house and has behaved herself beautifully. She's never been any trouble.'

'You mustn't let her on the beds or the sofas.'

'No, Pearl, I promise. I'll keep her in the laundry if you like. How are you, anyway?'

Somehow they'd got through that first evening, but the tension had ramped up the next day almost as soon as Troy had left for work and Billie had headed off to the bistro. Freya, left alone with Pearl in her beautiful home with its soaring cathedral ceilings, glass walls and spectacular ocean views, had wondered about the possibility of a cosy chat over a cuppa.

The expensive white linen sofas were like islands in the huge space, however, and not exactly cosy. And the 'chat' had begun with a long and painful lecture from Pearl about the importance of keeping insurance up to date, as if somehow that neglect and its disastrous results had been entirely Freya's fault.

Then they'd retired to Pearl's office for an even longer treatise on how to run the business side of Island Thyme. Admittedly, Freya didn't have a background in food preparation or food services management, but Billie and the chef would look after that side of things.

Pearl instructed her in the banking, the quarterly BAS reports to be sent to the accountant, the checking of emails and orders, and the staff pays on Sunday nights. Nothing was left out and it was all very important, of course.

Freya wouldn't have minded the detailed instructions so much, if she hadn't been spoken to like a totally clueless novice. Anyone would think she was still a reckless kid who jumped on the backs of motorbikes without caring about a helmet, who put vodka in her school water bottle, or who needed to be rescued from drowning in an outback creek.

Mind you, given the tone of their recent phone calls, Freya had been all too conscious of her sister's reservations about her general competence, so she'd been prepared for the lectures regarding the business. But for Pearl to stand there now, with her mouth all shrivelled and drawn in tighter than a cat's bum while casting doubts over Freya's ability to water pot plants?

Bloody hell, there were only three plants. Pearl had obviously embraced the new minimalist trends in decor, which were far too boring for Freya's tastes. She'd felt the same way about Island Thyme when she'd been taken on a tour. Not that she would mention this, of course, but for her, the best beachside bistros were also galleries for local artists and crafts people. She would have liked to see sculptures and paintings on display, pottery and candles and hand-crafted lanterns. Lots of pot plants.

And here at home, Pearl's living space was almost cell-like in its Scandi-style restraint. Her greenery consisted of one rubber plant, an asparagus fern and a yucca.

You know those plants are almost impossible to kill, Freya wanted to tell her, but then she'd remembered her own despair over Amber's pot plant neglect, so she once again cut her sister some slack. 'I promise I'll do my best, Pearl,' she said instead, but perhaps this sounded slightly facetious, as it was met by another searching frown.

'I love pot plants,' Freya added more warmly and with an extra dose of sincerity. 'I'll enjoy looking after them.'

Her sister gave a cautious nod and an even more cautious smile, confirming for Freya that her worst fears about her stay on the island were, unfortunately, correct. Pearl was as nervous as a goose in a doona factory.

Problem was, Freya was pretty damn sure the nerves weren't really about her ability to look after the business. The true source of Pearl's agitation was Billie – and the simple fact that she would be leaving her daughter and Freya alone together.

For the first time.

Ever.

Even though Billie was all grown up now, with a strong mind –
make that a *very* strong mind – of her own, this new arrangement
of leaving them together and in charge of the business demanded a
huge, previously untested leap of faith from Pearl.

The tension between the sisters was decades old, of course.

There had never been a row, exactly. Pearl had always remained
civil to Freya, if not exactly sisterly, but while Freya had hoped they
might form a deeper bond after the surrogacy arrangement they'd
shared all those years ago, the opposite had happened. Her generous gesture had, ultimately, caused a sad drifting apart that had
never really been bridged.

It wasn't worth dragging up that history again now. Pearl
wouldn't want to discuss it, but the bald facts were that Freya had
been too young and far too carefree at the time, and way too eager
to help her older sister out.

Ruby, their mother, had warned her, of course. 'Are you sure
you've thought this through, Frey? You've always gone at everything like a bull at a gate.'

Freya had liked to think that her generosity outweighed any
rashness on her part. At the time, she'd been filled with sympathy
for Pearl, understanding at a deep gut level how very thrilled her
sister was when she'd landed a husband like Troy, how overjoyed
she'd been to have found herself a steady, warm-hearted guy.

It had been clear to everyone that Troy would be a perfect family
man, a caring, loving husband and father. A salt-of-the-earth type
and a nurse, no less, with all the qualities that Freya and Pearl's
own father had so obviously lacked. So when Pearl and Troy had
no success in producing a family, Freya had been almost as disappointed as they were. And after several years of heartbreak, when
they'd almost given up hope, she'd been anxious to help.

Okay, sure – with the wisdom of hindsight, Freya would agree
that surrogacy was not a decision to be taken lightly, but she'd

always been the reckless one. And she *had* owed Pearl a huge debt ever since the drowning incident.

'A life for a life,' she'd insisted.

Altruistic surrogacy hadn't even been legal in Queensland at the time, but that hadn't fazed her. She'd happily gone to Canberra with Pearl and Troy for the IVF treatment.

Everything had been extremely civilised. No sex was involved. It was purely a medical procedure in which Freya was the 'womb mother', or gestational carrier as the white coats had called it, and the baby was Pearl and Troy's own genetic child formed from their egg and sperm.

'Your bun. My oven,' Freya had quipped, but in reality they'd been ever so sensible and serious about everything, with plans in place for every tricky possibility. They'd settled on how many embryo transfers they would attempt and what would happen if a scan result showed that something was wrong with the baby, even what would happen if the pregnancy was putting Freya's life in jeopardy.

Fortunately, none of these difficult decisions had been required. They'd been incredibly lucky. The first embryo transfer resulted in a positive pregnancy test and a relatively straightforward, uneventful nine months had followed. The baby was completely healthy, grew like Topsy and had kept Freya entertained with her near-constant internal acrobatics.

Okay, so yeah, Freya had loved the little tyke. How could she not? Secretly, from the day she'd first felt those thrilling, tiny flutters in her womb, she'd called her Butterfly. Just the same, she'd always, *always* thought of the baby as her niece and never as her own child. And when Billie – or Belinda as she'd been then – was born, sweet and perfect, with Troy's sandy hair and Pearl's upturned nose and her grandmother Ruby's deep-blue eyes, Freya had been quite relieved that she couldn't see herself in the baby at all.

She'd handed the tiny girl over quite readily, keen to get on with her own life again. And everything would have been hunky-dory – on the home front at least – if Pearl's insecurity hadn't reared its ugly head.

The big problem was that if Pearl wanted to be the baby's legal mother, she was still required to adopt her. Pearl had deeply resented this, and from that point on, she'd always been mega-nervous about Freya getting too close to her daughter. She'd insisted that Billie must never know the role Freya had played in her birth, and although Freya had agreed and had kept her word, the rift had grown. Never exactly huge or unbreachable, it had always been there.

A definite tension – which only got worse after Pearl realised that Freya would not be able to have a baby of her own. Perhaps she'd felt a little guilty, but almost certainly she'd feared there would be repercussions. She'd become even more insanely possessive of Billie, coming up with crazy excuses whenever Freya had tried to plan get-togethers.

And now, all these years later, that same tension was still causing trouble. But after everything Freya had been through in recent weeks, she was determined that this old hurt shouldn't be left to hang between them like an unexploded bomb.

Folding her arms and leaning back against the doorjamb at the entry to Pearl's office, she tried to look far more relaxed than she actually felt and she spoke calmly, but with quiet resolve. 'I'd like to make one thing quite clear, Pearl.'

'What's that?'

'You really can trust me. With the office.' Freya drew a quick breath. 'And with Billie.'

Her sister's eyes grew huge and worried. 'I – I – well, yes – I guess —'

'You guess?' Freya repeated, incredulous. 'Well, I *mean* it.'

Her sister still looked doubtful.

Freya stifled an urge to groan. 'Look, I'm truly grateful you've invited me here. Heaven knows, I need to keep myself occupied and I need a roof over my head. So I'm not going to blow it.'

Pearl had one of those foreheads that wrinkled very easily and deep furrows formed now as she frowned. 'I never suggested . . .' She left the sentence dangling.

'You don't have to *suggest*.' Freya was fast running out of patience. 'We both know you're worried sick that I'll say something to Billie, that I'll somehow spoil our agreement.' She swallowed, suddenly nervous. 'That I'll break my promise.'

To Freya's dismay, Pearl gasped and clutched at the back of a nearby chair, as if she desperately needed its support. Clearly, the mere mention of their pact was enough to rattle her.

A frustrated grunt burst from Freya. 'For God's sake, Pearl. What have I ever done to make you think I can't be trusted?' Her voice was raised now. Fishwife shrill? Maybe, but she couldn't help it. She was too tense and scared to speak calmly. 'When have I ever broken my word?'

'On the day she was born.'

Thud.

Now it was Freya who gasped, and her chest was so tight she could hardly breathe. A flash of panic followed and it was as if she was drowning all over again.

In that moment, she could no longer escape the real reason for the decades-long rift between her sister and herself. Pearl had never forgiven her for that one decision she'd made to experience Billie's birth on her own.

The fact that Freya had given the gift of her body and nine long months of her life, not to mention the hellish pain of the labour and delivery, had not, had *never*, been enough.

'It was twenty-four years ago,' she said, her voice barely more than a whisper.

'What difference does that make?' Pearl snapped back. Her jaw was tight now, jutting at a stubborn angle, and her eyes glittered with tears. 'Babies only have one chance to be born.'

Oh, God. Pearl would never see the other side of this picture.

'What's wrong with you, woman?' Freya cried. 'You have everything – a husband who loves you, a beautiful home, a lovely daughter —'

She wanted to say more, but the wave of emotions crashing over her strangled the words in her throat. With a broken cry, she turned and made her way as fast as she could stumble down the hallway and out of the house.

CHAPTER FOURTEEN

'Is that all you're having for breakfast, Billie?'

Billie glanced from the piece of toast she was cutting to Freya's bowl of glowing orange pawpaw topped with yoghurt and passion-fruit, and her stomach heaved unhappily.

She hoped Freya didn't notice anything amiss. Her morning sickness hadn't been too bad, luckily, more a lingering sense of exhaustion and nausea than anything, but toast was all she could face for breakfast these days. Preferably dry toast, although she'd added a smear of butter and Vegemite this morning, so as not to arouse Freya's suspicions.

'I'm good with tea and toast,' she said.

Freya's mouth tilted in wry smile, as if to suggest there was no accounting for some people's tastes, but she refrained from com-menting, for which Billie was grateful. This was their first morning alone since her parents had left and the atmosphere, as they break-fasted, was pleasantly relaxed, which was a huge relief. The tension in this household over the past few days had totally freaked Billie.

At least she'd managed to throw a rather nice farewell bash at Island Thyme. The chef, Gavin, had produced a slap-up dinner for her parents and their best friends, Pattie and Joe Harper, as well as Freya. And as far as Billie, who'd been waiting tables, could tell, they'd all got on quite well.

With Gavin's help, Billie had also created a rather awesome cake, if she did say so herself. It was shaped like an old-fashioned caravan, complete with sparklers and her mum's favourite peppermint icing, with *Happy Travels* spelled out in edible silver pearls. She knew her mum had loved it and there'd been plenty of laughter and good wishes from the other diners, many of whom were regulars, so that had been a good night.

Word had spread and the next morning there'd been a pleasing crowd of friends to wave her parents off at the ferry terminal. So the farewell had been a success, much to Billie's relief.

At home, though, during those last couple of days, her mum and Freya had barely spoken to each other and even her dad had been withdrawn. He'd made out that he was preoccupied with checking and crosschecking all their gear and the arrangements for the trip, but Billie still sensed there was something else bothering him. Unfortunately, she'd been too busy trying to hide her tiredness and nausea to pay really close attention to the others.

But she couldn't help asking Freya now. 'Um . . . I was wondering if you noticed anything different about Mum or Dad before they left?'

Freya frowned. 'Not especially.' Her expression was decidedly cautious. 'Why? Did you?'

Billie shrugged. 'Kind of.'

'What are you hinting at, Billie? Pearl's always been a worrier.'

'I know, but this seemed different somehow.'

'Do you think my arrival upset her?' Now Freya looked worried, too.

'Not really.' Billie didn't want to stir, or to cause unnecessary concern, but she was also tired of skirting the truth. 'Well, actually,

I guess I could see you and Mum weren't the best of buddies, which is a shame. But I actually thought something was bothering her even before you came. I thought I noticed it as soon as I got back from Greece.'

'Oh?' Freya's face, framed by her flame-coloured hair, was serious as she regarded Billie across the table. 'I'm sorry, I can't really help you. I guess I was too caught up in my own issues. I should have been more observant.'

'Nah,' said Billie. 'You've got enough on your plate and anyway, it was probably just my imagination.' She picked up a triangle of toast, set it down again. 'I know they're heading off on the trip of a lifetime, but maybe it's some kind of – I don't know – last-gasp remedy. I'd actually wondered if they might be thinking about a divorce.'

'Pearl and Troy?'

An eddy of panic whirled through Billie. Now that she'd said the words out loud, the possibility seemed all too real. But she couldn't imagine her little family breaking up. There were only the three of them. 'It seems to happen to the best of couples.'

'Well, yes,' Freya remarked with a rueful smile. 'Been there, done that.'

'Sorry. I wasn't pointing the finger.'

'Well, I am divorced, so your comment's relevant.' She was still smiling, though, as she said this, much to Billie's relief. 'And you're right – divorce is incredibly common these days. What's the statistic? One in three marriages? But not Pearl and Troy, I just can't imagine —'

'I know. They haven't been fighting as far as I can tell.'

'Neither were Brian and I, of course. We just kind of . . .' Freya waved her hand, as if searching for the right words. 'Grew apart.'

Billie was sure this was an oversimplification, but she didn't like to probe. 'I tried to talk to Dad about it. He insisted everything's fine.'

'Yes, I'm sure it is. I'm quite confident Troy's not having a midlife crisis.'

'Perhaps Mum is instead, insisting on taking off on this holiday – out of the blue.'

'I admit that surprised me,' said Freya. 'But I suppose she realised she's been working damn hard all her life and it was suddenly time for a little fun.'

'That's more or less what Dad said.'

'Well, that's reassuring. Troy's always been a straight shooter.'

'I guess.' Billie might have added that she couldn't be certain of her dad's total honesty lately, but she was distracted by the distant roar of a motorbike climbing the steep, winding road that rounded their headland.

The roar reminded her of a fellow who'd arrived by motorbike at the café, lateish the night before, looking impressively wild and macho in jeans and a leather jacket. 'We had a celebrity in the restaurant last night,' she said.

'Oh?' Freya's smile was even warmer now, as if she was pleased to change the subject. 'Not Elton John? Although I think he's already been up here for his farewell concert, hasn't he?'

'No, this person's not quite as famous as Elton, but way more good-looking.' Heads had turned last night when the motorbike rider arrived on the deck, all wide shoulders, craggy jaw and wind-blown hair flecked with grey.

He had the air of a man very at home in his own skin and it turned out he was also a mate of Gavin the chef. They'd met at the Arcadia Lifesavers, apparently. Cool as a cucumber, he'd wandered into the kitchen and chatted with Gavin. And then Gavin had stunned Billie by insisting his mate must have a table on the deck, even though he hadn't had a booking. An unheard-of coup.

'He's an artist, Sebastian Hudson,' Billie told Freya now. 'Have you heard of him? He's quite famous.'

Freya didn't answer at first, possibly because she seemed to have choked on a small piece of pawpaw. She made quite a business of swallowing and then took a sip of tea before she answered. 'I've heard of him,' she said at last.

Billie nodded. 'I thought you might have. We had to study his paintings at art college. I remember the teacher telling us back then that he'd spent some time here on the island when he was younger.'

'Yes,' said Freya, but she looked kind of shocked. Or unhappy. Or both.

'He's probably around your vintage. Did you ever meet him?' Billie asked.

'Once or twice,' came the vague response. 'I – I thought he lived overseas these days.'

'Yeah. Spain, I think. Somewhere exotic like that. But according to Sonia Brassal, who knows everything about everyone on this island, he's kept a little place here on Maggie as well.'

'I see.' Pushing her bowl away without quite finishing, Freya sat looking down at her hands in her lap. She seemed lost in thought.

'Handsome devil,' Billie added to make conversation. 'Some guys have got it all, haven't they?'

Freya's smile might have been a little strained, but she seemed once again quite composed. 'Sounds like he made an impression.'

'He did, rather. Way too old for me, of course.' As Billie said this she found herself thinking of Petros. Again. Unfortunately, she never really stopped thinking about him. He was always there. In her head, her heart.

Petros wasn't a motorbike rider like Sebastian Hudson. He drove a small utility truck, but he carried that same air of macho confidence, that hint of wildness, a certain vibe that could make a man unbearably attractive.

Stop it. Don't think about him. But it was too late. Already, she was slugged by a deluge of pain, by the deep, piercing ache that her memories of Petros always rendered.

From across the table, Freya was watching her. 'Is it too nosy of me to ask if you have a man in your life?'

Was her aunt a mind-reader? Billie couldn't quite hide her surprise, especially as this question was one that her mother had never dared to ask.

'No, no man,' she said quietly. 'At least, not any more.' And she gave the most deliberately casual shrug she could muster. 'I left him behind.'

'In Greece?'

'Yep. On Santorini.'

'Ah . . .' Freya's tone was gentle, her smile warm with sympathy.

'You've been to Greece, haven't you?' Billie asked.

Freya nodded. 'As a tourist, but no other woman I've met can lay claim to an actual romance on Santorini.' She turned for a moment, casting a considering glance to the scenery outside, the hillside of granite boulders rising out of the sun-bright sea. An unreadable emotion flashed across her face, then vanished, fast as lightning. She said, 'Greek men can be incredibly attractive.'

'Uh-huh,' came Billie's choked response.

Freya gave another thoughtful nod. 'A romance like that wouldn't be easy to give up.'

Billie decided she might as well be honest. Freya's husband had walked out on her, after all. She understood the pain. 'Leaving him was the pits.'

As she said this, she tried, desperately, to hold herself together. Freya had always been so strong and had suffered far huger catastrophes than the breakup of a holiday romance. But Billie was pregnant with Petros's baby and she had no idea what to do about it.

She didn't want to cry, to make a scene, but her eyes were hot with welling tears. Her mouth twisted out of shape.

'Billie, darling.' Freya was rising from her seat.

'I'm okay,' Billie spluttered.

The frantic hand wave she gave to deflect her aunt mustn't have been very convincing. Freya continued around the table and as the first sobs burst from Billie, Freya was already at her side, drawing a chair close, so she could slip her arms around her in a comforting hug.

Which was how Billie ended up weeping on Freya's shoulder, clinging tightly and bawling her eyes out, while Freya called her sweetheart and gently stroked her hair.

No fit of tears had ever felt so necessary. Or so good.

CHAPTER FIFTEEN

From Freya's perspective at least, their days fell into a comfortable pattern. She knew from painful personal experience that it was going to take Billie some time to get over her heartbreak, but after her initial storm of weeping, Billie seemed, on the surface at least, to pull herself together and get on with things.

Both Billie and Freya had received excited text messages and photos on their phones from Pearl and Troy, who were now in inland Queensland, exploring Carnarvon Gorge, having a brilliant time by all accounts. Freya spent an hour or so at Island Thyme each day, making sure that everything was in order and that Pearl's strict hygiene standards were maintained.

Gavin, the chef, a cheerfully rotund, thirty-something fellow with a closely shaved head, was helpful. In consultation with him, Freya kept an inventory of food supplies, as well as of the condition of the equipment. Part of her job was to ensure appropriate restocking and repairing, and living on an island was an added challenge in this regard, but not a huge one.

Provisions from the mainland could be ordered by phone or over the internet and would arrive with pleasing promptness on the ferry. Certain North Queensland suppliers would text her when specialty items such as zucchini flowers or blueberries were available and Gavin, who was flexible with his menu, would usually take advantage of these. The job was both challenging and interesting and already she felt quite relaxed about her new role.

Gavin was an excellent cook, but he'd mainly worked on coastal traders, mine sites and oil rigs, jobs where he'd been part of a team with a clear pecking order, so he appreciated Freya's managerial support. She was beginning to really enjoy herself, to think that perhaps this enforced change might be the start of better things.

True to her word, she also took conscientious care of the house, and the bloody pot plants, but there was usually time for her favourite walks. She could take her pick of trails that wound around the headlands linking bay to bay, or choose an easier stroll along one of the many beaches. On any of these ventures she took Won Ton, of course, and the little dog was ecstatic about all the new sights and smells.

The mood on the island was as slow and easy as Freya remembered. The Great Barrier Reef took the brunt of the rolling Pacific Ocean's force, which meant there was next to no surf crashing on the island's beaches. Instead of the roar and thump of the Sunshine Coast's waves, the sea arrived here on white coral sands in gentle, leisurely slaps.

This tranquil rhythm, combined with abundant sunshine and tropical warmth, made the pace of life incredibly soothing. Freya could feel herself beginning to let go, to relax – as long as she didn't think about her homeless future. Or about Seb.

She'd been shocked to learn that he was actually here on the island. A ridiculous reaction, really, given that it was more than two decades since they'd gone their separate ways.

Straight after the breakfast when Billie had shared the unsettling news, Freya had taken off the battered and tarnished little ring that she'd found among the ashes, and she'd hidden it in an envelope at the back of her underwear drawer.

She had no intention of seeing Seb again. She'd asked no questions and had no idea where the 'place' he'd acquired here might be, but it was better to be safe than sorry. The island was very small after all, and if she did happen to accidentally run into him, she couldn't bear the embarrassment of being caught with his ring on her finger, a fire-damaged ring at that. Lord, she could feel herself blushing at the very thought of being caught out.

The fire had obviously messed with her head. How else could she have ever decided that wearing that ring was any version of a good idea? She certainly didn't plan to spend the rest of her life looking over her shoulder and pining for a romance from her youth.

It was at the supermarket, when Freya was searching the refrigerated shelves for her favourite brand of yoghurt, that she ran into Sonia Brassal. A million years ago, they'd gone to school together. Later, with her teaching qualifications secured, Sonia had not only managed to wangle a posting back on Maggie Island, but she'd hung on to it forever. Word was, she'd known someone high up in the Department of Education.

'Freya,' she exclaimed now, all beaming smiles. 'I heard you were back.'

'That's right,' said Freya. 'And I'm loving it.' She was sure Sonia must be up to speed with all the news. Billie was right – the woman had always known everything about everyone on the island – but Freya supplied an explanation now for good measure. 'I'm helping Billie with the restaurant while Pearl and Troy take extended leave.'

'You and Billie? Really?'

Sonia's eyebrows rose high, and Freya could almost hear question marks pinging down the supermarket aisle.

Refusing to be rattled by such a dramatic reaction, she nodded. 'I'm quite hands-off in the kitchen, just looking after the business side of things.'

'That's – ah – nice.' Sonia's response was bland enough, but surprise and curiosity continued to flash in her dark eyes like neon lights. 'I'm sure Pearl's very . . .' She seemed to have to search for an appropriate adjective. 'Grateful,' she added at last.

'Yes, Pearl and Troy have earned a good break.' Freya was surprised Sonia didn't mention the fire, but perhaps she hadn't heard. Despite being a long-term resident on the island, she hadn't been among the group of friends who'd farewelled Pearl, so perhaps she wasn't privy to gossip in that particular circle. For all its laid-back lifestyle, the island could be quite cliquey.

'Anyway,' Freya said. 'It's great to see you, Sonia. I hope your family are all well?'

'Oh, yes. They're wonderful, thanks. Nicole and her —'

Now Sonia stopped mid-sentence, clearly distracted by something that was happening behind Freya. A beat later, Sonia's eyes almost popped out of her head and her mouth formed a perfect O.

'Goodness,' she said in a breathless whisper.

Intrigued, Freya turned, and then immediately wished that she hadn't.

It had been more than twenty years since she'd seen Seb Hudson in person but she recognised him instantly. He was at the end of the aisle, shopping basket in hand, checking through the cheeses. And Freya was instantly trembling with nerves.

So pathetic. Anyone would think she was fifteen again, blushing because Seb had winked at her as he strolled off the high-school football field.

Good grief. Freya could feel her face burning as memories flashed. Images she'd tried so hard to forget. Seb in their high-school art class, admiring her work and making her feel ten feet tall.

Seb helping her to adjust her goggles when he taught her to skin dive. The two of them building a camp fire on the beach at Florence Bay and then huddling close, watching the fire's bright flames while the Southern Cross climbed in the sky above them. Seb taking her into his arms, taking her to his bed.

Stop it.

Most likely she'd turned the brightest shade of beetroot possible and here was Sonia watching her, or rather ogling her, smiling and smirking, just as she had done at school all those years ago.

Get a grip, woman, for God's sake.

Forcibly, Freya dragged herself back to the present and to common sense. Why the fuss? What on earth was she thinking might happen? She was a mature woman. Over the hill in most men's eyes. She had lines on her face and grey in her hair – that she did her best to hide, mind you – and the beginnings of a bunion on her left foot.

But Seb Hudson wasn't just any man. He was her high-school sweetheart, her first lover and the man who'd asked Freya to marry him. And she'd broken off their engagement over what he'd seen as a reckless whim.

Life, Freya now knew, was nothing but a series of choices, of actions and consequences. When she'd naïvely taken on the surrogacy mission, she'd assumed that Seb would appreciate her thoughtfulness in giving back the ring and setting him free. But she'd also hoped that he'd hang around and take up with her again, after the baby was born.

Nine months is a long time, however, especially for a man in his early twenties. Long before those months were up, Seb had vanished out of her life.

For heaven's sake, so what? That romance was dead and buried long ago. *Hell, yeah.*

But damn it, she only needed one glimpse of Seb now, in the flesh, and her heart was thundering like a runaway horse.

'Well, well,' Sonia was saying beside her.

Freya refused to make eye contact with the woman, but she knew Sonia was relishing this situation. At least Seb hadn't seen her yet. Perhaps she could grab her yoghurt and scarper.

Too late. *Bugger.* Sonia was already waving and calling. 'Seb Hudson, how good to see you again. And look who's here.'

Regrettably, the earth didn't swallow Freya in that moment, despite her heartfelt prayer. She was left to stand there, trembling.

Seb wasn't good-looking in the traditional sense. He was tall enough, a couple of inches over Freya's five feet ten, but his features were too craggy to be handsome, his jaw too dark. None of this helped her, however. Even now, dressed in a simple white T-shirt and battered jeans, his thick hair flecked with grey, he still had the unconventional brute masculinity that branded him sexy as hell.

All this Freya noticed as her heart thumped crazily. *Stay cool. Stay calm.*

All you have to do is say hello. Forget that Sonia's watching. Just offer him a polite smile. And remember to breathe.

These instructions to herself proved unnecessary, though.

Seb offered Sonia a restrained but polite smile. 'Morning, Sonia.'

Then his gaze flicked ever so briefly to Freya and his eyes were hard as flint, showing no emotion whatsoever. He gave a curt nod. 'Freya.'

With that, he returned his attention to the cheese, made his unhurried selection and walked away. Without haste and without looking back.

Déjà vu.

CHAPTER SIXTEEN

It was Billie's day off. She'd been to Townsville and had caught a late ferry back. At this time of day, most of the island's commuters had already returned home, so the ferry was only half full and she sat, like a tourist, outside on the upper deck. Here, she breathed in deep lungfuls of sweet sea air and let the wind blow her hair around, while she made a deliberate effort to relax, to convince herself that she'd made the right decision. Everything would be okay.

By the time she reached the island's little harbour, dusk had painted the sky in gentle pinks and mauves, while turning the sea a sophisticated silvery grey. One by one, the island's house lights were coming on, glowing warmly.

Billie had always loved dusk. There was something magical about that time of day when the bright tropical sun dipped low and the strong colours of the hills and beaches were muted by shadows. Back in her high-school days she'd actually written a poem likening dusk to an elderly lady, elegant and a little subdued perhaps, but still with a glow about her as she awaited the coming of night.

She'd been inordinately proud of that poem, she remembered now. It wasn't an especially original metaphor, but her teacher had given her an A+, a rare feat during those years of rebellion.

Now the ferry docked and Billie followed the other passengers as they patiently filed off. It was only a short distance from the car park to her home, and as she steered her little vehicle around curving bends, there was still enough light to show tantalising glimpses of shimmering bays.

At the house, Freya's little dog was guarding the front door and she greeted Billie with a warning yap.

'Calm down, Won Ton.' Billie stooped to stroke her furry head. 'It's only me. You must know who I am by now.'

She went inside, the little dog following, tiny claws clicking on the timber floor. Freya was in the kitchen, barefoot and wearing a loose flowing kaftan in shades of green. On the bench beside her, a frosty glass of chilled white wine sat next to an arrangement of bowls holding various sliced vegetables. Capsicum, carrot, onion and pak choy. A pot of water was heating on the stove, probably in readiness for rice.

Freya's bright hair was twisted up into a loose knot and she managed to look wonderfully elegant, even though she was slicing shallots.

Brian had been an idiot to let her go, Billie thought. Then again, most men were huge disappointments, she decided now.

'Hey, Billie.' Freya was smiling as she picked up her glass and raised it in a welcoming salute. 'How was your day?'

This wasn't an easy question to answer honestly. Billie tried to sound offhand. 'Not bad.'

She hadn't been hungry at lunchtime, but now, seeing Freya's preparations, she realised she was quite famished. 'That looks delicious,' she said. 'Are you planning another of your fab stir-fries?'

'Yes, they're so easy,' said Freya. 'I have beef strips marinating in the fridge and I'll just throw it all together.'

'Yum.'

Freya gave another wave of her wine glass. 'You'll join me, won't you? I decided I've earned a drink tonight.'

Billie sighed. 'I'd love to. I'm sure I need one, too.' She was exhausted and she would have adored to curl up on the sofa with a hefty glass of wine, listening to music, or to Freya's conversation, while together they watched the last of the light sink into night.

'Wonderful.' Freya was already turning and reaching into an overhead cupboard for another glass.

'But I shouldn't,' Billie said quickly.

'Are you sure?'

Billie hesitated. She still hadn't shared her baby news with Freya and she wasn't in any rush to do so, but she'd just had the crappiest of crappy days. 'I'm pregnant,' she said quickly before she could change her mind.

'You're —' Freya paused and frowned, as if she feared she might have misheard.

'I'm pregnant,' Billie said again. She hadn't meant to make such a bald statement that would almost certainly spoil Freya's relaxed evening, but before she could add anything to soften her news, her throat seemed to close over. She swallowed and knew she had to get the worst of this off her chest now. 'Actually, the truth is, I went to Townsville today to have an abortion.'

Billie saw rather than heard Freya's gasp. She'd shocked the poor woman.

And now, instead of enjoying the peaceful evening, Billie was reliving the turmoil and pain of her day. Recalling that awful moment when she'd sat in the waiting room at the clinic, watching a young and frightened girl being wheeled on a trolley down a corridor and through swing doors. The girl could only have been seventeen or eighteen.

She had long, shiny dark hair and she was Asian and beautiful, and Billie didn't think she'd ever seen anyone look quite so scared. Or sad.

She'd told herself that tomorrow the girl would wake to a brand-new day and she'd get on with the rest of her life unburdened. Free. But as she'd sat in the waiting room with its pretty cane lounges upholstered in tropical hues, Billie had begun to sweat as she pictured the sterile operating theatre, the waiting doctor kitted in mask and gloves, the surgical instruments.

Quickly now, she continued with her story before she lost her nerve. 'There's a clinic in South Townsville and they're very good. Very professional. I'd been there for a previous appointment and the procedure was all arranged. If I was going to have – *it* – done, it was best to have it now, before I got to twelve weeks. But I turned up there today, and everything was all set, and then —'

Billie's lips trembled now, but she was determined not to cry again. 'I couldn't go ahead. I pulled out at the last minute.'

Pausing for breath, she was at least relieved that she'd got her story out without blubbering all over Freya for a second time. 'So, now you know,' she said.

Freya hadn't moved. She was still standing on the other side of the kitchen bench. 'Billie,' she said softly. It was quite possibly all the poor woman was capable of saying.

'I've shocked you, haven't I?'

'Not shocked, exactly.' Freya's smile was gentle. 'I'm not easily shocked these days, but I must admit you've surprised me.'

'I haven't told Mum and Dad – that I'm pregnant. I was worried they wouldn't leave on their holiday if they knew. They'd feel compelled to stay around. To worry and hover over me and protect me, or whatever.'

'I'm quite sure you're right about that.'

'And I didn't want to burden you with having to help me make such an enormous decision.'

Freya's smile was tinged with sadness. 'You really are all grown up now, aren't you?' She managed to make this sound like a compliment rather than a mere statement of fact. 'And you're going to have a baby.' Her eyes were shining a little too brightly. 'When Pearl and Troy do find out, they'll be over the moon.'

'I hope so.'

'They will, Billie. They'll be thrilled.'

Billie sighed. She felt exhausted but relieved to have this out in the open. 'I'm sure they'd be happier if I was settled in a steady relationship.'

'Oh, they'll get over that.'

'I guess they'll have to, won't they?'

Freya's smile grew warmer now. 'Babies have a way of making everything right.'

'You think so?' Billie wondered what grounds her aunt had for sharing such wisdom. One of the main thoughts that had stopped her from going ahead today had been the fact that she'd fallen pregnant so incredibly easily, while her mum had tried for years, apparently, and Freya hadn't been able to have children at all.

'Listen,' Freya said now, quite forcefully. 'There's no rush to eat. I can turn off that saucepan. Why don't we sit for a bit before I start cooking? What would you like to drink? Soda water? A cup of tea?'

'Sounds perfect,' said Billie. 'Soda water's fine, but I can get it, thanks. You don't have to wait on me.'

Bless Freya. She was so understanding. Billie felt a little guilty about her next thought – that she was more comfortable talking about such a difficult personal issue with her aunt rather than her mum, who was always such a worrier.

She filled a tall tumbler with soda water, added ice and a slice of lemon, and they settled on the sofas next to the huge picture windows. Tropical dusks were notoriously swift and, already, the daylight had almost disappeared outside. The first stars would show soon. Out on the horizon, she could just catch the silhouette of a sailing boat heading north, a sloop, its mainsail curved like a snowy wing.

Won Ton crossed the floor and leapt into Freya's lap, then curled, tucked her tail in, and settled, looking very pleased with herself.

'I know Pearl wouldn't approve, but I won't let her on the actual sofa,' Freya said as she stroked the little dog's back. 'But I don't think she can do much harm on my lap.'

'Of course she can't.' Billie realised, with some annoyance, that her mother must have issued dire warnings to Freya about her dog's presence in the house. 'Won Ton's a darling. I love having her here.'

'Thanks.' Freya took a sip of wine and then set her glass down on a small bleached-wood table. 'So, how are you actually feeling, Billie? Feeling physically, I mean. Have you had morning sickness?'

'I'm pretty good, actually. Tender boobs, a little nausea in the mornings, a bit tired, but nothing too drastic.'

'That's great.' After a beat, 'And now that you've made the big decision to keep the baby, how do you feel about that?'

'I'm still getting used to the idea.' Billie realised she was avoiding a direct answer. 'Actually, I think, if I'm honest, I'm shit scared. I certainly don't feel in any way ready to be a mother.'

'I don't suppose it's any consolation to suggest that there've been millions of women throughout history who've landed in the same situation.' Even as Freya said this, she looked instantly apologetic. 'Sorry, Billie. Why would I even bother to spout history when you're dealing with the here and now?' Quickly, as if to make amends, she added, 'Tell me to butt out and mind my own business.'

'No, it's good to have someone to talk with.'

'I suppose most of your girlfriends have moved off the island?'

'Yeah, you know what it's like. Straight after school, they all move away to get university degrees and sensible jobs.'

Freya accepted this with a gentle nod.

'And of course you're right about women throughout history,' Billie added. 'I'm really grateful that I live in Queensland in the twenty-first century, that I wasn't forced into some kind of back alley job and I at least had a choice.'

'Still, it can't have been an easy one.'

'Hardest decision I've ever made.' Billie gave her glass a gentle shake, making the ice cubes clink as the slice of lemon swirled. 'But I found myself thinking about you and Mum.'

At this, Freya looked quite startled, almost worried. 'Really?'

'You both had so much trouble falling pregnant. I was aware, even as a child, that pregnancy can be a really big deal.'

'Well, yes.'

'It's bizarre that here I am now, up the duff without even trying.'

Freya almost looked relieved now. She smiled. 'Life's full of little ironies.'

'True. And I've decided there's something crazily whacked about human fertility.'

'How do you mean?'

'Well, for starters, the whole connection to sex. That makes everything way too complicated and emotional. And too often, babies are either desperately wanted and hard to produce, or incredibly life-altering and inconvenient.'

'Yes, but those extremes are especially applicable to our family. Happily, most people enjoy some kind of middle ground.'

Billie sent her aunt a rueful smile. 'As you can see, I've been overthinking this subject.'

'That's perfectly understandable.'

'But I still think it would make much more sense if you could just buy a baby when you needed one.'

Freya laughed. 'Order one online perhaps?'

'Absolutely, or go find one under a gooseberry bush like in the old wives' tales.' In the next breath, Billie found herself apologising. 'Sorry. I know I'm talking gibberish. I think it's the relief of having finally decided. I promise I'm ready to face up to reality.'

Indeed, this evening on the way home on the ferry, Billie had found herself starting to fall in love with the idea of a baby. Despite her fears of inadequacy in the motherhood department, she'd been excited by the thought of *her* baby, her very own tiny being, curled like a bean or a fern frond, safely inside her.

'Speaking of reality,' Freya sounded cautious now, as if she was tiptoeing onto dangerous ground, 'am I right in assuming that the man on Santorini is your baby's father?'

'Yep.' This admission was accompanied by an instant slug of heartache and a deluge of memories of Petros at his most loving and gorgeous. Before he'd begun to tire of her. Billie grimaced. 'Yep, he's the father, but I haven't told him.'

'Okay.' Freya took another thoughtful sip of her wine. 'So are you planning to tell him? Now that you know you're keeping the baby?'

'I —' Billie wished, more than anything, that she could answer in the affirmative, that she could confidently share her happy news with Petros. 'I don't know,' she was forced to admit. 'I'm not sure it's something he'd want to hear.'

'That certainly makes it harder.'

'Yeah.' Billie shifted uncomfortably. 'Look, I might tell him. I guess he has a right to know, but I'm not going to rush.'

'That's fine, Billie. Please don't think I'm trying to push you.'

'No, I know you're not. But I guess I need to give myself time to get used to the idea first.'

'Of course you do. Will you keep working in the restaurant?'

'Sure. For as long as I can. I guess at some point a baby bump might get in the way.' Billie pulled a face as she said this. All the changes ahead were so daunting.

'See how you go,' said Freya. 'You don't want to overtire yourself.' With another of her lovely warm smiles, she added, 'But for what it's worth, I have every confidence you'll be a fabulous mum.'

CHAPTER SEVENTEEN

'I'm afraid Gavin has bad news.'

It was a month later, a month of relatively smooth sailing, when Billie greeted Freya with these tidings as soon as she arrived at the restaurant.

'What kind of bad news?' Freya hoped their chef wasn't ill.

'He wants to leave us.'

Freya groaned.

Billie looked bleak. 'I know.'

'Why?'

Billie was in the process of setting tables, but now she abandoned the cutlery and lifted her hands in a gesture of helplessness. 'I'll let Gavin explain. He's expecting you.'

'Bloody hell.' Freya mentally added even less polite swear words for good measure. This news was especially disappointing when the past month had gone so well. The weather had been perfect and Billie had been so much happier, especially since her recent scan at sixteen weeks when she'd been told that her baby was growing perfectly.

An extra bonus was that Freya had miraculously avoided running into Seb Hudson again. Meanwhile, tourists had flocked to the island and Island Thyme had been running brilliantly and was almost full every night. She really thought they were on top of things, that her life had finally taken a turn for the better.

Given that her life had been a complete shambles for the past twelve months, perhaps she should have been wiser, should have been ready, at least, for a few extra hurdles.

But to lose their chef? Surely that was one hurdle too many? Pearl, who was currently having a brilliant time in the Southern Highlands of New South Wales, would be devastated. She'd warned Freya that it was difficult to keep good staff on the island. At the time, she'd also said how lucky they were that Gavin loved living on Maggie and had no plans to leave.

Perhaps her sister should have known that a chef like that was too good to be true.

Freya felt quite sick as she went through to the kitchen. It didn't help that Gavin looked really uncomfortable, offering a smile that was more like a wince when he saw her, while scratching nervously at his chest.

She didn't beat about the bush. 'Billie's told me your news,' she said. 'You'll be leaving us soon?'

Gavin looked apologetic as he nodded. 'The thing is, I've had an offer too good to refuse. A fantastic job in Tasmania. In Hobart. At a top restaurant.'

Freya had been to memorable restaurants in Hobart, back in the days when she and Brian had liked to travel. She could still recall the delicious meals – aged beef and seafood seared on woodfired barbecues, wonderful cheeses, sticky puddings made with locally sourced berries.

'It's the kind of opportunity I've been hanging out for,' added Gavin.

'I'm sure it is and that's – wonderful.' What else could she say? Despite the dilemma his offer caused her, she couldn't help but be genuinely pleased for the guy.

She glanced at the counter behind him where he'd set his popular sourdough bread rolls to rise. Soft, plump and dusted in flour, even as raw dough, they made her mouth water.

The man was hardworking and talented and he was right to be ambitious. He deserved to progress.

But we need him here.

'The problem is, they want me to start as soon as I can,' he said.

Freya took a deep breath. 'How soon?'

'Next week.'

Good grief. 'But that's —' *Ridiculous* was the word that sprang to Freya's lips. Just in time, she tempered her response. 'That's a bit unreasonable, don't you think?' It was hard to take a firm stance, though, when she wasn't sure of the exact terms of Gavin's employment. 'You know it'll be almost impossible to find anyone decent to replace you so quickly.'

To her surprise, Gavin actually grinned. 'Well, that's the thing, you see. I do actually know someone who'd be a very good stand-in.'

'Really?'

'He's a mate of mine, from the Arcadia Lifesavers.'

This didn't sound at all promising. 'But is he a qualified chef?'

'He has a food handler's licence – for our sausage sizzles and fundraisers.'

'Gavin,' Freya could hardly believe she was hearing this, 'are you serious? You think a sausage-flipping lifesaver can take over in this kitchen? Do you really think he has the slightest chance of producing anything close to the wonderful meals that you've been serving?'

'I do, yeah. He's actually a really good cook. He spends a lot of time in Spain up in the San Sebastián region. You should sample the way he grills a whole fish.'

A nasty shiver skittered down Freya's spine.

'We're talking seriously good food,' Gavin said next. 'That area of Spain has some of the world's greatest restaurants and this guy's mates with a couple of their chefs. But he's also spent time in Italy and France, Morocco. He's picked up some great ideas.'

She forced herself to ask. 'What's this fellow's name?' But she already knew the answer. Almost fearfully, she said, 'It's not Seb Hudson, is it?'

'That's him.' Gavin was busily grinning again. 'You two know each other, don't you?'

Freya ignored this question. She was too busy remembering the embarrassment of Seb's snub at the supermarket. She'd never received such an obvious and publicly humiliating cold shoulder. Sonia Brassal's eyes had been out on stalks as she'd watched them. The woman was almost purring.

Suppressing another shiver now, Freya forced herself to ask, 'Have you actually spoken to Se— to Mr Hudson about cooking here – for us?'

'Yes, of course. I wouldn't have mentioned him otherwise.'

'And?'

Gavin was grinning yet again. He seemed very pleased with himself. 'And he said he'd do it.'

'Really?' The single word was a mere whisper now as Freya sank back against a cupboard, needing its support before her legs gave way.

She couldn't quite believe Seb had agreed to this. 'Isn't he too busy being a world-famous artist?' She couldn't help asking this, even though it sounded snarky.

'He's making time,' Gavin said. 'Reckons he owes me a favour.'

This was noble, Freya supposed, but she still found it hard to comprehend. Even if Seb was a staggeringly good cook and longed for a chance to show off his talents, he must be aware of her close association with the bistro. Gavin would have told him the set-up, including the fact that she'd taken over while Pearl and Troy were on leave.

'I'll admit he quizzed me about you.' Gavin looked as if he longed to ask Freya a question or three. Hell, he probably had a host of questions. For sure he was curious about her history with Seb Hudson.

She needed to clear her throat before she could speak. 'W-what did you tell him?'

This time, Gavin simply shrugged. 'I just said you were helping out, so Pearl could have a break.'

'I – I see.' She wondered what else Seb might know about her by now. About the divorce? The fire? Or perhaps he hadn't cared enough to ask beyond the basics. And it was the basics she had to concentrate on, too. 'Did he indicate how long he might be available?'

'He reckoned he could give it a month.'

A month? A month should be enough time to find a decent replacement. But a month with a cold and uncommunicative Seb Hudson working here in this kitchen? Five days a week? It was bizarre. Another impossible nightmare.

So much for her relaxed, happy island break. She'd probably end up having a nervous breakdown.

'Well, I'll see about preparing an advertisement straight away,' she said. 'And hopefully we'll find someone permanent well before the month's up.' With any luck a perfect candidate would turn up within a few days.

'I suggested that Seb should drop by this afternoon,' Gavin continued as if he hadn't noticed Freya's screaming tension. 'He can get to know the set-up here and we can talk about menus and ordering. Then he can stay on tonight as my kitchen hand. Get to see everything in action. He's a quick learner, and I'll grab the chance to show him a few presentation tricks.'

'But he's coming this afternoon?' Freya echoed faintly.

'Sure. That's okay with you, isn't it?'

'So soon?'

'Better sooner than later, I reckon.'

Freya didn't reckon so at all, but before she could speak up, a deep voice sounded behind her.

'Knock knock.'

She spun around. And there was Seb. A mere metre away, leaning a bulky shoulder against the kitchen doorway.

Her heart jolted in her chest. Such a foolish reaction given his own disinterest, but he was way too close for comfort. And she was too suddenly conscious of the man he'd become. His shaggy hair was flecked with grey, his face leaner and, inevitably, lined. His piercing grey eyes, however, were the same. No hint of a smile, of course.

He was dressed again in faded jeans and a simple T-shirt, a navy shirt this time. To Freya's dismay, she found herself imagining him in a chef's apron, tying the strings around his jeans-clad hips. *Good grief.*

Angry with herself, she quickly deleted that image. More than anything, she wanted to maintain a haughty and dignified demeanour, but when she tried to speak, her throat was bone dry. Nothing emerged.

Luckily, Gavin filled in the awkwardness. 'Hey, Seb, great timing, mate. I've just told Freya you can help us out.'

Freya merely nodded and Gavin continued. 'I'd do the introductions, but it seems you guys already know each other?'

At last Freya managed to speak. 'From long ago,' she said.

'Yes,' agreed Seb. 'Ancient history.'

That's right, she thought. Ancient history indeed. Anything they'd ever felt for each other had been dead and buried for decades.

'How are you?' Seb was looking directly at her now, but still with a kind of sleepy indifference.

'I'm very well, thank you.' She knew she sounded stiff and painfully formal, but for now it was her only survival tactic. 'And you, Seb?'

'Fighting fit, thanks.'

'Gavin tells me you're a star in the kitchen these days.'

Seb remained deadpan. 'Hardly a celebrity chef, but I manage.'

'It's very good of you to offer to help us out.'

'I'm doing it for my mate here.' This time Seb acknowledged Gavin with a smiling nod.

'Yes, we appreciate that,' Freya said tightly. 'But I know this wasn't planned and we don't want to inconvenience you. We'll try to find another chef as quickly as we can.'

'Sure.'

This conversation wasn't going anywhere and Freya wanted, more than anything, to flee. 'Look,' she said. 'It's good to see you, but I'll leave you and Gavin to have a good chat. Take a look at the pantry and the equipment. I'm sure I'm not needed at this stage.'

She was quite pleased with this exit strategy and was about to head for the door, when Gavin intervened.

'Hang on, Freya. I reckon you should be in on the discussion. You're the manager, after all.'

True, but she wasn't sure she had the stamina for a prolonged cold war. Reluctantly, she nodded, however. It would be stupid to make some kind of scene. 'Okay. You guys talk. I'll take notes.'

Somehow she got through the next hour or so. Seb really did seem to know quite a lot about the cheffing scene, certainly a great deal more than simply flipping sausages for the lifesavers.

She found herself involved as they discussed menus and food orders. Technically, Seb was a cook rather than a chef, as he didn't have official qualifications, but he had a few new suggestions for sourcing local North Queensland produce, which Freya realised she should have looked into before this.

Gavin showed him the temperamental gas stovetop that needed special treatment to light. He checked that Seb would be able to supply his own knives. Apparently chefs' knives were a very personal commodity and Gavin would be taking his with him.

They discussed the need to be flexible with what was in season, but also with the working hours. Inevitably there would be a table that came in late, or a sociable group that wanted to stay on. They agreed it was okay for Seb to put his own spin on dishes. Gavin had changed the menu quite often, so regulars wouldn't be hanging out for old favourites.

'I've eaten enough of your food to trust you,' Gavin told him. 'And let's face it, mate. Some of the best cooks are home cooks. The challenge will be putting up with the pace and the repetitious monotony day after day.'

Seb acknowledged this with a nod. 'I reckon I should be able to hold out for a few weeks at least. My main problem will be the desserts. I don't suppose we'd get away with fruit salad and ice cream?'

'Oh,' Freya jumped in. 'I love making desserts.'

It was only when both men smiled at her that she realised she'd let her guard down and had just made a really stupid mistake.

CHAPTER EIGHTEEN

Billie was cleaning salt spray from Island Thyme's windows, using her mother's old-fashioned method of a wad of newspaper and a homemade mix of methylated spirits, vinegar and water. Her fingers were black from the newsprint, but the windows were sparkling, and she was enjoying a sense of quiet satisfaction when she saw a stranger arrive on the deck via the stairs from the beach.

She supposed he was hoping the place was open, that he could grab a coffee or a snack. He didn't look like a tourist, though. He was dressed in long trousers and leather shoes, with a blue and white striped business shirt, worn North Queensland style, open at the collar and with the sleeves rolled to just below his elbows.

'Good morning,' he called to her.

'Hi.' Billie gave a nod to the empty dining room behind her. 'As you can see, we're not open, I'm afraid.'

'That's okay,' he said. 'I'm not looking for a meal.'

'Oh?'

'I was hoping to speak to Ms Belinda Mathieson.'

'Oh,' Billie said again. 'That's me.'

The newcomer smiled. He was youngish, early thirties at a guess. 'Pleased to meet you, Ms Mathieson. I'm Detective Senior Sergeant Dexter from the Townsville CIB.' And just like detectives on TV, he took an official ID card from his shirt pocket and flashed it at Billie.

Of course, she was instantly nervous. 'This isn't about my parents, is it?' Already her imagination was racing ahead, conjuring an accident. Robbery? Murder?

'Your parents?' The detective looked surprised. 'No. I'm assisting the Cairns coroner with a pending inquest.'

A *what*? Now Billie was completely confused.

This time he dug into his pocket again and produced a photograph. 'I understand you might know this man?'

Billie recognised the face instantly and went cold all over. Shaved head, dusty-blond moustache, pale, piggy eyes. It was the creepy bastard Reg Howe. When she'd arrived back in Queensland from Greece, short of cash and not really in a hurry to reach home, she'd crewed up the coast on his yacht, until she'd managed to escape his grubby clutches when they moored in Shute Harbour.

The detective was watching her closely now. Had her instant gut reaction given too much away? She was more cautious as she nodded. 'Yes, I know him.'

'Can you confirm this is Reginald James Howe, skipper of the sloop *Encounter* that recently travelled north from Mooloolaba?'

Billie nodded again. Had the detective found her name listed as crew in the logbook? 'That's him,' she said. 'But what's this about? Is he in trouble?'

'I'm afraid he's dead,' came the unexpected response.

Shock slammed through Billie. Reg Howe was a sleazy prick, but it was unsettling to know he'd died.

'That's why I'm here,' Detective Dexter said. 'I'm collecting information for the coroner. Is it convenient to talk?'

Billie lowered her gaze to her blackened hands. She was still holding the bottle of window cleaner and a sodden lump of news-paper. 'I – I guess.' The sun was rather bright on the deck at this time of day. She nodded to the empty dining room. 'We could sit in there. It's shadier.'

She wondered if she could escape to wash her hands, or per-haps she should just wipe them on the back of her jeans. Then she remembered the damp cloth she'd used to wipe tables down and quickly grabbed it and scrubbed at her fingers.

The detective made no comment and waited politely. He was nice-looking in an ordinary, everyday sort of way. No jaded weari-ness, rumpled clothes or stubbled jaw like the TV detectives, this chap was clean shaven, with short, neat brown hair and a familiar, Guy Next Door vibe.

With her hands a bit cleaner, they both sat at the nearest table.

'You looked upset when I showed you the photo,' he said. 'It's my job to find out as much as I can about the deceased – including what sort of person he was.'

Billie winced inwardly. She would have preferred to avoid any discussion of Reg Howe.

The detective offered a sympathetic smile. 'You can relax, Belinda, you're not a suspect. There's no reason to be afraid, but it would be helpful if you could answer a few questions.'

Setting her shoulders back, Billie braced herself for the unpleas-ant task. 'Okay.'

Rather than firing a question, however, the detective looked about him, gazing out through her now pristine windows to the perfect sweep of bay, the pale crescent of sand with rocky head-lands at either end, the spotless blue sky above. Holiday-makers were swimming in the gentle surf or lazing on beach towels. A boy threw a small ball and his golden labrador gleefully bounded into the shallows to retrieve it.

'This is an amazing location,' he said. 'I hear the food's great, too. Have you worked here long?'

'On and off since it opened. It's my parents' business,' she said.

'Lucky you.'

Billie sensed he was trying to help her to relax, but she was still on guard. How could she be anything else? She'd tried to clear the nightmare voyage with Reg Howe out of her head, but now she was forced to remember every sickening detail.

When she'd met Reg in Mooloolaba, he'd seemed fine, of course. Easygoing and friendly, even polite, going to the trouble of stocking up on the brands of muesli and coffee that she preferred. Everything had been fine until they were just south of Rockhampton.

She was cooking on the yacht's little gas stove when he came up behind her, slipped his arms around her and groped at her breasts. Luckily, she'd got rid of him with a fierce roar and an elbow in the ribs, and he'd laughed it off, claiming it was a joke.

Yeah, right. Sick kind of joke.

After that, Billie hadn't liked the way he'd looked at her. Such a slimey smile he had, and she'd started wearing long-sleeved tops and jeans instead of her usual tank tops and shorts. Then a couple of nights later, she'd woken in her bunk to find him on top of her, naked and reeking of beer. He'd been all over her, with one beefy hand under her T-shirt and another down her pants.

Billie had yelled and tried to push him off, but that only seemed to get him more excited. He wasn't a big man, but he felt as heavy as a mountain on top of her. She could scarcely breathe and he was panting and grinding away while she was screaming and struggling. In desperation, she'd poked him in the eye. Hard.

Reg had howled with pain, but it had worked. She'd been able to wriggle free and she'd locked herself in the toilet for the rest of the night.

After that, Reg probably would have skipped docking in Shute Harbour if he hadn't run out of beer, but it was then that Billie had seized her chance. As soon as the yacht was moored, she'd grabbed her small backpack with her money, phone and passport, a handful of clothes, and jumped onto the wharf and run.

Reg had probably feared she would talk. Seemed he'd only stayed long enough to get his beer and head off again.

She might have reported him. Thinking about it now, Billie knew she probably should have. It was sickening to realise that she'd already been pregnant at the time. But when she'd shared her sob story with a few of the girls over cocktails at the Airlie Beach backpackers' bar, they'd told her it wasn't worth the bother. No one would listen.

'They'll just say you were asking for it,' Jess from Edinburgh had told her. 'Hopping on a wee boat like that, just you and some geezer.'

Later that night Billie heard other similar tales of sex crimes against female backpackers and she had understood how damn naïve she'd been. She supposed this detective would think so, too. Perhaps she'd been so upset by the breakup with Petros she hadn't been thinking straight.

Now, instinctively, she touched her stomach. Just two nights ago, she'd felt the first tiny flutters. It had been the most amazing, unbelievably exciting moment and since then she'd regarded her body and its awesome responsibility with a whole new level of respect.

Surely this was the very worst time to find herself confronted by a plain-clothes copper and an inquest into the death of a horrible man.

Detective Dexter was still watching her. 'It appears,' he said, 'that Mr Howe didn't die from natural causes.'

Crumbs. He was murdered? Now Billie was more uncomfortable than ever.

The detective continued. 'His body was found floating not far from his moored yacht in Quarantine Bay just south of Cooktown. In cases like that it's classed as a "reportable death" and must be referred to the coroner.'

'I – I see.'

'So far, we have his identity, as well as where and when he died, and the coroner in Cairns will hold an inquest to determine the cause of death.'

Billie gulped. 'Right.'

'Our enquiries show that you spent time as a deckhand on *Encounter*. What can you tell me about that, Belinda?'

'It was awful,' she said. 'Probably the worst experience of my life.'

She sensed the detective's sudden relief. Leaning forward, elbows on the table now, he narrowed his gaze. 'I can't stress how important it is that you tell your story in as much detail as possible.'

'But he was well and truly alive when I left the boat.'

'Yes, I know your contact with him was well south of Cooktown, but the coroner will want to know how this man interacted with young women who crewed on his yacht.'

The detective pushed a small phone-like recording device forward on the table. Irrelevantly, Billie noticed that he had nice hands, squarish and strong and brown.

'In your own words,' he said. 'And your own time. What was your experience on board *Encounter*?'

She drew in a deep breath. 'Okay.' She couldn't get out of this and she wanted it over as quickly as possible. 'I crewed on Reg Howe's yacht from Mooloolaba to Shute Harbour and he sexually assaulted me.'

The detective was listening intently now.

'He didn't rape me,' Billie went on. 'But he tried to. He was naked in my bunk, on top of me and groping me, but I managed to poke him in the eye. Then I locked myself in the toilet for the rest of the night. As soon as we docked in Shute Harbour, I jumped ship.'

Detective Dexter looked solemn. 'Thank you, that's very helpful.'

She took another deep breath to calm herself.

'Is there anything you'd like to add?'

'No. Well, there had been another time earlier, when he had a grope. He really was a sleaze.'

'When you joined him in Mooloolaba, did you know you'd be the only crew?'

Billie swallowed, feeling guilty. 'Reg said there'd be two more joining us at Rockhampton, but then he never stopped at Rocky. He made up some stupid excuse about keeping ahead of the bad weather.'

'Was the weather threatening?'

'Not really.'

'Thank you,' Detective Dexter said again and he switched off the recorder.

Billie let out her breath in a heavy sigh. 'Do you think someone killed him?'

Uncomfortable seconds ticked by before he answered, as if he was considering how much to reveal. 'A Swedish backpacker has admitted to knocking Howe on the side of the head with a winch handle. She says he was attempting to rape her in the cockpit and she grabbed the winch in self-defence.'

Oh, God, the poor girl.

The detective sat straighter now, his brown eyes serious as he regarded her. 'Belinda, I'm going to need you to give evidence in the Coroners Court in Cairns.'

'In Cairns?' Billie cried, shaking her head. 'No, I —'

He held up a hand to silence her. 'I'm sorry, but your evidence could provide crucial support for the backpacker's story. As it stands, she risks being referred by the coroner to the Director of Public Prosecutions.'

Billie gasped. 'You don't mean she'd be charged?'

'There's always that risk.'

'Not for murder?'

'Perhaps a charge of manslaughter or unlawful killing.'

'Oh, God.' Billie closed her eyes. She felt overwhelmed, but she knew that her fear and stress would be nothing compared to the plight of the poor Swedish girl.

Opening her eyes again, she realised that the detective was waiting. 'It's a bad time for me to be away from the restaurant.' The last thing Freya needed was an absent waitress. Gavin's imminent departure was already causing stress.

'I know this is inconvenient,' he said. 'But if this skipper has a track record as a sexual predator, tricking young women into believing more crew were about to join them, your evidence will definitely help the Swedish woman's case.'

'I – I see.' Billie took a deep breath. 'What's this girl's name?' Somehow it seemed important to know this.

'Ebba Nilsson,' he said.

'Ebba,' Billie repeated, and a stranger she'd never met felt suddenly real.

'Your evidence could be vital.' The detective tapped the recorder still sitting on the table. 'You'll be compelled to attend, I'm afraid.'

So there it was. She had no choice. Billie shivered. 'How long will I need to be away?'

'At least overnight. It's hard to say. It all depends on the coroner and how things progress.'

Freya would have kittens.

'You'll be flown to Cairns,' he said. 'And your costs will be covered.'

Billie supposed that was something, at least.

CHAPTER NINETEEN

Freya enjoyed working in Pearl's kitchen. The layout was excellent, with a walk-in pantry, whiz-bang appliances and an induction cooktop that was a dream to use. As an added bonus, she had a spectacular outlook with sea views guaranteed to keep her mood upbeat as she worked.

And now that she was actually producing food to supplement Seb's efforts at Island Thyme, she was even more grateful for the fabulous workspace. Okay, her offer had been rash, but it was true that she'd always loved making desserts, and at least all those dinner parties on the Sunshine Coast hadn't been in vain. Mind you, Won Ton was sulking because they hadn't been for their usual long walks. The little dog now squatted in a corner of the kitchen watching Freya intently, no doubt hoping she would drop a tasty morsel.

It was only Freya's second day on the job, though, and she was still nervous about the level of professionalism required. The day before, she'd produced a classic tiramisu made with sponge fingers and mascarpone, as well as dainty little meringues to be served with mango slices and a berry compote. This morning she was tackling a white chocolate cheesecake with an accompanying brandy sauce.

Seb's contribution was fruit salad, which he'd claimed was merely a backup, but it had turned out, in fact, to be a classy affair with a delicious mint syrup. From all reports, the diners last night had been extremely happy with the desserts on offer, so with luck, they'd pull this off.

Freya was relieved, though, that she'd come up with the brainwave of making the desserts at home and delivering them each day when she dropped in to check the orders. Gavin had made this arrangement official by declaring that Seb, as a cook rather than a qualified chef, could not legally have an apprentice in his kitchen.

By keeping out of Seb Hudson's orbit as much as possible, she was hoping to maintain a polite, if cool, working relationship. Obviously, neither of them was keen to spend too much time together, but so far, so good.

The main hiccup had been Pearl.

Freya couldn't avoid telling her sister about Gavin's departure. After all, Pearl was phoning him regularly to keep a long-distance eye on things. Predictably, when she'd spoken to Freya she'd moaned noisily over the loss of their chef, but when she heard about Seb, she'd exploded.

'Seb Hudson, Freya? You've got to be joking!'

Freya felt obliged to defend the decision. 'Gavin swears he's a very good cook. Actually, I know he is, Pearl. He made dinner for us on Monday night – the most amazing grilled fish and —'

'I don't care about his grilled anything. So what? He could have Michelin stars coming out his bum for all I care. That's not the point.' Pearl was yelling so loudly, Freya had to hold her phone away from her ear. 'We can't have you and Seb and Billie all working there together. It's impossible. The three of you after all these years. My God, it's a recipe for absolute disaster.'

Freya was glad she'd rung Pearl while Billie was at work. She was glad, too, that they weren't using FaceTime. Pearl's screeching voice was distressing enough without graphic visual accompaniments.

'I'm sure you're exaggerating, Pearl,' she'd said. 'What kind of disaster are you imagining? What on earth do you mean?'

'You know very well. There are still folk on the island who remember everything.'

Everything? Freya knew there were a few long-term islanders who might remember that she and Seb had once been engaged and that she'd given birth to a baby that Pearl had ended up adopting. But if they wanted to make a thing of it, surely they would have done so by now?

She tried to placate her sister. 'But no one knows the actual —'

'For God's sake, Freya. *We* might know the true story, but other people only know what they *think* happened.' Pearl's voice was shrill now. Distraught. 'Seeing you all together will stir everything up. Tongues will wag. They'll put two and two together and come up with God knows how many. Billie will hear about it —'

At this point Pearl had burst into tears and Troy had taken over her phone. Freya was close to tears herself, but luckily, Troy was his usual calm self and he'd listened to reason when Freya explained that Seb Hudson was only a stopgap. She was doing everything possible to find a replacement chef.

'I know Seb is not an ideal substitute,' she said. 'But I assumed that keeping the business open would be Pearl's top priority.'

'Yes, you're right,' Troy assured her. 'And I'm sure it'll be fine. You're doing great, Freya. Thanks.'

'The last thing I want is to ruin Pearl's holiday.'

'You haven't ruined anything. She'll get over this.'

Remembering Billie's concerns about her mum, Freya felt compelled to ask. 'Pearl's all right, Troy, isn't she?'

'Yes, yes, she's fine. Don't worry.'

His answer had been swift. Almost too swift? Had she imagined the new brittle edge in his voice? It was so hard to tell.

By the time they'd finished the call, Freya was quite shattered, but the contact with Pearl had confirmed one thing. Billie was right when she'd declared that her mother mustn't be told about her pregnancy.

She reminded herself to take a deep breath. *One step at a time.*

At least she'd learned a thing or two from the crazy mess that her life had become over the past twelve months. She could view herself now as a battle-hardened soldier. A veteran, who'd learned that the best strategy for coping with ongoing disaster was to focus on whatever simple job came to hand.

And right at this moment, her task was to carefully combine melted white chocolate into a cream cheese mixture. After that, it was a matter of slowly beating in vanilla and heavy cream. Then she would set the cheesecake in a pan filled with warm water before baking it, and leave it to cool for an hour before it could go into the fridge.

She had plenty to keep herself busy and worrying about Pearl wouldn't help anyone.

'You're really good at this, aren't you?'

The grudging respect in Seb's voice was a surprise, but Freya had to admit the cheesecake did look rather professional, topped with curls of white chocolate, strawberries, piped cream and a dusting of icing sugar.

'Here's the sauce,' she said, trying to sound offhand, as if his praise hadn't filled her with ridiculous delight. 'You'll need to heat it up gently when it's time to serve.'

'Is that a brandy sauce?' Seb asked, sniffing.

'Yes. Is that okay?'

'Perfect. Thanks, Freya.'

So silly to be excited simply because he'd actually spoken her name. For heaven's sake, she wasn't still fifteen. She knew it meant absolutely nothing.

And yet hearing her name on his lips *felt* significant, lighting a kernel of warmth deep inside her.

'Right,' she said, dismissing such nonsense and adopting her most efficient and grown-up tone. 'Do you have a shopping list for me?'

'I do.' Spinning around, Seb grabbed a notepad from the counter and ripped off the top page. 'I hope you can read my scrawl. I have all the steak and lamb I need and a fisherman will be dropping off an order shortly. It's just a few grocery items. If there's no fresh asparagus, snow peas or runner beans will be fine.'

'Goodo.' Freya ran her eye down his list. Miso, Dijon mustard, canned tomatoes, coconut milk, several types of cheese, a range of vegetables. It all looked pretty straightforward. 'Anything else? Any problems with equipment?'

'No,' he said. 'All good so far.'

'Excellent.' Tucking the list into her shirt pocket, she turned to leave, relieved that they had once again conducted this meeting with businesslike briskness. 'I'm planning a flourless chocolate cake for tomorrow.'

'Sounds great. We'll probably use the last of the tiramisu tonight, so that'll fit in well.'

She gave a tight nod. 'Be seeing you then.' She was almost out the door when he said her name.

'Freya.'

She tried not to react, but her skin had other ideas. Her arms were tingling with goosebumps as she turned back.

Seb was still standing in the middle of the kitchen, hands resting lightly on lean hips. All shaggy haired, with a day's growth of beard. No sign of a chef's white apron.

'Yes?' Freya asked in a strangely tight voice.

'Billie's told me about everything you've been through.'

So silly of her to now feel like crying. She swallowed. 'I assume you must be referring to the divorce and the fire?'

Seb nodded. 'I just wanted to say how sorry I am.' To his credit he looked and sounded quite genuine.

'Thanks.' Very deliberately, Freya shifted her gaze to a spot on the wall just beyond his left shoulder. Her emotions were all over the place. Eye contact was dangerous.

'You deserved better,' Seb said gently.

She'd been steeled for resentment or derision. The last thing she'd expected from this man was sympathy. Now her eyes really did begin to water and she had to blink hard. *Damn.*

A deep breath helped, even though it sounded slightly ragged. 'Life's not about getting what you deserve, though, is it?' she said.

'Not for everyone, no.'

The tension in the air was so thick now she could have cut it with one of Seb's kitchen knives. But surely she was overreacting? He was merely trying to say the right things.

'At least you've had the success you deserved,' she added. 'I'm really pleased that your career's gone from strength to strength.'

'Thanks,' he said, but he frowned and let out a huff that might have been a sigh.

'And Pearl and Troy are grateful that you're helping out here.' She might as well get a few points up while she had the chance.

'I'm doing this for Gavin,' Seb said tightly. 'Not for Pearl.' His gaze narrowed. 'But it seems you've made a lifetime habit of helping your sister out?'

The barb hit home and Freya flinched. 'It's hardly a habit. And I'm sure Pearl sees this arrangement very much as the other way round. She's providing me with a roof over my head and a steady income for six months.'

He pulled a face, clearly not impressed.

Now was definitely the time to retreat. 'Anyway,' said Freya. 'I'd better go and put these orders through.' Once again she turned to leave.

And again Seb's voice sounded behind her. 'She's a great kid.'

This time Freya froze and her heart banged so loudly she was sure he must hear it. 'Are you talking about Billie?'

'Of course. Although I shouldn't call her a kid. She's a fine young woman. Hardworking, fun. She's terrific.'

When Freya looked back, his mouth was tilted in a lopsided smile, but the expression in his eyes was impossible to read.

Nevertheless, she saw it as a white flag. A fragile truce.

'Catch you later,' she said and she smiled.

CHAPTER TWENTY

Billie wasn't looking forward to telling Freya about the inquest. She'd already given her aunt enough hassles with her pregnancy news and now Freya had the added pressure of having to produce daily desserts on top of her management responsibilities. Not to mention that the poor woman was still getting over a divorce and the loss of her house.

Yikes. How much pressure could one woman take? Billie's private concern that she couldn't tell Freya about the court hearing without reliving the sordid experience on the yacht yet again was a minor issue by comparison.

The best thing she could do, she decided, was to first find someone to fill in for her at the restaurant. And with this, she was in luck. Josie Barnes, the local baker's granddaughter, was home on leave from uni. Josie was studying some obscure strand of philosophy, but she'd also worked in cafés in Brisbane, and she was more than keen to earn a few holiday dollars.

So with that sorted, it was crunch time. Freya arrived at Island Thyme mid-afternoon, looking rather pleased with herself as she delivered yet another of her fabulous dessert offerings.

Billie was polishing wine glasses and she waited till Freya returned from speaking with Seb in the kitchen before she shared her news.

Okay, deep breath. 'I'm afraid I'm going to need a day or two off,' she said.

Freya immediately looked concerned. 'Are you unwell, Billie? Is it the baby?'

'No.' Billie hadn't found an easy way to say this, so she just blurted out the bare facts. 'A detective was here earlier this week and I'm needed in court. I have to give evidence in Cairns.'

'You what?' Clearly appalled, Freya sank onto the nearest dining chair. The poor woman looked pale, as if this was one shock too many.

'I'm really sorry to lay this on you out of the blue.'

Freya stared at her. 'What's it all about?'

The story didn't take long. Billie took a seat and Freya remained very still with her hands folded in her lap, her forehead creased with a frown, her eyes round with worry.

'You poor girl,' she said when Billie finished, and then she let out a sigh and remained slumped in her chair, as if she needed a moment to take everything in.

'I can't imagine what the poor Swedish backpacker is going through,' Billie said.

'No, but still . . .' Freya gave a sad little shake of her head.

'I've found someone to fill in for me here at work,' Billie added, needing to inject a positive note, and she quickly explained about Josie.

'That's a relief. Well done.' Freya drew a deep breath, let it out slowly. 'Do your parents know about this?'

'No.'

'Does that mean you haven't told anyone?'

'Back in Shute Harbour, I talked about it with some of the other backpackers. They seemed to think it wasn't worth making a fuss.'

'Billie.' There was a note of reproach in Freya's voice now. 'Women need to speak up about these things.'

'Yeah, yeah, I know.' Billie did feel guilty. But she wasn't convinced that an official complaint in Shute Harbour would have spread quickly enough to stop the Swedish girl from boarding *Encounter* in Townsville.

'It's just – so – so *icky* to have to talk about it,' she said. 'And I knew I'd cop a load of lectures about how stupid I was to get on that yacht in the first place.'

Freya's face softened with sympathy. Reaching out, she took Billie's hands in hers. 'I guess you're right,' she said gently. 'It's all very well for outsiders to point the finger.' She offered a small smile. 'But at least you'll have a chance to speak up in Cairns.'

Billie closed her eyes. She'd never been inside a courtroom and she felt sick at the very prospect.

'You can do this, sweetheart.' Freya gave Billie's hands a gentle squeeze. 'You'll be great. I know you will.'

'Thanks.' She would try to hang on to those words.

Despite her aunt's reassurance, Billie spent a sleepless night before heading to Cairns, tossing and turning, worried that she'd freak in court and stuff up her answers.

The next morning, still sick with nerves, she decided that rather than wearing her usual jeans she would borrow a blue linen shift dress from her mother's wardrobe. That was one advantage of being the same height and build as her mum.

'Oh, yes,' Freya said when she saw Billie. 'That's just the right conservative touch. Good choice.'

'And it hides my baby bump,' Billie told her.

Freya's eyebrows lifted high and she looked amused. 'You have a baby bump?'

'The beginnings of one,' Billie said as she patted her ever so slightly curving tummy.

Later, at Townsville airport, Detective Dan Dexter was waiting to meet her. Billie politely extended her hand. 'Good morning, Detective Dexter.'

He'd smartened his blue business shirt with the addition of a red and white striped tie, and carried a navy sports jacket, no doubt a concession to the formality of the day's proceedings. This was the tropics, after all, and men in the north rarely wore formal suits. 'Good to see you, Ms Mathieson.'

His smiling brown eyes and Guy Next Door vibe were just as she'd remembered from their previous meeting. Not her type, of course. Romantically speaking, she preferred males with a bit of an edge, but this fellow certainly helped her to feel more at ease.

Impulsively, she said, 'You should call me Billie. Everyone else does.' And as they shook hands, she added, 'Ms Mathieson makes me feel ancient.'

He gave a her lopsided smile. 'How about we compromise with Belinda? Protocols, professional distance and all that.'

Billie shrugged. No point in making a song and dance about it.

'And you can call me Detective Dexter.' After a beat, 'No, call me Dan.' And this time his smile came with a hint of unexpected sparkle in his eyes that made Billie smile brightly back at him.

Surprised, she dropped her gaze and fiddled with the shoulder strap of her overnight bag. She'd been advised to come prepared for a stay over, although she was still hoping that her commitment in Cairns would be finished in a day.

Looking around her, she noticed a newsstand. Dan had a folded newspaper under his arm, so clearly he planned to read, and she was deliberating whether to buy a magazine for the flight when the PA system crackled and a woman's voice announced it was time to board. Oh, well, she thought as the passengers began to line up, she would just have to rely on her phone if she got bored.

The flight to Cairns was short, at least, less than an hour, and the plane was a small Dash 8. In no time, they were taking off, lifting high and then higher above the Townsville coastline and out over the sea.

Billie, seated next to Dan, had a window seat that offered her a brilliant view of Cape Pallarenda and Magnetic Island. She knew the island like the back of her hand, had walked the network of tracks that traversed its densely treed hills and had swum in every bay.

'It's beautiful,' Dan said, looking over her shoulder. 'We're lucky to have that island right on our doorstep. I must take Molly over there again. It's been too long.'

'Molly?' Billie asked, wondering about a girlfriend.

'My daughter.'

'Oh.' She wasn't sure why she was surprised that Dan had a daughter. She hadn't really tried to classify the guy, but she should have known he was the sensible sort who would be settled in a family relationship.

'How lovely.' She said this warmly to cover any slight hesitation. 'Yes, you must definitely bring Molly to the island. Kids always love it. How old is she?'

'Five.' He smiled fondly as he said this and Billie's thoughts flashed immediately to Petros, wondering what kind of father he would make. Would his face soften with such obvious love whenever he spoke of his child?

As always happened these days when she thought about him, her heart gave a nervous little flip. She knew she had to make contact with him soon. Very soon, actually. He had every right to be informed that she was having his child. But she was scared.

Of what? Rejection? Yeah, probably. Plus the sickening possibility that a brand new, bikini-clad holiday-maker had already stolen his heart, or at least found her way into his bed.

The plane climbed higher, flying north, hugging the coastline to their left and the sparkling sea to their right. Below them the vast ocean shimmered in shades varying from sandy white through to pale aqua and deepest turquoise. Billie recognised Palm Island and its neighbours. Soon they would be passing over Hinchinbrook and the Barnard Island Group, and there'd be other smaller atolls and patches of reef.

She thought about the slimy slug Reg Howe sailing through these pristine waters and the Swedish backpacker who'd been on board. The poor girl had come to Australia for an adventure and now she had to face a court hearing and the prospect of potential charges. And not just any charges. Manslaughter. How bloody terrifying was that?

It could have been me, Billie thought for the umpteenth time. It could, so easily, have been me.

Beside her, Dan had unfolded his newspaper and seemed to be absorbed. Clearly he was resuming his professional distance, which was fair enough, but it meant there was little chance for cheering conversation. Billie took out her phone and flipped to a games app.

'Have you been in court before?'

Dan asked this as they travelled by taxi from the airport down a long, straight divided highway lined with palms and massive trees and a statue of Captain Cook.

Billie shook her head. 'Never.'

'Don't worry. Most people are nervous at first, but just stick to your story and you'll be fine.'

It was all very well for him to tell her this. He was in and out of courts all the time. Billie couldn't help feeling nervous, and her nerves mounted as they made their way through the imposing front door of the Cairns Courthouse to the main reception.

She hadn't been expecting a security check. She'd already been through airport security that morning and that was enough, surely? But now a thickset, officious English chap with thinning red hair and rimless glasses was opening her shoulder bag and actually taking things out. Money purse, makeup, car keys, sunglasses.

Holy crap. Was this really necessary? Billie couldn't help scowling as he rummaged with his big paws through the movie tickets, shopping lists and biros at the bottom of her bag. Eventually, he decided she was boring and handed the bag back without bothering to close it. At least Dan offered her a sympathetic wink.

'We can leave our overnight bags at security,' he said, nodding to a small desk against a far wall.

Here they were given baggage tickets, before they went on to reception where a stern-faced woman in navy and pearls told them that their hearing would be held in Courtroom Three.

'We'll take the lift to the first floor,' Dan said now with a nod towards the lift doors.

As they stepped out of the lift into some kind of corridor, Billie wished she felt calmer. Their footsteps seemed to echo on the polished floors and as they turned a corner, she saw a row of solemn-looking folk sitting on a bench and her stomach tightened. It all looked incredibly grim and when Dan suddenly stiffened beside her, she felt a jolt of genuine fear.

Next moment, he gripped her arm. 'Just stop here a minute,' he said quietly. 'Stand over there, close to the wall. I won't be long.'

What the heck? Billie might have protested, but she'd sensed authority in Dan's quiet voice. She'd been given an order.

Her heart was racing now as she stood with her back to the wall, just as he'd instructed, while he walked up to two guys who seemed to be blocking one of the entrances a little further down the hallway.

One of these guys was massive, an obvious bikie in an ornate vest, complete with cropped hair, forked beard and arms covered in tattoos. Beside him was a much more conservative-looking fellow, neat haircut, small stature, wearing a tie and business shirt tucked into dark trousers. Chalk and cheese.

Dan approached the pair and stood tall, with his hands resting lightly on his hips and his legs planted firmly apart. Almost immediately, the bikie took two steps backward, much to Billie's surprise. The smaller guy didn't move, but his gaze narrowed menacingly.

She had no idea what Dan was telling them, but a sideways nod and a simple wave of his hand suggested they were being told to leave. The little guy's jaw tightened and for a minute Billie thought he was going to refuse. Dan took a step closer, hands clenched at his sides now and for a breathtaking second, she wondered if he was going to deck one of the men.

But before this could happen, they turned and walked meekly back towards the lift, while Dan spoke into his phone, no doubt passing on information.

'What was that all about?' Billie asked him as he came back to her.

'Don't worry. Nothing to do with the inquest.'

'But —'

'I don't think those two characters expected to see me here today.'

'And you moved them on?'

With his hand at her elbow, Dan steered her down the corridor. 'There's a big drug case being tried in Courtroom Two,' he said as they walked. 'That pair would have been hoping to intimidate one of the witnesses.'

Yikes.

'Anyway,' he said. 'It's nothing you need to worry about. Just part of my job.'

By now they had reached a small vestibule outside yet another closed door. Dan stopped. People were standing about in groups, talking quietly, staring at phones, clearly waiting for something to happen.

Billie spotted a young woman about her own age, tall and slim with a lovely suntan. She was dressed in grey and had long, blonde hair and a healthy outdoorsy glow about her.

'Is that her?' she whispered to Dan. 'Is that Ebba Nilsson?'

He nodded.

Ebba was standing stiffly with her arms folded. Billie noted an obvious tightness about her shoulders and the expression in her eyes signalled massive tension. Billie longed to send the girl a smile, or a friendly wave, but she was talking rather earnestly to a fat, middle-aged guy with glasses, presumably her lawyer, as well as an older couple, who were also tall and tanned.

'Are they her parents?'

'Yes,' she was told. 'They've flown out from Stockholm. I believe they're both doctors.'

'How awful for them.' Billie tried not to stare, but it was hard to keep her eyes away from the trio. She imagined how her own parents would have reacted if they'd been called to Greece because she'd accidentally killed someone. God, it didn't bear thinking about.

'They must be beside themselves,' she said, and she would have liked to offer them a word of sympathy, but Dan steered her to a row of seats some distance away.

'I'm afraid you can't speak to them,' he said, as if she was a book he could read.

There were no windows nearby and Billie experienced a moment of almost claustrophobic panic as she sat beside Dan. She was a beach girl, a lover of fresh air and sunshine, or at least a glimpse of the outside world, but this place was as closed in and serious as a hospital or a jail.

A policeman marched past, steering a fellow in handcuffs towards another courtroom. The handcuffed guy was Indigenous and probably still in his twenties. Billie supposed he was a prisoner. She shivered. 'How long do we have to wait out here?' She was anxious to get her part in this over and get out of here.

Dan shrugged. 'Hard to say, I'm afraid. You'll have to be patient. Ebba will give her evidence first.'

'Really? But will her lawyer allow her to tell her story?' On TV shows, lawyers always seemed to counsel their clients to not say a thing.

'This isn't a trial,' Dan reminded her. 'It's in Ebba's best interests to get her story across exactly as it happened.'

'But I have to wait here till it's my turn to speak?'

''Fraid so.'

'I can't go outside for a bit? Catch some fresh air?'

'Hey, don't be scared. You'll be fine.'

Dan said this like he meant it and when his eyes met Billie's, she read an implicit message – he was there for her, he was on her side.

I mustn't be a wimp.

She forced herself to remember Reg Howe and the shock of waking to find him on top of her. The ghastly stench of his beery breath, the revolting weight of his sweaty nakedness, the horror of finding his eyeball, slippery and soft beneath her finger. She'd been terrified she might have blinded him. How much worse had it been for Ebba to realise she'd killed him?

It wasn't long before she asked, 'I suppose there's a loo?'

Dan nodded and pointed to the right. 'Halfway down that corridor.'

'Thanks.' She needed to go so much more often now that she was pregnant.

'And don't let the blue light freak you,' Dan said.

'Blue light?'

'In the toilet. So the users can't find their veins.'

'Oh?' Was there no end to the freakishness of this place?

Billie was glad he'd warned her. The blue light was rather daunting and she got in and out of there as quickly as she could.

Dan was busy with his phone as she returned to her seat. He flashed a quick smile as he slipped it away.

'How much longer?' she asked.

'Hard to say. But don't sweat it, Billie. You'll be fine. A counsel assisting the coroner will ask questions and go through your statement with you. And they'll give you a copy of the statement you made to me, and you can refer to it if you need to.'

That was something at least. Perhaps she didn't need to panic that her mind would freeze and she'd be a total stuff-up.

'Just remember,' Dan said next. 'Ebba Nilsson, her family and the coroner are very lucky to have a witness of your calibre.' He gave her another of his nice-guy smiles. 'I'm really glad I found you.'

CHAPTER TWENTY-ONE

Freya was still in bed, mulling over the day ahead and wondering whether she could get away with baking a simple key lime pie, when she heard the front doorbell ring. She wanted to ignore it. After three busy days of coping with multiple responsibilities, she was allowing herself a bit of a lie-in.

Light was streaming through the bedroom shutters that Freya hadn't bothered to close, but she was sure it wasn't very late. A quick check of her phone on her bedside table confirmed it was twenty to eight.

Too early for callers, surely? She couldn't imagine who might be at the door. Even if Billie was back from Cairns, she wouldn't need to ring the bell. She had a key to let herself in.

But now it wasn't just the doorbell. Won Ton had joined in the fray with a fit of yapping.

'Stop that,' Freya reprimanded her little dog, as she reluctantly swung her legs over the side of the bed. Since the fire, Won Ton seemed to have forgotten the lessons she'd learned at the puppy training school.

Annoyed, Freya shoved her feet into silk slippers, reached for the lime-green kimono hanging on the back of her bedroom door and thrust her arms into its loose sleeves before tying the sash around her waist.

She refused to answer the door without a quick dash to the bathroom to splash cold water on her face and then a hasty brush of her bed-messed hair, but that would have to do. She was feeling quite grumpy as she headed down the hall, accompanied by an eager Won Ton, and her mood dropped even lower when she opened the door to find the very last person she expected.

Seb's hair was wet and shaggier than ever and he was dressed in a loose grey T-shirt over board shorts. Somehow, it didn't help that, now, approaching fifty, he still looked as good in this casual beach gear as he had in his twenties.

For heaven's sake, the man had worked until almost midnight. What was he doing, up so bright and early, looking astonishingly fit and as if he'd already been for a swim?

Freya tightened the sash of her dressing gown. Her good morning was a tad frosty.

'Morning, Freya. I'm sorry to intrude. I know it's early.'

'What's happened?' Surely there had to be a problem of epic proportions for Seb to visit her like this? Already Freya's mind was whirling through possibilities. A fire in the kitchen? A robbery?

'It's that new girl, Josie,' he said. 'The one who's filling in for Billie.'

Freya knew perfectly well who Josie was. 'Yes, what about her?'

'She's quit.'

Freya's jaw dropped so hard it almost cracked. 'But she's only just started.'

'I know, but she was a disaster last night. Knocked an almost full bottle of shiraz over an entire table. Managed to smash a couple of glasses at the same time and ruin a customer's white silk shirt.'

'Bloody hell.'

'And then she dropped two plates full of food. Seafood linguine and a vegetarian curry.'

'Oh, God.'

'After that she had a kind of meltdown. Left the place blubbering. Just raced off into the night and then rang to say she wasn't coming back.'

Freya groaned. Surely this sort of thing only happened in slapstick comedies? Not in real life? She found herself conjuring a mental image of a kindly celestial being who might pluck her out of this situation and deposit her gently on another tropical island, preferably one where all she had to do was read books and lie under a coconut palm.

Okay, so that wasn't going to happen.

She stared at Seb in dismay. 'How could Josie have been so clumsy? She was supposed to have loads of experience working at cafés in Brisbane.'

'Can't help thinking she was on something.'

'On? You mean drugs?' Pearl would have a double fit if she heard about this.

Seb merely shrugged. Clearly he didn't want to get the girl into too much trouble. At the very thought of Pearl's rage, Freya felt instantly defensive, too.

'I hope she's all right,' she said.

Surprise glimmered in Seb's eyes. 'Kind of you to worry about her.'

'Young people can find themselves in all kinds of messes.'

'True,' he said and for a moment, as his gaze met hers, she was sure she could sense unspoken questions. About their own youth?

But then the moment was gone and he added more dryly, 'But the not-so-young can find themselves in trouble, too. We'll need to source a replacement fast. 'I don't suppose Billie's finished in Cairns?' He didn't sound very hopeful.

Freya shook her head. 'I had a call from her last night. Apparently the case was unexpectedly adjourned yesterday. The poor Swedish girl broke down while she was telling her story and the coroner decided the experience was so stressful she needed time to compose herself.'

'Right,' Seb said grimly.

'Billie thinks it will take at least another day.'

'Well, we only need to get through two more days this week.'

This was fortunate, of course, but for Freya, the prospect of successfully negotiating those next two days without a waiter was as daunting as if those days were months.

'Look, you'd better come inside,' she said. 'We can hardly conduct a business discussion on the doorstep with me in my dressing gown.'

'It's a very respectable dressing gown.' Seb's eyes betrayed a sudden flash of amusement. Then, more seriously, he added, 'Sorry to call so early. I didn't like to bother you last night, but I can come back later.'

'No, we need to sort this out now.' Freya didn't add that Seb could have simply phoned her. She was actually pleased that he'd come to the house for a face-to-face chat. It felt like a step in the right direction.

Although, as he followed her through to the kitchen, she couldn't help remembering those days when any chance for the two of them to be alone together had automatically fired an inflammable lust fest. Now, she would have preferred to change out of her pyjamas and to try a little harder to tame her messy hair. And then she reminded herself that this new crisis at the bistro was a far bigger problem than any opinion Seb might have about her appearance.

'Would you like coffee?' she asked him.

'Only if you're having one.'

'Well, yes, I definitely need one. Is the old-fashioned style in a percolator okay?'

'Best way to make it.' Seb grinned. 'Unless you're an impatient millennial.'

Which they weren't, of course. They were well and truly middle-aged, with a buried history they were both ignoring, or pretending to ignore at any rate.

As Freya scooped ground coffee into the percolator's basket, Seb perched on a stool at the kitchen bench. 'Nice place,' he said, casting an admiring glance around the lovely living area and to the views beyond.

'It's amazing, isn't it? Pearl and Troy have scrimped and saved and worked damn hard for it, mind you.'

'I don't doubt that for a minute.'

She set the percolator on the stovetop at medium heat and wondered if she should offer Seb something to eat. But no, it was best to keep this meeting as simple and businesslike as possible, a brief but necessary practical discussion. If only she could see a ready solution to their current dilemma.

'I don't suppose you have any suggestions for another waiter?' she asked as she collected Pearl's boring grey and white coffee mugs from an overhead cupboard.

Seb shook his head. 'I've tried calling a few mates, but haven't had any luck.'

'I'm afraid I don't really know anyone on the island these days. I don't even know people in Townsville.'

'I'm pretty much in the same boat. I come here each year for a couple of months in the winter, but I only have a small circle of contacts. Mostly, I'm here to retreat and to paint.'

And yet this year Seb was doing exactly the opposite. Freya wanted to ask about him about that and she was desperately curious about his house on the island, but he hadn't come here to socialise.

'So how many bookings do you have for tonight?' she asked instead.

'Quite a few already. I'm not sure of the exact number, but we always have walk-ins.'

'And you don't really want to turn them away.' Pearl had warned Freya, using an especially lecturing tone, that a welcoming and relaxed flexibility was a vital ingredient for any island business. Freya adjusted the heat beneath the percolator. 'I could ring Billie to see if she can suggest anyone else, but if she can't, she'll only fret and feel guilty.'

Seb shook his head. 'Don't bother her.'

'So there's really only one solution then.'

'What's that?'

'I'll have to wait tables.'

His gaze narrowed. 'You have enough on your hands with the desserts and the orders.'

'I'll have to do a bit more, though, won't I?' She wasn't looking forward to the extra load, but if she'd managed to cook and serve for dinner parties, while running Brian's business, she should be able to cope with a couple of nights of waiting in a café.

Thank heavens plain black trousers and a black T-shirt had been among the op shop staples she'd purchased before leaving the Sunshine Coast. She hadn't planned on wearing them together or without bright accessories, but they were exactly what Pearl expected of her waitstaff.

Seb was pulling a face. 'Are you sure?'

To her own surprise, she found herself smiling. The situation was verging on the ridiculous. 'I can't promise I won't drop anything.'

Now Seb was smiling, too. But a smile from him was dangerous. Freya felt unexpectedly uplifted. And then she reminded herself she was getting carried away.

She forced her thoughts back to practicalities. 'With luck, Billie will be home tomorrow, so I might only be needed for one night.' She turned off the stove. The coffee was almost ready, but she would let it sit for a moment. 'Do you take milk or sugar?' Strange that she knew almost nothing about him now.

'No, thanks. Just black.' He paused, before asking, 'So how's Billie coping in Cairns?'

'Okay, as far as I can tell.' Freya poured the coffee carefully. She felt truly sorry for Billie. Such rotten luck to find herself pregnant to a man she clearly adored, but who'd already rejected her. And now this ghastly business. It was too much. She said, 'Billie's very concerned for Ebba, the Swedish backpacker.'

'It's a bad business. Did she talk to you about her time on that yacht?'

'Not until a couple of days ago, when she really had no choice.'

'Just shows,' Seb said, frowning, 'you never know the baggage people are carrying.'

'That's for sure.'

He looked at her strangely as she said this and Freya might have been imagining things, but she sensed there were questions he wanted to ask her. And she certainly had a thousand queries she wanted to direct his way – about the decades since they'd split.

Before she could begin, Won Ton trotted into the kitchen, no doubt drawn by the smell of coffee and the possibility of food. The little dog looked from one human to the other with bright, hopeful eyes.

'So what's your dog's name?' Seb asked, and the chance for a deep and meaningful moment seemed to evaporate like the popping of a soap bubble.

'She's called Won Ton,' said Freya.

He looked amused. 'An interesting choice to name your dog after an Asian dumpling.'

Freya's response was an eye-roll. 'I thought artists were supposed to see *beyond* the literal. Won Ton suits her perfectly. She's so
little and cute.'

'Of course. And I'm just being a smart-arse.'

Freya took care with her makeup before heading to work. Actually,
she went a little overboard, with eyeliner, mascara and smoky eye
shadow, plus her most flattering lipstick, which had, luckily, been in
her handbag on the night of the fire. She swept her bright hair up,
too, and added a pair of gold hoop earrings. She told herself that a
waitress needed to look as classy as possible, but she suspected she
also needed to upgrade the messy image she'd presented to Seb this
morning. She wasn't out to impress him. Truly! But as a divorcee
who'd been thrown over for a younger model, she did have a dented
ego to protect.

As it turned out, Seb was far too busy in the kitchen, darting from stovetop to counter to yet another stove, to even register
Freya's efforts. Or if he did notice, he made no sign. And Freya was
soon too busy to care.

By the evening's end, she had a whole new respect for wait-
ers. She'd known she would be on her feet the whole time, rushing
about, taking orders and delivering meals, while maintaining an
outer impression of assuredness and calm. But she hadn't quite been
ready for the level of interpersonal skills required.

More than once, she mentally cursed Pearl for being too stingy
to employ more staff. It was exhausting trying to remember exactly
what all the menu items involved, and dealing with super fussy customers – the glass that wasn't quite clean enough, the meat too
undercooked, the couple who found the sea breeze too cool and
wanted to move from the deck to inside.

Somehow, Freya managed to remain smiling and polite.

'I'm sorry about that, sir. Let me get you anther glass. Won't take a moment.'

'I'm sorry the lamb's not to your satisfaction, madam.' Clearly, the woman had a unique interpretation of medium rare. 'I'll take that back to the kitchen and our chef will prepare another. We'll be as quick as possible.'

'There's a table inside, sir. Will that be better for you? Lovely. Come this way, please. I'll bring your drinks and your meals.'

Halfway through the evening, Seb gave her a wink and a thumbs up. 'You're doing great, Freya.'

'Thanks,' she said, and decided not to mention that her feet were killing her.

On the whole, though, the experience was a rewarding one. It was gratifying to see so many people thoroughly enjoying themselves. Customers raved about Seb's Spanish-inspired entrées of breaded cod, tiny Iberian ham tarts and peppers stuffed with crab. His mains were also very well received and Freya was chuffed to hear her desserts scoring compliments.

Bonus, she didn't drop anything. Not even a wobbly moment. Such a relief.

By the time the last diners left, however, she was totally exhausted, but then there was all the tidying up. Luckily, Seb attended to the stoves and benchtops and stacked all his cooking gear in the dishwashers, so Freya was left to wipe down the tables in the dining room, fill the laundry bags and tidy the bathrooms.

As she emerged from dealing with this last task, Seb was waiting for her. 'That's enough for one night,' he said. 'I'll bring the deck furniture inside and we don't need to do anything more till tomorrow afternoon.'

'Thank God for that,' she said. 'I'm stuffed.'

His smile was sympathetic. 'You've earned a drink.'

This was a surprise. If she hadn't been so tired and aching, she might have been more on her guard. Instead, she returned Seb's smile. 'Yes, I'm sure I have.'

Seb pulled out a couple of chairs from the nearest table, even grabbed spare cushions. 'Sit and put your feet up. I'll be right back.'

The invitation was just too alluring. Freya hadn't the energy to question it, and as Seb disappeared, she sank with relief onto the nearest chair, stretching her legs out and letting her aching feet rest on a cushion on the opposite chair.

'Oh, yes.' She allowed herself a private moan of pleasure. 'This feels so good. Better than sex.'

She gave a tired giggle, quite pleased with her little joke and feeling safe in the knowledge that Seb was out of earshot.

Until a familiar voice commented, 'Really?'

Damn it, he hadn't been as far away as she'd imagined. And now he was coming around the corner with a bottle of wine and two glasses. 'Maybe you've been having the wrong kind of sex?'

Freya could feel her face burn bright with embarrassment. Worse, she was awash with memories of their youth when she and Seb had discovered sex together. Oh, my God, the thrills. The obsession. Oh, help. Just thinking about it now sent heat licking deep.

Stop it.

Seb was obviously referring to her more recent sex life, and she wasn't about to tell him how on the money his comment was.

'Scratch that remark,' he said, adding an apologetic smile, as if he regretted his impulsive quip. 'Guess I'm still in smart-arse mode. But hold that pose and I'll be right back.'

In this he was as good as his word. Setting the bottle and glasses on the table, he quickly returned with a platter of delicious entrées.

'Oh, yum.' Freya reached for a little ham and cheese tart. 'I've been eyeing these off and dying to try one.'

Seb was pouring the wine as she took her first bite, so he probably missed the look of bliss that undoubtedly came over her. 'Wow!' she said. 'Oh, that's sensational, Seb.'

'You can't beat *jamón ibérico*.'

'I'm sure you can't. It's so full of flavour.'

'Those hams are cured for at least two years. Sometimes four.'

'Well, they're worth the wait. And what's this lovely cheese you've teamed it with? It's so soft and mild, but tasty, too.'

'Sheep's cheese. *Manchego*.'

'Oh, yes, I remember ordering it for you. Mmmm, it's so good.'

'In Spain I'm friends with a farmer who makes his own sheep's cheese. It's a fascinating process.'

'How wonderful. And I suppose these little offerings are served as tapas in Spain?'

Seb nodded. 'Although where I live in the Basque Country, tapas are called *pintxos*.'

He handed Freya a glass of wine. 'Here's cheers.' He clinked his glass to hers. 'And bravo on a champion effort tonight.'

She smiled. 'We both deserve a bravo.' She took a sip and the wine was crisp and cold and tingly on the tongue. She closed her eyes, enjoying a moment of peace and satisfaction, took a deeper sip of wine and let it slide down her throat.

Perfect.

As Seb helped himself to a piece of breaded cod and Freya chose a pepper stuffed with crab, she said, 'So your cooking skills are undeniably impressive, but what can you tell me about your painting career? I don't mean a blow-by-blow history. But I know you're hugely famous now.'

'What would you like to know?'

She paused, searching for the right question. 'I guess I'm mostly wondering how you feel about your art now, about being an artist as a way of life? I suppose you still love it?'

Seb drank a deep draught of wine before he answered. He gave a brief shrug. 'I do still love it. No doubt about that. But if you want a very brief history, in the early days, I guess I painted to please my ego. I tried every style going, all kinds of experiments. But when I headed to America and found myself in an artists' colony in California, I really pushed the boundaries.'

Freya recalled photos of Seb in California, and in particular, that he'd been photographed with a different woman on each occasion. She supposed the boundaries had been pushed in all kinds of directions, in his private life as well as his art.

'You never married.' She couldn't resist this challenge.

His eyebrows lifted. 'I've had a couple of near misses.'

Including me? She did her best to ignore the little stab in her chest. She had absolutely no right to feel any version of envy for the other women in Seb's life.

But what was it like for him, she wondered, to have a string of lovers? Serial relationships certainly fitted the popular image of an artist, but was it an ultimately satisfying existence? Was Seb happy?

She didn't dare to ask.

He said, 'To answer your original question, I guess my breakthrough came once I'd worked at developing a strong and recognisable style.'

'Bold and vigorous landscapes and seascapes?'

His smile was mildly amused as he acknowledged this with a small nod. 'And by now, being an artist is how I am wired. I don't need to work as hard as I used to, but I can't really stop.'

'Except that you have,' Freya said, pointing with her wine glass towards the platter. 'Instead of painting, you're cooking for us – or, at least, for Gavin.'

'And it feels good to do something for someone else. As you're no doubt aware.'

His gaze met hers as he said this, and his grey eyes were fired by a sudden emotion and a complicated expression that sent unexpected shivers through Freya. Was he remembering the nine months she'd given up for her sister? The nine months that had torn the two of them apart?

If she tried to talk to Seb about that, she would become way too sad and weepy. And his response, for all she knew, might still be anger. They could end up fighting and spoil the night. Quickly, she forced her thoughts in a different direction.

'So I believe you have a house here on the island?'

Seb frowned, as if the sudden change of topic had caught him off guard. After a bit, he nodded. 'Yes, a little place in Nelly Bay.'

'That sounds nice.'

'It is, rather. Very private. I bought it for my mother originally.'

Freya remembered Seb's mother. Elise Hudson was an artist, too, but more of a sculptor than a painter. She made wonderful pieces using driftwood and seaglass and anything else that washed up on the island's shores.

Like Freya's own mum, Elise had also been single, and the absence of fathers had been a situation the young Freya and Seb had shared. Just one of the many small connecting threads that contributed to the closeness they'd enjoyed in their youth.

'How is your mother?' she asked.

'She died last year.'

'Oh, Seb, I'm sorry.'

'She'd always had a weak heart.'

'Did she really?' Freya remembered Seb's mum as always being wonderfully sun-browned and slim and super active. 'She always looked so fit to me.'

'I know. She'd never mentioned anything about her heart. I only found out in later years. In fact it's actually because of her heart condition that I owe Gavin such a huge favour. About three years ago, he found Mum collapsed on the beach at Cockle Bay. Being a life-saver, he jumped straight into resuscitation and had a helicopter over here in no time.'

'How wonderful,' said Freya. And Seb's willingness to help out at the bistro finally made sense.

Perhaps it was the second glass of wine and the extra helpings of delicious food that helped to mellow their mood. Freya told Seb about her own mother, who now lived in Broome on the other side of the continent, shacked up with a Japanese pearl farmer, not espe-cially well off, but ridiculously happy. Then they talked about lighter topics, such as Spain and other places they'd travelled to, about Pearl and Troy's adventure and the whole grey nomad scene.

Freya wouldn't have minded if Seb had asked her about Brian, but perhaps he wasn't interested, or perhaps he didn't want to cause any more awkwardness.

Obviously the wine coupled with exhaustion had gone straight to her head, because she also wouldn't have minded if Seb had asked her back to his place. It showed what a lonely and messed-up old bird she was, but she couldn't help remembering those heady days when they couldn't keep their hands off each other, when she'd loved him so fiercely she couldn't imagine her life without him.

This evening, Seb made no such offer, of course. He didn't even suggest they polish off the rest of the bottle, which was extremely sensible, as they still needed to drive home.

Freya told herself she was glad that at least one of them was sensible and grown up now, but as they climbed into their respective cars and set off in opposite directions, she just wished she *felt* glad and sensible and grown up.

CHAPTER TWENTY-TWO

'Where are the seahorses? Daddy, I can't see the seahorses.'

It was Saturday afternoon. Billie had finished mopping the restaurant's floors and she was folding starched linen napkins, ready for setting the tables, when she heard a small child's piping voice outside.

Looking out, she saw that a man and a little girl had arrived on the deck. The child was on tiptoes, leaning through the railing and peering out to sea. She wore a pink cap and her brown curly hair was tied in two small bunches on either side of her head. Billie thought she looked super cute in pink shorts and a purple T-shirt trimmed with aqua ruffles.

'I can't see any seahorses,' the little girl called loudly, and she rattled her bucket and spade to emphasise her displeasure.

Billie couldn't help smiling. There was a good chance that she had bossed her own dad like that when she was small. But she also couldn't help noticing that this girl's father, in sunglasses, a chest-hugging T-shirt and board shorts, was quite the man. Attractively tanned, and fit-looking, he was definitely worth a second glance.

Except that Billie's second glance gave her a jolt. Was that really Detective Dan Dexter?

She looked again.

Wow. Yes, it was definitely Dan. She'd had no contact with him in the past two weeks since she'd flown back from Cairns, apart from a formal phone call to inform her that the coroner had ruled that Reg Howe's death was due to 'misadventure'.

Billie had been hugely relieved to know that Ebba Nilsson had escaped being charged and was free to return home with her parents. With that news, she'd been keen to put the whole stressful experience behind her. Until now, she'd more or less forgotten about Dan's suggestion that he should bring his little daughter to the island.

And now he was turning from the view of the bay, and when he saw Billie, he waved. Then he spoke to the little girl and took her hand, leading her across the deck.

Billie met them in the open doorway. 'Hello there.'

'Hi,' said Dan. 'We're spending the weekend over here and I thought we'd say g'day.'

'A whole weekend on the island? How lovely.' This was such a surprise. In Cairns Billie had seen very little of Dan outside the courthouse. They'd stayed overnight, but he'd dropped her at a motel, informing her of the restaurant attached, and had promptly taken off. She had no idea where he'd stayed. Professional distance and all that.

Now, Billie smiled at his small companion. 'So this must be your daughter?'

'The one and only Molly Dexter,' Dan said with unmistakable fatherly pride.

'Hello, Molly.'

'Hello.' The child, who'd been so bossy mere moments earlier, seemed shy now, but she offered Billie a small smile.

'This is Ms —' Dan began, but Billie quickly intervened.

'Don't you dare call me Ms Mathieson,' she scolded. The poor man was being bossed from all sides today.

He smiled. 'Molly, this is Billie.'

Billie was surprised he'd actually remembered her preference, but she was sure she shouldn't be impressed by this small detail. She turned her attention on his daughter. 'And you're looking for seahorses, Molly?'

'She's obsessed with seahorses,' said Dan.

'I can see that.' A seahorse was emblazoned on the front of Molly's pink peaked cap and there was another on the front of her ruffle-trimmed T-shirt. Even her rubber sandals were decorated with tiny seahorses.

The little girl was very cute, with a ready smile and mischievous, twinkling eyes. She looked like a girly version of Dan, actually, except that her long-lashed eyes were a beautiful blue instead of deep brown.

Molly's small toenails were also neatly painted in glittery silver nail polish. Dan wouldn't have attended to that detail, surely? Billie wondered where Molly's mother was.

'Daddy told me I could see seahorses,' Molly said, pouting to show her disappointment.

'Well, yes,' Billie agreed. 'There are seahorses on the island, but they're only tiny, so I don't think you'll be able to see them in the ocean.'

'I think Molly expected to find them surfing the waves,' Dan said. 'She has a picture book that's given her quite the wrong impression.'

Billie smiled, remembering her own childhood when she'd been convinced that platypuses were almost as big as crocodiles, until she'd eventually seen one in the wild. 'Well, there's an aquarium in Nelly Bay,' she said. 'I'm pretty sure you'll find they have seahorses.'

Dan nodded. 'That's what I was hoping.' He looked past Billie to the tables inside and the pile of napkins she'd been folding. 'I guess you're busy.'

'Not so busy I can't offer you a coffee. And perhaps a little dish of ice cream for Molly?'

He looked surprised and Billie couldn't blame him. She'd surprised herself. The offer had just jumped out.

'The café's closed, isn't it?' Dan asked.

'Officially yes, but unofficially —' She gave a shrug and smiled.

She couldn't help remembering how Dan had been a pillar of strength during the hearing in Cairns, helping her to remain calm and focused, so that, in the end, giving evidence had been easier that she'd thought it would be. Ebba Nilsson's lawyer hadn't challenged any of her evidence, but had simply asked her to tell the court about her emotional response during the assault and after she'd broken free.

Words had tumbled from her then . . . . telling of the shock and embarrassment, the anger and terror, the humiliation . . .

'I'm sure I must have felt like every woman who's ever been subjected to sexual violence,' she'd said, and she'd looked directly at the female coroner, then back to the male lawyer. 'It's not easy to describe. I guess you'd have to be a woman to truly understand.'

To her surprise, there'd been a scattering of applause from the back of the court. The coroner had hit the bench with her ornate gravel and called for order, but no frown had been directed to Billie, and the coroner had given her an ever-so-slight nod of her head.

Billie had honestly felt as if she'd finally grown up on that day in Cairns and Dan Dexter's steady presence had been part of that milestone. Lately, one way and another, her life hadn't been much fun and it had been ages since she'd done anything impulsive. Why not be hospitable?

'Come on in,' she said to Dan.

Which was how the three of them ended up sitting at a table together, with Dan enjoying coffee and Billie herbal tea – she was conscientiously avoiding too much caffeine – while Molly had a little dish with two scoops of ice cream, chocolate sauce and a cherry on top.

Watching the little girl's joy as she dug her spoon into the delicious concoction, Billie couldn't help wondering about her own baby. She'd chosen not to know the sex, but now she found herself imagining a child, a girl perhaps, in five or so years' time, ready for a day at the beach, perhaps, enjoying ice cream and grinning at her with that special gleam of childish joy, a blob of ice cream on her chin.

She noticed Molly's silver-tipped toes wriggling with delight. 'Did you paint Molly's toenails, Dan?'

He glanced at his daughter's feet and grinned. 'Not a chance. My mum did that.'

'*Your* mum?' Billie didn't mean to sound so surprised, but this wasn't the answer she'd expected at all. She couldn't help wondering again where Molly's mother was.

'Mum picks Molly up from kindy each day and looks after her till I finish work,' he said.

Was Dan a single dad? Divorced, perhaps, and sharing custody of Molly with his ex? Billie didn't like to ask such questions in front of his little girl. They talked instead about safe, banal things – the accommodation where Dan and Molly were staying, the best bay for kids' swimming – and Molly told Billie about the seahorses in her book.

'There's a special one called Sandy and he has a curly tail that's magic.'

'He sounds amazing,' Billie told her.

'He is. He's got superpowers.'

'Wow. So he can swim really fast?'

'Yep and he rescues baby fishes and chases off sharks and baddies.'

'Sounds quite the hero.'

Molly nodded solemnly.

'You should be able to see his cousins when you go to the aquarium.'

Now the girl's eyes almost popped with delight. 'Daddy?' she demanded. 'When are we going to the 'quarium? Can we go now?'

Dan looked to Billie before he answered and as their gazes connected, she saw a flash, a leap of something like hope in his eyes. 'Would you like to come with us, Billie?' he asked.

She told herself it was the unexpectedness of his invitation that made her cheeks flash hotly.

'I know you have work commitments,' he added politely.

'Well, yes, I'm busy this afternoon,' she said. 'But I'll be free tomorrow morning.' Yikes, she'd jumped in again, feet first, hadn't she, without really thinking this through?

'You'll come with us then?'

'Ooh, yes,' piped in Molly. 'Come with us to the 'quarium, Billie.'

Billie swallowed guiltily. There'd still been no mention of Molly's mother, so it was quite possible that Dan was a single dad and it was also possible that he might be flirting with her. Flirting in a reserved and polite, nice-guy kind of way, of course. But that sparkle in his smile would soon vanish if he knew she was pregnant.

Right now, however, he was waiting for her answer. Even his daughter was all wide eyes and big smile, with her dripping spoon poised in midair.

'That would be lovely,' Billie found herself saying.

'Great.' Dan flashed Billie an even warmer smile. 'How about mid-morning then? Say, ten?'

Billie knew she wasn't handling this well. Last week she'd bought a couple of bigger tops and so far her bump was relatively easy to conceal, but she couldn't let Dan continue to think that she might be a dating prospect. First chance tomorrow, she would have to let him know she was pregnant and thus a no-go on the relationship front.

The conversation would need to be discreet, of course, when Molly was out of earshot, but it was time to come clean and set the man straight. Perhaps he might also be more forthcoming about his own situation.

It seemed weird to be planning to spill this news to a guy she'd just met when she still hadn't told her parents, or her baby's father for that matter, but it would be good to clear the air.

'Ten would be perfect,' she said.

The island's aquarium was a relatively simple affair set in sheds at the end of a path that wound through tropical gardens lush with palms, cordylines and flowering gingers.

Molly, wearing yet another seahorse-inspired T-shirt and almost bursting with impatience, skipped ahead of them up the path.

'You've done well to find her so many clothes with seahorses,' Billie told Dan.

'I have her granny to thank for that. She seems to find them online.'

'Sounds like your mum's a pretty special grandmother.'

'She is rather.'

By now Molly was well ahead of them, having reached the ticket office, where she was animatedly explaining to the kid who served there that she'd come to see the seahorses.

After an anxious night, Billie decided to grab this brief window of opportunity. 'Dan, may I ask about Molly's mother?'

'She died,' he said simply.

'Oh, God. I'm so sorry.' Perhaps she should have been prepared for this news, but divorce was so common she hadn't considered death for someone so young. Now the unfairness of this landed on Billie's chest like a physical blow.

'A car crash.' Dan kept his gaze lowered. 'A guy on meth ran a red light. Molly was only six months old and she was in her capsule in the back seat. Didn't get a scratch.'

Oh, Dan. Rendered speechless, Billie couldn't begin to imagine the horror for him, the unbearable shock and grief of losing his partner, combined with the sudden responsibility of caring for a baby daughter. She could almost feel her own heart breaking. 'That's terrible,' she said softly as her eyes filled with tears.

'It's been hard,' he said. 'But we're doing okay.'

Yes, of course he was doing okay. To Billie, he seemed to be coping wonderfully.

She blinked hard and stared at the bright red and cerise leaves of a cordyline plant, willing her eyes to dry.

Ahead of them, Molly was calling, 'Come on, Daddy! Hurry up!'

Billie swallowed and somehow managed to smile, and mere moments later, with their tickets purchased, they found themselves inside, surrounded by a watery wonderland. On either side, walls were lined with floor-to-ceiling tanks filled with the delights of the Great Barrier Reef. Coral and rocks and clams, and fish of every size, shape and hue.

Molly was delighted by the whole spectacle, but she was on a special quest, of course, so she hurried ahead again, past the underwater beauty until she reached her goal.

She squealed. 'Daddy!' she called again. 'Billie, hurry. Come here.' The little girl was quivering with excitement as she beckoned them. 'Look!' she ordered in a dramatic stage whisper, as Dan and Billie drew closer.

And there they were, a little family of elegant seahorses riding up and down in a tank of bright pink coral.

Billie grinned. 'They really are special, aren't they?'

'But they're so tiny,' squeaked Molly.

'And incredibly cute,' suggested Billie.

Molly nodded as she continued to stare, obviously needing a moment or two to realign her expectations with this diminutive reality. She was still smiling, though, and after a bit, she pointed to the biggest seahorse and announced quite assertively, 'That one's the daddy.'

'Perhaps,' said her father, crouching beside her with his arm around her shoulders.

Such a sweet picture they made, daddy and daughter.

Don't think about Petros, Billie scolded herself, as she dredged up another bright smile.

'That big seahorse might actually be the mummy,' Dan was telling Molly. 'I've read up on them.' He sent Billie a conspiratorial smile. 'Apparently, male seahorses like to choose large females as their mates.'

'They probably think the big girls are healthier,' suggested Billie.

'I guess, but the female lays eggs in the male's pouch and he then fertilises them and also incubates them.'

'So, he has all the work without any of the mating fun?'

'Apparently.' Dan's eyes were bright with amusement and more than a hint of interest.

And now Billie was cursing herself for making what could easily be interpreted as a flirtatious comment. What was wrong with her? 'Not a bad set-up for the lady seahorse,' she said in her driest tone.

The aquarium had a little courtyard café and morning tea seemed in order. Coffee for Dan and apple juice for Billie and Molly, plus a little dish of shortbread cookies shaped like various sea creatures. Of course, Molly chose the seahorse.

Billie, who'd selected a starfish, was wondering if there would ever be a chance to have the setting-things-straight conversation she needed with Dan. She was beginning to think she might have to save it for a phone call, when Molly piped up.

'Daddy, can I play on the swings?'

'Sure,' he said. 'As soon as I've finished my coffee.'

The little girl pulled a face. 'I don't need you to push me.'

Dan looked towards the play area where a boy and a girl about Molly's age were scaling a climbing frame while their parents nursed their coffees at a nearby table. It was pretty clear Molly was hoping to make new friends.

'All right then,' Dan told her. 'Off you go, but make sure you stay where I can see you.'

It was only as Molly raced away, whooping with delight, that Billie noticed she'd left her seahorse biscuit untouched on her plate.

'Maybe she couldn't bear to eat it,' she said.

Dan smiled wryly. 'I thought seeing real seahorses might be an anticlimax, might even cool her obsession.'

'Or fan the flame,' Billie suggested.

'Yeah, I guess either way it won't last forever.'

'She'll move on to princesses?'

He grinned. 'Then pop stars.'

'And boys in general.'

As soon as Billie saw the unmissable message in Dan's eyes, she realised she'd dropped another clanger. Or was he reading a subtext that she hadn't meant to imply?

Damn. It was time to come clean before things got totally awkward.

Unfortunately, her mouth was suddenly dry, her throat tight. She swallowed. 'Dan.' She swallowed again. 'There's something I really should tell you.'

She was instantly wincing. Such a clumsy start. But Dan still looked perfectly calm and unworried.

'I'm pregnant,' Billie added quickly.

The poor man's face was suddenly blank with shock, and the muscles in his throat jerked as he swallowed. 'Sorry,' he said. 'I – I had no idea.'

'Of course you didn't.'

He gave a strange little huffing smile that quickly came and went. 'And your baby's father . . .?'

. . . Is out of the picture? Billie wanted to answer this smoothly, but she found herself floundering. 'He's away at the moment,' she said after what, she was sure, was too long a pause. 'Overseas.'

'Right.' Dan was already sitting straighter, squaring his jaw and making a business of watching Molly at the playground. 'Well, I guess congratulations are in order,' he said.

'Thanks.' It was crazy to feel so uncomfortable, but Billie knew there'd been a connection, the shimmer of possibilities that she'd now quite thoroughly squashed.

CHAPTER TWENTY-THREE

'Fancy seeing you here.'

A familiar voice brought Freya whirling round. *Damn.* Seb had caught her out.

'I'm taking Won Ton for a walk,' she defended herself.

'I can see that. Morning, Won Ton.' Seb was unshaven, barefoot and wearing a white shirt left hanging open over bleached denim cut-offs. With a backdrop of cobalt sky, white sand and coconut palms, he looked like an ad for the relaxed island lifestyle. 'Nice morning for it,' he said.

It was a spectacular morning, clear and sunny and not too hot. Better still, this was the first of two precious days off from the restaurant and free time had never been more welcome. Freya had enjoyed a luxurious lie-in and a wonderfully leisurely breakfast with Billie, but eventually she'd given in to Won Ton's pleading eyes.

Now, as she avoided staring at Seb's naked chest, she hoped he didn't expect an explanation as to why she'd chosen this particular beach at Nelly Bay for their walk. After all, there were any number of bays available for a pleasant beach walk. Alma Bay was the closest to Pearl's house, but there was also Geoffrey Bay, and a short drive could have seen Freya at Picnic, Florence or Horseshoe bays.

She certainly wasn't going to admit to a burning curiosity as to which house in Nelly Bay might be Seb's. Since they'd shared their late-night supper, there'd been no more unguarded moments between them. They'd resumed a commendably sensible and businesslike relationship.

And thank heavens for that. It would be crazy and would serve no purpose to stir up messy emotions from their past. Freya was intensely relieved that she hadn't embarrassed herself the other night and she'd given herself stern lectures ever since.

Despite the lectures, there'd been dreams, however. Such cruel things dreams could be, opening windows into bliss she'd neither asked for nor expected. Just last night she'd dreamed she and Seb were in Florence Bay at sunset, sitting cross-legged on the sand. Could she even sit cross-legged these days? They'd been cooking their dinner of fish over an open fire and she'd been wearing his ring, loving the glistening, perfect little diamond. Loving him.

Longing for him.

When he'd taken her into his arms, the most glorious joy had blossomed inside her, rising through her like the moon lifting from the distant horizon.

Waking up had been such a downer.

'I didn't mean to intrude on your walk,' Seb said. 'But I was having a coffee on the deck when I saw you.' His shoulders lifted in a casual shrug. 'Thought you might like to join me when you've finished.'

'Oh?' Freya hoped her response sounded equally casual. 'So you live at this end of the bay? How – lovely.'

'Very last house.'

'Lovely,' she said again, feeling foolish for exhibiting such limited vocabulary, but unable, when trapped by his steady grey gaze, to unearth a more intelligent response.

Seb smiled, stepped back and lifted a hand in a parting wave. 'Take your time. See you whenever.'

She hadn't planned a very long walk, but now she made sure she went to the opposite end of the bay and out along the harbour wall. Here, Won Ton was in ecstasy, despite being kept on a leash, as the wall was home to rock wallabies and exquisite scents abounded.

Freya might also have enjoyed the walk if annoying tension hadn't tugged away inside her, pulling tighter and tighter. It was so difficult, coming to terms with Seb's re-entry into her life. She was far too conscious of the memories they'd shared, of the giddy and shining, youthful love she'd so recklessly shattered.

Surely, she should be able to conduct herself calmly now if she and Seb were to have a proper conversation? Cleared the air, so to speak. Laid a few ghosts and got important points out in the open. Actually, if Freya was truly honest, a desire for a cathartic chat with this man was probably the real reason she'd come to his bay.

By the time she turned back, she was quite decided. This was as good an opportunity as any and she would at least try to initiate some kind of grown-up discussion.

The sun was quite hot now as she made her way back along the wall and then down the beach to the very end. To Seb's house.

Gulp.

The pain of losing her own home had been gradually receding and while she'd enjoyed living in Pearl's home, she hadn't felt especially envious. Stunning as it was, her sister's house had never really felt like home.

But this house, right on the beachfront, at the very end of a no-through street and bordered by a tangle of scrubby bush, was, to Freya's mind, damn near perfect.

Unpretentious, low-set and of modest proportions, Seb's house had a deep verandah that ran across the entire front and a wall of bi-fold shutters that rolled back to expose glimpses of a living area with polished timber floors, tropical cane furniture and beautiful artwork.

Freya supposed privacy wasn't really an issue, as hardly anyone came to this sleepier and almost secluded end of the little bay, and the sense of being at one with the beach and the bush was deliciously inviting.

Seb appeared on the deck to greet her, and she was relieved to see that he'd done his shirt up. She retrieved the dog lead from her pocket. 'You'd probably prefer Won Ton to stay outside?' she suggested.

'Hell, no.' Seb reared back in exaggerated shock. 'We can't leave the little lady out in the street.'

He smiled then, and something in his eyes sent the smile rippling through Freya. No, she mustn't be ridiculous. It was time to finally prove to herself, to Seb, to anyone who might care, that she was mature and worldly-wise and well past girlish flutters.

Stepping onto the deck, she paused to compose herself and to admire a hanging mobile made from birds styled out of driftwood.

'This must be your mother's work,' she said.

Seb nodded. 'The very last piece she made.'

One of the larger birds – which was, in reality, nothing more than a single weathered branch of pale and twisted wood – had been given beautiful wings of woven string. 'It's gorgeous,' Freya said gently. 'Elise must have loved knowing that she passed on her artistic talent to you.'

'A lucky gene,' Seb suggested, but although the comment was made lightly enough, Freya didn't miss the shadow that crossed his face.

Disquiet thudded in her chest. As far as she knew, Seb had never fathered a child and she had no idea how he felt about this.

Suddenly she was nervous about raising the big unasked questions that lay between them. Perhaps, after all these years, she no longer had the right to probe too deeply. Or perhaps she wouldn't want to hear Seb's answers.

Her confusion returned as they continued into the house, where the aroma of coffee melded with the scents of citronella and incense sticks. Several of Seb's landscapes hung on the walls and Freya stopped again to admire the way he'd captured one of the island's headlands. So breathtakingly real, with an almost sculptural quality, yet transfused with a soft, dreamy glow.

'Wow,' she whispered, and she almost told him about the art lessons she'd started – after all, their romance had begun during their high-school art class – but Seb was already in the kitchen, and so she followed.

This central space was quite simple, with timber cupboards and white benchtops, but lifted by clever touches of colour. A bright-green teapot, a tiled splashback in shades of aqua that spoke of the sea, a coral-pink vase holding a single spray of the yellow orchids that grew in rocky crevices all over the island.

'This is lovely, Seb. Just —' Freya didn't want to be too effusive, so she scratched the word 'perfect'. 'Just so relaxing.'

'Yep, it works for me.' He poured coffee into mugs.

'Do you have a studio?' she asked.

'The shed out the back.'

Following the direction of his nod, Freya saw, through a window, a wonderfully ramshackle shed almost hidden by a clump of banana trees, but offering a glimpse of old-fashioned wooden louvres and flowering vines crawling over a rusty iron roof.

'Very authentic,' she said.

Seb merely grinned, but despite the relaxing ambience, Freya didn't feel any version of calm as they carried their mugs back to the lounge area and made themselves comfortable in well-cushioned cane armchairs, while Won Ton settled at her feet.

And although Seb seemed outwardly composed, she sensed tension simmering just below the surface.

'This is kinda weird, isn't it?' she said.

He frowned. 'In what way?'

'Us.' Freya waved her mug-free hand, a helpless flap. 'I never expected to see you again.'

'Ditto,' he responded cautiously.

An awkward silence fell. Freya wondered why he'd invited her. Had he wanted to talk?

She tried again. 'You have to admit it's strange, Seb, to find ourselves working together after all these years, seeing each other every day.' She didn't add that it was even stranger to know that he'd voluntarily put himself in this potentially ticklish situation. And she certainly wasn't going to mention that now they'd negotiated the initial frostiness, she'd spent way too much time remembering their youth and the fateful day she'd tried to hand his ring back.

To her dismay, Seb made no comment. Worse, his gaze narrowed and became wary now, as if she had pushed in a direction he didn't want to follow.

She sighed. She was tempted to give up, to paper over the cracks and pretend everything was fine. And it *was* fine. If she and Seb ignored their history.

But that wasn't realistic, surely? And after having her house and her life reduced to ashes, Freya was beginning to understand that the best way out of any mess was to simply push right through it.

'Seb, should we talk?'

At first she thought he was going to be facetious, to merely suggest that they were already talking, weren't they?

'You'd like to tell me about your marriage?'

Thud.

'Actually, no.' Brian and the divorce were the very last things she wanted to talk about, but Seb wasn't about to let her off the hook too easily.

'What went wrong?' he asked.

Freya gave a frustrated shake of her head. 'Oh, lots of little things, I suppose.' And now it was she who tried to be flippant. 'I got tired of Brian leaving cupboard doors open all the time.'

'Yeah, right.'

She shifted in her seat. 'I – I guess we might have been bored with each other. Well, obviously, he was bored with me. He took up with a thirty-something blonde.'

Again, the expression in Seb's eyes suggested he wasn't buying this excuse.

Freya found herself saying, 'And I guess Brian took not being able to have kids pretty hard.'

Seb was staring at her now, clearly shocked and, quite possibly, appalled. 'Are you telling me that you couldn't have children?'

'I am, yes.' Taking a deep breath, Freya added, 'But just last week, Brian's new wife had a baby. A little boy.'

Jo had rung Freya with this news, passing on the message as gently and diplomatically as she could.

'I have a friend in Nambour Maternity,' Jo had told her. 'And I asked her to let me know. I didn't want you to hear about it weeks later after the whole world already knew.'

Strangely, the news hadn't hurt Freya nearly as badly as it might have done before the fire, or before she'd learned about Billie's pregnancy. Perhaps she was mellowing. But her infertility news had clearly rattled Seb, which was understandable. He knew she'd had no problems getting pregnant with Billie.

'What was the problem?' he asked, clearly baffled.

This was not the direction Freya had planned for their conversation, but having opened the can of worms, she could hardly close it. 'I ended up developing the same problem as Pearl,' she said. 'Endometriosis.'

'Jesus.'

To Freya's dismay, this news launched Seb out of his chair and onto the verandah. As she watched him stride away, she felt her throat close on a hot knot of pain, but she couldn't move to follow him, was sure he wouldn't want her to. Was he angry?

Watching his stiff back and straight shoulders as he stared out to sea, she couldn't help remembering the shocked accusations he'd delivered all those years ago . . .

'You're offering your body to your sister?'

'Not my body, exactly. Just my uterus, Seb. It's not as if I'll be having sex with Troy.'

'Oh, so that makes it all okay?'

'Well, yes, I think so. Pearl's desperate.'

'Poor Pearl. And you didn't think you might speak to me first? You just went ahead and offered? Signed on the dotted line?'

'I'm sorry.' Freya knew she'd been impulsive, but when she'd been hit by her wonderful idea, she'd been fired with an almost holy zeal. She'd been so aglow with self-righteousness, with sisterly love and the magnificence of such a wonderfully generous mission that she'd just dived straight in. And expected poor Seb to understand.

God, she'd been naïve. Apart from delivering a healthy baby girl, she'd handled every aspect of that scenario so heavy-handedly. And, foolishly, she'd thought Seb would come back to her when it was all over. Instead, in one fell swoop, she'd lost her fiancé and had put her relationship with her sister under a strain that had never resolved. And she'd carried all that baggage into her marriage.

Perhaps a psychologist might have told her that Brian could sense she'd never given him her whole heart.

'So, I presume you want to talk about us?'

Freya jumped and so did Won Ton, who'd been snoozing at her feet. Seb was back, standing before her, his expression intense, almost threatening.

Despite the slamming of her heart, she gave a tight nod. 'We left so much unsaid at the time. Back then.'

'As I remember it, we said plenty.'

'But we were so busy arguing, Seb. I was pig-headedly determined to go ahead with the surrogacy. And you . . .' She paused, giving him space to respond.

'And I was in shock.'

'Yes.'

At least, he now lowered himself back into a chair. 'Have you any idea how it felt to learn that the woman I planned to marry was prepared to give her body to bear another man's child before she'd had a child of her own?'

'A child of yours,' Freya clarified.

'Well, yes.'

She resisted the temptation to suggest he'd behaved like any young male primate similarly threatened. 'We were young, Seb. We'd never really talked about having our own family. And I was healthy. I guess I thought . . .' She paused, tried again. 'I guess I naïvely assumed I could have it all – Pearl's baby, you and our – our own family eventually.'

Seb made no response, simply sat there frowning at some distant spot on the floorboards.

Watching him, Freya wondered yet again if she was foolish to try to rake up their past. Was she actually being selfish? Trying to ease her own guilty conscience?

But even as she asked herself this question, she found herself saying, 'You do understand why I broke off the engagement, don't you?'

'You lost patience with me.'

'No, not that.' She had tried to explain at the time, but Seb had been far too angry to listen. 'We were so young, Seb.'

'I think you've mentioned that.'

'But surely that's the point? I was totally gung-ho about my body, but I *did* feel bad about not considering how you might react. And I also felt guilty about keeping you tied to a woman who was going to have someone else's child.'

With a sense of urgency, Freya groped for the right words. 'I lost my freedom with the pregnancy, but I convinced myself you should be free to date other women, to have the chance to think twice about whether you really wanted me.'

The look Seb shot her now was filled with heat. Anger? Hurt? Freya couldn't be sure, but it was reminiscent of the look his mother had given her all those years ago, after she'd lost Seb.

When she'd gone to Seb's mother, weeping, Elise had been sympathetic, but quite firm. 'You hurt Seb badly, Freya. I'm sorry, but you made a serious mistake when you chose to go ahead without even discussing the surrogacy with him.'

'I know. I can't believe I was so stupid.'

'I'm afraid it's a hard lesson to swallow, but there are some things in life you just can't undo. Sometimes we make serious mistakes and we just have to learn to live with the consequences.'

Freya's problem now, all these years later, was that the consequences of her rash decision had never really finished. Here she was, back in Seb's orbit, but finding him suddenly bored by this conversation.

'Water under the bridge,' he said, and he sounded tired and so fed up Freya was silenced.

Defeated.

Clearly, there was no point in finishing her confession. Thank heavens she hadn't admitted the other, more shameful reason she'd embraced the surrogacy plan with so much gusto – that for the first time in her life, she'd found a way to be superior to her big sister. Pearl had always been better than Freya at just about everything – at school, at home, always conscientious and neat, a dream student and daughter.

Of course, Seb would be even less impressed by this ignoble motive. In fact, it was pretty damn obvious he wasn't nearly as interested as she was in retracing their past. He was prepared to be pleasant, to offer her coffee or a snack, but he saw no value in conducting a post-mortem. And perhaps that was wise.

Freya finished her coffee and set the mug aside. 'I should be going,' she said. 'Thanks for the coffee.'

'My pleasure.'

'And I'm sorry . . .' She gave an awkward little shrug. 'You know – about dragging up ancient history.'

Seb's response was an impatient nod. 'Yeah, we really don't need to go there.'

'No,' she said, unhappily.

And then, as if he needed to make his point clear, 'I'm cool, Freya. It's great to see you again, to know that you're fine, but I'm very happy with my life and I don't have regrets.'

'No. No, of course you don't.'

'And I'd like to keep it that way.'

'Yes, that's – that's – very sensible.' He was brushing her off, gently, but unmistakably. Utterly chastened, Freya discovered she was hurting in ways she'd never imagined. 'I – I didn't mean to —' But what could she say? Honestly? While her feelings for this man and the ramifications of her decision had continued to flow on like a river into tributaries with unexpected turns, Seb had left her far behind long ago.

Her sentence remained unfinished, but as she stood to leave, she managed, with significant difficulty, to offer him a smile. She hoped it was convincing.

CHAPTER TWENTY-FOUR

This was it. D-day for Billie. She couldn't put off the phone call to Petros any longer. Her pregnancy would soon be obvious, word would spread and even though the news was unlikely to reach Santorini, Billie had learned from her stuff-up with Dan and Molly that no one benefited when vital communication was delayed.

She had felt terrible, witnessing Dan's retreat, seeing the warmth in his brown eyes replaced by confusion and then by a disinterest that bordered on contempt.

As for poor Molly, the little girl certainly hadn't understood why her father had become suddenly sharp with her.

'But, Daddy, we can't leave yet. Billie's going to show me the bay where the seahorses swim.'

'*I* can show you,' Dan had insisted.

Billie had attempted to ease the situation. 'I don't think you'd actually be able to see the seahorses in the ocean, Molly.'

'No,' Dan said. 'Seahorses can be quite deceptive.' He'd shot an accusing look in Billie's direction as he said this and while she might have tried to apologise, tried to explain, she could see he was too pissed off to listen.

He'd just wanted out of there.

Which was fair enough, but it meant that Dan still didn't know the true story about Petros. He assumed that her baby's father would soon return to her, and the stupid thing was, she hadn't meant to mislead him. She'd got herself in a bind, all because she'd delayed the damn phone call to Greece.

So now, Billie was determined. She drove to Horseshoe Bay on the far side of the island, keen for total privacy when she made this call. The road wound around and over the headlands, offering teasing vistas of brilliant blue sea and curving beaches below before it slipped back down from the hills to the wide, aptly named, horse-shoe-shaped bay, which was now drowsing in afternoon sunlight.

Throughout the drive, she found it hard not to think about Santorini and the fun of warm nights at a taverna on the water's edge, sharing a bottle of wine, a plate of dolmades or fried tomato fritters. Picnicking on clifftops, hiking along the picturesque caldera, swimming in the Aegean. Not to mention the long blissful nights of making love.

Don't think about that now, Billie warned herself. And she wouldn't allow herself to imagine the many ways Petros might react to her news. She knew it was unrealistic to expect him to be pleased. After all, he'd initiated their breakup and had made no attempt to contact her since she'd left Santorini. Just the same, she couldn't damp down a tiny flame of hope.

As soon as she'd parked her car, she found a perch on a smooth boulder with a view out over the serene tropical waters and tried to ignore her thumping heartbeats as she coded in Petros's number. Greece was eight hours behind Queensland time and she'd chosen late afternoon as the best chance to catch him.

At least he answered quite promptly . . .

'Ya!'

Billie's throat was instantly sore and tight and she had to swallow. 'Hi, Petros, how – how are you?'

'Who is this?'

'It's me. Billie.'

'Oh, hi.'

'How are you?' she asked again.

'I'm fine, thanks. Rather busy,' he added in his careful English.

'Sorry if I've caught you at a bad time.' She wondered why on earth she was apologising. 'I won't keep you long. But I have some news. Something I need to tell you.'

She hesitated then, hoping for an encouraging hint of interest, but Petros made no comment. Swallowing again, she said, 'I'm pregnant, Petros. I'm having your baby.'

This momentous delivery was met by unsettling silence.

Billie held her breath and stared resolutely out to sea where a handful of yachts bobbed at their moorings. Beyond them, an empty ocean stretched, silent and still to the horizon.

Finally, Petros spoke. 'You can't be serious?'

For pity's sake. Why would she make this excruciating overseas phone call if she wasn't desperately serious? At least his response swept aside any lingering sentimentality that might have otherwise swamped her, and she refused to grace his dumb question with an answer.

'Are you sure it's mine?' he asked next.

God, the man was so self-centred and insensitive, Billie wanted to scream.

'Yes, Petros,' she said. 'I'm absolutely, one hundred percent certain this baby is yours, but you can have a DNA test, if you like.'

'No, no,' he said quickly, as if it might have dawned on him that he'd annoyed her. 'That's not necessary. I believe you.'

At this, despite all evidence to the contrary, Billie couldn't quell a foolish flicker of wishful thinking.

'But I need to explain something,' Petros added. 'I can't possibly marry you, or care for your child.'

Your child. With just those two words, he made his message painfully clear and Billie finally let go of a deeply suppressed and impossible hope.

Now, as tears flooded her eyes, she hugged her rounded tummy. Her baby was never going to know its father. Petros would never smile at her little one the way Dan Dexter smiled at Molly.

Sitting there, on a bare rock, looking out at an almost empty sea, she'd never felt so very alone. 'I – I see,' she managed.

'I am already engaged to be married,' Petros continued. 'The wedding is next month.'

Next month? *Next? Freaking? Month?*

This time Billie almost dropped the phone. 'But – but it's only a few months since we —'

Petros interrupted her. 'This arrangement – it was made a long time ago.'

'Arrangement?' Was he committed to some kind of family-arranged marriage? 'Are you telling me that you've always known about this? You were engaged even before we met?'

'Yes,' he replied with an air of impatience.

Oh, God. How stupid had she been? And how the hell could she have been crazily in love with this guy? With this egotistical, two-timing, too handsome prick?

Billie was tempted to hurl her phone into the ocean, except that she'd be the only one who would suffer.

Promptly, she disconnected, without even bothering to say good-bye. Swiping at her eyes with the backs of her hands, she sat there for ages, teeth firmly gritted, staring at the cloudless pale sky, letting the truth of Petros's message sink in.

So. Now she knew. Now she couldn't avoid the glaringly obvi-ous. Despite his murmurings of affection, Petros had never let her into his heart. She'd never been more than a holiday fling.

And caring for this baby was entirely up to her. Her pickle.

She might have felt scared, overwhelmed, but as she gave her tummy another rub, she felt an answering tiny kick and, amazingly, was aware of an inrush of strength, a dawning sense of power. *Stuff Petros.* She knew she could let him go now, not merely because she had no choice, but because she was bloody well good enough without him.

'We're gonna be okay, little one,' she said, and she even managed to smile. 'You might be my little Pickle, but I reckon we've got this covered, you and me.'

CHAPTER TWENTY-FIVE

Freya finished watering Pearl's pot plants, wiped a few drops from the timber floor and allowed herself a small, bored sigh. The three plants needed next to no attention. They offered no wilting leaves to trim, no curling tendrils to rearrange. No flowers to admire. They didn't even present any colour variegation. They were so plain-green and ordinary they might as well be plastic, which was, possibly, the reason Pearl liked them.

It was silly to mind, Freya knew, but she'd been in a bit of a slump the last week or so. She wasn't sure why. She had plenty to keep herself occupied, what with the bookkeeping and managing the orders, as well as continuing to make the restaurant's desserts. She seemed to have this extra task under control, though, and today she'd made another big tiramisu, which was always popular, while there was still half a lemon curd cheesecake in the fridge at the restaurant.

Returning to the kitchen, she was stacking the utensils she'd finished with into the dishwasher just as Billie came in, carrying a basket of washing fresh from the clothesline. This, Billie deposited on an end of the bench and then went to the sink to help herself to a glass of water.

'Warming up outside,' she commented before tipping her head back and drinking the glassful in greedy gulps.

'Yes,' Freya agreed. 'I think winter's well and truly behind us.'

Billie laughed. 'All three days of it.'

This was almost accurate. Winters in the north were so mild, Freya had rarely needed so much as a cardigan. She smiled at Billie now, aware of the warm glow she often felt in the girl's company.

Freya would never admit it to anyone, because it wasn't the right way to think – and it was also the very mindset that Pearl had always feared – but she did feel a measure of possessiveness towards Billie. And she was entitled to, surely?

She hadn't simply given up her womb for a baby's gestation. She'd given up nine months of her life, nine alcohol-free months at that, as well as the man she loved. So surely she'd earned at least a small sense of ownership? Crikey, you could own a square foot of a Scottish island simply by buying a particular brand of whisky. On that basis, Brian owned several square feet of the Isle of Islay and he had the certificates to prove it.

These were not helpful thoughts, though, and Freya knew she was unwise to dwell on them.

'By the way,' Billie said, inadvertently providing a digression as she set the glass back in the sink. 'I rang Petros yesterday afternoon.'

She seemed quite calm as she said this, but Freya knew the girl must have been nervous. The conversation couldn't have been an easy one and there'd been no mention of it at breakfast.

'How did Petros take your news?' she asked carefully.

Billie's response was an elaborate eye-roll. 'Like a gold-plated arsehole, to be honest.'

'Oh, Billie.' Freya was sure the girl must have been devastated, although she had to admit she looked more angry than upset.

'I'm actually okay about it,' Billie said. 'Maybe it was the kind of closure I needed, but I'm over him now. Well and truly.'

Remembering how deeply distressed Billie had been, Freya very much doubted this quick turnaround, although her niece certainly looked quite composed.

'You won't believe this, Freya.' Billie's lovely blue eyes were lit by a new intensity as she perched on a kitchen stool and leaned forward with folded arms resting on the bench.

'I'm all ears,' Freya said.

'Petros had the hide to tell me he's engaged and getting married next month.'

Freya stared at her, appalled. 'Next month?'

'Yep,' said Billie. 'Charming news, isn't it? And he's been planning to marry this other girl all along. I think it's some kind of stupid family arrangement.'

'Bloody hell.' Freya gaped at her. 'And he'd never seen a reason to tell you this?'

'That, my dear aunt, is a very good point, but I didn't bother to question him. I hung up on the prick.'

Despite the hard edge in Billie's tone, Freya knew she must be hurting. She wanted to take Billie in her arms, to tell her that while the pain of rejection might never really leave her, it was survivable. She knew that for a fact, had lived with it forever.

Carefully, she said, 'I'm so sorry to hear that, Billie.'

'Thanks. But I'll live. I had a good talk to Seb last night, which helped.'

'With Seb?' Freya echoed faintly. She wasn't quite ready for this surprise, or for the small stab of jealousy that came with the knowledge that Billie had turned to Seb first.

If Freya was honest, though, the downward slump in her mood lately had come after Seb's gentle but unmissable brush-off. Since then she'd spent far too much time coming to terms with the fact that her hopes regarding him had been unreasonable, a pathetic case of self-deception. There would be no rekindling of their youthful romance.

'Yeah,' Billie was saying. 'I decided I should tell Seb I'm pregnant. It made sense, seeing that we work together so much of the time.' She gave a small shrug. 'I'd just come back from talking to Petros and as soon as I told Seb about the baby, the rest of the story just kind of tumbled out.'

Freya nodded, imagining the exchange and trying not to mind that Billie had not confided in her first. 'I suppose you shocked Seb,' she said.

'He was so kind, Freya. Pretty amazing, really. He made me a special caramel latte, cos I told him I'm avoiding caffeine, and we sat down and had a lovely, long chat.'

'How – nice.'

'Yeah, it was great. We talked about everything – how shitty life can be, and how it's not about the cards you're dealt, but the way you play your hand.'

'Did Seb tell you that?'

'More or less. I was surprised, too.' Billie was grinning now, no doubt enjoying her private knowledge and Freya's incredulity. 'And we even talked about being a single mum.'

'Really?' Freya supposed she shouldn't have been shocked. She knew Billie and Seb had developed a friendly working relationship, but she'd never pictured Seb in any kind of counselling role. 'So what kind of advice did he give you?' She hoped she didn't sound too desperately curious.

'Oh, it wasn't advice exactly. More of a helpful chat. About his dad dying in the Vietnam War and how his mum brought him up on her own. I mean, I sort of knew about Elise Hudson, living here on the island, and about her art and everything. But Seb talked about how strong she was and what a good time he had growing up with her. Just the two of them. Living here on the island helped, I think. Their lifestyle was simple, but Seb made it sound like so much fun and I found the whole story quite inspiring.'

'Well, yes, I'm sure you must have. That's – lovely.' Freya could imagine the idyllic picture of his childhood that Seb might have painted, and she supposed it was sensible to give Billie positive scenarios. 'And your grandmother Ruby was a single mum, too, for many years,' she said.

'Oh, yes, of course.' Billie's eyes widened with gratifying pleasure. 'I'd totally forgotten that Granny used to be single. How cool! You and mum had no dad either and you turned out all right.'

Freya knew this was not the moment to mention the years of poverty, of living in van parks, of surviving on tinned fish and baked beans and wearing charity-bin clothes. To this day, Freya couldn't eat sardines. She offered her niece her warmest smile. 'I know you're going to be a wonderful mum, Billie. Your baby's lucky.'

Billie smiled back at her and drew a deep breath, as if she was drinking the praise in, letting it settle inside her. 'Thanks.'

'And, of course,' Freya added, feeling so much better now, 'You don't need to stay single forever.'

This time Billie's smile turned wry as she patted her swelling belly. 'Well, I won't be picking up any hot guys in the foreseeable future.'

'You just never know,' said Freya, who thought that Billie looked perfectly lovely right now, in denim shorts and a baggy white T-shirt, with her long tawny hair left loose and windblown.

'Anyway,' the girl said, moving back to the washing basket and extracting tea towels, which she proceeded to fold, 'I'm starting to feel a whole lot happier about the situation.'

'Good for you,' said Freya. 'I'm proud of you.'

As Billie began on the bathroom towels, folding them carefully into thirds, no doubt the way her mother had taught her, Freya wished she could also offer a few final words of wisdom. She would have liked to produce something pithy like Seb's bar-room philosophy about playing the cards you're dealt.

Nothing came to mind, however, and she found herself turning instead to her own recent difficulties after the fire and the wonderful support she'd received from Daisy and Jo.

'You'll probably find it important to stay connected with your friends,' she suggested. 'Especially if you have friends who are mums, even if they're married.'

'Yeah.' Billie gave a thoughtful nod. 'But I'm afraid most of my friends have left the island.'

'So you think you'll stay here?'

'I think so. For the moment at least. It seems to make sense.'

'Well, your parents will certainly be pleased and they'll be doting grandparents.'

Billie grinned. 'Oh, my God, ain't that the truth?' As she said this, she pulled an awkward face. 'And that's the other phone call I'm going to have to make very soon.'

'Absolutely,' said Freya. 'But don't let on that Seb or I know anything about the baby.'

'No,' said Billie. 'I'll be careful. I'd hate to upset their holiday. I just hope the news doesn't bring Mum tearing home.'

CHAPTER TWENTY-SIX

'It's been ages, Billie. We should catch up.'

When Sonia Brassal's daughter phoned Billie, announcing that she was home on the island for a short break and wouldn't it be great to meet up for a coffee, Billie might have excused herself. Nicole Brassal had never been what she'd call a close friend, but she had been part of the general gang of island kids who'd hung out together, fishing and skin diving and building rafts, sailing small dinghies, lighting camp fires on the beach.

And when Nicole's call came a mere day after Billie's conversation with Freya, her aunt's comment about keeping in touch with girlfriends was still nagging at her. Billie knew she'd been remiss about keeping in contact, but she'd always told herself there were justifiable reasons. Almost all her mates had left the island straight after high school and then, a few years later, so had Billie, following her desire to travel.

She'd found she was quite good at making new friends wherever she went, both male and female. Backpackers mostly, from all walks of life and from all over the world. Billie had found these folk, for the most part, fascinating, easygoing and fun, and quite generous with sharing all manner of practical info re hostels, rideshares, the best place to buy hiking boots, the nearest pharmacies.

Usually these friendships were little more than very brief acquaintances, but Billie had struck up a few longer-lasting relationships. A standout girlfriend had been Claire, a cheeky, freckle-faced Irish girl Billie had met in Bangkok. She and Claire had spent ten weeks together, travelling through Thailand, trying out a cooking class in Chiang Mai, hanging out on the gorgeous beaches at Phuket, attending a yoga retreat in Koh Samui. But since Claire had gone back to her university course in Dublin, they'd only exchanged random emails.

It had been the same with the others Billie had met – a certain two-timing Greek included. *Friends for a season.*

So, with Freya's comment in mind, Billie found herself responding positively to Nicole, who was one of the sensible island kids who'd gone to university and found a well-paid job. Nicole worked for a marketing company in Melbourne, and she'd also scored a respectable husband. They had a little boy called Preston, who, according to Nicole's Instagram posts, was some kind of two-year-old genius. Billie had always rolled her eyes at these 'mumfluencer' updates, but now that she, too, faced impending motherhood, she was trying to show more interest in other people's kids. Especially now that she'd cleared the final hurdle and had rung her parents to share her pregnancy news.

The call, which Billie had made straight after her conversation with Freya and before she lost her nerve, had begun with predictable drama. Her mum had screamed down the phone line.

'A grandma, Billie? What are you talking about? You can't be —? You're not —' And then a choked gasp. 'You're not really pregnant, are you?'

'I am, Mum. I'm having a baby.' And after Pearl had calmed down enough to put her phone on speaker, so that Troy could listen in, too, Billie told them about Petros. She did so as briefly as possible, leaving out the additional chapter of Reg Howe and the yacht and the trip to Cairns, and, thankfully, they let her get her story out with minimal interruptions.

Her mum had a little weep, of course, but she assured Billie she was shedding happy tears – *on the whole*. Then her dad had quizzed her about doctors and scans and whether she planned to attend antenatal classes and, all things considered, the phone call had gone pretty well.

'I'm fine, guys,' Billie reassured them. 'Honestly. I haven't said anything till now, because I wanted you to enjoy your holiday and the last thing I want is for you to worry, but I'm keeping really well. I'm happy. The baby's growing perfectly and I'm already halfway there.'

And don't you dare come rushing home, she wanted to add, knowing that they'd made it to Tasmania and were loving the island state, but she didn't want to risk putting the idea in their heads.

So, now that the important conversations with Petros, her parents, and Freya and Seb were finally behind her, Billie felt as if a huge weight had rolled from her shoulders and she was quite receptive to a dose of girl talk with Nicole.

Island Thyme was closed for the day, although Freya and Seb were meeting this morning to discuss the applications that had come in for the chef position, as well as any menu changes for the coming week. Billie, however, was happily commitment free, and she was determined to enjoy the morning and to be especially nice to Nicole's little genius. So she was surprised, when she arrived at Picnic Bay, to discover that Nicole had not brought Preston, but was alone and looking almost unrecognisably glamorous, as if she'd stepped straight out of a fashion magazine.

Nicole's hair was far darker than it had been in their school-days and was styled in a smooth, trendily layered bob. Her makeup was immaculate, if a tad try-hard, and she was wearing a botanical print sundress, glamorous high-heeled sandals, green to match her dress, and was sporting green nail polish as well.

Billie, in denim shorts, simple flat sandals and a white eyelet cotton smock that hid her tummy, felt as if one of them had walked onto a movie set wearing the wrong costume. Nicole greeted her effusively, however.

'How gorgeous to see you again,' she said, giving Billie an enthusiastic hug. 'It's been way too long.'

'Yes, ages,' said Billie. 'How are you? How's Jason?' Thank heavens she remembered the husband's name. 'Did he travel up here with you?'

'Of course,' said Nicole, as if there was no other possibility. 'We both managed a week off, which was brilliant, but I knew Jason wouldn't want to sit around here this morning, listening to a whole lot of girl talk, so I left him on Dad duty. He's taking Preston to Arcadia.'

Billie assembled a quick smile. 'How lovely.' Of course, Nicole's husband would be perfect. He probably fixed dripping taps, too. And picked up his socks and jocks. Pointless of her to think of Detective Dan Dexter just then, but he was also probably one of those dream men, caring and considerate, who would cook dinner for you if you were tired. *Sigh*.

They ordered their drinks. Billie, not wanting to draw attention to her caffeine avoidance, chose tea. Proper leaf tea in a pot, which was nice. Nicole ordered a skinny latte with a double shot and they sat at an outdoor table shaded by a huge banyan tree.

'I hope a parrot doesn't poop on us,' Nicole said and they both laughed, which was a good start, and they were quite relaxed as they settled to enjoy the perfect view of curving beach and headland and sleepy blue sea.

Billie decided to launch the conversation. 'So, you'll have to tell me everything, Nicole. About your job and what it's like living in Melbourne.'

'Oh, Melbourne's uh-mazing,' the other girl gushed. 'So much culture, you wouldn't believe.'

'I don't suppose I would.'

'Have you ever been there?'

'No, I haven't actually.'

Nicole looked so shocked it was almost comical. 'Oh, but, Billie, you must come to Melbourne. You'd just love it. It has such a fantastic vibe and the city shopping is amazing. As for the theatre – oh, my God. And the autumn leaves. I adore autumn, but you never really get an autumn here in the tropics, do you?'

'I guess not.' Billie decided not to mention the sea almonds and other northern trees that turned bright red in the spring, no doubt preparing for torrid summers rather than freezing winters.

'As for my job,' Nicole gushed on. 'It's crazily busy like you wouldn't believe.' On saying this, she cast an amused glance down the quiet tree-lined esplanade where a couple of families were eating ice creams, a small group of backpackers whizzed along on bicycles and a solitary dog sniffed at rubbish bins. 'I always get such a shock when I come back to the island,' she said. 'It's so easy to forget how quiet it is here.'

'But perhaps that's also why so many Victorians spend their winters here.' Billie couldn't help being defensive and at least Nicole had the grace to smile.

'Anyway,' she said. 'Enough about me. If you've seen my Instagram posts you'll already know most of it. But you're the dark horse, Billie. I want to hear what you've been up to.' Nicole leaned forward, all girly smiles. 'Is there a man in your life?'

'Not at the moment.' Billie was pleased that she managed a smooth response. 'There was a guy in Greece.' She gave a dismissive wave of her hand. 'But I left him behind.'

'Probably for the best.' Nicole was clearly an expert on such matters. 'But I bet he was easy on the eye.'

'Oh, yeah. Very.' Quickly, Billie added, 'But it was just a holiday thing.'

'So you're still on the hunt?'

'Not at all.' Billie might have answered this too quickly, but she couldn't ever imagine hunting for a man, thank you very much.

Nicole looked as if she might have wanted to counter this, but fortunately, she didn't persist. 'And what about your career?' she asked next.

Now Billie snorted. 'My career? I help out at my parents' bistro.'

'But that's just while they're away on holidays, isn't it?'

'Well, yes, more or less.'

'Weren't you studying art?'

'Way back, straight out of school,' Billie said, nodding. 'But I didn't stick at it.'

'That's a pity.'

'Nah. I didn't have what it takes. Not to be a serious artist. Anyway, I wanted to travel.' Billie could travel on a shoestring, but she'd always liked to earn a good amount before she left. She'd hated the idea of sending messages home, begging her parents for a little more money. They wouldn't have minded, but it was a matter of pride. 'I knew there was hardly any chance of earning decent money as an artist,' she said. 'Not unless you're brilliant.'

'But you had so much potential.'

Billie frowned. Nicole had never been in her art class, not even at school, so how would the girl know anything at all about her potential? Unless . . .

Good grief. Hadn't Sonia Brassal made almost exactly the same claim on that night at the restaurant?

'Did your mum tell you about my potential?' Billie asked.

Nicole's brightly painted lips twisted into an awkward smile that might have been apologetic. 'Well, yes,' she said. 'I mean – it makes sense that you would have an artistic gene.'

'It does?' Billie thought about this. 'Freya is fairly artistic, so I suppose it might run in the family.'

'Well, yeah, obvs. Of course you'd get it from her,' Nicole responded more confidently. 'Not to mention your dad.'

'My dad?' Billie frowned again. Poor Troy couldn't draw to save himself. Even his stick figures weren't very convincing. 'You mean those bright colours he painted our house all those years back?'

'No, not Troy.' Nicole dismissed him with a flick of her green-tipped fingers. 'Your real dad.'

Your. Real. Dad. The words slammed into Billie with the force of lightning bolts.

'W-what are you talking about?'

Instantly, Nicole's eyes widened, huge and horrified, as if she'd realised she'd made a massive mistake. 'I – I j-just assumed . . .' she stammered. 'You must know – you're working with them at the restaurant and everything.'

Billie thought she was going to be sick. Her head spun as she tried to make sense of this crazy statement. She wanted to ask vital questions, but she didn't think she could bear to have the answers spelled out.

Unfortunately, it was all too easy to stitch together the implications in Nicole's message. Her so-called friend believed Billie's real parents were Freya and Seb.

How fucking ridiculous. And suddenly Billie was angry. No doubt Sonia bloody Brassal was responsible for this misinformation.

Nicole looked stricken. 'Oh, God, Billie, I'm so sorry. We were sure you must know.'

'Know what, exactly?'

But now Nicole shook her head.

Anger flared. 'For God's sake, girl, why don't you just spit it out? What am I supposed to know?'

'About —' Another frustrating pause.

'Yeah, go on.'

'About the adoption.'

Billie's head fairly exploded now. 'Adoption?'

Miserably, Nicole nodded.

'You're saying that Freya's my mother, but Pearl and Troy adopted me?' Billie was surprised she could speak so calmly, when inside she was panicking.

Nicole was absolutely no help. She was a mess now. Blubbering. Covering her face with her hands.

Billie sagged, all breath knocked out of her. Was this true? Could it possibly be true? Both Freya and Seb had lived on the island back before she was born, but they'd been seeing her every day for weeks and were as cool as bloody cucumbers. Then again, she couldn't help wondering if something like this was at the heart of the never-ending tension between her mother and Freya.

Oh, God, did this mean her mum wasn't really her mum? Her dad, her darling Troy, not her dad?

For pity's sake, this couldn't be true. But if it was, Freya must have been pregnant, but perhaps Seb rejected her. Was that why they'd both been edgy about seeing each other again? And why they'd been so understanding about the whole Petros thing?

Was history repeating its bloody self?

Tears were streaming from Nicole's thickly mascaraed lashes. 'I'm so sorry. I feel terrible.'

You feel terrible? Billie wanted to scream. *What about me?*

She was desperate to get away, but there were too many things she needed to know.

Sick to the stomach, she forced herself to ask, 'Is that what everyone on the island thinks? That Freya is my real mum? That she let Mum and – I mean, Pearl and Troy – adopt me?'

Nicole's tears made dark, sludgy tracks down her cheeks. 'N-not everyone.'

'Who then? Just you and your mum?'

'Maybe a couple of others.'

Billie wanted to slap her. Instead she stood abruptly, making her chair fall backwards to clatter on the cement paving.

'I'm so sorry,' Nicole said again.

'Bit late for that.' Billie left the chair upended as she fled.

CHAPTER TWENTY-SEVEN

Everything was settled. Freya had quite enjoyed talking with Seb about the applications for the chef job. They'd narrowed down the candidates to three people they thought warranted interviews, but as neither Seb nor Freya were experts, they would organise a conference call with Pearl and she would make the ultimate choice.

Easier decisions had been the menu changes for the coming week. Seb was introducing duck breasts, a calamari salad and nannygai, a delicious local reef fish, while Freya would add treacle tartlets and a raspberry and coconut slice to her repertoire.

It had been a good morning and as she rechecked her shopping list, she experienced a rewarding sense of satisfaction. 'I feel hungry just thinking about all this delicious food,' she said.

Watching her, Seb smiled. 'Perhaps I should take you out to lunch.'

That was a suggestion Freya hadn't expected, but what a delightful one it was. She knew, though, that she mustn't read anything into it. She hadn't allowed herself any silly Seb-related fantasies lately and now she tried hard not to look too pleased. 'What a great —'

Freya didn't finish her sentence. She was distracted by a noisy clattering on the stairs and then loud footsteps stomping over the deck towards them.

Billie burst through the doorway. Her face was bright red, her blue eyes glittering and her chest heaving as she stood there, glaring at them, hands tightly clenched at her sides.

'So you're both still here,' she said tightly before Freya could speak. 'Good.' But there seemed nothing good about her intentions. Her face quivered with visible anger and she almost spat the word out.

'Billie,' Freya cried. 'What on earth's happened?'

'I've finally learned the truth,' the girl answered in a cold hard voice Freya barely recognised.

The truth? A ghastly shiver snaked through Freya. Surely Billie didn't mean —

No, she couldn't possibly.

Billie's eyes were bullet hard. 'You were never going to tell me, were you?

'Tell you what?' Freya certainly wasn't going to admit to anything till she knew exactly what Billie had heard. 'Billie, calm down,' she said, while her own heartbeat took off like a flight of screeching bats. 'What on earth's the matter?'

Billie stepped closer, reaching out to grab the back of a chair so tightly her knuckles showed white. 'The matter, my dearest aunt, is that someone has finally told me the truth. About me. About my birth.' She ground this between tight jaws. 'The *matter* is that for my entire life I've been living a lie.'

'No, that's so wrong.' Freya wished she didn't sound so terrified. 'You haven't, Billie. Not at all.'

Beside her, Seb joined in. 'What is it exactly that you've been told?'

'Didn't you hear me? The fucking truth, of course.'

'Which is?'

Billie rolled her eyes, gave a huffing, cold little laugh. 'That you two are my actual parents.'

'Your *what*?' Seb and Freya cried in unison. They turned to each other, their faces mirror images of shock and confusion, then back to Billie, who, for the first time, looked less certain.

But the change was only momentary. She was quickly glaring again. 'You're not going to deny it?'

Seb frowned at her. 'Of course we are.'

This time, Billie froze, staring at him in obvious despair, swallowing hard. Tears shone in her eyes, but before Freya could find the right words to calm her niece, Billie swung on her heel and stomped out of the room.

Seb reacted more quickly than Freya. Jumping to his feet, he hurried after the girl. 'Billie, come back.'

'Fuck off.'

This was flung over her shoulder as she ran across the deck.

Seb followed. 'Don't overreact,' he called. 'You shouldn't try to go anywhere in that state.'

At the top of the stairs, Billie turned back. 'Why would you care?' she bellowed. 'Why would either of you care? You clearly abandoned me. Gave me away.'

'Billie.' Seb continued towards her, his arms extended, his voice gentle, reasonable, in the tone he might have used if he were taming a wild animal. 'You've got it wrong, love. Believe me, I'm not your father. Pearl and Troy are your parents.'

Freya, watching from the doorway through tear-blinded eyes, had to lean against the timber lintel to steady her shaking body. She had never felt more terrified. Billie had obviously been exposed to dangerous gossip.

This was *exactly* what Pearl had feared would happen if she left Billie, Seb and Freya alone. And Freya had blithely dismissed it as an impossibility, a petty little worry. *How stupid am I? Don't I ever learn?*

Seb, out on the deck, had an arm around Billie's shoulders and was talking to her quietly, calmly. Then Billie was crying and he was cradling her to his chest, hugging her, just as a father might.

After a little while, they turned and came back and Freya stepped out of the doorway to let them into the dining room. Billie's face was pale and blotchy now and her eyes were shiny with tears. Freya went through to the kitchen, filled a glass with water, found a box of tissues.

When she returned, Billie and Seb were both sitting at the table where Freya had left her notepad and pen.

'Here,' she said gently, setting the glass and tissues in front of Billie.

'Thanks.'

As Billie wiped her eyes and blew her nose, found a fresh tissue and repeated the procedure, Freya took a seat at the small table. Her gaze met Seb's and she tried to signal her thanks. He gave a small shrug, and the message in his eyes suggested that he'd done as much as he could. It was over to her now. Which was fair enough.

If only she could trust herself to get this right. Was it going to be possible to keep her promise to Pearl? In this moment, she felt as if her life had been one long series of mistakes.

Billie sipped a little water and set the glass down.

Drawing a deep and hopefully calming breath, Freya asked, 'Who told you this nonsense, Billie?'

'Nicole Brassal,' she said, then she shook her head. 'Actually, Nicole's married now. I can't remember her new surname, but she was only repeating what her mother had told her.'

'Well, Sonia's quite wrong,' Freya said firmly. 'Pearl and Troy are most definitely your parents.'

'Are you sure?' Billie still looked miserable, as if she didn't know who to believe.

'I would never lie to you about something as important as that, Bills.'

Her niece sniffed. Gave a small nod. 'That's good to know.' Leaning her elbows on the table, she closed her eyes and massaged her forehead. She looked exhausted, with fragile blue veins on her eyelids and shadows beneath her eyes.

Sitting back again, she looked from Freya to Seb, her expression still haunted and suspicious. 'It still doesn't make sense. Why would the Brassals make up something like that?'

With all her heart, Freya wished she could tell the whole story, but she'd promised Pearl, had sworn she would never break that promise. 'Sonia's a dangerous gossip,' she hedged.

Seb nodded. 'Always has been.'

Thank you, Freya told him silently, and she wondered if he was remembering high school when Sonia had dobbed him in for smuggling a bottle of rum to the school social. Or had he heard all kinds of rumours flying around at the time of Billie's birth?

'I still don't get it,' Billie persisted. 'Mrs Brassal has lived here for yonks. She went to school with you and Mum and she was my teacher.'

'That's true,' Freya agreed. 'But she still managed to get the wrong end of the stick.'

Of course, Freya knew that the islanders had known about her pregnancy – how could they not? – and had decided she'd given birth to Seb's baby, then left it with her sister to bring up. It was the story Pearl had wanted them to believe, and it made sense that the Brassals might expect Billie to know this, too.

She felt a little desperate, though, as she faced Billie now. 'Honey, you know what the island's like. It's always been rife with gossip and most of the time that gossip's half-cocked. Or totally wrong, as it is in this case.'

Again Billie slumped forward, head in hands. 'This is driving me crazy.'

Me too, thought Freya.

'How about a cup of tea?' suggested Seb.

They all agreed and he went to the kitchen, where he found a packet of Ginger Nut biscuits at the back of a cupboard and put the kettle on. As they drank the restorative brew, they avoided the explosive topic of Billie's birth and talked about Pearl and Troy in Tasmania, speculating on where they might be by now. In the Tamar Valley? On Bruny Island? In Hobart, enjoying the cafés and galleries?

'I don't dare ring them about this,' Billie said. 'I just know Mum would feel she had to come home.'

Freya nodded. The secrecy had been Pearl's idea from the outset, and in many ways, she would have liked Billie to make the phone call and confront her parents with her questions. But perhaps it was best not to stir this particular pot. With any luck, the whole drama, or rather melodrama, would die down. Disappear.

Or was she fooling herself, yet again?

'Pearl was terrified that something like this would happen,' Freya told Seb as they watched a subdued and calmer Billie finally leave. 'I laughed at her before she left on her trip. Told her she was an over-anxious old biddy.' She winced as she remembered this. 'Damn it, why am I always so smugly certain that I know better, when the truth is that I can't get anything right?'

'That's rubbish,' Seb told her.

'It's true.' Freya had never felt more weighed down by guilt, by the certainty that she'd been a source of disappointment for too many people. First Seb, then Pearl and, eventually, Brian. 'I'm hopeless.'

'Hopeless? You? What nonsense.'

It was gratifying to have his support, but she knew he was only trying to say the right thing, while she was all too conscious of the many, many mistakes she'd made. 'It's true,' she cried again, feeling utterly wretched. 'Just ask my mother. She'd soon tell you I've always been reckless and impulsive, rushing in without thinking things through. I've managed to hurt everyone close to me. Including you. And now I'm supposed to be mature and sensible, but I don't seem to have learned anything.'

She realised, to her dismay, that she was on the verge of tears.

'Freya, you're being far too hard on yourself. I'm fine. I've told you that. So is Pearl. And rather than hopeless, you're as full of hope and as strong as anyone I've met. Look at what you've dealt with in just this past year alone, not to mention taking on all the extra duties here at the restaurant. You deserve applause, not condemnation.'

'But Billie —'

'You're not responsible for island gossip. Or for the fact that Billie's parents have chosen to hide an important truth from her.'

'But maybe I should go after her. She's in a state. I should make sure she's okay.'

'And what can you say to help her that you haven't said already? She's an adult, Freya, not a child any more, and she needs time to process this. Actually, what she really needs is a down-to-earth conversation with Pearl and Troy. You've done as much as you can for now.'

'Oh, Seb!'

He was being too kind and concerned. Freya wasn't sure she could handle it.

'Don't cry,' he implored.

But she couldn't help it. She was a mess, coming undone, so worried about Billie, about Pearl, and she'd been trying to be strong for too long. It seemed she'd been putting on a brave face all her life, but most certainly since the divorce and then the fire. And now Seb was being too nice to her and —

'Freya, I don't think I've ever seen you cry.'

'I d-don't want to,' she spluttered.

'Come on then,' he said, slipping an arm around her shoulders. 'Let's get you out of here.' He gave her shoulder a gentle squeeze, a simple gesture she found ever so comforting.

'Let me take you to Horseshoe Bay,' he said. 'I'm starving and I'm sure you are, too. I'll buy you fish and chips at the pub and we can watch the yachts, and then we can take a lazy stroll along the beach from one end to the other. Or lie under a palm tree. Or swim. Whatever you like. Maybe by then we'll have earned a drink while we watch the sunset.'

Freya reached for a tissue. 'You'd do that just for me?'

Seb's smile was one she remembered from long ago. 'I'd love to.'

It was only as they left the restaurant that Freya remembered Seb's sole mode of transport was a motorbike.

'Oh, dear,' she said as he approached his gleaming black and silver Harley-Davidson.

Seb shot her a look of pure amusement. 'You're not chicken, are you?'

'I might be.' She'd been habitually reckless when he'd known her in their youth, but she was a sedate middle age now and her own, perfectly good Forester was parked mere metres away.

'I have a spare helmet,' he offered.

'Oh, that makes all the difference.' But her sarcasm was lost on Seb.

He merely grinned and assumed she was coming with him. He handed her a helmet, which felt enormous, and she almost said no. But this was Seb and he'd just been so thoughtful and kind.

'Here. I'll help you with the chin strap,' he said, and because he was so close now – touching close – Freya held back her protest.

In no time the helmet was in place and he was swinging a leg over the huge machine. 'Hop on.'

Freya obeyed, despite her quaking knees. At least the seat was comfortable enough.

'Get close to me so you can hang on.' Seb, looking back over his shoulder, must have seen the tension – or possibly terror – in her face. 'I'm quite good at this, Freya. I promise you'll be safe.'

She managed a weak smile.

'And it's fun,' he said next.

'Promise you'll stop as soon as I start screaming.'

'You won't scream,' he responded, all confidence and smiles. *Oh, help.* Despite her fear, a tiny part of her was secretly thrilled, so she obediently slipped her arms around his waist and then they were off, roaring through Arcadia, while she clung on for dear life. But she soon had to admit it wasn't nearly as precarious or scary as she'd expected.

Trees, rocky cliffs and sweeping seascape vistas flashed past as they took the curving road over hills and around headlands. Hanging on tightly to Seb, breathing in fresh air scented with eucalyptus and salty sea, Freya knew he was right. She wasn't going to scream.

CHAPTER TWENTY-EIGHT

Billie felt guilty about snooping in her mother's office. She'd never done anything so underhand before, but then she'd never been in this amount of turmoil either. For pity's sake, how many people were told they were adopted only to have that story quashed, most unconvincingly, and left dangling with no conclusive answer?

She was sure Freya and Seb had been hedging – not lying, perhaps, but she'd seen a cagey look flash between them that suggested they weren't telling her the whole truth. Which left her in an impossible situation. As if she'd fallen into some kind of vortex that kept spinning and sucking her down, with no hope of a way out.

Billie's anxiety certainly wasn't eased when she remembered the long history of tension between her mother and Freya. She'd been conscious of it even during her childhood and she was sure there was still a missing piece to this puzzle. But she needed hard evidence. A piece of paper, a birth certificate, or some other legal document that would tell her the absolute truth.

Thus, the snooping. Her mother kept a personal folder in her filing cabinet, separate from all the business papers. The folder held wills and power of attorney and other important papers – Billie had seen the tag, neatly printed in Pearl's careful script. But there was no sign of it now.

Her parents had probably taken the folder with them, or stowed it at the bank for safekeeping. Damn it.

Disheartened, Billie wandered back to the living room with Won Ton following at her heels. The view, for once, wasn't bright and sunny blue, but quite overcast. Clouds scudded across the sky, chased by a wind that whipped the sea into choppy grey peaks. When had that begun? Rain was quite possibly on the way and Billie wondered where Freya had got to, and when she planned to be home.

'We've been abandoned, Won Ton,' she said, stooping to give the little dog a comforting scratch between her ears.

Normally, Billie didn't mind her own company, but today she was restless and would have liked someone to talk to. Okay, she would have liked to probe her aunt till she wormed the truth out of her.

Was Freya in hiding?

Billie took a photograph album from a shelf in the TV cabinet. Her baby album, with a padded pink satin cover and lace-trimmed hearts. Incredibly kitsch and sentimental. She hadn't looked at it in recent times, but she knew the photos pretty much by heart. Now she would look again, just in case they held a vital clue.

Since she was an only child, there was a ridiculous number of photos of her as a baby, starting when she was really quite tiny, lying on a quilted rug, or in a bassinet or pram. In her mother's arms. Later, she was propped on her granny Ruby's knee.

One photo Billie was especially fond of showed her laughing in her father's arms, with a youthful Troy looking down at her with a soppy, doting grin.

The album was incredibly sweet and terribly normal. No photos at the hospital where she'd been born, mind you, but that didn't really prove anything. And there were no photos with Freya, which was kind of strange, now that Billie thought about it.

After all, Billie had been the first in her family's new generation. Surely an aunt deserved a guernsey in at least one of the family snaps. Unless Freya had already left the island by then. Billie was a bit hazy about the exact date of her aunt's departure.

She gave up when she got to photos of her chubbier self crawling and then learning to walk. With a hefty sigh, she closed the album, which had been no help at all. Or perhaps she was just a hopeless detective.

Hang on a sec.

Speaking of detectives.

Billie jumped to her feet, momentarily elated. Dan Dexter might be the perfect person to turn to with a problem like this. Not only was he easygoing and considerate but, given his line of work, he was bound to have all kinds of useful knowledge. Bonus, he'd given her the number he reserved for personal calls.

Then, just as quickly, she flopped on the sofa again, deflated. Dan Dexter might have been perfect, if they were still on speaking terms.

She hadn't heard from him since she'd told him about her baby, which was perfectly understandable, especially as she'd hinted that the baby's father was still in the picture.

'What am I going to do, Won Ton?'

The dog's ears pricked when she heard her name. Her little tail wagged.

'Do you think I should ring Dan anyhow? Because he's very approachable and I'm kinda desperate?'

Won Ton made a gentle little yip, which might have been a message about her hunger, but Billie took it as encouragement.

'Okay,' she said. 'I'll ring him.' And she did so before she lost her nerve.

'Hello?' said a small childish voice.

'Oh,' said Billie, surprised. 'Is that Molly?'

'Yes. Who's speaking, please?'

The kid was very well trained. Another tick for single dad Detective Dan. 'It's Billie, Molly. Billie from the island.'

'Ooh,' the little girl squeaked. 'Hi, Billie!' Then loudly, 'Hey, Daddy, it's Billie from the island on the phone.'

In the background, Dan's voice sounded. 'Tell her I'll be there in a minute.'

'Daddy will be here in a minute,' Molly reported dutifully. 'He's cooking our dinner. We're having sausages.'

'Oh, sorry.' Billie had been so caught up in her own problems, she hadn't even bothered to check the time. Now her mind flashed to an image of Dan in the kitchen. He probably had to cook most nights, poor guy. 'Tell him I'll call back later.'

'Billie will call back later, Dad.'

'Here, I'll take it.' Dan's voice sounded close now. 'Can you set the table, Mollz?' A beat later, 'Hi, Billie.'

'Hi.' This time she was surprised by how good it was to hear his voice. Deep, warm, calm. 'Look, sorry, Dan. I didn't mean to interrupt your dinner. I'll call back later.'

'No, no, you're fine. Dinner can hold. How can I help you?'

Now that it came to the crunch, Billie faltered. 'This is going to sound pretty weird, but it's sort of a police matter.'

'Weird is part of my job description.'

Billie could feel all manner of clenched muscles relaxing as she settled back on the sofa. Okay, here goes. No beating about the bush. Deep breath. 'I was wondering if you could find out whether

I've been adopted. Is there a registry, or something? Or if you can't help me, is there a website?'

Several seconds passed before Dan responded and Billie couldn't blame the poor man for needing time. Her request was totally out of left field.

'So, you think you might be adopted,' he said, 'but you don't know for sure?'

'Yeah, I told you it was whacked.'

'I take it you can't just ask your parents?'

'Well, I can, I guess, but I haven't as yet.'

'Are they still touring around the country?'

'Yeah, and I hate the thought of upsetting them.'

This brought another pause from Dan. 'Are you sure it would upset them unduly, Billie?'

No, she wasn't sure, although she couldn't imagine her mum taking this calmly. 'It's mainly that there are rumours here on the island,' she said. 'And they're doing my head in.'

'You do sound pretty stressed.'

Did she? Just as well Dan hadn't heard her earlier in the day. 'Sorry,' she said. 'I've let myself get pretty stirred up over this. I shouldn't have bothered you.'

'Don't hang up.'

'No, I haven't.'

'Look,' he said. 'This isn't really my field. I'm not a private investigator, but there is definitely a process for people who actually know they're adopted to find their birth parents. They're entitled to the information once they turn eighteen. It's a bit of a balancing act between privacy laws for the mother and an individual's right to know, but the procedure's all in place.'

'I see.'

'But I'm not sure how that would work if you don't actually know whether you're adopted. That's tricky.'

'Yeah, it's crazy.'

'I could put you in touch with a private investigator,' Dan offered next. 'They often work with adoption issues.'

'Okay. Thanks. I'll think about it.' Billie was beginning to wish that she hadn't bothered him. It was time to stand on her own two feet, do her own research, face her own demons.

'Where are you?' Dan asked. 'In Townsville?'

'No, still on the island.' She couldn't help wondering what he might have suggested if she'd been closer.

'*How* are you?' he asked next. 'What does your partner have to say about this?'

Her partner? *Gulp.* Of course, Dan had no idea, but at least she was used to telling this story now. 'There is no partner,' she told him.

And again there was silence.

'We've broken up,' Billie added.

'I'm sorry to hear that.' Dan's tone was careful now. Carefully neutral. 'But he knows about your baby?'

'Oh, yes. He knows. He's just not . . . interested.' Billie was tempted to tell Dan the whole story, but she stopped herself just in time. She'd already landed enough of her crap on his shoulders.

'That's tough,' he said.

'Yeah, but that's how it is.' God, he must think she was a total screw-up. Sitting straighter, Billie injected brightness into her voice. 'I'm okay, though, Dan. I'm getting used to the idea of being a single parent. I might even call on you for a few tips.'

'Sure. I'd be happy to help, if I can.'

'Thanks. You're a champion.' *Good grief.* Now she sounded like a cheerful sports coach. So lame. 'I really do appreciate you taking the time to listen.'

'No problem,' he said. 'I hope you get everything sorted.'

'Thanks.'

'And for what it's worth, Billie, I reckon you should speak to your parents. You've got enough on your plate without having that kind of tension hanging over you.'

'Thanks,' she said again. 'I'm sure that's good advice. And say goodbye to Molly for me, won't you?' She wasn't sure she should have added that. Was it going too far?

'I will,' Dan said. 'Take care.'

After they'd disconnected, Billie sat in a kind of daze, thinking about Dan and how he cared for Molly and was getting on with his life after a truly heartbreaking tragedy. And here she was, dithering, and foolishly bothering him about asking her parents one difficult question.

What was she? Woman or wimp?

'I'm going to do it, Won Ton.' Beside her, the little dog sat up expectantly. Shit. Won Ton was on her mum's white sofa and Freya had been so anxious about keeping her off.

Picking the small dog up, Billie cuddled her close. 'Wicked little thing,' she murmured. 'But I'm going to do it.'

A phone call to her dad would be safest and, once that was behind her, she would know the worst. Or, thinking positively, she might be flooded with relief. Either way, she would take Won Ton for a walk as soon as the call was over, if it wasn't raining. Or maybe they would go even if it was raining, and Billie would buy Thai takeaway.

She felt distinctly better now that she had a plan.

CHAPTER TWENTY-NINE

Freya had opted for a beach walk after lunch. The meal of fish burgers shared with Seb, and eaten at a timber bench with views out to the sea, had been more than merely pleasant. She'd loved every minute, but she wasn't sure she could handle Seb's other suggestions of lying under a palm tree or swimming. Such activities hinted at an easy intimacy that they, sadly, no longer enjoyed. Such pleasures, surely, were best left behind them.

So they walked to the far end of the bay, which was the longest stretch of beach on the island. The sky was overcast and a fresh wind whipped at Freya's hair and tugged at her shirt tails, but she was already stirred after the tumultuous morning, so the windy beach and choppy seas rather suited her mood.

They didn't talk much as they walked. They'd exhausted the subject of Billie and Pearl and there was only so much they needed to share about the many years they'd spent apart. Freya was happy to enjoy the easy silence of this newfound companionableness and to absorb their surroundings. Happy to absorb the long stretch of sand crisscrossed by footsteps, the distant hills, the low dunes with grasses and trees bending in the wind, the hush and rush of the sea.

After the sleepy, tropical warmth of the past few weeks, she found the change in the weather quite exhilarating.

It was only when they reached the rocks at the far end of the bay and turned back that they saw how very dark and looming the clouds to the south were now.

'Do you think we'll be able to make it back before it rains?' she asked Seb.

'I'm not sure. Would you mind getting wet?'

'Not really. I guess we could always make a dash for it, but I'm not much of a runner these days.'

'Want to try?' he asked, smiling, and holding out his hand.

Her heart gave a ridiculous, girlish skip. 'All right, but if I take a tumble, you might have to help me up again.'

Seb sent another smile. 'I promise.'

So they ran, holding hands. They might have been young lovers, except that they were no longer young, or in love – but it didn't seem to matter. Freya and Seb were running in the wind, reckless and carefree, and she couldn't quite believe how happy she was.

The sand was firm beneath her feet and although she was a little breathless, she felt wonderfully strong. Invincible. Invigorated. Such a change from the downcast mood of an hour or so earlier. She knew that Seb's advice was very sensible. She could do nothing more for Billie until the girl had spoken to her parents. Which meant that, for now, Freya was free of responsibility. Light as a bird.

Until she stumbled.

At the very moment when she was beginning to feel entirely confident, her left knee suddenly gave way. Without warning, it just crumpled.

She cried out as she sensed this happen, and Seb, as good as his word, swung heroically into action. One moment the sand was rushing up to meet her – the next, she found herself supported in his arms, breathless, a little dizzy and clinging tight.

'Oh, dear,' she gasped and Seb drew her close, till her head was on his shoulder, her chest heaving against his, and she could feel their heartbeats pounding together in frantic unison.

'Thank you. That was my reality check.' She was a little breathless and panting now.

'You're not hurt, are you?'

'No, I'm fine, thanks to you. But I guess I was right about the running. I'm not young any more.'

'Old or young, you're damn beautiful, Freya.'

Lifting her head, she stared at him. His face was so close now, she could see the lines around his mouth, the crow's feet, the flecks of grey in his windblown hair. She looked straight into his eyes, clear silver and grey. No longer smiling, but intensely serious.

'Seb,' she whispered. Her throat was so tight it was all she could manage.

His eyes shimmered as he lifted his hands to either side of her head, and he kept his gaze locked with hers as he held her face mere inches in front of him. 'You're like a drug I can't get out of my system.'

She gave a shaky smile. 'That's not very romantic.'

'It doesn't feel romantic. Romance is happy, all sweetness and light, but this is painful. Deep in the gut.'

She knew exactly what he meant. She shared the same pain.

'I need you, Freya. I'm afraid I always have.'

Oh, Seb. Her knees almost gave way again. Her eyes were blurred by tears, but she blinked them away. No more weeping. This moment was too huge. A fantasy she'd never dared to dream.

'And I need to tell you something,' she said.

'I'm listening.'

'Having Billie might be the best thing I've ever done, but losing you was the very worst.'

She saw the pain in his smile, the sheen in his eyes and her yearning heart nearly broke. But then Seb was kissing her, or perhaps she was kissing him. It didn't matter. She was consumed by the utter bliss of his lips on hers again at last, the thrill of his arms binding her close. *Seb, Seb.* Had there ever been such a longing?

Theirs was a kiss for the ages, layered with memory and buoyed by hope. Freya no longer cared that the heavens had opened and the rain poured down. Winding her arms around his neck, she pressed closer still and their kiss turned wickedly wild. Crushing. Hungry and desperate. Not at all the sedate kiss befitting a mature couple on a public beach. A kiss filled with decades of defeated desire.

It might have been years before they finally broke apart, drowned-rat wet, with their hair plastered to their skulls and their clothes so sodden they were rendered transparent. But they were grinning like fools.

'We should get back to my place.' Seb reached for her hand again and there was nothing Freya wanted more.

They began to run and this time, luckily, she didn't fall.

If reaching Seb's house had been a matter of dashing up the beach and scrambling out of wet clothes, Freya wouldn't have had time to be nervous. But they were on the far side of the island, which was going to require a return journey, back over a hill, whizzing around a curving headland, dipping down through Arcadia and over yet another hill before they finally reached Nelly Bay.

All this on Seb's motorbike, no less. For heaven's sake, why had she recklessly jumped behind him on his bike, when they might easily have travelled in her sedate SUV? And now she had way too much time to think.

Such dangerous things thoughts could be. Freya was mega excited about being with Seb again. Their kiss was a gift beyond her wildest hopes and dreams, but going back to his place was a differ-ent matter. Now she had time to worry about her middle-aged body, her no longer pert boobs, the creases on her neckline, her not so firm thighs.

Oh, and the mechanics of lovemaking were another thing to fret about. After so many years of marriage, habits were established. But Seb wasn't Brian, thank heavens, and now she wanted to start afresh. But what were her chances, at this time of life, of becoming a lively and alluring siren?

Was it even remotely possible?

'Don't,' said Seb, shooting a glance back at her as the bike finally came to a juddering halt in his driveway.

'Don't what?'

'Don't start worrying.'

'I'm not.'

His smile suggested he knew she was lying, but all he said was, 'Good.' He cut the motor. 'You should have a warm shower.'

Freya nodded, imagining her body, white and shrivelled beneath the wet clothes. 'Great idea.' She wondered if Seb planned to shower with her, and how would she feel about that?

The bathroom was at the end of a hallway, white tiled and spacious with a long, slender glass panel that looked into a private palm-filled courtyard. Just gorgeous. Seb handed her a fluffy white towel, a cake of frangipani-scented soap and a towelling bathrobe.

'Take your time,' he said. And then he left.

Right. So this wasn't going to be a passionate, up against the wall in the shower affair.

As she slipped out of her clothes, Freya supposed it was possible that Seb was having second thoughts. Perhaps all he planned now was to get her warm and dry and then offer her some kind of supper.

Of course, Seb was a man of the world and the seduction of new women was a hobby for him, while Freya knew nothing about such things. But he'd told her he needed her, that he'd never stopped needing her. And that kiss had been blistering. Off the scale.

Don't worry, he'd said.

So she wouldn't.

And she did take her time, enjoying the stream of hot water, the sensuously fragranced soap, the luxurious bath towel. There was a hair dryer, which she used, quickly, without styling, and she was quite fresh and glowing by the time she emerged.

'What would you like to drink?' Seb called, and she found him in the kitchen, showered and dressed in beach shorts and a white shirt, left hanging open to reveal a tantalising hint of tanned torso.

Freya looked about her, expecting to find glasses and a wine bottle at the ready, but the benches were bare. She turned back to Seb. Her Seb. Thought of his kiss, of his arms about her, of their hearts beating together. She crossed the floor to him and smiled. 'How about we save the drinks for later?'

Seb grinned and before she could make another move he was reaching for her, gathering her in. 'Thank God you haven't changed,' he murmured close to her ear.

Delicious shivers flashed through Freya now, diving deep, pooling in heat. Already, with a little help from Seb, the robe was slipping from her shoulders, and Freya, in the middle of his kitchen, happily wriggled out of it, no longer caring about anything but her need for skin contact, for his hands holding her, finding her.

Just like that, the wildness was back and they were making their way, desperate and excited, to the bedroom.

Here, Freya couldn't help being momentarily distracted by the room's beauty. Gleaming, honey-toned timber floors, a massive bed with a snow-white spread, cushions in lime-green and aqua, and Seb's paintings of the tropics. Lush green palm fronds, an aquamarine sea, bright pink and orange flowers.

'Oh!' She came to a stop in front of the flowers.

'What is it?' Seb asked her.

'These heliconias. Those gorgeous colours. I decorated my bedroom in pink and orange just before the fire.'

He lifted a hand to gently touch her hair, to trace the curve of her cheek. 'I always think of you as bright and colourful.'

She laughed, recklessly happy. 'And I think of you as dark and sexy.'

'Is that a challenge?' He was sliding his hands over her shoulders now.

'Might be.'

'I'm up for it,' he murmured as he traced feather-light tracks down her arms, letting his fingertips travel in a delicious slow tease, making her desperate for more. Everywhere.

And now, no more banter. They were too busy kissing, seeking, pressing close and then closer as they tumbled onto the bed. Together.

Billie was still up when Freya finally got home, so she was glad she hadn't stayed with Seb for the whole night, much as she would have loved to.

The girl was on a sofa in the living room, watching late-night TV with Won Ton curled up beside her. In front of her, the coffee table was littered with takeaway Thai cartons, a crumpled soft-drink can and shiny chocolate wrappers. One look at Billie's face and Freya knew she was still stressed.

'Hello, stranger,' Billie said.

'Have you been waiting up for me?'

'What else can a girl do when she has an aunt who hives off like a troublesome teenager?'

Freya wasn't about to apologise for the most thrilling night of her life. She merely smiled. Meanwhile Won Ton, having woken at the sound of Freya's voice, now abandoned Billie, hopped down from the sofa, where she should never have been, and padded over the floor to her.

'Have you spoken to your parents?' Freya asked Billie.

She nodded. 'Yep. I spoke to Dad and, of course, he put me on speaker.' She clicked the remote to silence the television, unwound her graceful, sun-tanned legs and sat up, appearing to notice, perhaps for the first time, the litter on the coffee table.

Freya knew a moment of impatience. 'And what did they tell you?'

'Nothing, really. They want me to wait till they get home, so we can have a proper face-to-face conversation.'

'Really?' Freya couldn't believe this. 'Surely they could reassure you that they are your actual parents?'

'Well, yeah. More or less, but I know there's stuff they're not telling me.'

'But that's so unreasonable of them, Billie. They'll be gone for ages yet.'

'They won't, actually. They left Tassie straight after my first phone call. About the baby. My baby, that is. They're already in northern New South Wales and they'll be home in three days.'

CHAPTER THIRTY

Billie wasn't sure how she got through the next three days. Despite her desperate curiosity, she was disappointed that her parents had abandoned their trip of a lifetime. As far as she was concerned, it was crazy beyond words, but she'd refrained from telling them so, and she hadn't heard from them again.

Meanwhile, her one – unsatisfactory – conversation with her parents circled round and round in her head. Her father hadn't been nearly as straight down the line as she'd hoped he would be. 'What's this about?' he'd wanted to know. 'Why are you asking such a question?'

Billie had been too uptight to be patient. 'Just tell me, Dad.'

'You're our daughter, Billie. Your mother's and mine.'

'Your biological daughter?'

'Yes, love.'

'So I'm not adopted?'

But this vital question hadn't been answered with the unequivocal certainty Billie so desperately needed.

'What's happened?' Her mother had intervened at that point, her voice anxious and high pitched, somewhere in the background. 'Who have you been talking to, Billie?'

'Nicole,' she said. 'From school.'

'Sonia Brassal's daughter?'

'Yes.'

Painful seconds limped by before either of her parents spoke again. 'Look, everything's fine, Billie,' her dad said, finally. 'The Brassals are just guessing, grabbing at straws.'

But guessing about what? Billie almost screamed.

It was then that Troy asked her to wait, to be patient for just a few days until they could sit down and talk about this calmly, face to face.

Which was all very well for them, as they already knew the answers, but patience was hard to come by if you were the person left clueless and hanging. Billie was beside herself. Her need-to-know factor was off the scale.

Since then, the only things that had kept her remotely sane had been her work at the restaurant and the thought of her little baby, steadily growing and rolling and bumping inside her. For the baby's sake, she couldn't let herself go to pieces. She had to stay strong, but, man, it was hard.

To cap things off, Pearl and Troy weren't going to arrive till late in the day, when Billie would be at work. Which meant another evening of waiting tables, of trying to concentrate on orders, of being efficient and pleasant, of having to smile, smile, smile.

At least Seb had been quite sympathetic, but he hadn't budged when it came to offering Billie any more info, claiming it had really nothing to do with him, which Billie found hard to believe. As for her aunt, Billie might as well go whistle for the wind.

'Please don't keep asking me, Billie. I can't tell you any more, I swear.'

'You and Seb are in cahoots about this, aren't you?' she'd accused.

Freya had smiled then, a smile that softened her features and shone with deep happiness. 'Where did you hear an old-fashioned word like cahoots?'

Billie rolled her eyes. 'You're avoiding the question.'

'We're not in cahoots about you, Billie. I confess we've been rather obsessed with getting to know each other again.'

Her aunt, the cool aunt Billie had always considered the epitome of sophistication, now looked coy.

'My God, you're sleeping with him, aren't you?'

'I am,' Freya said simply.

And for a moment, Billie was quite distracted, as she tried not to think about Freya and Seb in bed together. 'I bet it's amazing.'

Freya grinned. 'Uh-huh.' And then, before Billie could get back to her more important questions, Freya waved to her and was out the door with her little dog following. 'Won Ton needs a walk,' she called over her shoulder.

But now Billie's shift was over and she was driving home and her parents should be there, and given the build-up of the past three days, she was almost sick with tension.

As she rounded the final bend, she saw lights streaming from the big living room windows out over the headland's huge boulders. Below the house, her parents' Pajero was parked in the carport. Okay, so they were here and hopefully waiting up for her.

Billie felt hollow and shaky as she pulled into the small off-road parking space, edging her car next to Freya's. Were they looking out for her? Was someone, even now, putting the kettle on in preparation for The Talk? To calm herself, she took several deep breaths, but they weren't much help.

Won Ton was at the door to greet her, but for once Billie didn't bother to return the little dog's courtesy. Her focus was elsewhere, searching. But the living room was empty and there was no sign of the kettle humming to life in the kitchen.

Seriously?

'Hello?' Billie called. 'Anyone up?'

She heard bare feet padding down the timber-floored hallway and Freya appeared, her flame-coloured hair tumbling to her shoulders as she tied a kimono over her pyjamas. 'Hi, Billie.'

'Where are Mum and Dad?' Billie demanded. 'They haven't gone to bed, have they?'

'I don't think so.' Freya looked back down the hallway. 'I'm pretty sure I heard them talking just a few minutes ago. Would you like me to check?'

Billie nodded, too tense and frustrated to trust herself to speak. She went to the kitchen to pour herself a glass of water and wished she could replace it with a medicinal slug of scotch. From down the hallway, she heard the murmur of voices. Freya and Troy. Then more footsteps.

Her parents, like Freya, were in their pyjamas and summer dressing gowns, which wasn't so very surprising, given that it was almost eleven, although this wasn't quite the way Billie had pictured the meeting. Her mum was finger-combing her hair, as if she'd been lying down and hadn't had a chance to tidy it. But shouldn't they be rushing to hug her? To congratulate her on her happy baby news?

'Hi, sweetheart.' Her dad did come forward then. And, yes, he hugged Billie and kissed her cheek, but she sensed an unsettling restraint in his manner.

'Hello, Billie.' Her mum looked thin and far too tired, as if the holiday hadn't done her any good at all. Or perhaps those dark shadows under her eyes were entirely due to the strain of the past three days.

'Hello, Mum.' They kissed and hugged and then Pearl stepped back a little, letting her pale gaze rest on Billie's belly. 'Look at you,' she said and her eyes now glittered with tears. 'You look like you're keeping very well, darling.'

'I am, thanks. Really well.' Billie wished she could return the compliment.

They stood in an awkward little cluster, and Billie was wondering if she should speak up when Troy said, 'It's already rather late, so we'd better sit down and have this chat.'

Thank heavens. Billie had feared that her parents might try to delay this conversation by regaling them first with travel stories, or suggesting they wait till morning.

'How about I put the kettle on?' offered Freya.

'Not for me, thanks,' said Pearl.

Troy also shook his head. 'Maybe later.'

So they settled on the sofas, with Pearl and Troy sitting quite close together and Freya and Billie opposite. The living room had been restored to its usual pristine perfection. No dog hairs on the sofa, thank God, and not a chocolate wrapper in sight.

It felt almost unreal to realise that this conversation was finally about to begin. Billie swallowed nervously.

Her parents exchanged cautious smiles. Then her dad sat forward. 'First up,' he said. 'We want to reassure you that you are definitely our biological daughter, Billie.'

'Okay.'

'But you were born via IVF.'

Holy shit. Billie swallowed again, this time with astonishment. 'You mean I was conceived in a lab?'

Her parents nodded.

Wow! Billie was still taking this in when her father added, 'And because of your mother's endometriosis, surrogacy was necessary.'

Oh. My. God. In all the adoption scenarios Billie had imagined, she'd never considered surrogacy. For a moment she was too stunned to respond, and then she was too busy thinking about her cells coming together in a Petri dish and then growing in some other woman's body. It didn't seem possible, but on another level it was strangely, crazily awesome.

Billie looked at her parents, huddled together, seeming smaller somehow now as they held hands, their anxious expressions mirroring each other's as they watched for her reaction. Then she looked down at her body, the body she'd lived in so comfortably for twenty-four years. She wondered why it didn't feel somehow alien. A scientific experiment.

'So this woman,' she said. 'This surrogate mother. How did you find her?'

CHAPTER THIRTY-ONE

Freya flinched as Billie fired her all-important question. This was it. The pointy end of their conversation. The moment when Pearl could no longer hide the truth.

Freya had been nervous from the moment she'd first greeted Pearl and Troy, imagining her sister's heated arguments and accusations. But as if by tacit consent, they'd managed to avoid dwelling on the difficult topic dominating everyone's thoughts. While they'd waited for Billie, they'd mostly talked about the trip and Island Thyme, about Gavin's replacement and Freya's bookkeeping. Pearl had even grudgingly admitted that Freya's efforts in the restaurant had been above and beyond. Apparently, she'd read glowing reviews on Island Thyme's website. Even Freya's pot plant care got a tick of approval.

'Although I hear you've taken up with Seb,' Pearl had said, letting her lip curl to show her displeasure. 'I'm sure that threw an extra spanner in the works.'

'I don't believe so,' Freya answered at her dignified best.

Pearl made no attempt to hide her opinion, rolling her eyes exaggeratedly and shrugging. 'You've just got rid of one hopeless bloke. Thought you'd enjoy being a woman on the loose.'

Freya smiled at her sweetly. 'And that's exactly what I'm doing.'

The matter, to her relief, was dropped then, but after a light meal, Troy and Pearl had retired to their bedroom. Apparently, Pearl had needed to rest, which Freya had found a little surprising, but she wasn't able to corner Troy to quiz him for details.

Now, here they were, and Freya could only guess what her sister must be thinking – that she'd been dead right about the dangers of inviting Freya into her home. And Freya couldn't help feeling guilty now that Pearl's worst fears, the fears she had scoffed at, had, indeed, been realised.

It was pretty darned obvious that this fraught situation would never have arisen if Freya had stayed safely in South East Queensland. But it was too late now for regrets and Billie's fateful question awaited an answer.

But who was going to break the news to Billie? After keeping her own promise of silence for so many years, Freya was reluctant to go back on her word. But neither Troy nor Pearl seemed keen to speak up. Meanwhile, poor Billie was sitting stiffly on the very edge of her seat, eyes wide with gut-wrenching tension, hands tightly fisted on her knees, as she looked from her mother to her father and then to her aunt.

It was then that it happened.

Billie's gaze met Freya's and held and, despite Freya's best efforts to keep her face deadpan, something clicked. A blink of connection. A spark of awareness flared in Billie's lovely blue eyes. Her jaw dropped.

'Oh, my God!' she gasped, as she stared at Freya. 'It was you, wasn't it? You were my surrogate mother.'

Freya couldn't have spoken then, even if she'd wanted to. Her throat was too raw and painfully tight.

From across the room, a strange kind of wail broke from Pearl, who looked ill, hunched over, hugging herself.

'It was Freya, wasn't it?' Billie demanded, shooting the question now to her parents. 'Freya was pregnant with your baby – with me – and that's why the Brassals assumed she was my mother.'

Billie sent an impatient glance from her parents to Freya and back again. 'For God's sake, please, someone —'

'Yes, Billie,' Troy said quickly. 'Freya was the surrogate. Your womb mother.'

At this, Billie's shoulders sagged and she let out a noisy huff, as if she could now release the breath she'd been holding. Then, with a dazed shake of her head, she turned from them all to stare outside into the darkness beyond the window, where the night sky and the black sea were faintly tinged by a slice of moon.

Freya supposed the poor girl needed a little time to take this news in.

Billie's eyes were silver with tears as she turned back to them. 'Why didn't you tell me? I can't believe you never told me. Why would you keep something like that a secret?'

A long, uncomfortable pause followed. Freya waited for either Troy or Pearl to speak up, to explain the unexplainable. For a mad moment she wondered if Pearl would finally be honest and admit to her unreasonable possessiveness, but her sister remained silent, huddled. Diminished.

Knowing that Billie was at the end of her patience, Freya felt compelled to speak up. 'I think the secrecy must have been my fault, Billie.' She decided it was her task to at least try to explain the way she saw this. 'On the day you were born, I was supposed to contact Pearl and Troy as soon as I went into labour. I knew they wanted to be there for your birth. But I'm afraid I didn't let them know until after you'd already arrived.'

Billie's response was a puzzled frown. 'That's not so terrible, is it?'

'I broke my promise, you see,' Freya continued, but she couldn't help feeling annoyed that she'd been reduced to a grovelling apology for a decision she still felt was justified. She certainly wouldn't try to explain why she'd wanted to keep both the agony of her labour and the momentous experience of Billie's birth to herself. That she'd felt she'd earned one small but shining moment of triumph. No one else could be expected to understand.

'I made a decision that Pearl couldn't forgive,' Freya said. 'I lost her trust.'

'Just like that?' Billie asked in clear disbelief.

Troy spoke up. 'I'm sure it's hard for you to understand, Billie.'

'You bet it is.'

'The whole experience was so emotionally laden,' Troy added.

'I can imagine.' Billie let out an angry sigh, not trying to hide her exasperation. 'To be honest, I think you're all pretty fucked in the head.'

'Oh, Billie,' Pearl cried now. 'Can't you even try to understand?'

'Oh, I'm trying, but I doubt it'll ever make any real sense.' Billie's lower jaw protruded stubbornly. 'But at least you've finally told me the truth.' In a dramatic gesture, she flung an arm towards the magnificent windows and the view beyond. 'And in case you haven't noticed, dear family, the world hasn't come to an end.'

With that, she rose rather majestically, cast a weary, almost despairing glance at the three of them, and then turned to leave. 'Thanks for the info. I'm going to bed. Goodnight.'

As Billie left the room, Freya waited for the expected remonstrance and tears from Pearl, the cries of 'I told you so', but her sister merely remained in a collapsed heap, as if drained of all fight or strength.

Troy slipped his arm around his wife. 'You need to get to bed, too, love,' he told her gently. 'We can finish dealing with this in the morning.'

Pearl simply nodded and, like an obedient child, allowed Troy to guide her back down the hallway.

'Goodnight, Freya,' he called to her.

'Goodnight.'

His smile was gentle, a mix of sympathy and concern. 'Thanks for your help.'

'No problem.'

Then they were gone, shuffling down the hallway, leaving Freya as deflated as a popped party balloon.

'Freya.'

Billie's voice.

Freya squinted through the grey early-morning light and saw Billie at her bedroom door. 'Morning,' she said, yawning as she lifted herself up onto one elbow.

'I hope I didn't wake you?'

'No worries. I think I was almost awake. Do you want to come in?'

'Do you mind?'

Before last night's revelations, Freya might have hesitated, out of deference to Pearl's sensitivities. This morning such caution seemed excessive. 'Of course not,' she said, throwing back the sheet and light cotton cover as she shifted over in her bed to make room.

'Thanks.' Billie was wearing a long grey T-shirt over short cotton pyjama bottoms. Her tawny hair was loose and hanging past her shoulders. Despite her pregnant tummy, she looked impossibly young as she settled beside Freya with her tanned legs crossed at the ankles.

'Have you had a bad night?' Freya asked.

'Terrible.' Billie adjusted the pillows and wriggled her shoulders as she made herself comfortable. 'My mind's been going at a million miles a minute. What about you?'

'I haven't had the best of sleeps.'

'I suppose I must have calmed down eventually,' Billie admitted. 'I did sleep for a bit after I finally got my head around the surrogacy and everything.'

'It must have been a shock for you.'

'Too right. Although now that I know, I can't believe I hadn't guessed something like that. Looking back, it kinda makes sense.'

'That's good to hear.'

Billie turned to Freya with a soft smile. 'And I wanted to thank you.'

'Oh.' Freya tried to return her niece's smile, but her lips were suddenly trembling, tugging down at the edges.

'What you did for me – for us – was huge,' Billie said. 'I know it's stating the obvious, but I wouldn't be here if it wasn't for you. And yet I know it was so much more than just that.'

Freya swallowed the building ache in her throat. 'It's only what women have been doing since time began.'

'No, it's not,' said Billie. 'I'm pregnant now, don't forget, so I know what you went through. The morning sickness, the careful diet, the exhaustion. And, crumbs, most women get the reward of a baby at the end of their nine months, but you knew from the start that you'd be giving me up. I'm not sure I could do that.'

'I enjoyed it.' Freya couldn't believe how emotional she felt. How many years had she longed for a few words of gratitude, just like this? Now, she wilfully pushed past her need to weep. 'I felt so sorry for Pearl and Troy,' she said. 'I knew how disappointed they were that they couldn't have a family.'

'But then, after everything you went through for them, you couldn't have a family of your own. That's hardly fair.'

'My infertility had nothing to do with your pregnancy, Billie. Those issues came later.' Freya did manage to smile now, but it felt very out of shape. She shrugged. 'Them's the breaks.'

'I still think it's unfair.'

'Oh, I don't know. I was pretty upset at the time, I must admit, but maybe it was for the best.'

'How can you say that?'

'Well, look what happened to Brian and me. At least we didn't have to put our kids through the misery of a divorce.' No point in suggesting that there might not have been a divorce if they'd had kids.

Accepting this, Billie seemed content to lie in companionable silence until she brightened suddenly and placed a hand on her belly. 'Someone's waking up.'

'Your baby's kicking?'

'Yeah.' Billie sent Freya a shy grin. 'Want to feel?'

'I'd love to.' Gently, Freya laid her hand on her niece's curving belly and through the thin layer of T-shirt she felt an unmistakable bump. 'Ooh,' she said. 'A little footballer, perhaps?'

'Or a gymnast.' Billie grinned. 'I don't suppose you remember what it was like when I was kicking inside you.'

'I certainly do. It was a beautiful experience. I could never forget it.' And then Freya told Billie something she'd always wanted to share. 'From the first time I felt those tiny bumps, I called you Butterfly.'

'Butterfly?' Billie's eyes were extra shiny now. 'Wow. That's so sweet.' Leaning closer, she slipped her arms around Freya and gave her a hug. 'I just love knowing I was your Butterfly.'

They both had to blink then and swipe at their eyes, but after a bit they were grinning.

'I'm afraid I call my baby Pickle,' Billie said.

'That's original.'

'I know, but it's not exactly motherly. This pregnancy seemed such a problem for me at first, you see, but it was *my* problem. My pickle.'

'And now it doesn't feel quite so much like a problem?'

'No, thank goodness. I'm quite used to the idea and starting to get excited, actually.'

'That's wonderful.'

'Anyway, thanks for this lovely chat.' Billie sat up. 'I might go and put the kettle on and find myself some breakfast. I didn't have any supper last night and I'm ravenous.' She swung her feet over the edge of the bed. 'Can I bring you a cuppa?'

'Thanks. I won't say no.'

'No probs.' Halfway to the door, Billie paused and turned back. 'There's one thing I still don't understand.'

'What's that?'

'The huge secrecy.' She lifted her hands in a gesture of helplessness. 'I mean, I get why Mum might not have wanted everyone on the island to know all the details about the surrogacy. But it was still a bit rough to just let people think you gave me up for adoption.'

'The thing was, your mum did still have to legally adopt you, because she hadn't actually given birth.'

'Oh?' Billie's eyes widened. 'Right. Okay. But why couldn't she and Dad have told me the truth?'

Freya hesitated, but she knew Billie had waited too long for these answers. 'I think Pearl was scared,' she said.

'Really? Why?'

'This is going to sound off, and I could be wrong, but I suspect she was afraid you might stop loving her if you knew the truth.'

'Oh, God.'

At that moment, a knock sounded on the bedroom door. Billie glanced at Freya. 'Probably Dad,' she said, and when she opened the door, sure enough, Troy was standing there, already dressed for the day in a polo shirt and shorts.

'Hello.' He looked surprised. 'I was about to ask Freya if she knew where you were.'

'We've been having a debrief,' Freya told him.

Troy's eyebrows lifted, but he said quite promptly, 'That's great.'

'Have you been looking for me?' Billie asked.

He nodded.

'You want to talk to me about Mum, don't you?'

'Among other things.'

Watching Troy closely, Freya saw a flicker of disquiet in his steady eyes.

'I thought we might go for a walk,' he said.

'Sure. Give me a moment to get changed.' Billie turned back to Freya. 'Sorry. I won't be making you that cuppa after all.'

'I can make Freya a cuppa,' said Troy.

'Freya can make her own cuppa, thanks,' said Freya.

They all smiled then and with that Billie was gone.

And Troy, watching his daughter, drew a deep breath that made his chest, quite visibly, rise and fall. Something was still bothering him, Freya decided, and almost certainly, the problem involved Pearl.

CHAPTER THIRTY-TWO

Billie grabbed an apple from the fruit bowl before she and her dad left the house. Outside the sun was a vibrant rosy ball rising triumphantly above the horizon. The silver sea was calm and stained with pink, the sky cloudless and clean. A new day. And Billie was no longer in the dark about her arrival into this world.

The truth was settling inside her, beginning to feel more comfortable. As she set off with Troy down the familiar sandy track that wound between giant granite boulders, she might have felt quite buoyant and optimistic, if she wasn't worried about her mum.

She felt a little guilty that she'd chosen to speak to Freya first this morning, but her mum had looked so tired last night that she hadn't wanted to disturb her.

'I'm glad you had a little chat with Freya.'

Billie turned to her dad in surprise. Was he reading her mind?

'I was just thinking that it might have been a mistake,' she confessed. 'I should have gone to talk to Mum first.'

Troy shook his head. 'I'm sure you needed a word with Freya.'

'I did want to thank her. For everything.'

'That's nice, love.' As they ducked beneath the dangling leaves of a paperbark, he said, 'I imagine the two of you have been getting on pretty well.'

'We have,' Billie agreed. 'I've really enjoyed getting to know Freya better. And she's worked damn hard while she's been here. What with managing all the orders and the books, as well as taking on the desserts.'

'I know. She's been brilliant. We never expected anything like that and we're very grateful.'

Good, Billie thought, *and I hope you've told her so.*

They walked on, rounding a corner that presented a spectacular view of a tiny bay, way below. 'So you're feeling better this morning?' her dad asked.

'Yeah. I'm slowly getting my head around everything. It took a while to sink in – the surrogacy and everything.'

'Yeah, it's huge, Bill.'

'It's still a head spin. I mean – I didn't even know surrogacy was happening back then.'

'It wasn't legal,' Troy said. 'Not in Queensland, at least. We had to go to Canberra.'

'Really? All three of you?'

'Yep.'

'That's – that's groundbreaking. And kind of awesome.'

They had reached their favourite lookout spot, where a broad shelf of rock made a comfortable seat, and Billie wasn't surprised when Troy suggested they stop for a bit. By now the sun had climbed higher and a huge cargo ship was sliding across the horizon, heading for Townsville's port. Billie munched on her apple.

'So how are you keeping?' her dad asked.

She grinned. 'I'm doing brilliantly, thanks, Nurse Mathieson.'

'You certainly look well.' He was smiling, too, but then his expression grew more serious. 'This fellow. The baby's father. I'm sorry things didn't work out.'

To Billie's surprise, the sudden mention of Petros slid through her without causing pain. 'Yeah, well,' she said. 'I'm over him now. I'm getting mentally geared for single motherhood.'

'You'll be great,' her dad said.

From the trees behind them, a pair of kookaburras burst into raucous laughter.

'Pooh to you,' Billie told them, unimpressed by their timing. 'I will too make a great mum, thank you very much.'

Her dad grinned. 'Of course you will.' And then, more seriously, 'You know you don't have to move out.'

'But I think I should.'

At this, Troy frowned and Billie shifted uneasily. She supposed it made financial sense for her to stay under her parents' roof, but she was afraid they would drive her nuts with their endless fussing. Now, as she planned for her baby's arrival, her independence had never seemed more important.

'No need to make a decision just yet.' And although her dad smiled, there was a tilt to his mouth, a hint of sadness that caused an anxious stirring in Billie. From the moment she'd arrived home from Greece, she'd been worried that something was bothering her parents. Now, she had the awful feeling she was about to find out.

'Dad, you wouldn't be beating around the bush, would you?'

This brought another flickering semi-sad smile. 'Never could outsmart you, could I?'

'I don't know about that, but you're making me nervous.'

'Sorry.'

She turned to him now, waiting for him to continue, but he stared out to sea, not meeting her gaze, frowning, as if he was trying to figure out the best way to tell her whatever it was that he needed to say.

Billie couldn't bear the suspense. She had to ask. 'It's not you and Mum, is it? You're not getting a divorce after all?'

'No, love. But there is something I need to explain – about your mum.'

Panic punched into Billie like a physical blow. 'She's not sick, is she?'

'Yes, she is, love.'

Oh, God. 'Not cancer?'

'No, not cancer, but her kidneys are in a bad way.'

Her kidneys. Billie calmed down a tad. She knew very little about kidney issues, but she had a vague idea they were manageable.

'That's actually why she was so keen to have the holiday,' Troy went on. 'She wanted a bit of an adventure before things got too bad.'

'Oh, shit, Dad, that's awful. Poor Mum.' Her mother's sudden urge to take off made horrible sense now. 'And poor you,' Billie said. 'I suppose you had to be Mum's live-in nurse.'

'Well, yes. I was able to keep an eye on her.'

This was so different from how Billie had imagined their holiday. She didn't want to start blubbing over her poor dad, though. She drew a steadying breath. 'Am I right in guessing that you didn't just cut the holiday short as an overreaction to my pregnancy news, that Mum actually needed to come home?'

'Yeah,' he said softly.

Billie reached for his hand and gave it a squeeze and they sat for a bit, hands clasped, shoulders pressed together, looking out to sea where another huge liner chugged south.

'So what sort of treatment will she need?'

'We're still working that out. She can't have dialysis here on the island. So if she wanted to stay on Maggie, she'd have to travel over to the Townsville Hospital Renal Unit for four hours of treatment, three days a week.'

'Yikes.' Her dad had never complained about having to travel back and forth to the hospital for his work, but he was a saint, and he enjoyed his work. Nursing and mixing with a whole range of different people in dramatic situations seemed to suit him.

It would be different for a patient, though, especially one who was already tired and unwell. For each trip, her mum would have to undertake the ferry journey, plus the drive across the city, before going through several hours of treatment, and then she'd have to face the journey home again. 'Would you move to Townsville?'

'That's an option, but as you can imagine, your mum would hate to leave here. Her best bet is a transplant.'

A transplant? Yes, of course. People had two kidneys, didn't they? Suddenly the situation seemed a little brighter. 'So Mum needs a donor?'

'Yeah.' With a small sigh, Troy said, 'I'd do it in a heartbeat, but unfortunately I'm not a match.'

'And I'm probably the obvious choice, but I'm pregnant. Damn. Can Mum wait a few more months?'

'Don't even think about it, Bills. We wouldn't dream of letting you give birth and then hand over a kidney.'

'But what if I'm a perfect match?'

Her dad was firm. 'We'll explore every other option first.'

CHAPTER THIRTY-THREE

'Knock, knock,' Freya called at Pearl's bedroom door.

She was carrying a tray with a teapot, two mugs, milk, sugar and a small plate of biscuits. The offering was a brave gamble on her part. She had no idea whether she'd be welcome. 'Are you awake, Pearl?'

'Yes,' her sister replied. 'Come in.'

So far, so good. Freya set the tray down before opening the door and was pleased to see that Pearl wasn't lying in bed, ill and weak, but sitting up, bolstered by pillows, and busy tapping on her phone.

Gathering up the tray once more, Freya quickly toed the door closed before Won Ton could follow her into this hallowed sanctuary. *Sorry, little mate.*

'Thought you might like a cuppa,' she said to Pearl.

'Oh, that's kind of you.' Pearl eyed the laden tray and frowned. 'Are you joining me?'

Freya knew it was weird to feel nervous, but she couldn't help it. 'I wondered if we might be able to have a chat?'

'Oh?' Pearl looked surprised and not entirely pleased. Her eyes betrayed a flash of worry, but she was civil enough as she said,

'All right.' Then she waved her phone. 'Can you give me one moment? I'm just sending off text messages to finalise the interview times for the chef's job. The sooner we can relieve you and Seb, the better.'

'Sure.' Freya couldn't deny she'd be quite happy to be free of her dessert-making duties. The novelty had certainly begun to wear thin.

'I'm sure you're looking forward to getting back to the Sunshine Coast and all those girlfriends you have down there,' Pearl added.

This rather took the wind out of Freya's sails. She'd been pre-occupied with everything that had been happening here on the island, her reconnection with Seb included, and she'd hardly given any thought to leaving. Fortunately, Pearl went back to her texting and didn't seem to require an answer.

Freya was aware of her heart beating a little too fast as she set the tray on a white cane table where two matching chairs were positioned to make the most of the view. The bedroom was lovely. Too much white for Freya's tastes, but wonderfully spacious, with floor-to-ceiling windows, sliding shutters, walk-in wardrobes and an ensuite.

'I'll get up in a sec,' Pearl said.

'No rush. Finish what you're doing.'

'Where are Troy and Billie?'

'Gone for a walk.'

Pearl nodded, as if this news wasn't unexpected. Freya unpacked the tray and chose one of the chairs, upholstered with pale-blue cushions. Her stomach was a nervous knot, which was ridiculous. Anyone would think she was in a courtroom about to be tried for some heinous crime, not having a cup of tea with her sister.

Through the deep windows, she watched a lizard emerge from the shade of a pandanus palm and begin to sun itself on a smooth granite boulder. She managed to smile.

It wasn't long before Pearl set her phone aside, heaved herself out of bed, and found slippers and a cotton dressing gown.

'Is Billie still angry with us?' she asked as she joined Freya.

'She seems to be calming down. We've just been talking, actually.'

'This morning?'

'Yes. She was up early.'

Pearl's mouth tightened at this, but she didn't look unduly upset. She seemed stronger, Freya was pleased to note. Still too thin and pale, with shadows under her eyes, but not quite so exhausted and weak.

Unfortunately, these small signs of improvement didn't help Freya to feel any calmer, though. Her hand shook a little as she poured the tea. *For heaven's sake.* 'You still have white with one?'

'Yes, thanks, but you don't have to wait on me.'

'No problem. There, it's all done.'

They sipped their tea in silence. Outside, the lizard scurried off, while on the beach below, a powerboat delivered a group of skin divers, who proceeded to don masks, snorkels and flippers.

Drawing a deep breath for courage, Freya launched into her reason for invading her sister's private domain. 'Pearl, I wanted to apologise. You were obviously right that I would upset everything by staying here on the island with Billie. I should have listened to you. I know these rumours and trouble wouldn't have happened if I'd stayed away.'

Pearl's bony shoulders lifted in a shrug. 'What's done is done.'

'I know, but I still wanted to apologise.'

Her sister accepted this offering with a small, resigned nod. 'Maybe it was for the best after all.'

This was a surprise. An incredibly welcome one, of course. Freya had been braced for Pearl's resentment and anger, and she'd been wondering how she could safely work in a suggestion that Billie had a right to know the truth, that all children deserved to know their history.

'So you agree it's good that Billie knows about everything?' she asked cautiously. 'Especially now she's going to have her own baby?'

'Her pregnancy certainly makes a difference.' Pearl's lips tilted into a curve that might have almost been a smile. 'I can't quite believe I'm going to be a grandmother.'

'It's exciting, isn't it?'

As Pearl helped herself to a finger of shortbread, she said, 'I don't suppose you know whether Billie's having a boy or a girl?'

'Heavens, no. She wouldn't tell me without telling you first. But she decided she doesn't want to know.'

This was received with a small, satisfied nod. 'It's sad about the baby's father, though.'

'Yes, it is,' Freya agreed. 'But I suspect Billie's better off without Petros.'

'I suppose you would know a lot more about that than I do.'

Pearl did sound frosty now and Freya hunted for a positive way out of this corner.

'Billie's young and lovely. I'm sure she won't be on her own for long.'

'She might be. She has a very independent spirit.'

'Well, yes, but I guess that's fine, too. As long as she's happy.' When Pearl made no response to this back-pedalling, Freya added, 'You never know, she might take after our mother.'

'Yes, that thought had occurred to me.' The glance Pearl slid in Freya's direction was decidedly warmer, almost conspiratorial. 'We managed without our father.'

'We did, didn't we?'

They both smiled then. The smiles were no doubt rusty from lack of use, but laced with memories of those long-ago days when they'd been girls, living in van parks, a tightly knit trio – two sisters and their mum making the most of what little they had – facing the world together.

Before everything went wrong.

Freya lifted the teapot and she was no longer trembling. 'Would you like a top-up?'

'Thanks. You make a good cuppa.'

Happily absorbing this small compliment, Freya drew a deep breath and let it out slowly. Their conversation was going so much better than she'd dared to hope. *Tread softly, Freya.*

'Have you heard from Mum lately?' she asked as Pearl stirred her tea.

'Not really. You know what she's like. The occasional phone call out of the blue.'

This was true. Ruby had never been the sort of mother who needed to keep in daily or even weekly contact with her adult daughters.

'I've been sending her postcards from most of the places we stopped at,' Pearl added. 'And I'm sorry Troy and I didn't make it to Western Australia. I would have liked to see where she and Tatsuo live in Broome.'

Freya refrained from suggesting that Pearl needn't have rushed back. 'Maybe next trip,' she said instead.

'Mmmm.' A shadow seemed to fall across Pearl's face and she looked away, out to sea, frowning, as if distracted by some secret trouble.

For a moment, Freya thought Pearl might be about to confide in her, but as seconds of silence ticked by, she knew this wasn't going to happen and that prying would only make her sister clam up. 'Speaking of Tatsuo,' she said, keen to keep the chat flowing, 'it's rather an amusing coincidence that Mum called you Pearl and then years later fell in love with a pearl farmer.'

'It is, isn't it?' Pearl brightened again, as if grateful for the distraction. 'But Mum's always been a little obsessed with gemstones, hasn't she?'

'Has she?'

'Of course. Don't you remember when we lived in the van parks, and she was always trying to trade her little collection of rocks with the gem fossickers?'

'Oh, yes, that's right. She kept that little chocolate box filled with bits of topaz and sapphires. I think there were a few rubies, too. Just the rough stones, of course.'

'Yes. She could never afford to have them cut and turned into proper gems or jewellery.'

'It's coming back to me now,' said Freya. 'There was that con man, too, wasn't there? What was his name?'

'You mean Des, the so-called geologist?'

'Oh, God, yes. He had that dreadful moustache.' Freya pulled a face of disgust. 'How could Mum have ever trusted a moustache like that?'

'Heaven knows. It was all so sad. He promised he could get her a great price for her stones, so she handed them over, trusting him completely, and then he just left. Vanished. Never to be heard of again.'

'Bastard.'

To an outsider their conversation would seem utterly banal, Freya realised, but after decades of strained silence, this simple chat felt like a hugely significant step, an important stitch in the massive rift that had held her and Pearl apart for so many years. Might she dare to hope?

They'd finished their tea, but she was keen now to keep this chat ticking along. 'I don't suppose Mum's interest in gemstones was inspired by her name, Ruby.'

'It may have been.' Musing on this, Pearl said, 'You know Mum almost called you Amber.'

Freya was glad she'd finished her tea, or her gasp of shock would have splattered it everywhere. Bloody hell. 'Amber is Brian's new wife's name.'

'Really? That's rather a bizarre coincidence.'

Pearl looked amused now, but Freya was groaning. 'Oh, my God. Just imagine if Mum had called me Amber and Brian found himself trading one Amber for another.'

'Amber One and Amber Two.' Pearl actually chuckled at her small joke. Wow. Freya couldn't remember the last time her sister had seemed so relaxed. This was a minor miracle.

'But it's true,' Pearl said next. 'Mum had always planned to call you after another gemstone. She was Ruby, I was Pearl and you were going to be Amber, if you were a girl.'

'And Rock if I was a boy?'

This brought a wry chuckle. 'I can't remember. Maybe. But I do remember that while Mum was pregnant, she read a book she adored. Some sort of saga. I forget its title, but the heroine was called Freya and Mum thought it was the most beautiful name ever. Actually, I think she would have been devastated if you'd turned out to be a boy.'

'Well, I'm glad she didn't read *Forever Amber*. There would have been no escape for me.' And then, a beat later, Freya said, 'You know, in Norse mythology, Freya is the goddess of fertility.'

'Really?'

'Yeah. One of life's little ironies.'

Another silence fell and Freya began to gather up the tea things. This might have been a landmark conversation, but she didn't want to outstay her welcome.

Pearl said, 'If Freya represents fertility, it's a fitting name for you. After all, you brought us the gift of Billie.'

The cup in Freya's hand clattered on its saucer, almost breaking.

'And I should also be apologising,' Pearl said next, her voice tight, as her mouth twisted into an awkward little smile. 'I let one small thing come between us.'

Freya knew, of course, what this *one small thing* was.

Her decision on the day Billie was born.

And this moment now was so huge, she was incapable of replying. She was too busy biting her lips, too busy trying to stop herself from bursting into noisy sobs.

'The thing is, I've always been hopelessly jealous of you,' Pearl said next.

'Of me?' Freya cried, sure that there couldn't be a single reason why Pearl would be jealous. Pearl had always been the good sister – older, wiser, neater and tidier, better behaved, with better school results. A dream daughter.

'You were Mum's favourite,' Pearl said next.

'I was not.'

'Yes, you were. I always tried so hard to please her. I turned myself inside out trying to be good, but you didn't have to try. Mum loved you anyway.'

Freya stared at Pearl in astonished dismay. 'But Mum despaired of me. I was the naughty and reckless one. I caused her no end of worry.'

Pearl shook her head. 'You never really noticed, but I know I'm right. Even on that day you almost drowned, Mum didn't thank me for rescuing you. She just went mad at me for letting you go near the creek.'

'But you saved my life.'

'I know.' Tears shone in Pearl's pale eyes now. 'But Mum was so worried about what might have happened to you, she never once thanked me. And she cuffed me around the ears for good measure.'

'Oh, Pearl.' Freya wanted to protest that she couldn't believe this, but the huge sorrow in her sister's face told its own story.

'Once Mum had you warm and dry and tucked up in bed with a mug of cocoa and Iced Vovos, she took me outside and lectured the hell out of me. How I had no sense of responsibility and I should have known better. How I was supposed to look out for my little sister.'

'Plus a cuffing?'

'Plus a cuffing.'

'That's terrible, Pearl.' Freya didn't know what to say. She was reliving the terror of that day. The water closing over her, the struggle to breathe, the weeds dragging at her. How could their mum have been so unfair? Pearl's rescue had been truly heroic.

Her sister sighed. 'I know it's silly how we let these things stew inside us forever.'

No, it wasn't silly, thought Freya. It was tragic. Pearl should have been blissfully happy. She had a loving and faithful husband, a beautiful daughter, a successful business and a gorgeous home. But none of these wonderful things had helped her to overcome her lifelong gnawing insecurity.

Devastated, Freya wanted to launch out of her chair and give her sister a hug, but the urge was no sooner born than the bedroom door opened and Troy came in.

He stopped, somewhat startled when he saw Freya and the mugs and teapot.

Freya jumped up, blinking back the tears that had almost spilt. Time was getting on. No one had eaten breakfast yet and she had to make at least one new dessert this morning. 'I've been loitering in your bedroom,' she told Troy.

'That's fine.' He lifted a hand and motioned her to sit. 'I didn't mean to interrupt you.'

'We were just having a cuppa, but we've finished.'

Troy shot his wife a searching glance, no doubt worried by the watery gleam in her eyes. He frowned. 'So you've told Freya?'

The deep concern in his gaze suggested that he was not referring to any of his wife's lingering childhood issues, but to something else entirely. Something imminent and of vital importance.

Fighting a knife-sharp slice of panic, Freya turned to him. 'Told me what?'

CHAPTER THIRTY-FOUR

Sonia Brassal's house was on a back street in Arcadia, away from the waterfront and bordering on bushland. Many years had passed since Billie had last gone through the Brassals' low front gate and up the path that wound between clumps of traveller's palms. These days the path was made of concrete, but Billie remembered it as a river of bark mulch set with round timber stepping stones.

In the backyard, there had been a cool swing set and a home-made cubby house, as well as an above-ground swimming pool. The pool was nearly always full of leaves from overhanging trees, and most of the local kids had preferred to swim in the sea, but it had provided a fun freshwater alternative.

Billie could remember games of Marco Polo being played there. Eventually, once his kids had grown up, Mr Brassal had removed the pool and play equipment and set up a paved barbecue area instead.

Now, a child's tricycle was neatly parked beside the front steps. Billie wondered if Nicole's little boy, Preston, was home. The conversation she had planned wasn't really suitable for a child's ears, so she would have to be careful.

She mounted the stairs and crossed the verandah where numerous hanging baskets were lush with maidenhair ferns and trailing plants. Wrought-iron shelves near the front door held a lighted citronella candle, old gardening gloves, a pot plant or two, plus a trowel and watering can.

Through the front flyscreen door, Billie could see a ginger cat curled on a cane chair, looking out at her through sleepy yellow eyes. The weatherboard home was modest, but comfortable, and typical of the homes Billie had always known until her parents' recent move. But despite the familiarity, she felt nervous.

The house seemed very quiet. The only sound was music playing somewhere, possibly on a radio in the kitchen. She rang the doorbell.

Footsteps sounded and Sonia Brassal appeared, wiping her hands on an apron. She squinted a little, peering through the flyscreen, and her lips parted with obvious surprise when she saw Billie. 'Hello, Belinda.'

'Hello, Mrs Brassal. I was hoping Nicole might be home.'

'Oh, no, I'm sorry. Nicole and Jason left yesterday. They're back in Melbourne now.'

This was disappointing. Billie had been braced for an awkward but necessary chat. 'I'm sorry I missed her.'

Now Sonia opened the flyscreen door. 'Would you like to come in?'

Billie hesitated, wishing she'd texted Nicole to check her whereabouts, but she'd been so anxious to get this conversation behind her that she'd just headed straight over. She couldn't help her mother by donating a kidney, but she could at least set the record straight with the Brassals and she'd decided this would be best achieved face to face.

She gave a slight shake of her head. 'It's okay. I can phone Nicole.' But she was sure Sonia would know everything about her daughter's disastrous meeting at the café, so she added, 'I wanted to apologise.'

Sonia's mouth opened even further. '*You* wanted to apologise?'

'Yes. I – I —' Billie was uncertain now about how much she should tell.

'Nicole wanted to apologise to you,' Sonia said. 'She was terribly upset. She feels so bad.'

'Yes, but that was partly my fault. I – I overreacted.'

'It was all very unfortunate.' Sonia stepped back and gestured again for Billie to enter. 'Why don't you come in?' Her smile was surprisingly gentle. 'Then I can add my apology to the mix. I feel partly responsible for this.'

Billie couldn't really refuse and she wished she didn't feel so tense. Despite her friendship with Nicole, she'd never been able to shake off memories of Sonia Brassal as her rather strict primary-school teacher. Today, however, in a loose tie-dyed kaftan and with bare, somewhat gnarled feet, her face free of makeup and her grey hair caught up in an untidy knot, Sonia looked less formidable and more like any friend's mum. And as Billie stepped inside her home, she couldn't help liking the familiar tropical feel of the timber floors, cane furniture and woven mats. Deep casement windows looked out into the leafy green branches of a poinciana tree and she caught the scent of curry cooking.

'Come though to the kitchen,' Sonia said. 'Would you like a coffee?'

'A glass of water would be fine, thanks.'

The kitchen, at the back of the house, was just as Billie remembered. Plain pine cupboards without a hint of renovation. A chopping board, onion skins and spice bottles were scattered on a bench beside the stove where a pot of curry was simmering. Sonia had been listening to the ABC on the radio, but she turned this off and filled two glasses with cold water from the fridge, adding ice cubes with mint leaves frozen inside them.

As they sat at a small scrubbed pine table, she said, 'I really am very sorry that Nicole upset you the way she did. But I'm even sorrier that it was my fault. I should never have told her about Freya and Pearl and – and the pregnancy and everything.'

She dropped her gaze for a moment and swallowed, and when she looked up her eyes were extra bright. 'I'm rather ashamed of myself, Belinda. I should have known better.'

The last thing Billie had expected was to feel sympathy for this woman. 'I admit it was a shock, hearing about the adoption from Nicole,' she said. 'But I think it was the shock my family needed, actually. It means that I now know the truth after all this time.'

Sonia nodded, managed a watery, fleeting smile.

'And I think you need to know it, too,' Billie said.

At this, the woman's eyes almost popped with surprise. 'But I thought —'

'You thought that Freya was my mother and she gave me up for adoption.'

'Well, yes.' Sonia looked understandably puzzled. 'Isn't that . . .?'

She didn't finish her question and so Billie explained, carefully and quickly, giving the basic facts of the surrogacy without going into details of the emotional fallout.

'My goodness,' Sonia murmured when the story was told. Then she sat back in her chair, staring into space with a dazed smile as she absorbed Billie's news. 'That's quite amazing, isn't it?'

'Yeah,' said Billie. 'And once I got over the shock, I decided it was kind of awesome, really.'

Sonia's smile warmed. 'It certainly is. Quite awesome.'

'And I'm really glad I know about it at last,' Billie added. 'But I mightn't have found out if I hadn't had coffee with Nicole. So,' she gave a small shrug, 'I will let her know things have turned out okay.'

'Thank you,' said Sonia. 'I know she'll appreciate that.' Then her expression became serious. 'But I hope it wasn't the need to sort through this that brought Pearl and Troy back from their holiday.'

Billie supposed she shouldn't be surprised that Sonia already knew about her parents' return, but she had to think quickly now. Having enjoyed a good in-depth chat with her mum about everything that had transpired since their return, she knew that Pearl was now comfortable enough about sharing the surrogacy story, but she wouldn't want to broadcast news of her health issues.

'They were ready to come back,' she said, hoping this would suffice.

Sonia's eyebrows lifted. 'I thought they were planning a much longer trip. I hope it's not Pearl's kidneys?'

Billie stared at her, gobsmacked. *Good grief.* Was there no end to this woman's insider knowledge?

'Oh, God,' Sonia cried, as she realised she'd delivered yet another shock. She pressed her hands against her lips, palms together as if in prayer. 'I haven't done it again, have I?' she asked in a small, scared voice.

Billie needed a moment to recover her breath. 'You know about Mum's kidneys?'

'I do. Yes.' Once again, Sonia looked both worried and apologetic.

'I thought only Dad knew.'

'I – I more or less found out by accident.'

Such a puzzling comment. Billie had to know more. 'So when did this happen?'

Sonia leaned forward, elbows on the table, as she explained. 'I was at the hospital. It was a few months back. Just a routine check-up and I went to the cafeteria afterwards for a coffee, before heading home. Your mum was in there.'

'Right.'

'I knew, as soon as I saw Pearl, that she was terribly upset. She'd just had the diagnosis, you see. I'm not sure where your dad was just then. Somewhere in the hospital, but Pearl looked so lonely and worried. We ended up having a cuppa together.'

'And she told you?'

'She did, yes. We talked for quite a while. The poor woman. She was so worried – about everything – not just her health, but keeping up the business, about you and your travels, about whether she'd be able to stay on the island.'

Billie could imagine that it must have been comforting for her mum to offload these worries. From her own experience she knew there were times when talking to someone outside your normal circle could help in ways you never expected. But she was still surprised that her mum's confidante had been Sonia Brassal.

Now that she'd settled into her story, however, Sonia seemed quite keen to explain more. 'When I realised Pearl didn't have to start the treatment immediately, I suggested she might like to take a break. A chance to get away with Troy and relax for a bit. She seemed to like that idea, so then we started talking about where she might go. I was a bit shocked to realise she'd hardly been anywhere.'

'I know,' said Billie. 'She always claimed that the island was lovely enough for her and and why should she need to leave? But both Freya and I have done quite a bit of travel and I think she'd started to realise what she'd missed. The poor thing has worked so hard all her life.'

'Exactly,' said Sonia. 'Pearl regretted not seeing more of the world. That was when we came up with the grey nomad idea.

'You and Mum cooked that up?'

Sonia gave a sheepish smile. 'We did, yes.'

Billie hoped there were no more surprises. Her head was spinning.

'But is Pearl's condition worse?' Sonia asked now.

Billie nodded, although she had no plans to share information about treatments and transplants. A prudent daughter would leave now. She drained her water glass. The ice cubes had melted and she savoured the refreshing touch of mint on her tongue. 'Goodness,' she said as she glanced at the clock on the kitchen wall. 'I really must get going.'

To her relief, Sonia accepted this without further questions. She rose and accompanied Billie to the front door. 'Thanks so much for coming,' she said. 'I really appreciate it, Belinda.'

'And I'll be in touch with Nicole.'

'Thanks. She'll be so relieved.'

As Billie left, she was remembering the puzzling comments Sonia had made soon after she'd started back at the restaurant. *Travel is so good for broadening the mind and you always had so much potential . . . Although I'm sure your parents are very happy to have you home again . . .*

Huh! The first comment was based on the assumption that she was the daughter of a famous artist, while the second was fuelled by Sonia's knowledge of Pearl's illness.

Billie couldn't help wondering if Sonia and half the island also knew she was pregnant. Then again, after everything else that had happened recently, this news was rather small beer.

CHAPTER THIRTY-FIVE

'No!' Seb was adamant and, quite possibly, furious. 'No way, Freya. You can't be serious.'

It was late at night. A new chef was now on duty at Island Thyme, a very capable young woman who'd returned to Queensland after five years of cheffing in ski lodges in Europe, and to celebrate their newfound freedom, Seb had invited Freya to his place for dinner.

They'd dined on his deck and the meal had been delicious, accompanied by candlelight and wine, a wafting breeze and the soft whisper of the nearby sea. Such a magical night, relaxing and amusing, and made especially exciting by the teasing, pulsing promise of the lovemaking that Freya had known would follow.

Now, some time later, they were basking in the happy afterglow. Freya was cradled against Seb's shoulder and both of them were a little breathless and more than a little smug.

'My God,' Seb said. 'If this is growing older, let's have more of it.'

And Freya, chuckling happily as she snuggled close, decided that satisfaction was an overused but totally underrated word.

Almost straight away, though, she went and spoiled the happy moment by sharing her important news with Seb. No doubt this was unwise timing, but was there ever a good time to share difficult tidings? She'd already held off mentioning it for days, and she'd said nothing earlier in the evening so as not to upset their lovely mood.

In the darkness, however, and feeling so wonderfully close to Seb, the details that had been pounding away inside her had been ready to explode.

'You can't be serious,' he cried now.

'I would hardly be joking, Seb.'

'But it's crazy. It's unbelievable. History repeating itself.'

'I know, but I've had the tests. I'm a good match for Pearl.'

He gave a vehement shake of his head. 'Pearl would never expect you to give up a kidney. Not after everything you've already done for her.'

'You're right,' Freya said. 'Pearl doesn't expect it and she has said as much. Several times. But Troy's not a match for her. He's the wrong blood type. And Billie's pregnant. And – and I owe her.'

'For that drowning incident when you were kids?'

'Of course.'

With an angry grimace, Seb lifted his gaze to the ceiling. 'So help me, you raced off and discovered that you'd be a perfect match.'

'I did. Yes.' And already, a tentative date for the transplant surgery had been set.

'Freya.' The despair in his voice cut straight through her.

She knew the timing was impossibly cruel, just when they'd found each other again, a savage twist of fate, a horrible rehash of their youth. But this time Freya was quite determined that she wouldn't be reckless. Or inconsiderate. While she was trying very hard to be practical and mature, she also hoped to be sensitive.

Seb, however, had lurched upright and was sitting a metre from her, his strong, brown back stiff with tension.

Freya tried to explain. 'Being a kidney donor doesn't shorten a person's life expectancy, or mean they're more likely to have kidney issues in the future. I've talked to the doctors at length. There's no reason why I can't live a perfectly normal life with one kidney.'

But Seb didn't reply, and her stomach tightened with fear. Was she about to lose him again? It was inconceivable, surely? The mere thought brought pain, as if her heart, rather than her kidney, had been scooped clear out of her chest.

'Seb, it would only involve four to six days in hospital and then being careful with heavy lifting or contact sports for six weeks. And I don't play contact sports, so it's hardly a problem. It's nothing like the commitment of a nine-month pregnancy and giving birth.'

She saw his glare, the tightening of his jaw and the fear of losing him speared through her. 'And this time it could save Pearl's life,' she added for good measure.

He turned to her then, his expression bleak, unforgiving. 'Why does it have to be you? Why are you so hellbent on sacrificing yourself yet again?'

Freya winced as his barb found its mark. She'd never thought of herself as any kind of martyr, but surely it was obvious that she would want to help Pearl.

Of course, Seb couldn't be expected to comprehend how important her conversation with Pearl had been. He'd never had siblings. He probably wouldn't understand the deep and complicated bond. How, despite their differences, she'd always longed to be closer to her sister, or how the healing warmth of Pearl's surprising apology would stay with her forever.

'I just can't see any other viable option,' she said.

'But aren't there plenty of other kidney donors out there?'

'They're not thick on the ground. And hanging about for someone else would mean Pearl would go on a waiting list. I could save her that time and stress. She could have the transplant quite soon and be well and truly recovered by the time Billie's baby arrives.'

'That soon?'

'Yes, the recovery usually takes just a couple of months.'

The muscles in Seb's throat rippled as he swallowed. He gave a heavy sigh, ran agitated fingers through his shaggy hair. 'Look,' he said. 'Don't get me wrong. I'm very sorry to hear about Pearl's illness. Truly I am. But, Freya, you thought your womb was fine. You thought you'd be having children of your own, and look what happened.'

Yes, Freya had been trying hard not to think about that.

Shifting closer to her now, Seb reached out, gripping her shoulders so she was face to face with him, and the message in his eyes spoke of such unbearable tenderness that her heart rocked sharply in her chest.

'I can't lose you again,' he said.

'You wouldn't lose me. Honestly, Seb. There's hardly any risk for me.'

With gentle fingers, he traced a trail down her back, stopping at the spot where the vital organ in question lay.

'Scars heal,' she said, keeping her tone light. 'And anyway, they make the incision at the front.'

'Oh, Freya.' He bound her close to him now and she let her eyes drift closed, loving the warmth of him, the scent of his skin, drinking in the knowledge that these arms that held her so close were Seb's, miraculously returned to her.

'I know it's hard,' she said softly. 'I know it doesn't seem fair, but what else can I do?'

He sighed. 'We'll give this more thought. That's what we'll do. I won't let you be rash.'

We'll give this more thought. Freya had investigated this problem from every angle, so she had no idea how any more thought was going to help, but it was a concept she could live with for this evening, at least. Lifting her head, she kissed his jaw, nibble-kissing the rough line of stubble.

'Sounds good to me,' she murmured. 'But let's do that thinking in the morning.'

'Minx.' He was smiling now as he kissed her chin, her nose, her lips, as they fell back onto the bed in a happy tangle of limbs.

This time their lovemaking was infused with an extra layer of emotion, fear as fierce as love.

'Freya. Good heavens, I don't know what to say.'

When Freya rang Daisy with her news on the following after-noon, her friend sounded almost as distressed as Seb had. Freya, sitting on the beach at Alma Bay, watching seagulls take off, snowy white against the blue, tried to make light of her situation. 'Oh, you know me, Daisy. Always bouncing from one drama to the next.'

'But I thought life was calming down for you.'

'It is. More or less. This is a minor hiccup. No real drama for me, to be honest. Poor Pearl's the one with the worry.'

'Well, yes, that's true. How is she?'

'She's looking better, actually. The travel was tiring her out, so it's for the best that she's home again and getting her health seen to straight away. She's excited about Billie's baby, of course. She's already dived into making a patchwork quilt for the cot, would you believe? And she's poring over all sorts of baby shop catalogues, marking up the best buys.'

'Oh, bless her. I guess it's a good distraction. Helps to keep her calm.'

'Mmmm. I guess.' Freya didn't add that Billie was thinking of moving out, that she was feeling suffocated by her mother's intense interest in her pregnancy.

'And how's Seb?' Daisy asked. There had been previous girly phone calls where Freya had quizzed Daisy about her American 'friend' who'd come to stay with her and had remained for over a month. And in turn Freya had coughed up one or two details about her fledgling love life.

'Seb?' she said now. 'Oh, he's —' Dead sexy was the description that first sprang to mind, but as tense as a bowstring would be more accurate. When they'd parted that morning, Seb had been no happier about her plans. He hadn't tried to talk her out of the donation exactly, but he'd made his worry and disappointment clear.

Freya knew he wasn't so much anxious that something would go wrong with the procedure – the chances of that were incredibly slim – but rather worried that she might develop her own kidney problems down the track, even though she was in the pink of condition at the moment.

'He's not thrilled,' she admitted.

'That's understandable.'

'But I don't think he'll try to stop me.' *At least, I hope he won't.* Seb had headed over to the mainland for the day, ostensibly to buy more art gear, but Freya suspected that he needed time and distance to think. And she was scared, dead scared, that those thoughts might take him away from her. Again.

Was it possible that he didn't know how to be in a relationship unless everything was perfectly smooth sailing? After all, he'd made a lifetime habit of never staying with one woman for too long.

CHAPTER THIRTY-SIX

When Billie's phone rang on Saturday morning, she was absorbed in studying the ads in a real-estate agent's window, sussing out the flats available for rent. Her nesting instinct was in full swing, it seemed. Even though she hadn't yet reached the final weeks of her pregnancy, the desire to have a little place of her own, a home just for her and her Pickle, was growing stronger every day. She didn't have much money, but a one-bedroom flat would do.

Luckily, her parents had accepted this suggestion without too much fuss.

'As long as you don't race off overseas again, so we never get to see our grandchild,' her mum had pleaded.

Billie assured Pearl that she would stay put in North Queensland for the foreseeable future. And now, as she took down the details of a little A-frame cottage that appealed, her phone started to ring, and when she retrieved it, the caller was Detective Dan.

A glance at her reflection in the shop window showed that she was smiling broadly as she answered. The smile also registered in her voice. This was such a cool surprise. 'Hello, Dan. How are you?'

'I'm fine,' he said. 'Just ringing to see how you are.'

'Oh, that's kind of you.' The last time they'd spoken, Billie had been in a fluster over the adoption business. Afterwards, when she'd looked back on that phone call, she decided she'd been unforgivably intrusive. Teatime, for pity's sake. She'd hesitated to ring Dan back once everything was sorted.

Actually, she'd thought it was more than likely he'd put her little problem out of his mind while he got on with his far more important work of catching criminals. And yet here he was, thoughtfully enquiring.

'Actually, I'm fine, too,' Billie told him.

'Dare I ask if you've spoken to your parents?'

'Yes, I have and it's all good. Although it's an incredibly complicated story.' Too complicated to try to explain quickly over the phone. 'Pretty amazing, though. I should tell you sometime.'

She suspected she was babbling and sounding way too enthusiastic, but she couldn't help it. Dan was, on reflection, one of the nicest guys she'd ever met. It was hard to remember that his working life was all about investigating crime. It seemed so at odds with his clean-cut image as a family man.

'I don't suppose you'll be back on the island any time soon?' As the words left Billie's lips, she cringed. She'd sounded way too hopeful.

'Funny you should ask,' Dan said. 'I'm actually on the island right now. Molly talked me into another ferry trip and I have the day off, so I thought why not. We're about to buy fish and chips and eat them on the beach. I don't suppose you're free?'

For a moment Billie thought he was just being polite, and then she heard Molly's voice, squeaky and excited. 'Yes, Billie, please come and have fish and chips with us.'

Billie found that she was grinning. She could picture Molly leaning in to her dad's phone, could see her determined little face with curly wings of hair on either side, her bright and eager smile. And she honestly couldn't think of anything she'd like more than to have fish and chips with that pair. 'Where are you?' she asked.

'Arcadia.'

Which was only a few minutes away by car. And Billie still had a couple of hours before she needed to head to work. 'Sounds like fun,' she said. 'Thanks for the invite. I'll see you soon then.'

'Great,' Dan responded, and in the background Billie could hear a little girl giving a cheer.

The fish and chips were salty and crisp, just perfect with a generous squeeze of lemon, along with cold ginger beer to wash them down. The trio enjoyed this splendid meal, eating straight from the paper at a picnic table in Geoffrey Bay. The setting was magic, with a soft wind whistling and whispering through the thin she-oak needles above them, while broken coral tinkled and chimed as gentle waves washed it ashore.

Billie, used to the island's beauty, sometimes took it for granted. Today, however, she looked about her with the eyes of a visitor, taking in the sparkling turquoise water, the darker patches of reef, and the way the bay was perfectly framed by huge granite headlands covered in scrub and dotted with bright splashes of yellow from flowering kapok trees.

And also, well within her sights, was Dan.

Dan, dressed simply, in the manner of all beachgoers, in a striped T-shirt and board shorts, seemed more tanned and broader in the shoulders than she remembered. Or perhaps she hadn't been paying enough attention in the past? She wondered if detectives were required to work out. Even the shape of his hands, as he broke a piece of fish for Molly, seemed extra manly today.

While they ate, Molly told her, in no end of detail, about her trip with her father to the Townsville aquarium. How they had been given paper bangles to wear around their wrists and had walked through a glass tunnel that went right under the water.

'And there were sharks and turtles and all sorts of fishes. And I could see the sharks' tummies when they swam over us.'

'And you saw seahorses?' Billie asked.

'Yes, yes, yes!' exclaimed Molly, eyes shining.

'The seahorses were in a special tank of their own,' said Dan.

'And two of them were dancing with their tails hooked together,' added Molly.

'Wow.'

'They were so *sweet*,' the little girl squeaked.

'They were courting,' Dan said in an undertone, while his eyes flashed with secret amusement.

'Cute,' said Billie, and she found herself blushing, but she had no idea why.

The whole time they were eating, Molly, who'd come equipped with a bucket and spade, was eyeing off the shells scattered on the sand and quite desperate to collect them. A few times she announced she was finished and Dan gently encouraged her to eat a little more. But eventually he relented.

'All right,' he said with a good-natured smile. 'But you know the rules. Don't go too far, okay?'

'Okay.'

'On the count of three.' This was clearly a well-practised ritual. 'One, two —'

Molly took off and Dan sent Billie a shrugging grin. 'What happened to three?'

Billie was grinning, too. 'She's certainly a beach lover.' And as they watched Molly begin to sort through the shells that lay among the snowy-white driftwood and coral rubble littering the beach, she told Dan about the surrogacy and necessary adoption, about the fallout from Sonia Brassal's misinformation, about Freya's generosity and Pearl's secrecy and, finally, the new chapter about Pearl's health crisis.

Dan was a very good listener, hardly ever interrupting her and never once looking as if he was losing interest. But it wasn't possible to tell him her story without also thinking about his own situation, and how appalling it must have been for him to lose his wife, the mother of his baby girl. Billie couldn't help choking up when she thought about that.

'My family probably sound like something out of a soap opera,' she said, trying to lighten the moment.

Dan shook his head. 'It's a pretty amazing story.'

'I know. I look in the mirror now and think – did I really start life in a test tube? It's so surreal.'

'But what a great result.' He grinned at her then and something in his eyes, a flash, a spark, made her look away quickly before she blushed again.

She told herself she was being foolish. Imagining things. Dan wasn't cracking on to her. He was simply being Dan. Being nice. No, that wasn't the right word. Decent. Yes, Dan was decent, although Billie was sure he could be tough, too. She'd seen the way he stood up to those guys at the courthouse.

More to the point, she was pregnant and Dan knew it, and the last thing he would want was the burden of a woman with another man's kid. And she certainly wasn't looking for a partner. She planned to be a single mum and a damn good one at that.

She looked at him again now as he watched his daughter stooping to pick up yet another beach treasure. She saw the softening in his smile, and the way his brown hair caught hints of gold in the sunlight. She found herself asking, 'Isn't your job rather dangerous for a single dad?'

His brown eyes gleamed with amusement. 'It's not like *NYPD Blue*. I don't have guns pointed at me every day, if that's what you're thinking.'

'But you're still dealing with crime. You see bad stuff all the time and you have no partner to offload to when you get home. I just —'

Dan shook his head. 'Now you're starting to sound like my mother.'

'Sorry.' More carefully, Billie asked, 'So what do you like about your job?'

'Apart from the fact that I don't have to wear a uniform and I get to drive an unmarked car?'

They were both smiling now.

'Haven't you heard that men look good in uniform?' Billie teased.

Dan accepted this with a shrug. 'Truth is, I spend quite a lot of time on routine stuff – writing reports, making notes in files, checking photos. Taking phone calls from families of victims. Interviews and more interviews.'

'Middle-of-the-night phone calls?' Billie asked.

'Sometimes. Our weekends are rostered, so it's not all bad.'

'How did your wife find it?' Billie couldn't help asking this. 'Did she mind?'

Dan shot her a quick, searching glance, but if he was surprised or upset by her question, he didn't show it. 'She preferred not to know too much,' he said simply.

Billie couldn't resist trying to learn a little more. 'What was her name?'

'Jane.' His mouth formed a crooked smile. 'She taught kindergarten. Loved little kids.'

'Oh, Dan.' Feeling wretched, Billie switched her gaze to Molly, but she couldn't stop the sudden spill of tears. She grabbed one of the paper napkins that came with their meal and dabbed at her face, but the tears might have been hard to stem if Molly hadn't called out suddenly.

'Daddy! There's a little bird here and it's hurt.'

Frowning now, Dan rose from his seat. 'Coming,' he called, and Billie rose quickly, too, and went with him.

It wasn't easy at first to locate the little ball of feathers that Molly was pointing to, but as they got closer, they could see a rather ordinary small grey-brown bird huddled among the driftwood not far from Molly's feet. It was cowering close to the sand and quite visibly distressed.

'Has it got a broken wing?' Molly cried. 'Daddy, help it.'

The poor little bird was certainly struggling and one wing did appear to be dangling at an awkward angle. Billie wondered what had happened. Had the bird been grabbed by a hawk? Hit by a car?

Molly reached for her father's hand and gave him a shake as she looked up at him with imploring blue eyes. 'We've got to save him, Daddy. Can we take him to a bird doctor?'

Billie thought this might be quite feasible, actually. If they could catch the bird safely, there were several wildlife carers on the island who could help. She was about to say as much, when Dan, who was watching the bird carefully, shook his head.

'She's okay,' he said. 'She's not hurt. She's a mother sandpiper protecting her eggs. Or maybe her babies.'

'No, she's hurt,' Molly insisted.

'I know she looks hurt, Mollz, but she's acting.'

Molly scowled at her father in disbelief. 'Acting?' she repeated in amazement. 'Like people on TV?'

Billie was pretty amazed, too. She'd never heard of such behaviour from a bird, but Dan seemed quite certain.

'She thinks we want to hurt her babies,' he explained. 'So she's acting hurt to get our attention. She doesn't want us to find them and she's trying to lead us away.'

'Wow,' said Billie. 'How do you know this, Dan?'

'My parents had a fishing shack down at Cungulla. As kids we used to see shorebirds doing this sort of thing.'

'And I've lived on the island all my life and I've never seen it before.'

Molly, however, wasn't nearly as impressed. 'Where are her babies? I can't see them.'

'They're probably still eggs and they'll be hard to find,' said Dan. 'They'll just look like little pieces of rock or wood.'

Intrigued, Billie scanned the stretch of sand strewn with broken coral, pieces of dried seaweed and driftwood. Cautiously, she stepped forward, super careful about where she put her feet. Then, when she least expected it, there they were.

In a bare circle of sand. Two beautiful little speckled eggs, almost the same pale tan as the damp sand, with dark specks like strips of seaweed.

'Here they are,' she cried, but of course the little bird became more agitated now, piping shrilly and dragging her wing, and to Billie's dismay her eyes filled with tears. Again.

She was thinking of her own mum. Small, plain, tough Pearl, ferociously loving, and so scared of losing her precious baby that she'd gone to great lengths to keep danger away, even if that danger had come in the form of a loving aunt and surrogate mother.

From behind her now, she heard Dan call, 'Billie's found them, Molly. Come on. We'll have a quick look and then we're going to shift far away from here so we don't upset their mother.'

Billie was aware of Dan and Molly next to her now, but she was too blinded by tears to see them properly. She was still thinking of her mother, now so ill, of her unborn baby that she longed to see and hold, of Dan's poor wife, Jane, killed so unfairly in a car accident, and now, of this fiercely protective little mother bird . . .

Molly was squatting so she could inspect the eggs.

'Okay.' Dan was taking her hand, urging her upright. 'Let's move away now, so we don't upset the mother.'

'When will the eggs become babies?' Molly was asking as he led her away.

And Billie, stumbling beside them, was so overcome by the whole hugeness of motherhood that she thought her heart might burst.

'Billie's crying,' Molly announced a moment later and Billie, who hadn't brought the paper napkin with her, had to madly swipe at her face.

'I'm okay,' she told them. 'It's just pregnancy hormones.'

Through tear-blurred eyes, she was aware of Dan leaning in to check her, could see his concerned smile. She tried to smile back, but her mouth pulled out of shape. She must have looked hideous.

'Truly,' she said in a voice choked by tears. 'I'm fine.'

'Sure,' he said, but he slipped his arm around her shoulders anyway and gave her a sympathetic hug.

A simple gesture, but incredibly comforting and calming.

Billie blinked to clear the tears. 'Thanks,' she said, and she almost threw her arms around him and gave him a whopping great kiss, just because he was so lovely and understanding. But she behaved herself, which was just as well. She didn't want to give him wrong ideas.

Then they went back to the picnic table where they'd abandoned the remains of their meal, which they wrapped and stowed with their drink cans in the bins. Billie checked the time on her phone. 'Gosh. I'd better get cracking or I'll be late for work.'

'Daddy, can we come back another day to see the baby birds?' Molly was asking.

'Oh, I don't think we'd find them a second time,' her father told her.

'Maybe you can come and see my baby.' Billie couldn't believe she'd said this aloud, but the words were out now and she couldn't take them back.

Molly was staring at her with wide eyes and an open mouth.

'Whoops, sorry,' Billie said to Dan, but luckily he was grinning. Besides, her tummy had really popped out lately, so her pregnancy was hardly a secret.

'Daddy?' Molly was clearly bursting with questions.

But Dan was still smiling at Billie. 'I'll explain,' he told his daughter.

'Sorry,' Billie said again. 'I'd better dash. Oh, and thanks for lunch.'

'Our pleasure. Great that you could join us.' Dan walked with her to her car.

'Daddy!'

'In a minute, Molly. We're saying goodbye to Billie.'

When they reached her car, he said, 'Take care, won't you?'

'I will and thanks again.'

His brown eyes shone with a warmth that made her heart sing. 'See you later.'

'Great.' But she had no idea when that 'later' might be.

CHAPTER THIRTY-SEVEN

'So do you think this wall would be best?' Pearl, with a finger to her pursed lips and her head dipped to one side, studied an expanse of white-painted wall in her restaurant's dining room.

'Probably,' said Freya. 'You'll need to find a spot that can be seen through the windows from the deck as well.'

It was a Tuesday. The restaurant was closed and they were discussing the hanging of a painting that Seb was going to auction to raise money for the local lifesavers. Pearl mightn't have been too keen about hanging Seb's work in Island Thyme if she hadn't owed him a huge favour for filling in as their chef. But now that she'd actually seen the painting, she was quite enchanted.

Executed in Seb's trademark strong colours, it offered a bird's-eye view of Alma Bay, and the Nippers, the junior lifesavers, busy at their training on the beach. Freya had been quite amazed when she'd seen it.

Seb rarely included human figures in his landscapes or seascapes, but he'd done a wonderful job with this, using clever daubs of colour to portray the little Nippers in their bathers and red and yellow swimming caps. Their bodies were, necessarily, foreshortened by the overhead view and at first glance they might have been little crabs, or flowers scattered on the sand. But a closer look showed they were unmistakably children. Busy, mischievous, full of life and purpose.

'The effect's quite gorgeous, isn't it?' Freya enthused.

'It's fascinating,' Pearl agreed. 'And I'm not sleeping with the artist, so I'm not biased,' she added with a sly grin.

Pearl had been smiling quite a bit lately, which was rather wonderful, given the seriousness of her circumstances. Freya, on the other hand, had found it hard to stay cheerful, mainly because she'd seen almost nothing of Seb and she suspected that he was avoiding her.

Retreating . . . echoes of the past.

Since the evening she'd told him about her decision to donate, he'd either been busy collecting art supplies or locked away in his studio producing this masterpiece. Which would have been fine if it hadn't also meant that there'd been no further discussion about her plan.

We'll give it more thought, he'd said, but Freya still had no clue, really, about how his thoughts on the subject were progressing, so she could only assume he was backing away. Again.

'We shouldn't try to hang the painting till Seb gets here,' decided Troy, who'd arrived sensibly equipped with a bag of tools including a hammer, screwdriver and tape measure. 'He'll want to get the right light, or the right height or whatever.'

Standing in front of the painting, legs planted apart, arms folded over his chest, Troy seemed to be studying it, as if he was a learned art critic. But then he turned to Pearl and Freya with a cheeky smile. 'So what's the collective noun for a gathering of Nippers? A confusion of Nippers?'

Pearl obligingly laughed.

'A hilarity of Nippers?' suggested Freya.

'A noise of Nippers?' added Troy. 'A squeal?'

'A shrill?' said a voice from behind them.

In unison they turned and there was Seb. For Freya, the air in the room seemed charged with new energy.

'Ah,' said Pearl. 'The man himself.' And Freya wished she felt calmer.

Fortunately, neither Pearl nor Troy seemed to notice anything amiss with her, although Seb's piercing glance found its mark, landing inside her like an arrow. Discomfited, she kept well in the background as a discussion ensued about the best position for the painting, which was followed by an equally serious discussion, led by Pearl, about the wording of the sign that would accompany the artwork.

'We need to explain that the Nippers are a good cause,' she suggested, earnestly. 'It's not just a group of kids having fun. They're getting an early education about water safety and a good introduction to community service.'

Pearl managed to sound sanctimonious as she made this pronouncement, but no one was inclined to argue, so she offered to type up the sign on her computer and print it out. Then, between them, Troy and Seb set to with tools and tape measure to hang the painting in place. It looked brilliant.

'Great,' said Seb, stepping back and surveying the result, clearly satisfied. Then, turning to Pearl and Troy, he said, 'And while you're both still here, there's something else I'd like to discuss with you and Freya.'

Ping. A nervous tremor zapped through Freya. What on earth could Seb need to discuss with all of them? He was avoiding eye contact with her now, which was hardly a good sign.

'Perhaps if we could sit down?' he said, gesturing with the air of a genteel host towards one of the dining tables.

Seb, what are you doing?

Freya almost refused to join them at the table. She was terribly afraid Seb was about to announce that he couldn't agree to her donation plans. But he wouldn't be so arrogant, surely? It was her body, her decision.

Pearl and Troy were quite obedient, however, sitting where Seb directed, and Freya, reluctantly, followed. When she looked around at the assembled group, she saw restrained curiosity in Pearl and Troy's faces, and cautious determination in Seb's. For her own part, she suspected she looked as nervous as a woman on the edge of a crumbling cliff.

'So,' Seb said smoothly. 'I'll get straight to the point. Freya's told me about your difficult health issues, Pearl, and that she plans to donate a kidney.'

'Yes,' said Pearl, but then she turned to Troy and they exchanged a worried glance.

Freya was beyond worried. She was furious. How dare Seb barge in here all heavy-handed and masterful? 'Seb, you can't do this.' Her voice was too loud, but she was too stressed to make adjustments. 'You have no right.'

'Let him finish,' Pearl said rather sharply.

Somewhat startled by her sister's intervention, Freya closed her mouth, while Seb dipped his head, as if to acknowledge Pearl's support. 'The thing is,' he continued. 'I'm not happy about Freya making yet another generous sacrifice.'

'Neither am I,' said Pearl. 'Not really.'

Troy was frowning, leaning towards Pearl, speaking in an undertone, and Freya was sure he was advising his wife to be cautious, that she mustn't throw away her best chance of recovery.

And good on him. Seb was way out of line.

Freya glared at him. 'You should have spoken to me first. You know I'm a perfect match.' And she might have hammered this point home, if she hadn't seen the way he looked at her then – as if he was sending her an intense silent entreaty.

Or reminding her that this very moment was an uncanny echo of their past when he'd said those exact words —

You should have spoken to me first.

Somewhat shaken, she sat back and remained silent as Seb continued.

'Look,' he said. 'I understand this is primarily a family matter, but the thing is, I've been to the Townsville hospital and I've had the tests.'

Ignoring Freya's shocked gasp, Seb continued now in a voice of quiet authority. 'I received the last of the results this morning and I'm ninety-nine percent certain I'd be a good match for you, Pearl.' He held out both hands, palms up. 'Which means you have options.'

Freya gasped again, but could find no air. It was as if she'd dived too deep and could no longer find her way back to the sea's surface.

'You, Seb?' Pearl was saying. 'But why would you —'

And then Freya managed to drag in air in an embarrassingly noisy, gulping gasp, so loud that the others all stared at her.

'Sorry,' she said. 'I guess I got a shock.'

'And I should apologise for dropping the news on you out of the blue.' Seb's smile was gentle.

The shoe was well and truly on the other foot, Freya realised, and she didn't like it at all.

'I didn't want to say anything until I found out if I was suitable,' Seb went on. 'But my blood group is O positive, which means I'm pretty much anybody's when it comes to matching, and now I've passed all the other health checks as well. We would need to talk to your renal specialist, of course, Pearl, but the doctors I've spoken to seem to think I should be fine to donate.'

'But there's no need,' protested Freya. 'I'm perfectly —'

Seb raised a hand to halt her. 'I think we all agree that you've already been very generous, Freya.'

Pearl and Troy both nodded.

'But this is different,' she said.

'It is,' Seb agreed. 'Pearl's health is the most important issue here. And an important fact I've learned is that males often make better kidney donors than females.'

'Goodness,' said Pearl.

The room was silent now as they absorbed this. The only sound came from parrots bickering in a palm tree outside. And now tears glistened in Pearl's eyes, and Troy, who had his arm around her shoulders, looked close to tears, too.

Freya, quite sideswiped, slumped in her chair. She wasn't sure what to think or feel. So many emotions and thoughts churned through her. Seb's offer was beyond anything she'd ever imagined. It was crazy. He was prepared to undergo major surgery. For her sister's sake.

And for my sake, too.

She knew this was so. Seb wanted to protect her, to save her from possible danger in the future. And while he'd never actually told her that he loved her – not in so many words – she was all too aware that mere words could be hollow. Brian had claimed to love her when he clearly hadn't. This action, however, this offer of Seb's spoke more loudly than words ever could.

It was some time before the profuse thanks and tears and hugs were over. Seb would make an appointment with Pearl to see her specialist in Brisbane, and now Pearl and Troy, overwhelmed and grateful, had gone home.

Freya and Seb lingered on the restaurant's deck, leaning against the balustrade, arms on the railing, elbows touching as they looked out to the sleepy bay.

'I've never played chess,' Freya said, watching a majestic eagle circle the headland. 'But I suppose this is what it feels like to be checkmated.'

Seb frowned. 'You think this was some kind of contest?'

'Actually, no. Sorry. I didn't mean that at all. It's just that you caught me out completely. I never dreamed you'd do such an amazing thing.'

'Perhaps I know a woman who has set me a very good example.'

A rush of emotion filled her then, happiness tangled with gratitude and fear. *Please stay safe, Seb. I can't lose you again.*

A fresh breeze washed in from the sea, bringing the scents of salt and coral, and blowing her hair over her face. As she tucked it behind her ear, she smiled at him. 'And perhaps I know a shining gem of a man.'

CHAPTER THIRTY-EIGHT

Billie had found the cutest little A-frame house available for rent. It wasn't a unit in a block of flats, but a tiny standalone house set back behind a wonderful jungle of a garden. With its own small deck, it offered a kitchen, living room and bathroom on the ground floor and a loft bedroom above.

'It's gorgeous, isn't it?' she enthused to Freya, whom she'd invited to accompany her for an inspection.

Freya eyed the narrow ladder up to the bedroom. 'Would you really want to scale that thing with a baby in your arms?'

Billie wasn't prepared to admit that she'd asked herself this very question. She wanted this house. She loved it so much more than any of the flats she'd seen, which were all too small, or too shabby or too close to noisy pubs and bars.

'I can carry the baby in one of those slings,' she said. 'It would be quite safe.'

'But what about when your little one starts to crawl and climb?'

'I'd have one of those gates at the top of the ladder and – I don't know – a playpen or something at the bottom.'

'Hmmm.' Freya still didn't look too impressed, which was rather annoying. Fussing over a ladder was the sort of protest Billie expected from her parents. And avoiding such quibbles was one of the main reasons she'd delayed this inspection until they were away in Brisbane with Seb for their pre-surgery interview at the hospital.

Billie had hoped Freya might enjoy the distraction from worrying about Seb, but she'd also hoped her aunt might be an ally, and fall in love with this little house. In so many ways, it was perfect – private and affordable and cute as pie.

She could absolutely see herself and Pickle living here. It was close to her parents, but not too close. And she'd been reading on the internet about the tiny house movement that was growing in popularity all over the world, as part of a shift away from the consumerist mindsets of the past. It seemed there were countless reasons why she could feel good about living here.

Why should one little ladder be a problem? She'd be careful.

'What about when you're in the last few weeks of your pregnancy?' Freya asked now in a stern voice that was totally out of character. 'It won't be long now before you find yourself growing absolutely enormous.'

'But I won't be feeble.'

Freya still shook her head. 'I'm sorry, Billie. I think this place is very sweet. I can understand the appeal and the garden's lovely —'

'Yes,' Billie jumped in. 'The garden's gorgeous and I could grow my own herbs and vegetables.'

'Yes, you could, although I'm not sure how much spare time you'll have once the baby arrives. But even so – I'm sorry – that ladder's just too dangerous,' Freya finished firmly.

Dismayed, Billie folded her arms, propping them on her ballooning belly. She'd so wanted this place to be perfect. She loved the pretty but functional kitchen with its blue glass tiles above the tiny gas stovetop, and she adored the nifty bathroom tucked at the back. And the sitting area had a perfect space for spreading the baby's rug. She could picture her little one lying there on the patchwork blanket that Pearl was making, chubby legs kicking, grinning up at her, and learning to roll over.

But she had to admit, the front deck, while almost at ground level, would probably need some kind of railing. And that ladder was a bit of a risk, she supposed. *Damn it.*

'Have you considered looking for a place in Townsville?' Freya asked.

Dan had asked Billie this same question when he'd phoned for a chat. He'd been busy investigating a murder on a farm west of the city, and his mum had been minding Molly more than usual, but he'd still made time to contact Billie. He'd even asked if she might be free for dinner or a movie.

'Sometime next week?' he'd said. 'You could stay at my place, by the way. I have a spare room, so you wouldn't have to rush back to catch the ferry.'

So typical of Dan to issue an invitation that gave her options. Billie was incredibly tempted. And, if she was honest, when it came to thinking about her future, Dan Dexter had become a definite distraction.

Each day seemed to find her more confused. So many issues were at play. Her mother's health and her loyalty to her parents. Her desire to stake a claim for independence. And now, to add to the mix, sneaky thoughts of how happy she was whenever she was with Dan. She knew, instinctively, he was the kind of guy a girl could trust, and she was beginning to realise that trust might very well be the most important ingredient in a relationship.

Watching her, Freya said, 'I'm guessing that fellow you had lunch with last week probably lives on the mainland?'

Billie blinked in astonishment. 'Have you been spying on me?'

'Of course not. You were at a picnic table at Geoffrey Bay – out in the open for all the world to see – and I happened to drive past.'

Yikes. 'That was Dan Dexter.'

Freya frowned. 'The name rings a bell.'

'He's a detective.'

'The detective who took you to Cairns?'

'Yes.'

Her aunt's eyes gleamed with unabashed curiosity now. 'You're a dark horse, Billie. So you've been seeing him all this time?'

'No, not really. Not seeing him, exactly. Well, yes, sort of.'

Freya's smile was far too knowing. 'Good for you.'

'It's not serious, Freya. We're not really dating.' Not yet, at any rate. 'Dan's a widower. He has a little girl called Molly. And he understands that I'm not looking for —' Billie gave a helpless flap of her hands as she searched for the best way to explain. 'He knows that I plan to be a single mum.'

'I see.' Freya sounded more amused than approving. 'Well, at any rate,' she went on, 'you shouldn't rule out living in Townsville. You'd still be close enough to see Pearl and Troy regularly, and now that most of the people who were flooded last year have been able to move back into their homes, there are oodles of rental places coming back on the market.'

Yes, Billie had seen the ads in the newspaper.

She looked around again at the interior of the little A-frame. She'd spent the past few days weaving happy dreams about living in this space, but already she could sense it was losing its hold on her.

'I'm beginning to think I should maybe wait until after the baby's born before I make a definite decision,' she said.

'That's probably a very good idea.'

'The first step is getting Mum well again, of course.'

'Yes.' Freya looked as if she was trying to smile but couldn't quite manage it. She was worrying about Seb, of course, and Billie was instantly ashamed that she'd been fretting over the minor matter of accommodation when her family had so much at stake.

'Freya, Seb's going to be all right.'

'Yes, yes, I know he is.' But she looked agonised.

'It's an amazing thing that he's doing for Mum.'

Freya nodded and made another effort to smile. 'Were there any other places you wanted to see today?'

'No, thanks.'

They went back outside. Billie closed the front door, which was painted blue, and locked it. Linking her arm with her aunt's, they walked together back through the garden filled with bougainvillea and flowering gingers.

She was quite sure that Freya's life was going to be wonderful. Totally. Seb had confided to Billie that he wanted to take Freya back to Spain, but he was also happy to spend more time here on the island, or anywhere else she wanted to live. Spectacular happiness awaited her aunt, and no one deserved it more. They just had to get through the next few weeks.

CHAPTER THIRTY-NINE

Waking in a Brisbane hotel on the day before the surgery, Freya experienced a gnawing, sickening anxiety like nothing she'd ever known. Even though this day was merely the pre-surgical admission and tomorrow was the big day, she couldn't suppress the panic.

Of course, she'd told herself that the surgeons were bloody brilliant and that Seb would sail through this procedure and so would Pearl. Last week they'd had their final tests to make sure they were both still healthy and ready for the surgery, so every care had been taken. She knew she was being overly emotional, blown away by the enormity of Seb's generosity.

For his part, Seb had remained quite calm. Already, he was up and Freya could hear the shower running. Throwing off the covers, she swung her feet over the edge of the bed. She would make herself a cup of tea, but they weren't going to bother with breakfast. Just as well, she didn't have the stomach for food. Maybe later, she'd have something in the hospital cafeteria with Troy. They had two difficult days to fill.

As the kettle hummed to life, Freya crossed to the window and drew the curtains. Their room was many floors above the ground, but any chance of a view was obstructed by the surrounding tall buildings. She looked down to the street way below where steady streams of traffic flowed, cars and buses, small as toys. There were also joggers and cyclists and a few people, already dressed for work, hurrying along pavements, getting on with their day. Their nice normal day.

Not like mine. Fear vibrated inside her, sending fine tremors under her skin, and she wished the day was already over.

Her nervousness had started yesterday as their flight descended into Brisbane. Even though it had only been a few months since she'd left this busiest corner of the state, she'd become surprisingly accustomed to the sleepy quietness of life on Magnetic Island, to the simplicity of having only one narrow road that wound from bay to bay.

To Freya's surprise, the sudden sight of motorways and overpasses crowded with traffic, of skyscrapers and endless suburbs stretching as far as the eye could see, had felt alien and somehow threatening. Her tension had mounted as their taxi sped into the depths of the city.

Now the kettle boiled and she poured the steaming water over a teabag in a mug. The only milk available was one of those little long-life capsules that tasted artificial, but it would have to do. She didn't normally take sugar, but today she tore open a slim packet and added it to the mug. It would help disguise the milk. And the circumstances seemed to demand at least one small indulgence.

Sinking into an upholstered armchair that was gratifyingly comfortable, Freya crossed her legs, took a sip of the warm tea and closed her eyes, waiting for the beverage to work its universally lauded calming magic. But closing her eyes was dangerous.

Cut off from her new surroundings, her mind winged straight back to memories of Seb in their youth and to those heady days in their late teens when she'd first discovered that her schoolgirl crush was not a one-sided affair, but a fabulous mutual attraction.

And then the later years, that happy, carefree time in their early twenties, when they'd moved from the island into a tiny rented flat in South Townsville, working part-time jobs while Seb studied art at James Cook University and Freya undertook a business course at TAFE. They'd been quite busy with their study and their jobs and they hadn't had much spare cash, but they'd had tons of friends and could party on a shoestring. Freya had been quite sure she could see their happy future unwinding like a smooth and shining ribbon in front of them.

Until the weekend they'd returned to the island for her mother's birthday, and Freya had heard the latest chapter in the ongoing saga of Pearl and Troy's infertility.

Her eyes flashed open now, snapping her back to the present, to solemn reality. If she'd learned anything in the intervening years, she knew that life was all about the choices a person made. Every choice, big or small, shaped the person you became. Yet now it seemed that despite their quite different choices, her life and Seb's had come full circle.

Her only problem was that she found it hard to trust her new-found happiness. After the roller-coaster of her divorce and the fire, there were times when her renewed relationship with Seb seemed just too miraculous to be true.

'Good morning, Sunshine.'

Seb's voice saved Freya from drowning in these downward-spiralling thoughts, and she made sure she was smiling before she turned to greet him. 'Morning, Seb.'

Freshly showered and shaved, he looked admirably calm and relaxed. When Freya kissed him, she gave him an extra tight hug, burying her face in his chest and breathing in the lingering traces of the hotel's expensive soap that clung to his skin.

Her hapless mind flashed a picture of tomorrow when he would be wheeled on a trolley through the swing doors of an operating theatre, and a mighty lurch of longing threatened to erupt from her in a groan of despair. Despair for all the lost years, fear that something might go wrong now, that they would be denied the chance to make up for the past.

'Are you okay?' Seb asked, dropping a kiss on the top of her head.

'Yes,' she lied, but she couldn't look up at him. 'How about you?'

'I'm fine,' he said. 'Fighting fit.'

His smile was gorgeous and she made a deliberate effort to banish mental pictures of him lying on the operating table, unconscious. Vulnerable. Sliced open.

She smiled back at him, which was at least a step in the right direction. Today she hoped to keep that smile in place. If life was about choices, today, heaven help her, she *chose* to be brave.

Fear came in many forms, but so did courage. No more wimpy imaginings were allowed.

'I guess I'd better get ready, too,' she said, retrieving the mug and draining the last of her tea. Pearl and Troy were bound to be dressed and waiting, anxious to get to the hospital, so Freya showered and dressed in record time and vowed, with fresh determination, to ignore the hollowness in her stomach.

When she returned, dressed and ready, Seb was calmly watching the morning news. Donald Trump and Iran seemed to be the story of the moment. Again. He switched the TV off as soon as he saw her.

'All set?'

Freya nodded.

'Good. I've had a text from Pearl. They've already left for the hospital.'

'Gosh. Am I holding things up?'

'Not at all. I guess they were anxious, but there's no rush. We have plenty of time.'

Crossing the room, Seb took Freya's hands in his and seemed about to say something when he was distracted. His gaze dropped to her fingers, which he held lightly in his. 'What's this?'

He was staring at her ring – the ring he'd given her. She'd remembered to bring it with her and in the bathroom just now she'd slipped it onto the fourth finger of her left hand. She wasn't quite sure why – as a good luck charm, perhaps?

'Do you remember it?' she asked, feeling slightly overcome by her audacity. 'It doesn't look quite the same, of course. It was damaged in the fire.'

Seb was frowning as he stared at the small diamond, no longer shining, but clouded and cracked. Then he blinked, as if to clear his eyes. His Adam's apple jerked as he swallowed. 'You kept it?' His voice was rough around the edges.

'Of course I kept it, Seb. You wouldn't take it back and I couldn't bring myself to sell it.'

His mouth was contorted now as he gave the diamond a gentle rub with his thumb. 'And you found it after the fire?'

'I did, yes.'

'How on earth?'

'By scrambling about in the ash and debris.'

'Freya.' So much emotion was conveyed in that single word.

'It wasn't easy to find, but I'd always kept it in a drawer in my bedside table, so I had a rough idea where it might be. I was pretty damn determined.'

Tears glistened in Seb's eyes now. 'Thanks,' he said in a choked voice. 'That – that's a good thought to hold on to today.' And then he was hugging her, binding her close, as if she was the most valuable thing on earth, and her heart swelled to bursting point as it pounded against his.

*

'I'll buy you another ring,' Seb said as the lift began its descent to the ground floor.

A small laugh escaped Freya, born of conflicting emotions. Joy, disbelief, amusement, shock. 'Not an engagement ring?'

'Why not?' Seb looked surprised and she felt caught out by her own reaction, scrambling for some kind of explanation.

'Aren't we a little old for engagements?'

'I didn't know there were age limits.'

She gave another shy little laugh. 'Well, no, I don't suppose there are.' And then, 'But shouldn't some kind of proposal come first?'

'You're dead right,' Seb responded, and to her complete astonishment, he dropped to one knee in front of her.

'What are you doing?' she cried as the lift continued its downward rush. This was Seb. Alpha male. Man of the world. Slayer of hearts.

'Will you marry me, Freya?'

'Seb, don't be —'

At that very moment, the lift reached the ground floor and its doors slid open.

Ta da.

An elderly couple waiting outside were obviously quite startled to discover a man on bended knee with a hand pressed to his heart. A flustered glance beyond this pair showed Freya the hotel's marble foyer where expensively suited businessmen and women were scattered in sedate groups or in patient queues. A jeans-clad family, clearly travellers, were heading towards the lift, followed by a valet and a trolley laden with luggage.

All this she saw in an instant, as people turned to stare at them. Eyes popping, mouths gaping, delighted smiles sparkling.

Ignoring all of this, Seb remained on his knee, keeping his focus entirely on Freya. 'Will you?' he asked her again.

There had only ever been one possible answer. 'Yes, of course,' she told him, wondering why she didn't feel more embarrassed.

With a huge grin, Seb sprang to his feet and reached for her hand. It was only as he scooped up his overnight bag and they stepped out of the lift that he seemed to notice the amused onlookers. Raising his hand clasped with Freya's in a gesture of triumph, he grinned at their impromptu audience. 'She said yes!'

'Onya mate,' shouted a guy in maintenance overalls.

'*Felicidades!*' called a smiling, dark-eyed girl, who might have been Spanish.

There was even a small scattering of cheers and applause.

'You're an idiot,' Freya told him, turning her face into his shoulder to hide her happy blush.

But she and Seb were grinning from ear to ear as they floated, hand in hand, across the foyer and out through the sliding glass doors to the waiting taxi.

CHAPTER FORTY

By the mutual consent of everyone concerned, Island Thyme was closed on the day of the surgery. Billie was relieved. She wasn't sure she could have kept serving customers and smiling if she'd also been fretting and anxious about her mum. But this decision to close was followed by another welcome surprise. Dan had managed to organise time off as well.

'I thought you might need a distraction,' he said when he phoned. 'If you can make it over to Townsville, we could see a movie in the morning and have lunch on The Strand and then maybe hang out at my place in the afternoon.'

Despite her goal of independence, Billie couldn't help feeling grateful for his invitation, although she would have liked to be clearer about Dan's motives. She knew he wasn't merely playing the good Samaritan, but spending a day with her couldn't really be classed as a date. Not when she was pregnant with another man's child.

At any rate, she didn't hesitate. 'I'd love that,' she told him, and she truly meant it. She would go mental if she had to spend the nail-biting day alone, and Dan would be the perfect companion. 'Thanks so much.'

The night before the surgery she spent on her own, with only Won Ton for company. A sort of freedom, perhaps, and useful practice for her planned single parent lifestyle, so it made no sense that she was restless. She didn't only worry about her mum and Seb, but also that some dramatic development in the Townsville crime scene would mean that Dan had to work after all. The detectives on television never seemed to have time for any kind of social life.

But there was no sudden text message from Dan calling off their rendezvous, and Billie was up bright and early. She considered dressing up for the occasion, but was wary of sending the wrong message, so she wore her trusty maternity jeans and a plain, pin-tucked white smock. At the last minute she added flattering pink lipstick, but she didn't bother with other makeup, or 'war paint' as her dad had always called it.

She rang her mum before she left.

'I'm fine,' Pearl told her, and she sounded unusually bright, almost excited. 'All prepped and ready. The staff here are wonderful.'

'I'm sure they are,' said Billie. 'You're in very safe hands.'

'I am, darling. How are you?'

'Fabulous, thanks.' Billie decided not to mention her plans for the day. Her mother hadn't met Dan and the explanations might be unsettling. 'Love you, Mum.'

'Love you, too, darling. Take care, won't you? And don't worry about me. I'll be fine.'

'Okay.'

The confidence in her mother's voice was reassuring, but when Billie arrived at the Townsville jetty and saw Dan standing there, she experienced an even higher level of reassurance in his now familiar features. And when she stepped off the ramp and onto the wharf and Dan greeted her with a smile, his deep-brown eyes were so lively and warm that her heart gave a weirdly painful flip.

*

'Mum will be halfway through her surgery by now.'

'I'm sure it's going well.'

'Yes, of course. I'm feeling better than I thought I would, actually.' Billie smiled at her companion. 'Thanks to you.'

She and Dan were sitting at a restaurant table that offered a fresh sea breeze and views across Cleveland Bay. The movie they'd chosen had been most enjoyable – an amusing, farcical whodunnit, the perfect distraction – and with their delicious meal finished, they were lingering over another round of drinks, a cold beer for Dan and a lemon, lime and bitters for Billie.

'I feel sorry for Freya and Dad,' she said. 'So awful for them to have to spend the day hanging about at the hospital.'

'I imagine Seb should be back in recovery soon.'

'I hope so. Freya promised she'd let me know.' Billie checked her phone again in case she'd been too busy eating and chatting to hear the ping of an incoming text, but nothing had arrived. She gave a small huff of impatience as she set the phone aside. 'Enough of my family dramas. Tell me more about you, Dan.'

He looked mildly amused. 'What would you like to know about me?'

Why are you spending so much time with me when I'm the size of a house and there's no chance of us jumping into bed?

Perhaps, if Billie had been on her second or third glass of wine, a question like this might have tumbled from her, but she was stone-cold sober, thus inclined to be cautious. She longed to know more about Dan's wife, about his marriage, about his plans, but such questions felt too invasive. Too intimate.

'Oh, I don't know,' she said lamely. 'I guess I'm just looking forward to seeing where you live.'

'That's easy,' he said. 'If you finish your drink I'll show you. I need to get back anyway. Mum will be delivering Molly soonish.'

*

Dan's home, Billie soon discovered, was at Pallarenda, one of Townsville's beachside suburbs. The house was neat, low-set, pale brick, with a shady garden. All very practical and low maintenance, but not boringly so, with an open-plan kitchen and living area, ceramic tiled floors and sliding glass doors opening onto a tiled back patio that overlooked a well-treed nature reserve. The furnishings were simple and comfortable, with well-cushioned sofas in soft sand tones that were echoed in the bleached timber shelves and tables.

Touches of Molly's presence were everywhere in the form of brightly coloured children's books stacked on a low shelf, an overflowing toy box in a corner and the almost mandatory cushion in the shape of a seahorse. Billie felt immediately at home and she might have been effusive if she wasn't being so cautious. She didn't want to act like a woman with plans to move in.

She was sitting on a sofa, thumbing through a travel magazine, and Dan was making cuppas in the kitchen when his mother arrived with Molly.

'Helloo,' the woman called, smiling brightly as she pushed open the insect screen and came through the open front doorway without bothering to knock. 'You must be Billie,' she said straight away, offering Billie a warm grin as she held out her hand. 'Dan doesn't tell me much about his work, but he managed to mention that you were a great witness in Cairns. I'm Grace, by the way. How do you do?'

Billie wasn't sure what she'd expected, but Grace Dexter was a surprise. Remarkably attractive with a glowing, smooth complexion that belied her age, high cheekbones and a wonderfully wild mop of silvery curls. She was dressed in a trendy loose grey linen shift with a chunky coral necklace at her throat, and she looked quite marvellous.

'Hello,' Billie said as her hand was gripped warmly. 'Nice to meet you, Grace.' She meant it, having experienced one of those instantaneous reactions of feeling completely at ease with a brand-new acquaintance.

'Billie!' squealed a small voice, and the next moment Molly rushed out from behind her grandmother to hug Billie, a rather difficult undertaking, given the little girl's short height and Billie's huge tummy.

Kneeling, Billie accepted a squeezing hug and a sticky kiss on the cheek. 'Hello there, Miss Molly.'

'The baby in your tummy's getting bigger,' the little girl told her.

'Yes, it is rather, isn't it?'

'Molly!' warned a reproachful Dan from the kitchen. 'That's not very polite.'

Grace merely chuckled. 'You can always trust a child to tell it like it is. By the way, Dan, Molly's already had a little after-lunch nap, so I'm afraid she's full of beans.' Then, with an apologetic grin and a roll of dark eyes that were very like Dan's, she said, 'I'm sorry, but I have to dash, or I'll be late for my book club.'

Setting down a bulging shoulder bag that obviously contained toys and changes of clothes for Molly, she blew a kiss in the direction of the kitchen. 'I'll love you and leave you, Dan.'

'Thanks, Mum.' Dan came around the counter and kissed her cheek. And then, with another smiling wave for Billie and Molly, Grace was gone.

Such a relaxed and fuss-free encounter.

Having experienced a lifetime of reserve and caution from her own mum, Billie couldn't help but be impressed. She supposed Dan had inherited his mum's agreeable nature, and she might have made a comment along these lines, but just then she heard a text message arrive on her phone. A quick glance showed it was from Freya.

Her heart leapt to her throat as she clicked on it.

Seb's out of surgery and he's fine. Scary number of tubes attached to him, but that's to be expected. Sleeping off the anaesthetic.

I also quizzed a nurse and all seems to be going well with Pearl. Hang in there. Love, Freya xx

'Seb's out of surgery and he's fine,' Billie called to Dan. 'And everything's going well so far for Mum.'

Dan was pouring boiling water into mugs, but he set the kettle aside. 'That's great news.' And then he came to her and took her in his arms.

It was only a hug, a reassuring and comforting hug, but it reinforced for Billie how very much she liked this man, and how good it would be to let her head sink onto his sturdy shoulder, to press her face against the warmth of his neck. She was pretty sure it would only take a small signal from her before he —

'Don't you paint your toenails?' demanded a small voice at floor level.

Molly was squatting on the floor, her little forehead creased by a puzzled frown as she studied Billie's sandalled feet.

Billie grinned down at her. 'Not any more.' She patted her tummy. 'It's too hard to reach past my bump.'

'Daddy!' Molly cried, frowning up at her father. 'We should paint Billie's toenails.'

'No, it's okay,' Billie assured the child, wishing she could stay in Dan's arms a little longer. But he'd already released her, so she sent a quick message back to Freya.

Such a relief. So good to hear. Love you and thanks for letting me know. B xx

Settling once more on the sofa, Billie also considered sending a text to her dad, but Molly was clearly on a mission.

'Your toes would look pretty with nail polish, Billie. Come on, Daddy. We can fix them.'

'Let Billie enjoy her drink,' Dan told his daughter as he handed Billie a steaming mug of peppermint tea.

'She can drink her tea while we paint her nails,' decided Molly. 'I'll get the polish.' Without waiting for a response, she scampered off, disappearing down the hallway.

'Molly!' Dan called after her, but there was no reply.

'Sorry about this,' he said, shaking his head as he turned back to Billie. 'But don't worry. I won't let her make a mess of your feet.'

'I don't really mind.'

'No, don't encourage her. She'd be a disaster.'

'Actually, I thought your mother was the toenail-painting expert.' Billie could well imagine that Grace Dexter kept her own feet looking stylish.

'Oh, she most certainly is,' said Dan. 'But little kids can be so confident. Unjustifiably confident, of course. Molly was convinced she could play the violin after just a couple of music sessions at kindergarten.'

'Oh, well,' said Billie. 'I guess it's better than being shy and bashful.'

'Maybe,' he said. 'At least school next year will bring her face to face with reality.'

As he said this, Molly returned with a bottle of sparkly blue polish and a towel.

'Oh, that settles it,' said Dan. 'You can't give Billie blue toes. I know for a fact that she wouldn't want that.'

'No, no, the blue would look great. Wouldn't it, Billie?'

'Well . . .' Billie began tentatively, not sure how to answer. She didn't really mind. Blue was her favourite colour and nail polish remover was readily available.

Already Molly was kneeling, spreading the towel beneath Billie's feet and then shaking the little bottle of polish, ready to start work.

'Hang on, Mollz. Careful. Maybe I should do that.'

The little girl looked up at her father in amazement. So did Billie.

'But you don't know how to,' Molly told him.

'I painted the bathroom, didn't I? If I can paint a bathroom, I'm sure I can paint a toenail or ten.'

Billie might have protested, but Molly was clearly impressed by her father's boast and quite happily surrendered the bottle. A beat later, Dan was kneeling on the carpet beside Billie's feet, and by then she was overcome with curiosity to see how he'd cope with the challenge he'd set himself. Besides, the thought of him touching her feet was kind of mesmerising.

'Is there an undercoat that goes on first?' Dan asked as she took off her sandals. His eyes held a glint of amusement and something else. A hint of smoulder, perhaps?

Billie's throat was tight with a new, inexplicable tension and she had to swallow before she could answer. 'Just the colour will be fine, thanks.'

And then she felt a little breathless as Dan positioned himself on the floor at her feet, but she couldn't help smiling as she watched his concentration while he shook the little pot of polish, then unscrewed the lid and extracted the tiny brush.

With his other hand he picked up her foot. *Oh, help.* The touch of his hand cradling her heel was way sexier than it should have been. Flashes of heat shimmied up her leg.

Just as well Molly was there, watching them both with excited amazement.

'Hey, Daddy, you really can do it.'

'Told you,' said Dan, but he wasn't looking at his daughter. He was looking directly at Billie and the message in his eyes burned.

*

Somehow they got through the toenail painting. Dan did a creditable job and his skills were praised to the skies. Billie survived without going into labour, although she was quite sure that at least some of the physical sensations she experienced involved Braxton Hicks contractions. So bloody ridiculous. She had no idea that a woman so heavily pregnant could also be turned on by a man touching her feet.

And Molly, bless her, seemed to be in raptures over the whole process.

Once Billie's nails were quite dry, they headed for the beach, which was only half a block away, and they hadn't quite reached it when Billie received another phone call.

'Hello, Billie.'

'Dad.' Her grip on the phone matched the sudden tightness in her chest. 'How are you? How's Mum?'

'We're good, love. The surgery's over and Mum came through like a champion.'

'Oh.' A gasp of relief. 'That's fantastic.'

'Yeah. The surgeon came and spoke to me. He said the kidney's in place and everything's working and Pearl was making urine on the table.'

'Oh, Dad, that's wonderful.' She sent Dan a thumbs up signal. 'You must be so relieved.'

'Yeah. We've got a lot to be grateful for.'

'We certainly have.'

'And how are you, love?'

'Oh, I'm fine, thanks. I've been thinking of you all day.' She didn't like to admit that she'd also been enjoying herself, despite the worry. 'Give my love to Mum, won't you?'

'I will, love. You'll probably be able to ring her tomorrow.'

'Oh, I will, definitely.'

They said their goodbyes and Billie let out another breath of pure relief. For a moment, the view ahead of her went misty, but she couldn't think why on earth she would cry when everything had turned out so well. Sniffing, she wiped at her eyes with the backs of her hands and joined Dan and Molly, who were waiting to cross the road.

'All good,' she told Dan, and he took her hand in his while Molly held his other hand and together they crossed to the beach. Here they were met by a welcome stiff breeze, sand and seagulls and the smell of salt in the air. Billie could see across the bay to the island and there was also a view down the beach that stretched in a long curve to Townsville's Kissing Point and then on to Cape Cleveland south of the port. Billie stood, taking it in, enjoying the overarching sky, the murmur of the sea, the pale sand backed by tea trees and palms, and Castle Hill standing like a sentinel guarding the city.

'Why would you need to come over to the island when you have this lovely beach almost on your doorstep?' she asked Dan.

He looked at her and she saw the leap of light in his eyes as he smiled. 'Can't you guess?' he said.

And then she knew.

CHAPTER FORTY-ONE

On the day Billie went into labour, she rang her mother. Or at least she tried to, although Pearl wasn't aware of this at the time. Freya was spending most of her time with Seb these days, but on this particular afternoon she was helping Pearl with the bistro's book-work, a task she had continued with during Pearl's recovery. Meanwhile, Billie had gone for a walk.

'Don't go too far,' Pearl had warned her. 'There's a storm on the way.' But Billie had just shaken her head and laughed at such fussing, saying she still had three weeks till her due date and she'd go stir crazy if she had to sit around the house all afternoon.

'I'll keep an eye on the weather,' she'd promised, and the sisters, who had been tiptoeing slowly, cautiously, towards a new kind of closeness, returned their attention to Pearl's laptop and the piles of bills and receipts.

It was only when this work was completed and Freya suggested a cuppa that they lifted their heads and became aware of the dark, menacing clouds outside, and the wind whipping the sea into choppy waves.

Rising stiffly from her chair, Pearl went to the window to peer out at the cliffs and the track Billie had taken. She sighed. 'She should be back by now.'

'Yes,' agreed Freya.

'I suppose she's all right.'

'Well, yes, she'll be fine. She knows that track like the back of her hand and she's taken her phone.'

'But there are spots all over that track where the network drops out.'

'Oh?' Freya felt a flurry of concern now. She decided they should at least try to phone Billie, but when she did so, she could only get Billie's voice message. 'Perhaps I should go and just make sure she's all right?'

Pearl's tense shoulders lifted in a shrug. 'She hates us fussing.'

'I know.'

Pearl turned from the window with her arms tightly crossed as if she was hugging herself. Her forehead was deeply wrinkled with worry. 'Of course this would have to happen as soon as Troy started back at work.'

Freya shrugged. 'Sod's law.' She was trying to stay calm, but Billie had been gone rather a long time. Now from outside came a roll of thunder followed by a lightning flash and, almost immediately, rain began to fall.

'Oh, God.' Pearl was hugging herself even more tightly now and her eyes were huge with worry.

That settled it. 'I'll go and check on her,' Freya said. 'At least I can take her a raincoat.'

'Yes, that's a good idea. Thanks, Freya.'

In a matter of moments she was ready and armed with a spare raincoat. It was too windy outside to bother with an umbrella, so she tied a scarf around her head. It wouldn't hold off the rain, but at least it would keep her hair out of her face.

Poor Won Ton had been cowering behind the sofa ever since the first thunderclap, but now she whined in protest at being abandoned. 'Sorry, sweetheart.'

'Come here, Won Ton.' Pearl, with a remarkable show of sympathy, scooped up the little dog and actually cuddled her close, making soothing noises and promising her a treat.

Astonished, Freya slipped out the door, marvelling at her sister's change of heart, but as rain needled her face, her focus was on finding Billie.

Hunched in the rain and hugging her swollen belly, Billie couldn't believe she'd been so stupid. She'd taken such care of herself throughout her entire pregnancy. She'd been a bloody martyr going all those months with no alcohol or coffee, and now, on this most crucial of days, when her baby was choosing to be born, she'd walked way too far and had found herself caught in a storm. Terrified and in pain.

Horrible, horrible pain.

Over the past few weeks, she'd experienced plenty of Braxton Hicks contractions, but the midwife had assured her they were merely signs that her body was getting ready, so today, when she'd felt the first few pangs, she'd never dreamed they were the start of actual labour. She still had three weeks to go, for fuck's sake, and she'd been warned that first babies were often late.

It wasn't until she was quite some distance from home and on a clifftop perched above dark, angry seas that she'd realised the pains were getting closer and stronger.

I'm so sorry, little Pickle. This wasn't what I'd planned for you at all.

Of course Billie had turned back as soon as she'd realised her mistake, but walking on the uneven track was suddenly much more uncomfortable than it had been before. The baby seemed to have slipped lower in her pelvis and the pain – *oh, dear God, the pain* – was like nothing Billie had ever known or imagined. Huge and cruel, gripping her with a vice-like force. And the deep, slow breathing exercises that she'd practised at the antenatal classes were no help at all.

Nobody had warned her that it would be this bad. And, damn it, the rain was getting heavier.

Her clothes and her hair were soaked through. Worse, she'd seen no sign of anyone else on the track, probably because no one else would be stupid enough to set out on this path when a storm was on the way.

Billie thought about ringing home, but what was the point? Her mum and Freya would freak if they knew her situation, and even if they rushed out here to help her, what could they do? They weren't midwives. Billie knew with sickening certainty that her only option was to keeping walking between the contractions. But, oh, God, what a marathon it was going to be. Could she make it?

Another pain cut in – deeper, harder, lower. Billie groaned aloud. *Bloody hell!* She'd wanted independence, but not like this. Perhaps she'd better ring her mum after all. But when she tried to use her phone, a message informed her she was out of the network's reach. *Shit.* As she faced this inescapable reality, she was drenched by very real fear. What if she ended up having the baby out here? All alone in the rain?

'Oh, Pickle,' she whispered, close to tears. 'I'm so sorry.'

Ahead of her, the track was turning soft in the sheeting rain, but she had no choice but to struggle on.

It was some minutes later, as she was rounding a huge boulder, that she heard a voice. 'Billie!'

Peering, she could just make out a figure in a raincoat hurrying towards her. 'Freya?' she whispered.

'Oh, dear God,' cried her aunt. 'I'm so glad I found you. But what's happened? Are you okay?'

Before Billie could answer, another contraction gripped her, then consumed her, driving every other thought from her head. It was only when it finally stopped that she realised Freya's arms were about her and that she'd probably been moaning.

'Darling, you poor thing,' murmured Freya as she lifted wet strands of Billie's hair from her face. 'When did this start?'

'I'm not sure,' Billie whimpered. 'It feels like ages. I tried to ring Mum, but there was no reception.'

'But your waters haven't broken?'

'No, thank God. I've been trying to get back home.'

'And you will get back.' Freya sounded quite confident as she said this, or perhaps she was merely determined. Either way, they were the words Billie needed to hear in this moment. 'Here,' Freya said. 'You may as well put on this raincoat, even though you're already soaked. Lean on me, and we'll walk whenever we can, between your contractions.'

'That's what I've been trying to do, but they're getting closer.'

'How close?'

'I'm not sure. Pretty close.'

'You don't want to push, do you?'

'No, not yet.'

'That's good. That's great.' Freya was frowning, though. 'Maybe I should ring Pearl and tell her to call the ambulance.'

'I think we're still out of the service range.'

'I'll keep trying.'

'Mum will panic. She'll imagine the worst.'

'You're right. She will, won't she?' Freya compressed her lips as she considered this. 'Okay, I'll wait till we're closer, but don't worry, Billie, you're almost there and you're going to be okay.'

Their progress was necessarily slow. Luckily, the sandy soil on the track wasn't too boggy, but the normally familiar and friendly scrub and boulders seemed to close in on Billie today. She felt so much stronger, though, now that she had Freya to lean on. Even so, she couldn't help thinking about how this was supposed to happen – in a lovely, orderly maternity ward, with clean sheets and nice nurses supporting and encouraging her. Dan had even suggested she could stay at his place when she got close to the due date, so she didn't have to worry about the ferry trip from the island.

Instead . . . she'd landed herself in this mess, all because she'd been stubborn.

They continued on. Every so often Billie had to stop and cling to Freya as she breathed and huffed through another contraction, but at least she wasn't quite so terrified now and she knew they were making better progress.

'Look,' said Freya. 'We're at the last bend in the track.'

Freya had never been so relieved to see Pearl's house and she sent up a silent prayer of thanks. Pearl must have been watching out for them, as the front door immediately swung open and Pearl came rushing out of the house, heedless of the rain.

'Oh, my God,' she cried as she reached them. 'What's happened?'

'Everything's all right,' Freya told her in her calmest voice. 'But the baby's on its way.'

Predictably, Pearl shrieked and clapped her hands to the sides of her face.

'Mum, don't panic,' pleaded Billie.

'Perhaps if you could ring the ambulance?' suggested Freya.

Pearl gaped at her, her eyes glazed with shock, but then she seemed to blink as the message registered. 'The ambulance? Yes, of course. I'll ring them straight away.'

With that she turned and fled back into the house and Freya helped Billie along the final few metres and up the steps.

So good to finally make it. Freya breathed a huge sigh of relief. If Billie had to give birth in this house with an ambulance guy assisting instead of a midwife, so be it. At least she was no longer out in the rain on top of a cliff. She would be dry and safe and there'd be medical expertise on hand.

'How about a nice warm shower?' she said to Billie.

'I'd love that,' Billie said. 'But do you think it's okay?'

'Sure. Then we can get you dry and into a nightie ready for the ambo.'

Billie nodded, clearly not in any mood to argue, and Freya helped her to the bathroom, but Billie was no sooner undressed and enjoying the streaming warm water than Pearl came hurrying down the hallway, her expression clearly agitated.

'What is it?' Freya asked, stepping out into the hallway.

'Bob, the ambulance officer, is busy dealing with a heart attack over at Horseshoe Bay.'

'But surely there's more than one ambulance on this island?'

Pearl shook her head and her face crumpled. 'No,' she wailed. 'Just the one vehicle. Diane Jones is rostered on call, though, so they're ringing her instead.'

'Bloody hell.' Freya might have expressed her frustration more forcefully if Pearl hadn't looked so distressed. She had no idea how long it would take this second officer to wake up, or drop whatever she was doing and get ready for work. She wondered if she should call Seb. She could do with his steadying presence right now, but adding a man with zilch midwifery skills to this mix wasn't going to help Billie. 'I'm assuming this Bob guy will come as soon as he possibly can?' she asked Pearl.

Her sister nodded.

'What about Troy?' Freya asked. He might not be a midwife, but he was an emergency nurse.

'I tried to ring him, but he didn't answer. His shift should be over by now, though, so I left a message, but he still has to catch the ferry, so he won't get back here in a hurry.'

'You're right.' Freya straightened her shoulders, and somehow pinned on a smile. 'There's no need to panic. This baby will probably take hours to arrive. We just need to keep Billie comfortable and by then we'll have your ambulance people and possibly Troy both here.'

'I – I guess.'

Freya took her sister by the shoulders and gave her another encouraging smile. 'We can do this, Pearl. Babies are born at home every day.'

'But what if something —'

Freya touched a warning finger to her sister's lips. 'We're going to be positive, okay? Just the way we were for you and Seb.'

Pearl nodded. 'Okay. But —'

'No buts,' Freya told her. 'Go and check the mattress protector on Billie's bed.'

'It's new and I know for a fact that it's waterproof.'

'Good. Get towels then and extra pillows. Maybe some blankets. We want to make sure Billie's totally comfortable.'

Billie felt much better after her shower, despite a massive contraction that had almost brought her to her knees.

Freya fetched her a clean nightie and rubbed her hair dry with a towel.

'Where's the ambulance?' Billie asked her.

'He – he'll be here as soon as he can.' Looking almost guilty, Freya quickly added, 'I can blow-dry your hair if you like.'

'I think I need to get onto the bed first.' But Billie had no sooner said this than she felt a brand-new sensation, as if the bottom half of her was being wrenched away from her with massive force. She only just had time to grab at Freya for support before her knees gave way. 'Oh, God!'

In the next breath she was seized by an overwhelming urge to bear down. 'I think the baby's coming,' she moaned.

CHAPTER FORTY-TWO

The baby couldn't be coming already. For a moment Freya was so busy panicking she couldn't think. Good grief, she was in no way qualified to actually supervise a birth.

'Bring Billie down to my room.' Pearl, who had no idea of this latest development, called down the hallway, 'I have it all ready.'

Luckily, the sound of Pearl's voice snapped Freya out of her terrified daze. Her sister would probably panic for both of them. Someone needed to remain clear-headed.

'Are you okay to walk?' she asked Billie as she linked arms with her, gripping her firmly.

'I think so.'

'We'll take it carefully. Sing out if you need to stop.' And then she remembered something from her own labour all those years ago. 'If you feel another urge to push, you should pant.'

Billie nodded.

Halfway down the hall, Pearl met them with her arms full of towels.

'Ring the ambulance again, or try triple zero,' Freya told her. 'We're going to need instructions.'

Pearl's eyes widened with horror. 'She's not – it's not —'

'The baby's coming,' Freya told her as Billie sagged against the wall, holding her belly and panting fiercely.

'Oh, God.' Pearl looked ready to burst into tears.

'Ring Emergency,' Freya reminded her sternly. 'They'll tell us exactly what to do.'

Pearl hurried away to do this, thank heavens, and Freya guided Billie the short distance to the bed.

Billie could never have imagined any sensation so intense. In a matter of moments, she'd been overtaken by an incredible force that every cell in her body urged her to give in to. She was only dimly aware that Freya was spreading towels on the bed and her mum was talking to someone on the telephone.

She tried to pant, to hold back, but it wasn't working any more. There was nothing she could do but push.

And push. And pu-u-u-sh.

'You're doing brilliantly,' Freya told her.

Billie groaned. 'What's happening down there?'

'I can see your baby's head,' Freya said with a warm smile.

'And it has dark hair,' cried her mum, who was back in the bedroom and looked almost euphoric.

Gosh. Her little Pickle was almost here. A real little person. With a head. And dark hair. Despite her exhaustion, Billie experienced an unexpected spurt of excitement.

Her mum and Freya were looking excited, too. But then Billie's excitement was superseded by another violent urge to push.

'That's it,' cheered Freya. 'Good girl.'

'I can see your baby's face,' called her mum. 'It's so cute.'

'And the shoulders are almost there now,' added Freya. 'Everything's happening just the way it's supposed to. You're doing so well, Billie. Good girl. Another push and —'

Billie couldn't push again. Totally exhausted, utterly drained, she flopped back onto the pillows. Her Pickle had dark hair. A cute face. That was nice to know, but now she just needed to sleep.

She might have dozed off, she wasn't sure. From nearby, she could hear the murmur of anxious voices, but she was bone weary and she needed to rest. Maybe she could finish this tomorrow . . .

A moment later, however, she was gripping her knees and pushing again, assisted, thank heavens, by another fierce contraction.

'That's it, Billie,' cried Freya. 'Here it comes. Good girl.'

Face screwed tight with the effort of another mighty push, Billie felt the baby slip from her and heard cries of triumph from her mum and her aunt.

'Oh, darling!' her mother sobbed. 'She's gorgeous.'

'She?' Billie was instantly wide awake. 'Is it a girl?'

'A perfectly beautiful little girl.'

A little girl. Billie took a deep, happy breath as she absorbed this news. Secretly, she'd hoped for a girl, but she'd been fairly sure she was having a boy. A miniature Petros.

'Is she breathing?' she remembered to ask.

'*Waaaa!*'

'There's your question answered.' Freya was grinning from ear to ear.

'Wow!' Billie tried to sit up. 'And she looks fine?'

'She looks perfect as far as I can tell. All her fingers and toes. Hey, Grandma.' Freya was speaking to Pearl now. 'Show your daughter her baby.'

'Oh!' Her mum's face was a picture of ecstasy and reverence as she appeared at Billie's side. 'Here, darling,' she said gently, and Billie felt a wondrous warm weight on her chest.

Looking down, she saw her baby, all shiny and wet, but so, so cute. Her little Pickle. A tiny daughter. Red and perfect with a scrunched-up face. A cap of dark hair and tiny neat ears, fat little hands, teeny perfect feet.

Here, safe.

'Thanks,' she said to Freya, who had tears in her eyes now. 'Thanks to both of you.'

'No, we should be thanking you,' insisted her mum, whose eyes were extra shiny now as she beamed at Billie while she slipped an arm around Freya's shoulders and gave her sister a hug.

Billie was sure they were remembering her own birth and the decisions and regrets that had marred their relationship for decades. She smiled at her mother. 'I'm so glad you were here today.'

Pearl nodded, blinking as she managed a teary grin. 'This is, without a doubt, the grandest day of my life.'

'Anybody home?' called a masculine voice down the hall.

'Oh,' said Freya. 'That must be Bob, the ambulance man. In here,' she called.

'I thought it sounded like Dad,' said Billie.

And she was right. It was indeed Troy who hurried into the room, followed by a female paramedic. Troy's face was tense with concern, until he stopped, taking in the scene. And then his expression was one of utter delight.

'Oh, darling, you clever, clever girl.'

It was several days before Dan was free to visit, arriving late in the afternoon with an enormous bunch of the sweetest pink rosebuds and several gift-wrapped packages.

'One from me, one from Mum and one from Molly,' he told Billie.

'How lovely.'

Pearl was agape with curiosity, but she seemed to approve of Dan, especially when he was introduced to her as Detective Dan

Dexter. She happily set his flowers in a jug for Billie and then dis-
creetly retreated while Billie took Dan alone to her bedroom where
her new little daughter was sleeping.

They'd already spoken on the phone and Dan knew all about the
drama of the home delivery.

'Wow,' he said now as he looked down into the bassinet. 'She's
very cute.'

'She is, isn't she?' Billie could spend hours staring at that sweet
little face. As they watched, however, the baby frowned, wrinkling
her forehead and scrunching up her nose, twisting her mouth and
transforming herself from newborn cherub to ancient lady.

Oh, dear, Billie thought, but Dan merely laughed.

'She's gorgeous.'

She might have fallen in love with him in that moment.

'Have you settled on a name for her?' he asked.

'Peppi.' Billie spelled it for him. 'I wanted something unusual,
but sweet, a name that made me smile.'

'Sounds like a perfect choice then. Peppi.' He repeated the name,
as if testing it, and then, most obligingly, he smiled. 'I really like it.'

'Thanks.' It seemed important that he approved.

And then he turned to Billie, giving her his full attention. 'You're
looking great.'

'I'm feeling really well.'

'You look beautiful, Billie.'

When he smiled at her like that, his brown eyes filled her with
warmth and made her feel all fluttery and melting, and Billie wanted
nothing more than to lean in to him, to bury her face in his chest, to
feel his arms around her.

She resisted, however, and they sat on the bed as she opened the
presents he'd brought. From Grace there was a gorgeous little pair
of white lace-trimmed socks that somehow carried an air of glam-
our, and from Molly a plush, long-eared, cheeky-faced rabbit.

'How perfect,' Billie said. 'I'm sure Peppi will love this bunny.' And she wondered if Grace had had a hand in its selection.

Dan grinned. 'Luckily the baby store didn't run to stuffed seahorses.'

They shared a laugh and again Billie resisted an urge to hug him. Instead, she asked, 'How is Molly? I thought she might have come with you.'

'Oh, don't worry,' he said. 'She was desperate to come, but I told her she'd have to wait.'

Billie wasn't sure if she imagined it, but she sensed a hidden message in this statement. Uncertain, she picked up the final gift, Dan's gift, and wondered what it might be. There was a good chance he had chosen something practical like nappies or onesies. He'd already raised a baby, after all.

As Billie tore away the last of the paper, however, she discovered bubble bath and bath salts, a gorgeously scented candle and a voucher for a massage at a luxury spa.

'Oh, Dan.' She was suddenly quite overcome.

'Most people will give you things for your baby,' he said. 'But I thought you deserved a gift, too.'

'Aren't you lovely?' This time Billie leaned in and kissed his cheek, and yes, she let her lips linger at his jawline slightly longer than was strictly necessary while her heart began a crazy kind of thumping.

She sat straight again, sensed a tension in Dan as powerful as her own and found herself trembling. 'Thanks,' she managed in a breathless whisper.

He was watching her carefully. 'And how are your plans?' he said. 'I don't suppose you've had time for any more house hunting.'

'Not really.'

'But are you still planning on living alone?'

'I – I guess.' Billie looked away, feeling totally flustered. In recent weeks, her aim of single parenthood had faltered somewhat, primarily because of this man. But in just a few days, the demanding reality of caring for a newborn had convinced her she'd been dreaming to think that she and Dan might have a future.

When she turned to him again, he was still watching her, as if he was trying to read her.

He reached for her hands, held them firmly, confidently, in his and gave her his most gorgeous smile. 'I was hoping I might change your mind about that.'

CHAPTER FORTY-THREE

Given the scarcity of Freya's possessions, packing for her departure to Spain was going to take very little time. Her main concern was Won Ton.

Initially, she'd investigated the requirements and restrictions of the various airlines, but that was only the start of this particular venture. Freya also needed to get her head around all the customs and quarantine controls at both ends of the journey, not to mention the vet checks, or finding an appropriate container, or organising all the required export, import and transit health certificates.

Won Ton's microchip needed to be updated to international standards, and the poor little sweetheart had to be vaccinated for rabies. A daunting prospect on so many levels.

'Is it worth all this bother?' asked Pearl as she stood at Seb's kitchen counter, taking excruciating care to slice purple cabbage as thinly as possible.

'I don't really have much choice,' said Freya.

'But the poor little dog will be terrified.' Turning from the counter, Pearl gave an agitated wave of her hands, causing shreds of cabbage to fall from the chopping knife. 'She'll hate being stuck in a crate and shoved into the cargo hold for such a long flight.'

Freya blinked at her sister's surprising concern, but she was inclined to agree. 'I'm sure the airline will take every care,' she suggested without much conviction.

'Oh, I suppose they will,' said Pearl. 'But then Won Ton will have to go through the whole nightmare again every time you want to come back here.'

Which did seem to be an inordinate and possibly unnecessary ordeal, especially as Freya and Seb were hoping to make regular trips back and forth between Spain and Queensland. Seb was being quite tolerant about the whole situation with Won Ton, and Freya was grateful for his forbearance, but she was beginning to wonder if she was being fair to her little dog. Surely it was cruel to drag the poor mite back and forth?

'Perhaps I should ring my friend Daisy,' she said. 'She might be prepared to adopt Won Ton.'

'Or you could leave her with me.'

Freya stared at Pearl in disbelief. They were preparing salads for a family dinner. Seb was out on the deck heating up the barbecue, and on the kitchen counter beside the women sat glasses of white wine chilled with ice cubes. These they had sipped as they'd chopped and chatted. Behaving like normal sisters. A minor miracle, surely? Now this astonishing offer. 'You don't mean that, do you?' Freya couldn't help asking.

Pearl shrugged, then set the knife down and crossed her arms, hugging herself, as her face twisted into a squashed and somewhat embarrassed grin. 'Well, I have got used to her,' she said. 'She's quite a sweet little dog, really.'

Good heavens. 'And at least she's learned to stay off your sofas,' Freya suggested.

'Yes, there's that.'

'You'd be okay to take her for walks? She wouldn't tire you too much?'

'No, Freya. I'm fine for a daily walk.'

'So you'd really be prepared to keep her for the whole six months while we're in Spain?'

'Isn't that what I've just said?' Pearl's natural abrasiveness flared for a second or two, but then she relented. 'Yes,' she said more gently. 'I'd be happy to look after Won Ton. It's the least I can do after everything that you and Seb have done for me.'

'Gosh.' Freya sucked in a necessary gulp of air. 'That's wonderful, Pearl. Thank you.' Freya's voice was choked and tight as she said this. She knew she would miss her little canine companion terribly. But she couldn't deny that Pearl had offered a perfect solution.

She blinked back the threat of tears, knowing it was time to set aside her sense of loss, to embrace all the other wonderful things happening in her life. In all of their lives.

'Won Ton might even be company for you now that Billie's moved over to the mainland with Dan,' she said.

'Yes.' Pearl nodded. 'That thought occurred to me, too.'

Freya looked out through the open-plan house to Seb on the deck and beyond to the beach past the line of she-oaks. From here she could just make out the figures of Billie and Dan at the edge of the water. Billie was carrying Peppi in a papoose-like sling, which the baby seemed to love now that she'd passed the early weeks where she'd pretty much slept from feed to feed.

A stiff breeze was lifting Billie's hair and, as Freya watched, Dan slipped an arm around her shoulders and kissed her. Everything about their body language screamed happiness, and further along the beach Troy and Molly were also a picture of joy as they knelt in the sand, building a massive castle to be decorated with shells and coral, while Won Ton frolicked around them.

'It's wonderful that they're so happy, isn't it?' Freya said. In truth, she'd been amazed by how quickly the new little family had blended. Molly seemed to adore being a big sister to Peppi, and Billie and Dan exuded that special glow that accompanied falling deeply in love.

Pearl was nodding as she followed the direction of Freya's gaze, and her face relaxed into a smile. 'Troy and I get to see Peppi at least once a week, so we're happy, too.'

Billie's move had worked out better than Freya could have hoped. Most weeks Pearl travelled over to Townsville where she met Troy when he finished his shift, and together they drove to Dan's place. Other weeks, Dan, Billie, Molly and the baby happily came over to the island, as they had today. It really was fine on all fronts.

Now, from out on the deck came the tummy-teasing scent of onions hitting the hotplate. 'I'd better see if the chef needs a top-up,' Freya said, and she collected the wine bottle from the fridge and slipped outside where the sky and the sea were just beginning to deepen into twilight.

'Those onions smell great,' she told Seb as she refilled his glass.

He grinned. 'And how lucky am I to have a woman who anticipates my every need?'

'Only because you're tall, dark and handsome,' Freya told him, and she was grinning, too.

From the beach, Troy called, 'Is it almost dinnertime?'

'Yes,' they called back. And Seb slipped his arm around Freya's shoulders as they stood close together, watching the first pink of sunset reflected in the sky.

Beside them, the barbecue flames flickered and Freya's mind instinctively flashed back to the night of the fire and her burning home. That brutal destruction and her divorce had both been so final, leaving her with no room in her head or her heart to imagine second chances or new beginnings.

Now, as the others turned from the sea and began to trudge back across the sand, she was filled with gratitude for her new life, for her old love and for their boundless possibilities.

ACKNOWLEDGEMENTS

I wrote this story through the upheaval of selling our home on the Atherton Tablelands and relocating back to Townsville. This was a busy time of mixed emotions on many levels and I found, to my surprise, that returning to my desk and to these characters was like sitting down for a cuppa and a chat with old friends, a perfect escape between those bouts of busyness. So my first vote of thanks must go to my muse, who has stood by me for many, many books now, and to Freya, Billie & Co. for staying the course with me. You were so real to me, I could have hugged you.

As always, my husband Elliot was ready to listen to my moans when I was sure the story would fall apart, or be too short, or generally hopeless. He's my unfailing cheer squad and I'm forever grateful. Any research required for this novel was my own, however, and if I've made mistakes, they're mine as well.

Huge thanks are also due to everyone at Penguin Random House who has helped to make this book the best it can be. Thanks to Ali Watts, Nikki Lusk and Melissa Lane for your insightful and sensitive attention to the words on these pages, and thanks as well to publicist Sofia Casanova and audio producer Radhiah Chowdhury.

Finally, thanks to you, my wonderful readers, for picking up yet another of my books. Without you, none of this could happen.

BOOK CLUB NOTES

1. The story begins with Freya's decision to experience the baby's birth on her own. Do you think she was justified in making this choice? How does it shape the rest of the story?

2. In many ways, this is a story about choices. How many characters faced difficulties in this regard?

3. Surrogacy was a relatively new option for Pearl and Troy. What do you think of their decision to hide the truth from Billie?

4. How did the Magnetic Island setting shape the story? Do you think that growing up on this island may have influenced Billie's sense of adventure or lack of ambition? Or were there other factors at play?

5. If you had the chance to ask the author of this book one question, what would it be?

6. Which character in the book would you most like to meet?

7. If you could read this story from another character's point of view, who would you choose?

8. Did the characters seem believable to you? Did they remind you of anyone?

9. What aspects of the story could you most relate to?

10. Which other books by Barbara Hannay have you read? How did they compare to this book?